AMERICA AND I

AMERICA AND I

SHORT STORIES

BY AMERICAN JEWISH

WOMEN WRITERS

EDITED AND WITH AN INTRODUCTION BY

JOYCE ANTLER

BEACON PRESS · BOSTON

Beacon Press
25 Beacon Street
Boston, Massachusetts 02108-2800

Beacon Press books
are published under the auspices of
the Unitarian Universalist Association of Congregations.

97 96 95 94 93 92 91 90   8 7 6 5 4 3 2 1

Text design by Lisa Diercks

Library of Congress Cataloging-in-Publication Data
America and I: short stories by American Jewish women writers / edited and with
   an introduction by Joyce Antler.
      p.   cm.
   ISBN 0–8070–3604–8
   1. Short stories, American—Jewish authors.   2. Short stories, American—
Women authors.   3. Women, Jewish—Fiction.   I. Antler, Joyce.
PS647.J4A47   1990
813'.01089287—dc20   89-78237

For the women of my family—
my grandmothers, Tillie and Anna;
my mother, Sophie;
my aunts, Dina, Essie, and Gladdie;
my sister, Phoebe, and niece, Kim;
my daughters, Lauren and Rachel.

Contents

Part 3: Wider Glimpses: 1960–1979

Part 4: The Past as Present: The 1980s

Acknowledgments

Many friends and colleagues aided my work on this book. For their comments on the introduction to this volume, I thank Sylvia Barack Fishman, Michael T. Gilmore, Robbie Pfeufer Khan, Sonya Michel, Tema Nason, Gail Reimer, and Stephen J. Whitfield. Daniel Margolis and Patricia Horelly Margolis supplied constant encouragement and good friendship. Thanks also to Jayne Anne Phillips and Saul Touster for story suggestions. I am grateful to Brandeis University for a Mazer Faculty Grant for research support, and for the assistance of the reference and interlibrary loan staffs at the Brandeis University Library and of Ann Abrams, librarian at Temple Israel, Boston. My editor at Beacon, Joanne Wyckoff, contributed excellent advice at every turn.

This book would not have been completed, and probably would not even have been started, without the enthusiastic support and assistance of my husband Stephen, whose interests in the world in general and in Jewish life and writing in particular continue to parallel my own. The usual good cheer of our two daughters, Lauren and Rachel, made the production of the book all the easier. I hope that they will enjoy reading these stories as much as I enjoyed assembling them.

Introduction

A woman and a Jew, sometimes more
of a contradiction than I can sweat out,
yet finally the intersection that is both
collision and fusion, stone and seed.
                                Marge Piercy[1]

W HAT DOES IT MEAN to be both a woman and a Jew, the question
    Marge Piercy addresses in her poem, "The Ram's Horn Sound-
ing"? As the concerns of the women's movement have expanded to
include issues of religious as well as social and political identity, feminists have found the secondary role of women within Judaism and
secular Jewish culture to be problematic. "We will not let ourselves
be defined as Jewish women in ways in which we cannot allow ourselves
to be defined as women," theologian Judith Plaskow insists.[2]

The struggle to confront and resolve conflicts between Jewish heritage and female identity has figured prominently in the outpouring
of fiction by contemporary American Jewish women. In their short
stories and novels, these women explore their histories, expressing and
exposing the contradictions which are both "stone and seed," as Marge
Piercy writes. Their work provides a new mapping of the Jewish female
self, a self connected, though often in ambiguous ways, to Jewish
tradition.

While the contemporary feminist movement has generated an un-
precedented number of Jewish women writers whose fiction probes
this dual heritage, earlier generations of talented female authors also
addressed questions of Jewish and female identity. Although this legacy
has been obscured by the prominence of male Jewish writers, it is rich,
vital, and innovative, speaking expressively to women's experience and
to the experience of American Jews.[3]

1

For these several generations of women writers, fiction has been a powerful vehicle with which to chronicle their environment and stretch the limits of their social and moral universe. Often these writers have grasped and represented aspects of reality hidden to others. As critic Mary Dearborn has stated, literature by ethnic women can reveal the contradictions of American culture in heightened form because of their double "otherness"—these writers have been outsiders both as women and (in this case) as Jews.[4]

Several Jewish women writers are highly regarded as literary stylists or are known for their bold experiments in form; Grace Paley for open-ended inventiveness, Cynthia Ozick and Francine Prose for combinations of the natural and supernatural, Susan Fromberg Schaeffer for the exploration of time, memory, and consciousness. Perhaps for some of these writers, it is the peculiar contradiction of being Jewish and female that demands unusual, imaginative treatments.

In the hands of these gifted stylists, the short story emerges as a major work of art, demonstrating superb technique, perfect timing, poetic immediacy of imagery and metaphor, and a rich complexity of emotions and ideas. It is no accident, perhaps, that such authors as Anzia Yezierska, Tess Slesinger, Hortense Calisher, Tillie Olsen, Cynthia Ozick, and Lynne Sharon Schwartz have gained as much or more acclaim for their short stories as for their novels. (Stories, indeed, have earned several writers in the present collection the reputation of "writers' writers.") Perhaps because the short story articulates ordinary private matters in a pointed and compressed form, it appeals especially to women writers. While women have been central to the development of the novel, often, as Tillie Olsen points out, their time commitments have prevented the uninterrupted concentration that long fiction requires.[5] It has also been suggested that women writers may be drawn to the short story because it allows them to probe the texture and nuances of a moment of experience, to find significance in the seemingly trivial matters of everyday life.[6]

Over the years, the narrative styles and sensibilities of American Jewish women writers have changed considerably. As this collection allows us to see, their themes have remained remarkably consistent: the pull between assimilation and tradition; loss of identity; the exploration of unfamiliar cultures; the search for the moral meaning of

2

Judaism and Jewish life; antisemitism; feelings of marginality (as Jews and/or as women); generational conflict; the importance of social commitment, and of writing itself.

These writers, like their male counterparts, have only occasionally been concerned with specifically religious or spiritual aspects of Judaism, tending instead to focus on secular or cultural themes. Many would probably consider themselves American rather than Jewish writers, yet consciousness of the Jewish tradition, cultural or religious, has deeply influenced their work. As Susan Fromberg Schaeffer explains, she does not write primarily about Jewish themes, but her Jewishness is "like the wallpaper in every room [she] has ever been in."[7]

The stories collected here reveal this influence at its most striking. Incorporating characters, settings, or themes that are identifiably if not explicitly Jewish, they provide a particularly female version of Jewish identity, centered in the private and familial meanings of women's experience.[8] While American Jewish male writers have also written about familial and generational conflicts, their work uses male experience as the norm and often presents women in stereotypical roles.[9]

Together with the novels of such contemporary writers as E. M. Broner, Norma Rosen, Marge Piercy, Erica Jong, Anne Roiphe, Lore Segal, Judith Rossner, and Alix Kates Shulman, the stories in this anthology address problems of women's coming of age; of intimacy, sexuality, friendship, and work in adulthood; and, especially, of parenthood and mothering. As the many protagonists of this volume struggle to find their way in the world, fighting economic and social barriers, religious prejudice, and limiting traditions or family entanglements, they provide a rich portrait of courage, resiliency, and growth. Writers in every generation explore the often tense balance between women's needs for individual expression and achievement and their desires for a larger rootedness within family life or Jewish culture and religion.

In choosing the selections for this book, I have sought to present a broad range of stories spanning successive eras. Changing generational sensibilities are highlighted in the four chronological sections of the book. I have focused on American Jewish women authors who are devoted practitioners of the short story form (though most also write other forms of fiction) and I have included writers of established reputation as well as those whose works may be less familiar. I have also limited this volume to authors writing in English, rather than Yiddish.[10] The book's title, taken from a story by Anzia Yezierska, points to one of its main themes—the effort of Jewish women to find their way in America and to make America their own. The fiction in this collection—the first historically based anthology of short stories by American Jewish women—reveals the success of this attempt.[11]

From the Ghetto and Beyond: 1900–1929

Among the first to chronicle the experience of Jewish women in English were Mary Antin and Anzia Yezierska, both Eastern European Jews who came to America during the peak years of immigration in the 1890s. Born in Polotzk, Russia, in 1881, Antin was 13 when she arrived in America. Five years later she had published her first book, *From Plotzk (sic) to Boston*, a series of letters to her uncle in Russia (originally written in Yiddish) describing the family's passage. In 1912, she authored a best-selling autobiography, *The Promised Land*, an optimistic account of the opportunities offered Jewish immigrants, largely through education, to become Americans. Antin's story in the present volume, "Malinke's Atonement," affords a remarkable contrast to the hopefulness that abounds in her autobiography. In this story, set in a European shtetl much like the one in which Antin spent her childhood, the piety of Malinke's hard-working, widowed, mother and her offspring only deepens the suffering that poverty inflicts upon them. Malinke defies religious tradition by ignoring a rabbinical decision. After she has publicly atoned for her sin, the rabbi, admiring her spirit, promises to educate her. Antin emphasizes how unusual this promise is to one of Malinke's gender, and how, in the old country, such a promise was always controlled by male benefactors.

Like Antin, Anzia Yezierska was born in Russian Poland, probably in a village called Plinsk, in the early 1880s. Set in the New World, much of Yezierska's fiction reveals the subordinate role of Jewish women within the family, a consequence of their secondary place within the religion.[12] In *The Bread Givers*, a novel published in 1925, Yezierska's heroine, Sara Smolinsky, laments the fact that "God didn't listen to women . . ."

Women could get into Heaven because they were wives and daughters of men. Women had no brains for the study of God's Torah, but they could be the servants of men who studied the Torah. Only if they cooked for the men, and washed for the men, and didn't nag or curse the men out of their homes; only if they let the men study the Torah in peace, then, maybe, they could push themselves into Heaven with the men, to wait on them there.[13]

In the exciting, expanding world of urban America, it became possible for women to challenge traditional definitions of their duties. "I'm smart enough to look out for myself," seventeen-year-old Sara challenges her father, a scholar whose devotion to the Talmud (like that of Yezierska's own father) impoverished the family yet allowed him to tyrannize it. "Woe to America where women are let free like men," is the father's rebuke.[14] Sara's demand for autonomy reflects the refusal of some members of the new generation of Jewish women to accept the strictures of patriarchy. "In America," she tells her father, "women don't need men to boss them."[15]

Renouncing neither her independence nor her distaste for what she regards as his fanatical adherence to his traditions, Sara becomes reconciled with her father. In the last lines of the book, she feels the Jewish tradition like a "shadow still there, over me," not just her father, she recognizes, but "the generations who made my father whose weight was still upon me."[16] In "America and I," reprinted in this volume, we see that writing allowed Yezierska to connect to the shadow she could not erase, to find America and to create her own identity.

I began to build a bridge of understanding between the American-born and myself. Since their life was shut out from such as me, I began to open up my life and the lives of my people to them. And life draws life. In only writing about the Ghetto I found America.[17]

For Antin and Yezierska, the choice of writing as a career was not without cost. Antin's authorship brought her huge success, but alienated her from her own people. She married a German-born Lutheran scientist, from whom she separated during World War I, and had little contact with Jewish culture during her adult years. A devastating portrait of her by a contemporary suggests a "conceited," "unsympathetic" and pretentious matron, revolted by any reminders of her Russian-Jewish past.[18]

Yezierska did not veer so far from her roots, but still found it difficult to resolve the conflict between her roles as Jewish woman and writer. Unlike the father of Sara Smolinsky, Yezierska's own father never accepted her achievements.

Despite family opposition and later frequent critical rejection, Yezierska persisted in her attempts to portray the meaning of Jewishness in the New World and to render immigrant speech and dialect in authentic form. Her story "The Fat of the Land," which gave classic expression to the subject of acculturation, won the Edward J. O'Brien Prize in 1919 for the best short story of the year; so impressed was O'Brien with Yezierska's story that he dedicated his 1919 anthology to her.[19] This story, and the publication of her collection, *Hungry Hearts*, the following year, established Yezierska as one of the nation's preeminent chroniclers of immigrant life. Though her fame would be temporary, her stories helped to establish a cultural bridge between Jews and non-Jews, and demonstrated a new model of independent Jewish womanhood—the Jewish woman as writer.[20]

The conflict between the bonds of tradition and the beckoning promises of American womanhood also appears in the fiction of two American-born, Midwestern Jews, Edna Ferber and Fannie Hurst. Born in 1885 in Kalamazoo, Michigan, Ferber was the daughter of a Hungarian Jewish father who had come to the United States in his late teens and an American-born mother whose prosperous merchant banking family, of German Jewish extraction, had immigrated in the 1840s. Hurst, born in Ohio in 1889, and reared in St. Louis, was the child of a factory owner and his wife, whose Jewish families had come to America from Bavaria in the 1860s. Although neither Ferber nor Hurst experienced the anxieties of immigration and acculturation at first hand, both identified themselves as Jews, and occasionally turned to Jewish themes and characters—particularly female ones—in their fiction.[21]

In Ferber's case, childhood experiences of antisemitism sensitized her to the perils and privileges of her heritage. "Being a Jew makes it tough to get on, and I like that," she once remarked.[22] Rachel Wiletzky, the protagonist of "The Girl Who Went Right," in this collection, is one of the few Ferber heroines who is recognizably Jewish. Like Emma McChesney (whose exploits Ferber turned into a series of popular stories published in *Cosmopolitan* and *The American Magazine* before World War I), Rachel Wiletzky becomes a saleswoman, one of the new breed of assertive working-class heroines whose lives Ferber was among the first to depict. With her "ghetto voice" and slender sensitive hands that bespeak an inheritance of "at least five generations of ancestors who have sat with the hands folded in their laps" while they studied Talmud, Rachel is different from her co-workers, yet she seeks to become like them, denying the poverty and foreignness of her heritage, even lying about her name. Not until she recognizes the superficiality and snobbishness of the world she seeks to join can she accept her past and reclaim her identity. "My name is Rachel Wiletzky," she proudly admits in the last line of the story.[23]

In 1910, against her family's protests, Fannie Hurst moved from the Midwest to New York City to pursue a career as a writer. Working as a waitress and saleswoman, she explored the slums of the city, coming to know and empathize with its residents. In 1915, shortly after the publication of her first collection of short stories, she married a recently emigrated Russian Jew, though she did not reveal the marriage for five years. By 1924 (the year in which Edna Ferber won the Pulitzer Prize for her novel, *So Big*), Fannie Hurst was one of the three highest paid writers in America, publishing widely in women's magazines. By 1940, she was *the* highest paid novelist in the country.[24]

Though critics often found Hurst's fiction sentimental and predictable, the public responded with continuing enthusiasm.[25] She wrote sympathetically of working women, deploring the discrimination which limited their options. Several of her works address Jewish assimilation in America. "Seven Candles," reprinted in this collection, focuses on the issue of intermarriage and its often wrenching consequences for family life. In this story, a second-generation son is forced to choose between his beautiful but vain Gentile wife, who ridicules Orthodox Jewish practice, and his observant mother.

In the first decades of the twentieth century, the problem of assimilation concerned Jewish women writers more than any other. While they recognized the opportunities offered to immigrants in America, these authors also portrayed the dark side of acculturation, suggesting that for women of the first generation, divorced from their communities and their religion, its tensions were hard to bear.

Troubles in the New World: 1930–1959

In succeeding decades, Jewish women continued to write about acculturation and problems of Jewish identity. During the Depression, however, many of these writers (like their male peers) were attracted to the radical political and literary movements of the time, a decade when such male Jewish writers as Mike Gold, Henry Roth, Daniel Fuchs, and Meyer Levin began to make their mark on American fiction. Of the major Jewish women writers born in the decade 1903–1913 and who therefore came of age in the thirties—Tess Slesinger, Leane Zugsmith, Hortense Calisher, Tillie Olsen, and Jo Sinclair —none would write predominantly of Jewish characters or milieus. Identifying with the poor and the oppressed, writers like Slesinger, Zugsmith, and Olsen joined the progressive writers—many of them Jewish—producing proletarian fiction.[26] With politics as a central literary concern in the 1930s, these writers resolved the problem of assimilation through their characters' identification with political ideas and movements. In the 1940s and 1950s, as the possibilities for radical action declined, they turned more openly to Jewish topics.

Born in New York of immigrant Hungarian and Russian parents in 1905, Tess Slesinger graduated from Swarthmore College and the Columbia School of Journalism. Before publishing her critically acclaimed novel, *The Unpossessed* (1934), she wrote for the *New York Evening Post Literary Review* and the *Menorah Journal* (the chief outlet for left-leaning Jewish intellectuals in the 1920s and early 1930s). Her 1928 marriage to Herbert Solow, assistant editor of the *Menorah Journal*, gave her access to the circle of "New York Intellectuals" associated with the *Journal* (among them, Lionel Trilling, Eliot Cohen, Philip Rahv, and Clifton Fadiman) whom she satirizes in *The Unpossessed*. This novel and her short stories, collected in *Time: The Present* (1935), reveal a strikingly modern sensibility critical of the sexual and emotional exploitation of women by male radicals and expressive of female experiences of love, marriage, sexuality, and childbearing. Contemporary critics compared Slesinger to Dorothy Parker—"the same type of wit, the same extremely feminine sensitiveness, the same ability to reflect their age"—but noted that Slesinger had chosen "worthier material for satire."[27]

"Missis Flinders," in this volume, appeared in *Story Magazine* in 1932, perhaps the first time a general circulation magazine addressed the issue of abortion. (Responding to requests that she expand the story, Slesinger wrote *The Unpossessed*; "Missis Flinders" is its closing chapter.) Though Miles and Margaret Flinders are not Jewish (as is Bruno Leonard, the leader of the intellectual circle she portrays in the book), Slesinger's depiction of the emotional pain which Miles's radicalism causes his wife is suggestive of the *Menorah* group's politics. The story was based on Slesinger's own abortion, which her first husband demanded.[28]

Leane Zugsmith, born in Louisville, Kentucky, also began as a journalist. In the late 1920s and 1930s, she published six novels and two collections of short stories, all with political themes. "Room in the World," reprinted in this volume, portrays the bitterness and humiliation a father's unemployment causes his wife and children. While the wife in this story must swallow her frustration in order to keep her family intact, Aline Weinman, the sympathetic Jewish heroine of Zugsmith's 1936 novel, *A Time to Remember*, goes out on strike although she knows her father will object.

Jo Sinclair's first published fiction, "Tony and the WPA," which appeared in the *New Masses* in 1938, resembles Zugsmith's "Room in the World" in theme. In Sinclair's story, the nameless, unemployed father, desperate for a job, is not specifically Jewish, but an oblique clue to his origins is provided. By the mid-1940s, Sinclair was publishing stories with identifiably Jewish characters and settings for such small magazines as the *Chicago Jewish Forum*, and *Common Ground*, a progressive quarterly which explored racial and ethnic issues. (None of her stories for such popular magazines as *Esquire*, *Reader's Digest*, or *The Saturday Evening Post* addressed Jewish themes.)

Sinclair (Ruth Seid) was the daughter of working-class, Russianborn parents who immigrated to Argentina and then to Brooklyn, where she was born in 1913. She grew up in a racially mixed Cleveland neighborhood, the setting for much of her fiction. After graduation from high school, she worked in a knitting mill and for the WPA as she struggled to put herself through college. When *Esquire* took one of her stories in 1938, she invented "Jo Sinclair" as a nom de plume, since the magazine would not publish fiction by women.[29] This pseudonym masked her ethnic identity as well as her gender.

With her first novel, *The Wasteland* (1946), which won the prestigious $10,000 Harper Prize, Sinclair incorporated Jewish issues into the fiction that she wrote for a popular audience. The *Wasteland* explores the crisis of identity experienced by John Brown (born Jacob Braunowitz), who changes his name to conceal his Jewish origins. Sinclair presents a realistic portrait of a second-generation Jew struggling to come to terms with the ghetto heritage of his parents, which he must reject, as he searches for more enduring meanings of Jewish life and ritual. Speaking in Jake's voice, the author draws an equally sympathetic portrait of Debby, a lesbian who has had to confront the perils of her own sexual nonconformity. In showing how a Jew or a lesbian stood outside the cultural mainstream in America in the early 1940s, Sinclair pioneered comparisons of sexual and ethnic difference.

In a second innovative novel, *The Changelings* (1955), Sinclair assumes the voice of Judith Vincent, a teen gang leader known as "Vincent," who shrugs off both gender and ethnic stereotypes. Dismayed by the crude racism of her family and community, she intervenes when one of the neighbors attacks a black man inquiring about housing. Vincent's friendship with Clara, a black girl as tough and spirited as herself, opens up the possibility that people of the young generation, the "changelings" of the title, can come together despite the prejudices that divide their elders. Sinclair's frank examination of black-Jewish relations, a subject she wrote about in many of her short stories, links questions of race to those of class and gender. It is the economic insecurity of her characters which fuels their ethnocentrism and desperate fear of change. The men of Vincent's neighborhood feel cheated by their failure to realize the American dream; in turn, they cheat on their wives, bully their daughters and sons, and turn to unlawful means to solve the "problem" of black intrusion.

"Second Blood: A Rosh Hashonoh Story," the Sinclair story which appears here, was published in *The Jewish Spectator* in 1944. It is the story of an assimilated Jew who discovers during the war that being

"American" is not sufficient, and gives blood a second time to assert his Jewishness.

For Hortense Calisher, autobiographical short stories were a means to her identity as a writer. Daughter of a second-generation German Jewish father and a first-generation German Jewish mother, Calisher married shortly after graduating from Barnard in 1932. Absorbed in her role as full-time wife and the mother of two children, she began publishing stories about Hester Elkins, a stand-in for herself, in 1948. Her first collection, from which "Old Stock" in this anthology is taken, appeared in 1951. Calisher alternated short stories with novels in the flourishing career which ensued; though both have received praise, the short stories have garnered more acclaim. Calisher, it is often stated, is simply "one of *the* best" modern writers of this genre.[30]

Written during the 1940s and 1950s, Calisher's Hester stories draw on her heritage as the daughter of a transplanted Southern Jew and his immigrant wife. Despite the family's comfortable life in New York City, antisemitism hovered in the background, a threat not only from the outside, but, as in "Old Stock," from within. Published in *The New Yorker*, this story outraged many Jews with its unflattering portrait of Jewish self-hatred. (Calisher wrote of antisemitism in several other early short stories.) Her 1969 novel, *The New Yorkers*, deals with the interlocking themes of Jewishness, class, sexuality, and gender.

The radical political consciousness that informs Tillie Olsen's stories and her one novel, *Yonnondio: From the Thirties*, recalls the proletarian fiction of Slesinger and Zugsmith rather than the acculturation themes of writers like Calisher. Though Olsen's first published stories appeared in the early 1960s, her political and literary perspectives had been largely formed during the Depression.

Born in 1913 to Russian Jewish immigrants who settled in Nebraska, where her father was secretary of the state Socialist Party, Tillie Lerner dropped out of high school to help support her large family. For the next several years she wrote poetry and worked as a political activist for the Young Communist League, landing in jail in Kansas City and California for her organizing activities. Olsen began *Yonnondio* in the early 1930s, but did not complete the novel until nearly four decades later. Married in 1936 to Jack Olsen (a printer and union man) and the mother of four daughters, she put aside her writing and took a series of jobs as waitress, secretary, and laundry worker to help support her family. Not until some twenty years later did she publish her first story. Her first book, the collection which takes the title of her signature story, "Tell Me A Riddle," came out in 1961, when Olsen was nearly 50 (although the story itself was first published in 1956).

"Tell Me A Riddle" is marked by Olsen's skillful use of the rhythms and locutions of Yiddish speech and her exploration of Jewish secular humanism. Though Eva, the central character of the story, is an atheist, she reaches back through her past to recover what she considers to be the spiritual essence of Judaism—its messianic mission and its concern for a wider humanity. On her deathbed Eva recalls the hopes and dreams of her revolutionary youth in Czarist Russia, when, as a socialist orator and organizer, she talked "not of family but beyond . . . of humankind." In this moment of epiphany she also solves the riddle of her family life. As she recaptures the zeal and commitment of her girlhood, the anger she has felt at sacrificing her own identity to her family's demands dissipates. Beyond women's anger and their first necessary steps toward independence, Olsen hints, lies a realm of interconnection, caring, and forgiveness.

Joining self-assertion with interdependence, Olsen's vision is a strongly feminist one. When women live only through their families, she suggests, they are denied their own individuality and any possibility for a larger connection to humankind. As Olsen herself recognizes, at its core this vision is also a Jewish one, drawn from her Jewish socialist background. As she explained in a recent interview, this background, which she calls *Yiddishkeit*, taught her "knowledge and experience of injustice, of discrimination, of oppression, of genocide and of the need to act against them forever and whenever they appear," as well as "an absolute belief in the potentiality of human beings." As Olsen says, "What is Yiddish in me . . . is inextricable from what is woman in me, from woman who is mother."[31]

"I Stand Here Ironing," the Olsen story reprinted in this anthology, presents a compelling portrait of a mother and her "thin, dark and foreign-looking" daughter which reflects the experience of many Jewish, and other ethnic, families in America. Though she has had little control over her own and her daughter's lives because she has had to work outside the home for many years, the mother in the story hopes that her daughter will be able to determine her own future despite the disadvantages of her background. She wants her daughter to be "more than this dress on the ironing board, helpless before the iron."

Wider Glimpses: 1960–1979

Even as the experience of the immigrant generations has receded in memory, provoking continuing predictions that American Jewish literature had reached the end of its authentic life, Jewish women writers have increasingly turned to themes of acculturation, conflict between generations, and the secular and religious meanings of Judaism.[32]

In the 1960s and 1970s, a new cohort of women, several of them deeply involved in labor zionism, feminism, and other social movements, gave these concerns more open-ended, optimistic portrayal, reflecting the expanding confidence of American women and the women's liberation movement.

Allegra Maud Goldman, the title character of Edith Konecky's 1976 fictional memoir about growing up in Brooklyn before World War II, is an example of the precocious pre-teen and adolescent Jewish heroine of this period. Miriam, the Bronx-born heroine of Johanna Kaplan's story in this volume, is similar—spirited, sensitive, highly intelligent and nonconforming. Set in a Zionist summer camp where Miriam, directed by an Israeli playwright, acts in a play about the Warsaw Ghetto uprising, the story allows Miriam to confront the destiny of the Jewish people as she reenacts a young girl's heroic struggle against the Nazis. During the 1960s, writers increasingly turned to the Holocaust and the State of Israel as they pondered the meanings of Jewish existence in the United States and the larger world.

The attempt to bridge cultural gaps is a theme of several stories in this section. In "Z'mira," Gloria Goldreich's narrator, an American Jew in Israel, comes to appreciate the perspective of her poor but proud Moroccan Jewish maid. In Joanne Greenberg's "L'Olam and White Shell Woman," a Jewish college student, working as a waitress in the southwest, sings the "Shema" and "Kol Nidre" for her skeptical Navaho co-workers in order to convince them that she is not an Anglo. "Our two people would have understood one another," she tells them; in fact, she believes, "My Abraham and Isaac were American Navaho."

13

The student's attempt to connect her own God to the religion of the Navahos reflects Greenberg's deep interest in the spiritual aspects of Jewishness.

The Past as Present: The 1980s

Cynthia Ozick has written consistently and imaginatively about Judaism as a religious heritage. Ignoring such popular American Jewish themes as assimilation, intra-family conflict, and social class oppression, Ozick focuses her attention on the spiritual conflict between Jewish values and "pagan" influences—the idols of art, nature, human ambition or greed—which tempt men and women away from God. In *The Pagan Rabbi and Other Stories* (1971), her first short story collection, she treats this theme with linguistic inventiveness and a highly original display of fantasy and realism; her three novels and other collections of short fiction also treat matters of Jewish faith and history in a uniquely contemporary way. Despite an orthodox Jewish orientation, Ozick is very much a postmodern writer who revels in the use of magic, the supernatural, and unorthodox literary devices to illuminate her moral philosophy.

Born in 1928 to Russian immigrant parents, Ozick is a first-generation American who grew up in the Bronx. While she proudly identifies herself as a Jewish writer even more than as an American one, she denies that she is a "woman writer," believing that such a label diminishes the universalist content of her work.[33] Nevertheless, much of Ozick's fiction addresses issues that bear upon female lives and gender relations. (The story, "Virility," for example, touches upon the gendered double standard of artistic merit, which Ozick later dubs the "Ovarian Theory of Literature.")[34] Ozick's "Puttermesser" stories also reflect both Jewish and women's issues. "Puttermesser: Her Work History, Her Ancestry, Her Afterlife," introduces Ruth Puttermesser, a Yale law school graduate and an assistant corporation counsel in a government office. Despite her success, Puttermesser seeks a connection with her Jewish past which her American-born, assimilated parents can not give her. Claiming her great-uncle Zindel (who died before she was born) as "all her ancestry," Puttermesser conjures up a scene, which Ozick exposes to the reader as fraudulent, in which Zindel

teaches her Hebrew. "Puttermesser and Xanthippe," a sequel, rein-
forces the author's warning about the limits of creativity and ambition.
When Puttermesser, now middle-aged, is demoted, she creates a
"child" creature, Xanthippe—a female golem—who makes Puttermesser mayor of New York. Xanthippe's insatiable appetites lead her
to destroy Puttermesser's reforms and plunge the city back into chaos;
Puttermesser renounces her powers and destroys her own creation.

For Ozick, the deepest evil goes beyond the sins of ambitious, but
essentially well-meaning, women and men. Her Holocaust story, "The
Shawl," reprinted in this collection, tells of a magic shawl that helps
Rosa, the main character, nurse her baby daughter in a concentration
camp. Through a startling immediacy of language and a combination
of the supernatural and realistic which allows the reader to imagine
the totality of a mother's love for her child and her helplessness in the
face of Nazi brutality, Ozick dramatically conveys the horror of the
Holocaust.

The author of three highly regarded collections of short stories,
Grace Paley is known for her personal, vigorous style, for experimen-
tation with form, and for the depth of feeling she brings to her un-
conventional plots and characters. Though her characters vary widely,
many of them are identifiably Jewish, and, in their interactions reveal
conflicts between the values of the immigrant generation and those of
their descendants. Paley's precise imagery and masterful use of Yiddish
dialect enhances the veracity of the changing Jewish milieus she de-
picts, yet her comic sense and open-ended, inventive style take her
stories beyond these settings. While she does not probe religious aspects
of Judaism, Paley's stories portray the profound moral dilemmas of
contemporary urban Jews and, most poignantly, of women.

Born in the Bronx in 1922, Paley is the daughter of Jewish parents
who emigrated from Czarist Russia, where they had been active in the
socialist movement. Though Paley's father became a successful American doctor, he and his wife retained their belief in socialism. "I just
kind of inhaled their early lives," Paley commented to an interviewer,
describing the source of her commitment to social justice and political
activism.[35]

It is especially through Paley's female characters that she articulates
the link between individual daily life and the historical process. Writing

self-consciously as a woman exploring the texture of women's lives, Paley brings a vivid feminist consciousness to her work. ("I think of myself as a woman who has been a writer and who has been in a tradition which is largely male," she noted in 1975.)[36]

The protagonist of many of Paley's stories, Faith Darwin, is a divorced wife and mother deeply involved in raising her children, devoted to her neighbors and friends, and urgently committed to her urban environment. In Paley's three collections (which span three decades), Faith moves out from her domestic role to become a social activist and aspiring writer.

As Faith matures, she accepts the burden of social responsibility inherited from her Jewish ancestors. To be truly American, she learns, is not merely a matter of unflinching optimism but also one of commitment to others, a theme which Paley explores and also satirizes in such stories as "Zagrowsky Tells," "The Long-Distance Runner" and "A Conversation With My Father." In this last story, in many ways Paley's most paradigmatic, the narrator tells her dying father, who protests against her experimental writing, that she despises a linear story line "because it takes all hope away. Everyone, real or invented, deserves the open destiny of life." She is searching for a new way of telling stories, especially women's stories, that will give an "open destiny" to her characters.

One of Paley's most recent stories, "Midrash on Happiness," reprinted in this volume, links Jewish, feminist, and activist themes. Writing in the form of *midrashim*, stories and parables that explain Biblical texts, Paley gives Faith the opportunity to examine her liberal politics, her optimistic belief in change, and her continuing reliance on female friends. Even though Faith guiltily recognizes that the planet may be falling apart, she finds happiness simply in having "women to walk with."

Paley and Ozick, born in the 1920s, are joined today by a fourth and a fifth generation of Jewish women writers. Rosellen Brown, Lynne Sharon Schwartz, Susan Fromberg Schaeffer, and Francine Prose (born in the late 1930s and 1940s) are responsible for a remarkable and growing range of novels, short stories, and poetry. The youngest authors in this anthology—Rebecca Goldstein, Ivy Goodman, Marjorie Sandor, and Lesléa Newman (all born in the 1950s)—have also produced important new fiction.

16

While these writers do not always focus on Jewish issues, a significant portion of their work portrays Jewish settings or characters. A growing number of them have become interested in spiritual themes. Concerned with the limits of feminist secularism, they join others in calling for a renewed Judaism relevant to women's lives. In contrast to stories written by Jewish women in the 1960s and 1970s, which focus on separations, contemporary works by these authors emphasize the ties which bind families and generations. Rather than denying the collective memory of their past, their characters seek—or are forced—to confront it.

Several stories in the last section of this volume concern memories of the Holocaust. The family secret learned by the narrator of Rebecca Goldstein's "The Legacy of Raizel Kaidish: A Story" (that in Buchenwald, her mother had informed on two young girls who were then gassed) undermines her mother's rationalist ethics. In Marjorie Sandor's "The Gittel," a young woman tells the story of her grandmother, Gittel, whose happy memories of her childhood in Berlin lead her, with three of her children, back to face certain death in Nazi Germany. The narrator identifies Gittel's misguided, dreamlike innocence as a family tradition that her father and her daughter have inherited. In Lesléa Newman's, "A Letter to Harvey Milk," an elderly Jewish man takes a writing class taught by a Jewish lesbian interested in preserving stories of the Jewish past. Harry, the story's narrator, writes a letter to his dead friend Harvey Milk, the gay city supervisor who was murdered in San Francisco. Writing allows Harry to recall a painful secret told him by a Holocaust survivor.

Other stories by contemporary Jewish women deal with the complex interactions between parents and their grown children as the latter seek to come to terms with their family histories and personal destinies. In Rosellen Brown's "A Good Deal," a father's revelation of his infidelity forces his son to re-evaluate their relationship and his own memories of the past. In Francine Prose's "Electricity," a young mother recently separated from her husband visits her family in Brooklyn and makes a connection to her father, who has bewildered the family by his sudden conversion to Hasidism. A family wedding becomes the occasion for the young heroine of Lynne Sharon Schwartz's story, "The Opiate of the People," to learn about her family's past. "Would it have cost you so much to tell me some of these things?" she berates her father, an assimilated Russian immigrant who has refused to reveal memories of his childhood. In Susan Fromberg Schaeffer's "Homage to Isaac Bashevis Singer," the main character, Mrs. Klopstock, recovers from a serious, but undiagnosed, illness after she prays to Isaac Bashevis Singer and begins to write herself. (The generational message is reversed when Mrs. Klopstock's middle-aged daughter accuses her mother of betraying family secrets.)

The past, these writers tell us, cannot be avoided, though its complex and painful truths may appear differently to parents and children, to women and men. As Ivy Goodman points out in the conclusion to her story, "Remnants: A Family Pattern": "Though the fabric tears, unravels, you can't forget things. You can never run away. They're behind me; they are with me. I am wearing them. They're my family."

Recovery of the past has been a prominent theme of other contemporary Jewish women writers; among them are Elizabeth Klein, Nessa Rapoport, Meredith Tax, Daphne Merkin, Allegra Goodman, Sylvia Rothchild, and Tema Nason.[37] The work of the writers in this section and their contemporaries points the way to a rich new vein in contemporary American Jewish writing. Their voices join those of other Jewish feminists whose critiques have revitalized Judaism and enriched the spiritual and cultural possibilities of the women's movement.

The tradition of American Jewish women's writing has emphatically come of age. Speaking in a variety of voices, male and female, heterosexual and lesbian, this fiction is diverse and richly detailed, comic and serious, exotic and familiar. Contemporary American Jewish women write about private affairs of the heart and about historical and political matters. Like their forbears, these authors experiment with form and technique; alternating, and sometimes integrating, realism with fantasy, the present with the past or the future. The tone of these stories is varied as well—intimate and personal, conveying the dailiness of everyday life and the intensity of emotional response, or abstract and distant, exploring intellectual truths and philosophical values.

Some of the authors represented here would consider themselves writers first, then Jews or women; for others, these identifications would be reversed. Within one author's body of work, the voices, settings, themes, and meanings may change. There can be no doubt, however, that these authors compel our attention with their imaginative and complex shapings of American Jewish experience, and especially, of the experience of Jewish women. Like previous generations of Jewish women writers, they chart the changing personal and collective meaning of their relationship to their world. Through literature, they have come to represent, and to possess, America.

Notes

1. Marge Piercy, "The Ram's Horn Sounding," in *Available Light* (New York: Alfred A. Knopf, 1988), 128.

2. Judith Plaskow, "The Jewish Feminist: Conflict in Identities," in *The Jewish Woman: New Perspectives*, ed. Elizabeth Koltun (New York: Schocken Books, 1976), 3.

3. On Jewish women writers and the image of Jewish women in literature, see *Studies in American Jewish Literature* 3 (1983); Charlotte Baum, Paula Hyman, and Sonya Michel, *The Jewish Woman in America* (New York: The Dial Press, 1976), chap. 7; June Sochen, *Consecrate Every Day: The Public Lives of Jewish American Women, 1880–1980* (Albany, N.Y.: State University of New York Press, 1981), chap. 6; Sonya Michel, "Mothers and Daughters in American Jewish Literature: The Rotted Cord," in Koltun, *The Jewish Woman: New Perspectives*, 272–282; Claire R. Satlof, "History, Fiction and the Tradition: Creating a Jewish Feminist Poetic," in *On Being a Jewish Feminist*, ed. Susannah Heschel (New York: Schocken Books, 1983), 186–206; and Connie Burch, "Women's Voices, Women's Visions: Contemporary American-Jewish Women Writers" (Ph.D. dissertation, Purdue University, 1987).

4. In her pioneering study, *Pocahontas's Daughters: Gender and Ethnicity in American Culture* (New York: Oxford University Press, 1986), Mary V. Dearborn provides a broad outline of an ethnic female literary tradition based on themes common to writers from different ethnic groups. She argues that gender and ethnicity bring together the concept of "otherness" in particularly dramatic ways. On the role of ethnicity in American literature, also see Werner Sollors, *Beyond Ethnicity: Consent and Descent in American Culture* (New York: Oxford University Press, 1986).

5. Tillie Olsen, *Silences* (New York: Delacorte Press/Seymour Lawrence, 1978).

6. According to Hermione Lee, feminist anthologies of short stories "appropriate the form as the special property of women writers." Lee also suggests that the short story's relation to folklore and fairytale (narratives told to chil-

dren) make it especially suited to women writers. See *The Secret Self: Short Stories by Women*, ed. Hermione Lee (London: J. M. Dent & Sons, Ltd., 1985), viii.

7. Susan Kress, "Susan Fromberg Schaeffer," *Dictionary of Literary Biography* 28 (1984), 280. Also see Harold U. Ribalow, "A Conversation with Susan Fromberg Schaeffer," in *The Tie that Binds: Conversations with Jewish Writers* (San Diego & New York: Barnes, 1980), 77–92.

8. Although the stories by Tess Slesinger, Leane Zugsmith, and Tillie Olsen do not contain a specifically Jewish milieu, they are nonetheless written from a Jewish perspective characteristic of Depression Era writers, as explained in this Introduction.

9. For a discussion of negative stereotypes employed by Bernard Malamud, Saul Bellow, Philip Roth, and other American Jewish male short story writers, see Bryna Lee Datz Blustein, "Beyond the Stereotype: A Study of Representative Short Stories of Selected Contemporary Jewish-American Female Writers" (Ph.D. dissertation, Saint Louis University, 1986), chap. 1. Representative of many articles on the subject, see Evelyn Torton Beck, "I. B. Singer's Misogyny," in *Nice Jewish Girls: A Lesbian Anthology* rev. ed., ed. Evelyn Torton Beck (Boston: Beacon Press, 1989), 291–297; Sarah Blacher Cohen, "Sex: Saul Bellow's Hedonistic Joke," *Studies in American Fiction* 2 (1974): 223–224; and Barbara Koenig Quart, "Women in Bernard Malamud's Fiction," in *Studies in American Jewish Literature* 3 (1983): 138–150. For a positive view of Bellow's portrayal of women see Ada Abaroni, "Women in Saul Bellow's Novels," in *Studies in American Jewish Literature* 3 (1983): 99–111, and Allan Chavkin, "the Feminism of *The Dean's December*," in *Studies in Modern Jewish Literature* 3 (1983): 113–127.

For a comprehensive discussion of American-Jewish literature, see Louis Harap, *Creative Awakening: The Jewish Presence in Twentieth Century American Literature, 1900–1940s* (Westwood, Conn.: Greenwood Press, 1987) and Harap, *In the Mainstream: The Jewish Presence in Twentieth Century American Literature, 1950s–1980s* (Westwood, Conn.: Greenwood Press, 1987). *Twentieth-Century American-Jewish Fiction Writers*, vol. 28 of the *Dictionary of Literary Biography* (Detroit: Gale Research, 1984), edited by Daniel Walden, is another helpful resource.

10. On Yiddish women writers, see Norma Fain Pratt, "Culture and Radical Politics: Yiddish Women Writers in America, 1890–1940," in *Decades of Discontent: The Women's Movement, 1920–1940*, ed. Lois Scharf and Joan M. Jensen (Boston: Northeastern University Press, 1987), 131–152.

11. Other collections of American Jewish women's writing include: Melanie Kaye/Kantrowitz and Irena Klepfisz, eds., *The Tribe of Dina: A Jewish Wom-*

en's Anthology, rev. ed. (Boston: Beacon Press, 1989); Beck, *Nice Jewish Girls*; and Julia Wolf Mazow, ed., *The Woman Who Lost Her Names: Selected Writings of American Jewish Women* (New York: Harper & Row, 1980).

12. Yezierska often exaggerated women's subordination for effect. Despite religious inferiority, Jewish women frequently played active economic roles. For accounts of women's place within the shtetl, see Baum, et al., *The Jewish Women in America*, chap. 3, and Sydney Stahl Weinberg, *The World of Our Mothers* (Chapel Hill, N.C.: University of North Carolina Press, 1988), 8–16. See also Jacob R. Marcus, *The American Jewish Woman, 1654–1980* (New York: KTAV, 1981), and on ghetto life see Irving Howe, *The World of Our Fathers* (New York: Harcourt Brace Jovanovich, 1976).

13. Anzia Yezierska, *The Bread Givers* (New York: Persea Books, 1975), 9–10.

14. Ibid., 205.

15. Ibid., 137.

16. Ibid., 296–297.

17. Anzia Yezierska, "America and I," *Children of Loneliness* (New York and London: Funk & Wagnalls Co., 1923).

18. Ruth Rosen and Sue Davidson, eds., *The Maimie Papers* (Bloomington, Ind.: Indiana University Press in cooperation with The Feminist Press, 1977), 158–167. (In a letter from Maimie Pinzer, a former prostitute, to Boston philanthropist Fanny Quincy Howe.)

19. Another important story about the rapid assimilation of a Jewish family in America is Thyra Samter Winslow's "A Cycle of Manhattan," published in her 1923 collection, *Picture Frames*.

20. On Yezierska's struggles as a writer, see the excellent biography by her daughter, Louise Levitas Henriksen, *Anzia Yezierska: A Writer's Life* (New Brunswick, N.J.: Rutgers University Press, 1988). Also valuable are Mary V. Dearborn's *Love in the Promised Land: The Story of Anzia Yezierska and John Dewey* (New York: The Free Press, 1988); Carol B. Schoen's critical biography, *Anzia Yezierska* (Boston: Twayne, 1982); chapter 6 of Sam B. Girgus's study, *The New Covenant: Jewish Writers and the American Idea* (Chapel Hill, N.C.: University of North Carolina Press, 1984); and the many articles about Yezierska and her work which appear in various volumes of *Studies in American Jewish Literature*.

21. Ferber's second novel, *Fanny Herself* (1917), fictionalizes her experiences growing up Jewish in the Midwest. She also deals with her Jewishness in her

autobiographies, especially the first, A *Peculiar Treasure* (1939), and A *Kind of Magic* (1963). Hurst writes of her Jewishness in her autobiography, *Anatomy of Me* (1958); Hurst's novel *Back Street* (1932), and various short stories include Jewish characters or themes.

22. Cited in Carolyn Heilbrun, "Edna Ferber," in *Notable American Women: The Modern Period*, ed. Barbara Sicherman and Carol Hurd Green (Cambridge, Mass.: Harvard University Press, 1980), 227. For a discussion of ethnic pride in Ferber's writing, see Diane Lichtenstein, "On Whose Native Ground? Nineteenth-Century Myths of American Womanhood and Jewish Women Writers" (Ph.D. dissertation, University of Pennsylvania, 1985), chap. 6.

23. Though published seventy years later, Lesléa Newman's, "The Gift," recalls Ferber's story. Newman's heroine (also called Rachel), who has spent much of her life avoiding things Jewish, goes to *shul*, where she meets several women friends. "Rachel has come home," Newman concludes in the last line. ("The Gift," in Newman's A *Letter to Harvey Milk: Short Stories by Lesléa Newman* [Ithaca, N.Y.: Firebrand Books, 1988], 31.) The protagonist of Sinclair's "Second Blood" also "come[s] home, at last" at the end of the story.

24. See Antoinette Frederick, "Fannie Hurst," in Sicherman and Green, *Notable American Women*, 359–361.

25. For an interpretation of Hurst's work and its appeal to her contemporaries, see Susan Koppelman, "The Educations of Fannie Hurst," in *Women's Studies International Forum* 10 (1987): 503–516. Koppelman notes that critics praised Hurst's early work. Also see Diane Lichtenstein, "Fannie Hurst and Her Nineteenth Century Predecessors," *Studies in American Jewish Literature* 7 (1988): 26–39.

26. For a fuller discussion of Jewish American male writers in the 1930s, see Harap, *Creative Awakening*, chap. 3.

27. Edith H. Walton, "The Satirical Stories of Tess Slesinger," in the *New York Times Book Review*, May 26, 1935, cited in "Tess Slesinger," *Twentieth Century Literary Criticism* 10 (1983): 441. Dorothy Parker was the daughter of a second-generation German Jewish father, Henry Rothschild, and a non-Jewish mother who died when Dorothy was five. Dorothy was sent to a Catholic school near her home in Manhattan and, like her father, generally scorned identification with Judaism and her Jewish relatives; nevertheless, at the end of her life she quipped, "I was just a little Jewish girl trying to be cute." Cited in Marion Meade, *Dorothy Parker: What Fresh Hell is This?* (New York: Villard Books, 1988), xix. Parker's stories reveal no Jewish content.

28. According to historian Alan Wald, Slesinger created in *The Unpossessed* "a prototype of the Jewish/intellectual writings of Saul Bellow." Cited in "Tess Slesinger," *Twentieth Century Literary Criticism* 10 (1983): 439. Also see Wald, *The New York Intellectuals: The Rise and Decline of the Anti-Stalinist Left from the 1930s to the 1980s* (Chapel Hill, N.C.: University of New York Press, 1987), 64–74; and Mark Krupnick, "The Menorah Journal Group and the Origins of Modern Jewish-American Radicalism," *Modern Jewish Studies Annual* 3 (1979): 56–67.

29. According to one newspaper account, Jo Sinclair "sounded like a good anonymous writer's name and she liked Upton Sinclair and Sinclair it was." See "Jo Sinclair Shuns Gotham: Ohio's A Tremendous Joint," *Cleveland Plain Dealer*, 27 Nov. 1960, cited by Elisabeth Sandberg, "Jo Sinclair: Toward A Critical Biography" (Ph.D. dissertation, University of Massachusetts, 1985), 53.

30. Robert Phillips, in his *Commonweal* review of *The Collected Stories of Hortense Calisher*, cited in *Contemporary Authors, New Revision Series* 22 (1988): 63.

31. Unpublished interview with Naomi Rubin, May 1983, cited in Bonnie Lyons's important article, "Tillie Olsen: The Writer as A Jewish Woman," *Studies in American Jewish Literature* 5 (1986): 91. Also see Deborah Rosenfelt, "From the thirties: Tillie Olsen and the radical tradition," in *Feminist Criticism and Social Change*, ed. Judith Newton and Deborah Rosenfelt (New York: Methuen, 1985), 216–248.

32. See, for example, Irving Howe's "Introduction," in *Jewish-American Stories*, ed. Irving Howe (New York: New American Library, 1977), 16–17, and Ted Solataroff, "American-Jewish Writers: On Edge Once More," *New York Times Book Review*, 18 Dec. 1988, 1.

33. In "Literature and the Politics of Sex: A Dissent," *Ms.* 6 (Dec. 1977): 79–80, Ozick identifies herself as a "classical feminist" whose goals concern humankind rather than a narrower "female sensibility." Also see Ozick, "Torah as Matrix for Feminism," *Lilith* 12/13 (Spring 1985): 47–48; and Ozick, "Notes Toward Finding the Right Question," *Lilith* 6 (Spring/Summer 1979): 19–29. The Fall 1987 *Studies in American Jewish Literature* 6 is devoted to "The World of Cynthia Ozick." See also Sanford Pinsker, *The Uncompromising Fictions of Cynthia Ozick* (Columbia, Mo.: University of Missouri Press, 1987).

34. See Cynthia Ozick, "Previsions of the Demise of the Dancing Dog," in *Art and Ardor* (New York: Alfred A. Knopf, 1983), 266–268.

35. Blanche H. Gelfant, *Women Writing in America: Voices in Collage* (Hanover, N.H.: University Press of New England, 1985), 22. On Paley's work, see Dena Mandel, "Keeping Up With Faith: Grace Paley's Sturdy American Jewess," in *Studies in American Jewish Literature* 3 (1983): 85–98; and Minako Baba, "Faith Darwin as Writer-Heroine: A Study of Grace Paley's Short Stories," *Studies in American Jewish Literature* 7 (Spring 1988): 40–55.

36. Cited in Adam J. Sorkin, "Grace Paley," *Dictionary of Literary Biography* 28 (1984): 227.

37. See, for example, Elizabeth Klein, *Reconciliations* (Boston: Houghton Mifflin, 1982); Nessa Rapoport, *Preparing for Sabbath* (New York: William Morrow & Co., 1981); Meredith Tax, *Rivington Street* (New York: William Morrow & Co., 1982), and *Union Square* (New York: William Morrow & Co., 1988); Daphne Merkin, *Enchantment* (New York: Harcourt Brace Jovanovich, 1986); Allegra Goodman, *Total Immersion* (New York: Harper & Row, 1989); Sylvia Rothchild, *Family Stories—In Every Generation* (Detroit: Wayne State University Press, 1989), and Tema Nason, *Ethel: A Novel About Ethel Rosenberg* (London: William Collins, 1990).

PART 1

From the Ghetto and Beyond: 1900–1929

Malinke's Atonement

Mary Antin

I

I T WAS NOT THE FAULT of Breine Henne, the egg-woman, if her
only daughter, Malinke, had to assume the burdens of housekeeping
before she cast her milk teeth. Breine Henne made a fraction of a
living for herself and her two children by a small trade in poultry;
whence her nickname. As her business obliged her to stand all day in
the market-place, it naturally fell to Malinke to cook and sweep and
wash. The law of circumstance was potent in Polotzk, next to the law
of the Czar.

Late one afternoon Malinke was kneeling on a chair by the window,
watching for her mother's return. It had rained all day, a cold autumn
drizzle, and she knew trade was dull in such weather; her mother ought
to be coming home. Presently she saw the familiar figure, and ran out
into the entry to open the door.

Breine Henne came up the yard with a flat, heavy tread. The water
churned in her broken shoes. Her limp skirt was a fringe of rags at the
bottom, dripping with the mud of the market-place. Her frayed jacket,
whose original color the owner herself could scarcely recall, looked
black on the shoulders from the rain it had soaked up, and the woolly
shawl tied about her head was hoary with moisture. She walked with
her red hands clasped on her stomach, a covered basket hanging on
one arm.

Malinke hopped on the threshold, impatient for her mother's society. The child was much alone.

27

"Let me brush off the mud for you with the besom," she offered, as her mother stamped her feet in the entry. "I have scrubbed the floor and sanded it all afresh, and you mustn't bring in any mud, mama."

"Good health to you, my little housewife!" the mother said, giving the child a wet caress. "And where did you get the sand? The box was empty yesterday."

"Oh, I ran errands for old Rachel, and she gave me a basin of sand. Isn't it bright, mama? But you are so wet! Did you sell the hen? What have you in the basket?"

Malinke paused in her chatter to lift the cover from the basket. She saw a ball of gray feathers, slightly speckled with white. A little sigh of disappointment escaped her, but she said nothing. Lifting the hen, she cut the rag that bound its feet and set it down on the floor. The bird shook out its feathers, stretched its wings, and pattered over to the corner behind the oven, to drink from the broken earthenware dish which Malinke hastened to fill with fresh water.

Breine Henne peeled off her wet garments and spread them around the hot oven, watching the child meanwhile with a smile half sad, half happy. How many times she had promised Malinke a treat—an apple or a pear—in case she disposed of the hen that didn't lay; and always she had disappointed her—until now. Her smile turned wholly happy as she thought of the treat in store for Malinke and Yösele.

"Feed her well, little daughter," she said. "Give her all the oats you have, and the others will get the scrapings Rachel gives you after supper."

"All the oats? Why all the oats for her alone?" Malinke looked for an explanation.

"Yes, stuff her all she'll hold. She's to be killed in the morning."

"You're joking, mama. You didn't sell her, so who's going to kill her?"

"The butcher, of course," laughed Breine Henne, as she tied a cotton head-kerchief under her chin, preparatory to sitting down to roast her bare feet. "Who else kills chickens? The butcher, of course."

Malinke's eyes grew large with conjecture, but she could not frame a guess.

"The butcher shall kill the hen, Malinke," Breine Henne repeated impressively, *"and you shall eat it!"*

28

The child changed color from surprise. Her mother was not jesting—
she would not tease her so. There was to be a chicken cooked for her
and Yösele and Mother. She was speechless for a quarter of a minute,
then she broke into a laugh of pure happiness, and clapped her hands
as if she were a real little girl of nine, instead of a responsible house-
keeper and an understudy to her mother in bearing the troubles of
their difficult existence.

"Oh, mama, it will be so good! For Sabbath, you mean, don't you?
Won't Yösele be surprised! Let me tell him, mama, do. I'll run to
meet him when I hear the boys coming home from *heder* [Hebrew
school]. Oh, how good it will taste!"

Intoxicated with unlooked-for happiness, she caught one foot in her
hand and danced around on the other till she lost her balance. Her
eye fell on the devoted hen, who, unconscious of her impending doom,
was polishing her yellow bill on a leg of the wooden bench against
the wall. Malinke caught her up in her arms.

"Oh, you dear old hen! You poor old hen! You wouldn't lay, you
wouldn't get fat, nobody wanted you, and now *I'm* going to eat you!"

She thrust her fingers knowingly through the soft feathers to the
warm skin. The exuberance faded from her face. She turned to her
mother with a wry little smile.

"She's *not* very fat, is she, mama? Do you think there will be *any*
yellow rings on the soup? I saw the chicken soup the women from the
sick-visiting society brought old Rachel when she was sick, and it was
all yellow on top—*fat!*—and smelt so good!"

"If we live, we'll see," was Breine Henne's philosophic reply. "There
will be the bones to lick, anyway. And now reach down under the
bed and pull me out the sack of potatoes, and I'll peel some while you
make the samovar. Yösele comes home all dried up—nothing hot to
eat all day, poor boy."

One potato apiece was as much as Breine Henne could allow for
supper, but her tongue being nimbler than her fingers, she had time,
while preparing those few potatoes, to rehearse a good deal of domestic
history.

"I don't know what people will say of such extravagance," she remarked to the pot in her lap. "Breine Henne the egg-woman, the
destitute widow, to eat chicken, and not even a holiday for an excuse!

It was Rebecca the apple-woman put it into my head, and I can't see but what she is right. 'How much longer will you lug around that hen?' she laughed at me. 'I have seen you six market days with the same lean hen,' she said. 'I know her by her single eye, and every housewife in Polotz knows her by this time. Naked bones, that's what she is. You'll never sell her. Take my advice, Breine Henne, go home and have her killed for Sabbath. You'll save all she'll ever bring you if you use her economically. You can stand another year in the rain and rot in your shoes, the hen will never be any plumper. Nobody wants to put a lean chip in the soup.' "

Malinke had been watching the much-criticized fowl peck at its food, rejoicing, with anticipatory relish, at every kernel that swelled its crop. Her pleasure was marred by her mother's quotation of the apple-woman's disparaging opinion.

"Is she as bad as that, mama?" she asked. "Won't there be any fat at all?"

"If there won't, there won't," replied the mother unemotionally. "I can't make the creature over now. Is it my fault that she always was lean, and would not lay? I stuffed her enough, I'm sure; more than the others. It was fated that we should eat her, else why wasn't she plump, so that I could sell her? Already last Atonement Day I had it in mind to kill the hen as a sacrifice, but I reconsidered, and decided it would be too great an extravagance. It is no trifle for a destitute widow to offer up a hen. So I offered a groschen, and you a groschen, and Yösele, being a scholar, and soon to be confirmed, offered a little dwarf rooster, the one the stray cat—a curse on her!—nearly chewed up when he was a chick. He wasn't fit for anything else, the crippled rooster, and God would accept him, I knew. Everything is acceptable to the Almighty that is offered Him by the poor man's self-denial."

Malinke showed interest in her mother's discourse.

"Then why didn't you sacrifice the hen?" she asked.

"I've told you why, you little fool. It would have been too much."

"Too much for God?"

"Silence, you imp! Don't let loose your tongue. I thought I could not afford the hen then. Extravagance is a sin. The Almighty knows how I have to struggle to keep body and soul together. I am behind with the rent, behind with the tuition. Reb' Zalmen Boruch sent me

30

word last week that if I don't pay him at least half of what I owe he can't let Yösele come any more. I don't blame the *rebbe* [Hebrew teacher]; he is a poor man himself. If I have to take Yösele out of school, the Most High will know it was not because I did not value sacred learning."

Malinke saw that her mother was getting ready to cry, and tried to divert her thoughts.

"I can peel as close as that, mama," she said, fingering the little heap of potato parings in her mother's lap. "I make it so thin you can see the light through if you hold it up."

She cocked her head as she applied the test to a curl of the peel.

Breine Henne brightened at once.

"Sound be your little head!" she blessed as she emptied her lap before rising. "I know you are a good housewife. Now you watch me to-morrow when I cut up the hen, and you'll learn how to make the most of a fowl. There will be the soup for Sabbath, and the meat, and the bits will last a few days. And then the feathers—a handful; but I won't have as much as a little pillow to give you, Malinke, when you make a match, unless I fill it by handfuls."

Malinke laughed. "I don't want to make a match, and I don't want any feathers. I just want to eat chicken every Sabbath!"

When Yösele came home, the story of his good luck met him on the threshold, and nothing was talked of during the supper but the next day's feast.

"Oh, mama, will you give me the neck?" begged Malinke. "I once ate a chicken's neck, at Aunt Leah's, and it had so many little bones, you could suck and suck and never know when you were done. Will you give me the neck?"

Jumping up from her stool in her excitement, the little girl bumped her mother's elbow, causing her to spill the boiling water she was at that moment drawing from the samovar.

"See what you are doing, you little fool!" scolded Breine Henne. "Do you want to scald me? Don't jump in the air like that. I'll give you what I'll give you, and an end of it. In the meantime you have potatoes and herring; eat and be thankful. Ever see such a wild goat? Have the neck and the tail too, only quiet down."

Yösele put in a brotherly joke.

31

"Why don't you bid for the whole chicken at once, and be done with it? I don't expect anything but a couple of drumsticks, the feet, and maybe the breast and the liver."

But this rehearsal of the chicken's anatomy betrayed him into a slip from his dignity. "The liver, mama," he begged eagerly, "will you give me the liver? I think you ought to give me the liver, because there's only one, and I'm an only son, you know. Will you give me the liv—"

"But I'm an only daughter, you know!" cried Malinke, once more jumping up in her place. "Mama, you give *me* the liver!"

Breine Henne emptied her saucer at a gulp, and set it down on the bare table. "Children, children," she cried, spreading out her hands in appeal, "will you get quiet to-night? You, Yösele, ought to be ashamed to be so greedy—a great boy of twelve! And, anyway, a scholar ought to be sated with Torah [sacred learning], and ask for nothing more. You, Malinke, are out of your head to-night. An only daughter, indeed! What are daughters worth? They're only good to sit in the house, a burden on their parents' neck, until they're married off. A son, at least, prays for the souls of his parents when they're dead; it's a deed of piety to raise sons."

"That's just what I think, mama," Yösele caught at her words. "And so you'll give me the liver?"

Breine Henne shook her head angrily by way of answer. She had begun the long grace after meals, and she would not speak till after the amen.

Yösele, reproved, began to pray in a loud voice, swaying back and forth, and from time to time closing his eyes tight, as if the better to concentrate on the holy words. Malinke also began to mumble the prayer, sitting on the edge of her stool and surreptitiously brushing the few crumbs from the table with one bare hand, catching them in the other.

Before Yösele was half through, Malinke ended with an explosive "amen," causing her brother to open his eyes at her in an incredulous stare, while his lips mechanically progressed with the prayer.

"Mama, she skips!" the male of the house broke out, as soon as he could speak. "She slurs the words, and she skips. I don't think she knows the prayer at all."

"I don't—I do," his sister defended herself. "I know it all, but I can

32

say it fast, can't I? When we have only half a herring and three potatoes, and say the whole prayer, what'll we say when we have a chicken? I'll pray slowly to-morrow, you'll see."

Yösele stared, amazed at his sister's audacity. Breine Henne gave her a couple of cuffs with the flat of her hand, and would have given more if Malinke had not skipped out of arm's reach.

"Hold your tongue, you bastard!" she cried, using a not uncommon epithet of reproach. "Ever hear such a mouth? Where does the imp get such words? What! will you measure the prayer according to your meal? You should thank God for every crumb that you put into your mouth. There are plenty in Polotzk who don't have any potatoes, nor any herring either. Already nine years old, and she hasn't learned respect for the Almighty! One might think she wasn't raised among Jews. Never let me hear you talk like that again, Malinke; do you hear?"

The culprit received this tirade at a safe distance, with an expression of forbearance rather than contrition. She traced patterns in the sand with one foot, where she stood, at the same time chewing on the end of a very thin pig-tail, until her mother stopped for breath.

"But, mama," argued the bold child, unabashed, "I don't grudge the prayer,—I'll say it twice, if you want me to,—but it seems foolish to thank God just the same for a little as for much. I think He won't believe that we mean it. You don't do that way to anybody else—to people. When Aunt Leah brought fruit and wine for Yösele, when he had the fever, you thanked her and blessed her, and prayed for her in the synagogue; but when a neighbor lends you a spoonful of salt you don't say so much about it. Don't you think God knows the difference, too?"

Breine Henne had opened her mouth several times during Malinke's discourse, not to speak, but to catch her breath. Her pale eyes stared at the child as if they saw a strange monster. She made an ineffectual clutch at Malinke, and finally collapsed on her stool, crying from helplessness.

"Hear her—hear her!" she wailed, a corner of her kerchief at her eyes. "What kind of a renegade have I brought into the world? Let somebody talk to her who knows how. I can't argue with her any more. I'm a poor, struggling widow—a friendless female—I'm obliged to spend my days in the street, in the market-place. How do I know what the girl does here all day—where she gets such talk? No child in Polotzk ever had such audacity. Such a mouth! And to think how I wept when her twin sister died! A fine life I would have of it if I had two like her! The Supreme One will punish us all for her sinful mouth."

After one or two unsuccessful efforts to sooth her mother, Malinke went about her usual evening duties with a composure that bespoke a conscience at rest. Her critical young soul by no means yielded in the argument that so outraged her mother's piety; but she knew when it was useless to speak. Having washed the few dishes from the recent meal, she quickly made her toilet for the night, by slipping off her coarse flannel dress and removing the clumsy boots from her bare feet, and tumbled into the only bed in the room, burying herself up to the nose in the miscellaneous collection of rags that composed the bed covering.

Yösele, rather ostentatiously reading his bed-time prayers, watched her prompt proceedings out of a corner of his eye, wondering, in a parenthesis of his evening devotions, why Malinke was such a queer little girl. He knew no one who asked such strange questions as Malinke, and no one who could satisfy her. His own teacher, a pious scholar, caught in the toils of one of her impudent inquisitions, was obliged to silence her by the only argument that ever made Malinke hang her head in submission.

"You are only a girl," the rebbe had reminded her. "Girls don't need to know things out of books."

Malinke was asleep by the time Yösele had finished his devotions; she was snoring gently before he had composed himself to sleep on the narrow wooden bench by the oven. The latter process required some time and thought, as Yösele, in spite of years of experience, had not evolved a satisfactory way of arranging his bedding, which consisted of a tattered quilt, a couple of burlap sacks, and his own jacket.

"If I lie on the sacks and cover myself with the quilt, I am warm, but my sides get sore," he complained to his mother. "If I lie on the quilt and cover myself with the sacks, it's soft, but my feet freeze. If I put my jacket on my feet, I have nothing for a pillow."

The vexing problem was solved this evening in one of the few ways possible, and presently Malinke's solo became a duet, Yösele snoring an octave or two deeper than his sister.

II

Breine Henne sat up some time longer over a bit of hopeless mending. "Patch upon patch," she muttered to herself, "like a head of cabbage."

She was about to blow out the lamp, preparatory to going to bed, when Malinke, with a long-drawn sigh, turned over in her sleep. Breine Henne went over and looked at her. The child was a small hump under the bed-clothes. Her thin little face was turned to the wall, and her colorless pig-tail, tied with a scarlet rag, straggled forlornly on the pillow.

"Seems like a baby, when she lies there like that," mused Breine Henne, stooping over the bed, her hands busy with the knotted fastenings of her undergarments. "No bigger than a baby, and speaks up like a man. And such queer ideas! God knows where she gets them."

She blew out the lamp and lay down beside Malinke. "May God refrain from punishing her for her talk!" she prayed as she fell asleep.

The next day was Friday—a short work-day, as the Sabbath began with the early sunset. It was the day appointed for the great feast, the children reminded each other on waking.

"Be sure you go to the butcher early, Malinke," Breine Henne called over her shoulder, as she was leaving for the day. "I'll be home at twelve to dress the chicken. That will give it plenty of time to cook."

Malinke, always a diligent little housewife, needed no prompting on this day. Returning from the butcher's, she passed a morning of volcanic activity. She had scrubbed and scoured only the day before, but in honor of the coming feast she scrubbed anew, first carefully brushing the sand from the floor into a basin, to be used over again. She repolished the almost spotless samovar with sand and cranberry juice,—she had to beg the cranberries from a neighbor,—and her small collection of cutlery came in for its share of rubbing. The little window-panes were so pieced that it was risky to touch them, but this was a supreme occasion, worthy of supreme daring. And looking through her clear window-panes, Malinke perceived that the street was very muddy. The street was no business of hers, because she was not a house-owner; but she cleaned the street for a generous distance to right and left of the house, exerting herself with besom and shovel till her little back ached. If she could have reached the sky to tear the

35

clouds asunder, she would have set the sun to shine into her shining room. Nothing was too good for the occasion.

From time to time, as she busied herself in the room or outside, Malinke ran to peep at the slaughtered hen, which lay awaiting further operations. If something should happen to the chicken now—a cat or a dog! Malinke wished her fowl were safely in the pot, but she did not yet know how to dress a chicken. She had picked the feathers clean; that was as far as she could go. And what if her mother should be late, and the chicken not have time to cook! The anxious little house-keeper was making up her mind to ask a neighbor to prepare the fowl, when Breine Henne, breathless with haste, came into the room.

It was a tense little face, with two great eyes—two hungry eyes— that bent over the wretched carcass, as her mother slit and cut and tore, laying bare the creature's anatomy. The mother, herself not a little excited, kept up a running commentary on the subject of chick-ens, with special reference to the one in hand; but Malinke uttered no word. She was in an ecstasy of expectation beyond speech.

"Not so bad, after all," Breine Henne commented, cheerfully mak-ing the most of the lean carcass. "Upon my word, she's not as bad as I thought. I'm glad I didn't sell her. We'll have a nice soup, and chicken meat for two or three days. I've seen plumper chickens, but still this one—"

She broke off abruptly, a look of keen trouble in her face. Her bloodstained fingers trembled as she tore at the intestines. They had felt a lump where there should be none.

"Lord of All!" she breathed, "what is this?"

Malinke watched her with a face gone pale. Her hands clasped tightly over her thumping heart, she waited for her mother's explanation.

"Look, look!" Breine Henne cried, "a wire—a bit of crooked wire, right in the intestine! Oi, woe is me! the chicken is *tref!*"[1]

Malinke felt a sickening sinking of the heart. For a quarter of a minute she remained standing as if petrified, then she threw herself on the bench and cried aloud.

Breine Henne took no notice of her at first. She sat staring at the dismembered chicken, wringing her hands and bemoaning herself.

1. *Tref*, unclean, in conformity with Jewish dietary laws, as distinguished from *kosher*, clean.

Presently she became aware of Malinke, now sobbing with her face in her arms.

"Don't cry—don't cry, Malinke," she soothed. "Maybe it isn't *tref*, after all. Take your shawl and run to the *rav*.[2] Perhaps he will decide that the chicken is *kosher*."

The little girl jumped up, a flame of hope in her tear-stained face.

"Oh, do you think so, mama? Do you really think it may be kosher? Oi, dear little mama! Where's my shawl? How shall I carry it? What shall I tell the rav? I'll run—I'll run."

Breiné Henne wrapped the chicken in a cloth. "Don't lose anything," she cautioned, "and don't be gone long. This is where I found the wire; see? Show him. Now run, and God grant that the rav finds it kosher."

It was some distance to the rav's, but Malinke ran all the way. Arrived at her destination, she burst into the house and thrust her bundle under the nose of the astonished servant.

"A *shala*" [question], she panted. "My mother sent me to ask a shala. Is Reb' Nossen at home?"

"Mercy on us!" protested the servant, an elderly person who was not used to being hurried, "one would think the town were on fire, to see the child. And if it is a shala, what then? Must you rush in on people and take their breath away? It's nothing new, a shala. Reb' Nossen settles a dozen every day. Sit down there on the bench, and I'll go and see if he is not busy. There's a novelty for you—a shala!"

Malinke thought the woman was gone an age, but at last she saw her returning through the long living-room, where the table was already set for Sabbath.

"Come, he will see you at once. See that you do not touch the clean table cloth as you pass. You are—I guess you haven't got your Sabbath dress on yet."

Malinke did not notice the look of disapproval which her conductor cast over her ragged person. She saw only an open door at the end of the room, and went in, always holding out her bundle before her.

Reb' Nossen was busy arranging a pyramid of books on a table. He greeted the child over his shoulder.

"Well, little girl, what is your question?"

2. *Rav*, the religious head of a Jewish community.

Malinke, in all her eagerness, remembered that she was in a great presence. She had never been in the rav's house before. A sudden shyness replaced her usual assurance.

"Well," repeated the rav, still without turning, "you came to ask a shala. What is it?"

Malinke advanced a step. "The chicken," she whispered. "My mother found a wire."

"So? Let's see it. Put it down here, by the window. This is the wire, is it? And how was it found? Show me exactly where it lay. H'm—h'm."

The rav poked the dismembered organs with a long forefinger, and carefully examined the spot where the bit of wire had been embedded. He peered long at the wire itself, with knitted brows and set mouth. Then, after wiping his fingers on a red bandana, he picked out a book from the pile he had been arranging, and began to turn its yellow leaves, humming a bit of Sabbath melody under his breath.

Malinke followed his movements with eyes of feverish expectancy. The rav's word was law in such a matter. Would he say tref or kosher?

Reb' Nossen turned the leaves and hummed to himself. His silvery earlocks mingled with his beard, which swept the table. A silk skullcap sat high on his broad brow. Face and hands were shining with health and cleanliness. The rav had just returned from the *mikweh*.[3] The peace of approaching Sabbath was in his soul.

Malinke did not take her hungry eyes from Reb' Nossen's face. Apparently the question was not a simple one, to be resolved at a glance. The rav ceased his humming. He pushed away his book and took another. He returned to the chicken, lying in the light of the window. Once he asked Malinke to show him again how the wire was found, and she answered that, and other questions, in a voice trembling with apprehension.

If Reb' Nossen had noticed the child's distress, and asked her questions about herself and her mother, he might have come to a conclusion promptly. Besides the nature of the foreign body, the position in which it was found, and the condition of the carcass, the rav had a right to take into consideration the circumstances of the owner of the animal. For the sacred office of the rav endows him with considerable

3. The ritual bath.

38

latitude in the interpretation of the Law. If the question is one on which authorities differ, or even if the rav to whom it is submitted disagrees with recorded opinions, the owner of the property in question is entitled to the benefit of the doubt, especially if he be a poor man. The Jewish Law was not framed to oppress God's chosen people. It was meant to keep them clean, by guarding them against every disease of mind and body. In the mouths of wise and liberal scholars, it can be interpreted in two words: Be pure.

Reb' Nossen peered very closely at his book, following the lines across the page with his finger. He was a trifle short-sighted. Perhaps that was why he did not notice that Malinke's shawl was in rags, that her shoes gaped, and that she looked at him with frightened, hungry eyes.

"Little girl," he said, after an interval in which the child suffered agonies of doubt, "little girl, tell your mother the chicken is unclean."

Malinke felt again that horrid sinking of the heart. Mechanically she tied up her bundle, and went out. She did not hear the rav call "Good Sabbath" after her.

Her feet carried her homewards. She did not think of the way. The bitterness of her disappointment made her blind and deaf. But suddenly, as she turned a corner, she was brought back to life by a strong smell of cooking coming from an open kitchen door. Involuntarily she drew a deep breath. Fish, chicken, and fresh bread. Malinke gave a gulp and stuffed the corner of her shawl into her mouth. She would not be seen crying on the street.

Her knees trembled as she walked on. She had eaten black bread and tea for breakfast, and bread with salt for dinner. She was tired from exertion, and shaken by emotion. The miserable bundle in her hand became a grievous burden. And what were they going to have for supper?

Oh, if only Reb' Nossen had found the chicken clean! Why was it unclean? All sorts of things were found inside chickens, and yet they were pronounced clean. Yösele once told her about a chicken that his schoolmate's mother cooked for a holiday. An earring had been found in the gizzard, and the rav had pronounced the meat kosher. Why was not her chicken kosher? How did the rav know?

Malinke's thoughts climbed from the plaintive to the curious, from

39

the curious to the rebellious, from the rebellious to the defiant. What was written in the books the rav consulted? She was only a girl—she would never know. Reb' Nossen said tref. How did he know? Suppose he had said kosher, then her mother would cook the chicken, they would all enjoy it, and no harm come to anybody.

Malinke stopped short in her walk, struck by an idea, a great and fearful idea. Nobody knew of the rav's decision but herself. *Suppose she should tell her mother it was kosher?* Her face flamed; the blood thumped in her ears. Stooping down, she undid the bundle in her lap. The chicken looked exactly as it had done when first opened by her mother. Why, why was it unclean? The rav's word made it so. Oh, it was cruel! She was so hungry—half the time she was hungry. She never had good things to eat. Why should the rav rob her of the chicken? It was just like any other chicken. He should not rob her! He might have said kosher, and he did not. Suppose she told her mother it was kosher?

She began to run, frightened at her own thoughts. It was a heinous sin she contemplated. The rav was the voice of God. He had declared the chicken unfit for a Jewish table, and she proposed to eat of it, and impose it upon her mother and brother.

"But what if the rav were mistaken?" the rebel in her cried. Malinke, who went much from house to house doing errands, and heard much talk, and asked questions freely, knew that it was not impossible for a rav to make a mistake. Only the year before, Polotzk was torn into two factions, the one adhering to Reb' Nossen, the other to Reb' Isaac, when the two dignitaries disagreed in the settlement of a shala. Malinke did not know just what the point in dispute was,—something about a burial,—nor whose opinion prevailed in the end. But one thing was clear from the dispute: a rav may make a mistake. And if Reb' Nossen were wrong in her case, was it just that she and Yösele and her mother should suffer for his error?

"No, no, no!" she cried in her heart. "I won't tell—I won't. If it's unclean, God will punish me, and then I shall know."

She kept on running, but she was no longer frightened. Arrived at her own doorstep, she paused once more. Clasping her bundle tightly to her breast, she closed her eyes and prayed.

"Good God, if the chicken is tref, punish me, and nobody else. Amen."

Breine Henne opened the door the moment she heard Malinke in the entry.

"Well, well?" she questioned eagerly. "What does the rav say?"

Malinke answered firmly, "Kosher."

Her mother was too excited to notice how pale the child was.

III

It was a happy family that sat down to supper when Yösele returned from evening prayer in the synagogue.

Breine Henne had replaced the cotton kerchief by her wig, which she wore only on holy days and ceremonious occasions. Yösele's patched trousers were mercifully invisible under the table, and from his thighs to his neck he was conscious of his Sabbath jacket. It had belonged to his father, may he rest in peace! but Yösele was a big boy for his age, and the jacket fitted not so badly, if he puffed himself out a little in front, and sat firmly on the tails of the coat behind, and turned up the cuffs of the sleeves.

Malinke was even more splendid than Yösele. She wore a blue woolen dress, trimmed with rows of gold braid on the skirt and a double row of gilt buttons on the waist. The dress was frayed and stained and choky,—Malinke was obliged to leave the waist and the neck-buttons unfastened,—but the gold trimmings redeemed every fault. She had earned the dress by hulling quarts and quarts of straw-berries for a neighbor, whose little girl's cast-off clothes fitted her well enough.

Dear to Malinke's heart was the dress, and dearer still the boots on her feet. Yes, a pair of Sabbath boots had Malinke, and such boots! They were whole, they were new, they were shiny. They had patent-leather tips, and patent-leather tops closing with three buttons on each side, and all the buttons were on. All the poor little girls in the neighborhood envied her those boots. They squeaked delightfully. They were the pride and joy of her heart.

How came Malinke by such superior footgear? "God is good," she somewhat tactlessly remarked, when Aunt Leah presented her with the boots, which had belonged to Cousin Fredke, who died of cholera. Aunt Leah never gave away anything till it was shabby enough for a beggar, but because poor Fredke had been fond of Malinke—"God is good," said the beneficiary of Aunt Leah's sorrow.

Arrayed in all her finery, Malinke sat down to the unwonted feast with a face of glowing happiness. There was no shadow in her heart. The anguish of the afternoon was washed away in a flood of peace. Having struggled so bitterly and come to a great resolution, she was abiding by it with all the courage of her fiery young soul. By her prayer on the doorstep she had bravely assumed all the responsibility for her conduct. If she had sinned, the punishment was to fall on her alone: no innocent person should suffer. She did not doubt for a moment that God had heard and would heed her petition. And until God gave her a sign of His displeasure, she would not call herself a sinner, but would enjoy herself to the utmost.

All joys come to an end, but the joy of sucking chicken-bones bade fair to outlast all others. The Sabbath candles, stuck in a basin of sand, for want of candlesticks, had burned down to half their length before Breine Henne could induce the children to give up the clean-picked bones to which they clung.

"M—m," protested Yösele, "there's more on it"; and "M—m," pleaded Malinke, "it still tastes of chicken."

The mother got up and brought the soup to the table, and set it steaming under their noses. Then, and not till then, did they consent to part with the bones.

"Oh!" triumphed Malinke, gloating over her plate, "there *is* a fat-spot in mine!"

"Take care," warned Breine Henne, "it's very hot. Blow on it, children."

The soup was pronounced delicious with every mouthful. Malinke dipped up very scant spoonfuls, to make it last. Yösele, finishing before her, made a dive at her plate to help himself.

"She had more than I," he grumbled, when his mother ordered him to let his sister's plate alone. And Malinke, not feeling safe enough even under her mother's protection, began to gulp her soup hastily, lest her brother rob her of any.

She had almost finished, when she gave a short cough, accompanied by a convulsive jerk of the head. She grew red in the face; her eyes started out; her tongue protruded. She was choking.

Breine Henne and Yösele jumped up in a fright, and began to thump and shake her.

"A bone!" wailed Breine Henne. "Oi, *weh!* She'll choke to death. Take a drink of water—there, try to drink. Woe is me, she's choking!"

Breine Henne set Malinke's plate on her head, while she and Yösele pounded her on the back and chest simultaneously. It was the best remedy they knew, and it failed to dislodge the bone. The mother next inserted her forefinger into the girl's throat as far as it would go, but without result. The child struggled convulsively. The sweat was on her blackening face, the tears in her eyes.

Yösele began to bawl with fright. His mother was out of her wits.

"Oi, weh! Woe is me! I always knew no good would come of that hen. Malinke! Malinke! little daughter! Take a drink of water. God Almighty, have pity on us! Run, Yösele, call the neighbors. Oh, Malinke, Malinke!"

Yösele ran out, calling, "Help! Help!"

Jacob the tailor, who occupied the rear of the house, answered the call, and his frightened family flocked after him to the scene of distress.

Jacob stopped in front of Malinke, helpless and aghast. Not so Peshe Frede, his wife. Without a word she grasped the strangling child by the ankles, and turning her upside down, swung her back and forth with all her might.

Presently Malinke gave a gasp, followed by a wailing "Oh—h!" Peshe Frede put her back in her chair, and everybody crowded around.

Slowly the red left Malinke's face. It faded and faded, till she was ashy white. She looked around the circle of faces, with a growing horror in her eyes. She tried to speak, but failed.

"There, there," her mother crooned, "sit still. You'll be better in a minute."

She began to fondle the child, wiping her moist face with a corner of her own apron. Malinke avoided her touch with a strange gesture, always staring with eyes of horror.

"God has punished me," she breathed in a strangled whisper. "I have sinned, and God has punished me."

"What is she saying?" they all asked one another. "Better put her to bed, Breine Henne. She will be all right when she has rested."

But Malinke pushed her mother away. Springing up, she threw out her hands in a gesture of despair, crying aloud, "God has punished me! God has punished me!"

The others drew away from her in amazement. "What do you mean? What does she mean?" they questioned.

Again Breine Henne tried to soothe the child, and again Malinke avoided her.

"Don't touch me!" she cried. "I am a great sinner. God has punished me."

Then she told them. Standing in the middle of the room, with wild eyes, panting and sobbing, she told them the whole story of the rav's decision and her false report. She did not excuse herself, although she tried to explain to them the thoughts and feelings that led up to her wicked resolution; but she saw that they did not understand.

"Do with me what you will," she cried. "I have sinned. God has punished me." With a sob that shook her whole frame, she threw herself prone on the floor in abject surrender.

No language but the Yiddish can reproduce the exclamations of horror, anger, reproach, that broke from the lips of the bystanders. Breine Henne sank upon a chair and threw out her arms across the table, moaning as one mortally hurt. Yösele shrank into a corner, his jaw hanging, his eyes roving around the room as if seeking support. The assembled neighbors turned horrified faces on one another, gasping and ejaculating. Jacob's two little girls clung to each other, backing away toward the door, as if they feared contamination. And the culprit shook the floor with her sobs.

"Oi!" moaned the unhappy mother, when she could speak. "Dark is my world; my eyes may not look upon the light of day. God in heaven, why didst Thou punish me with such a child? A monster— a renegade! Why dost Thou leave her in the world, such a wicked spirit? Woe is me, woe is me! dark is my world."

Peshe Frede, herself weeping from pious sorrow, tried to soothe her neighbor.

"What good will it do to cry? Calm yourself, Breine Henne. The Almighty knows it is not your fault. The girl is possessed by an evil spirit. I always warned you that she would grow up a renegade. A trifle is it, to impose *trefah* upon a clean house? Such treachery! An honest Gentile would not do such a thing. Mark my word, this will not be the end of her wickedness. She would poison all Polotzk if her evil heart told her to. But what is the use of crying? Calm yourself, Breine Henne. What is done, is done."

After a while, Breine Henne lifted her heavy head. Her eyes fell on the dishes standing on the table. She broke into fresh weeping.

"Tref—tref—everything tref! All the dishes defiled. Woe is me, she has ruined me!"

"Don't lose your head, Breine Henne," Jacob spoke up. "Defiled vessels can be purified. The crockery must be scalded, the knives must be stuck into the cracks of the floor for half an hour, the—the—the rest of the things must be taken to the rav to pass upon."

The tailor was not much of a scholar, but so far as he had ventured to advise, he was correct. Every housewife knew as much. A gleam of comfort came to Breine Henne's heart as Jacob spoke, but the mention of the rav brought her shame back to her. She wept and prayed and wrung her hands. Peshe Frede at last gave up the attempt to comfort her, and retired, followed by her family.

"The whole town will ring with this," the poor egg-woman wailed. "Peshe Frede will have it all over town tomorrow. They will call us *trefah fressers* [eaters of unclean food]. Everybody will point a finger at us. Where shall I bury myself? Good God, just God, I beg Thee open a grave for me, and let me sink in and hide my disgrace."

Far into the night Breine Henne wept, exhausting the vocabulary of lamentation. The candles burned out, the oil in the lamp was low, and still she rocked herself in her grief. Yösele had long since curled up on his bench, too stupefied by misery to bother with the bedclothes. Finally she dragged herself over to the bed and fell asleep, exhausted. At Malinke she did not look.

Malinke had not moved since she had thrown herself on the floor. She heard the hubbub excited by her confession, as one hears the rustle of summer leaves on the brink of a cataract. The greater tumult was in her own heart. Her own conscience hurled the bitterest reproaches at her. She knew, better than all her censors, how often she had questioned the written Word of God, defied the authority of her elders, and set up her own unhallowed standards. Nobody knew but she of the foreign petitions she injected into her daily prayers. For weeks past she had prayed, morning and night, that her hair might grow long, so that her playmates could not twit her about her pig-tail. Now, in her hour of repentance, she realized how irreverent were her prayers. She had mocked at Yösele's rebbe, a pious and learned man, because he could not answer her impertinent questions about the

45

Creation. Finally, she had disregarded the express commands of the rav himself, and betrayed her own mother and brother, for the sake of a chicken-bone and a plate of watery soup. Her most pitiless judge could not have drawn up a more bitter indictment than Malinke's conscience presented to her.

Now that she had had a sign from God, her remorse was bottomless. With all her soul she repented. She knew she would never be wicked any more, but she longed for a means of immediate atonement for the past. She threw her soul at the feet of God in utter humility at last, and she prayed Him to trample upon her and leave the mark of His chastisement on her.

IV

Worn out by her agonized thoughts, Malinke finally fell asleep. When she awoke, stiff with cold and sore from lying on the bare boards, the windows were opaque with dawn. She sat up, amazed to find herself on the floor. She made out her mother's figure lying on the edge of the bed. There was a curious atmosphere of disorder about the room.

Breine Henne moved on the bed with a groan. In a flash Malinke remembered everything. Her tormenting thoughts of the evening rushed back into her brain. The sense of guilt once more overwhelmed her. It seemed to her that she was not herself, but somebody else,— a monstrous, unclean creature, from whom the real Malinke shrank in horror. She longed to cry out, to struggle, to shake off the hideous thing that grappled her, but she was afraid to wake the sleepers. She must get out of the house, or she would stifle.

Slowly creeping across the floor, inch by inch, she reached the door. Noiselessly she lifted the latch and stole out. The chill of the autumn morning struck to her very bones. She wished she had taken a shawl, but she dared not go back.

Like a ghost she wandered away through the empty streets. She had never been abroad at such an hour in the autumn; she thought it was her sins that had turned the world so gray and unfamiliar. The watch-men had gone home with the first glimmer of day. In all the sleeping city, she alone was awake. It was a symbol of her isolation from the world of righteous men.

46

Her dress reminded her that it was Sabbath. The people would sleep late, but presently they would awake. The men would go to the synagogue, and so would some of the women. The children would put on their best clothes, and call to one another from the doorways, and go visiting until dinner-time. Where should she go then, she that was neither man nor woman nor honest child?

Crying softly, she wandered blindly on. At the bottom of a steep street, the river gleamed pale in the ghostly light. Malinke descended to the edge, and being unable to go farther, looked about her for the first time.

On the bank above her a low gray building was just visible between the palings of a sagging fence. Beyond the fence she could make out a gray ribbon trembling down a shallow gash in the bank. That was where the spring flowed out which was reputed among the Gentiles to cure blindness. The building behind the fence was the Old Synagogue. By these landmarks, Malinke identified the spot. It was where the Jewish women came on New Year's Day for the ceremony of shaking their sins into the river, that they might start the new year with clean hearts.

A sudden thought came to Malinke. A flash of hope lighted up the gloom of her troubled soul. Why could not she, like the pious women of Polotzk, shake her sins into the river and begin a holy life? Was repentance only for New Year? Did God grant pardons only on the Day of Atonement? She did not realize that she was once more committing the sin of religious innovation—once more reasoning outside the book. Swept away by a genuine longing to make her peace with God, she cast about for means to carry out the symbolic rites of the season of atonement, fervently praying that the Almighty should see and understand.

Contrition, prayer, fasting, and sacrifice. She could not think of any other processes that went to the solemn drama of annual repentance. Contrition? Her soul prostrated itself in deepest humility. And prayer? She prayed with all her being that God should have mercy on her and forgive her sins. Her every breath should be a prayer. Fasting also she could fulfill. She would fast as long as her body would hold out. A whole day—two days she would fast. Sacrifice was left. What could she sacrifice? What had she that would be acceptable to God?

47

Malinke's heart sank as she failed to find a solution to this problem. Was she to give up the hope of God's forgiveness because she had nothing to sacrifice? No, no! she must think of something.

Her pockets were empty, because it was Sabbath. She looked down on herself, and so got her inspiration. She would sacrifice her Sabbath clothes—the dress with the gold trimmings, *and the boots!*

Joy unspeakable lighted Malinke's pinched face. With feverish fingers she unfastened and tore off her dress, half laughing, half crying with excitement. Then, sitting down on the wet bank, she unlaced her boots and started to roll them up in her dress.

What pretty boots they were! The patent-leather trimmings were as shiny as water. They were almost new: the varnish was not all worn off from the instep. She had worn them very little, of course: only on Sabbaths and holy days. It was the only pair of boots she could remember that had come to her new. She always had other people's cast-off boots. If they were too big, she stuffed them with rags; if too small, she slit them in the tight spots. Her Sabbath boots, now, fitted her as if made to her measure.

Malinke could not forbear trying them on once more, for the last time. It was light enough now for her to make out the stitching on the patent-leather tops. It was a pretty pattern, all scrolls. She wondered if Fredke had loved those boots as much as she did.

With a deep, deep sigh, Malinke pulled off the beautiful boots again, and resolutely rolled them up in the blue dress. The sacrifice was ready.

But now a new difficulty assailed her. In what manner was the sacrifice to be performed? On Atonement Day, when money was offered, it was put into the poor-box; if a fowl, it was cooked and eaten at the close of the fast. What was she to do with her clothes? And the formula—she could not remember the formula by which the sacrifice was offered, because it was used only once a year. She also suspected that it would not fit the novel sacrifice she proposed to offer.

After some hard thinking she threw up her head with a gesture of finality, and turned an appealing face to heaven.

"Good God," she prayed, her teeth chattering with cold, "I have nothing to sacrifice except this. I don't know how to do it. I'll just tie a stone to it and throw it into the river. I beg Thee to pardon me if I do wrong, and accept my sacrifice like a real one. I would pray from the prayer-book, but it's at home, and there is nothing in it about atonement in the middle of the year. Forgive me for everything. Amen."

V

Malinke never knew how she got home that day, nor how the time passed. Her faith in the validity of her atonement had lifted her into a state of exaltation past all physical sensation. She heard herself, in a voice not her own, communicate the great news to her mother: that she had atoned, by prayer and sacrifice, and all was well. Her mother seemed unaccountably affected by the news. Malinke dimly perceived that her mother's fresh tears were not the tears of joy; but she was too far removed from the world to be troubled, or even puzzled. She was fasting, in accordance with her resolution. She felt as buoyant as a chip floating on the bosom of the river.

It was well along in the afternoon when Malinke awoke from her trance. She was lying on the bed, staring wide-eyed at the wall, when she became aware of some unusual commotion in the room. Presently her mother's voice penetrated her dazed consciousness.

"Do you hear, Malinke? Get up and go to the rav. He has sent for you. Do you hear?"

Breine Henne's voice, though on the verge of tears, expressed a sort of awestruck elation. Genuinely grieved by the sinful conduct of her untractable child, the poor mother yet felt a tinge of bitter pride in the enormity of Malinke's crime, that attracted the notice of the rav himself.

"Get up, Malinke," she urged in a deep voice. "Reb' Nossen wants to speak to you. His messenger is waiting."

The mention of the rav's name brought Malinke to her senses. She jumped up and looked about for the messenger. He was a sickly-faced youth, a poor student in the seminary, who lived on the charity of the community. As she looked into his dull, unspeculative eyes it came over Malinke that in the sight of the world she was still a sinner, a law-breaker at large, no matter how sure she was in her heart of God's forgiveness. She would have to answer to her neighbors for her back-sliding. The rav's summons was only the beginning. With quick imagination she visualized the mocking children that would follow her in the street, the mothers who would scowl her out of all companionship with their good little daughters; and she heard the taunts and jibes of inventive enemies. The expiation of her sin would be the long punishment at the hands of her neighbors. It was well for Malinke that she had so promptly made her peace with God. She had courage now to face the disapproving world.

She suffered her mother to wrap a shawl about her head and shoulders, but of the messenger she took no notice. Did she not know the way? She kept several yards in front of her guide, and presented herself at Reb' Nossen's gate with brave promptness.

The elderly servant ushered her into the rav's presence without a word. Even the customary "Good Sabbath" stuck in her throat at sight of the juvenile sinner. The woman knew Malinke's story by this time, as did every person of sound hearing and fair understanding in Polotzk. For Peshe Frede, the tailor's wife, had been to the synagogue, and started the story on a town-wide career by a score of sure, unobstructed channels. Before the Gentile chore-women had unsealed the Jewish ovens, to draw out the Sabbath pots, there was not a bit of stale gossip current in Polotzk. Malinke and her misconduct furnished the fresh topic for every domestic circle.

Reb' Nossen had heard the story from his good wife, who had it from her good neighbor, who overheard the women exclaim over it in the rear rows of the women's gallery in the synagogue after service. The rav was one of the most liberal that Polotzk had ever had. Hearing the story of Malinke, he was a little shocked, and more than a little interested. He had taken but scant notice of Malinke the day before, when she came with the chicken. Now he wanted to see what manner of child was this who could plot and deceive, and invite the wrath of God, and make public confession of her sins, all in one short Sabbath eve.

Malinke's heart beat quite evenly as the great man bent his short-sighted gaze on her. Her own look was clear and direct. She wished for nothing so much as that the rav should see to the very bottom of her soul. The peace that filled her heart—the gift of a forgiving God— would be the answer to his bitterest reproaches. And as Reb' Nossen continued to study her face, without speaking, Malinke's mind was flooded with a sudden intuition of the nature of the judge before whom she stood. She had tested his wisdom—God Himself had confirmed his judgment: how could he fail in understanding and mercy? She was eager to speak, to tell everything, but restrained her tongue out of respect.

At last the rav began to question her. Very earnestly he listened to her artless account of her family, and the history of the luckless fowl up to the time of Breine Henne's great resolution concerning it. He made her repeat certain details, and led her to quote freely from her mother's comments on their daily life. From time to time his fine head moved in a barely perceptible nod of comprehension, but he said nothing, except to direct the child's narrative, until she came to the account of her temptation and its tragic consequences.

Here, to Malinke's amazement, he took up the story himself.

"You were very hungry, little girl," he said, in as simple words as she herself would have used. "It seemed to you a cruel decision. You thought perhaps I had made a mistake, after all."

Malinke gasped. Such perfect comprehension she had never expected from anybody below God.

"Is that so, little girl?"

"Oh, yes, yes!" she affirmed eagerly. "I thought there might be a mistake. But I know now it was true—the chicken was unclean. That's why it choked me." A touch of confusion made her speech waver. She did not know just how to express her newer faith in the rav's wisdom. "But I know, Reb' Nossen, that it was true. You couldn't make a mistake."

Reb' Nossen put up his white hand to silence her.

"Hush, my child; do not speak so. There was a great mistake—a great mistake. No man has a right to give judgment who does not know his people. A wise teacher is like a physician, who has one medicine for the strong, and another for the weak. The Law must be read with one eye on the scroll, and the other on the world, lest the Torah become a writ of bondage, and the pent people rebel. The rabbi alone cannot keep the Torah holy. The people must be with him, and he with them."

Reb' Nossen spoke as if to himself. Malinke gazed at him in wonder, not half comprehending his meaning. After some moments of silence, the rav came out of his reverie. The child had been respectfully standing all this time, but now he bade her be seated. He set a chair for her himself, in the light of the window, near his own. He had been blind long enough with respect to this poor, uninstructed child. He, too, wanted to atone.

He brought Malinke back to her story.

"And so you ate of the forbidden meat, and thought you had a sign from God when you choked." There was not a trace of reproof in his voice.

"Yes, and then I was so sorry, and in the morning I prayed, and I had nothing to sacrifice except my things."

She was not surprised at his knowing more of her story than she had told him. The rav seemed to read her thoughts of yesterday.

"And those were your Sabbath clothes?"

For answer Malinke looked down on her very shabby dress. Anybody might know *that* was not her Sabbath dress.

"You had a pair of good boots, eh?"

"Oh, they were beautiful!" Malinke grew loquacious again. "They were the best I ever had. They were almost new. Aunt Leah wouldn't have given them to me, but Fredke died, and the other girls couldn't wear them, because Fredke was the smallest. They were trimmed with patent leather, and they fitted me—"

She broke off, unable to express the perfection of the relation between the now historic boots and her abused little feet. Unconsciously she looked down upon the ruinous boots that replaced them.

The rav's eyes followed hers.

"Do you regret the pretty boots, Malinke?"

The child jumped up in her excitable manner, her eyes full of protest.

"Oh, no, *no!*" she cried earnestly. "I'm glad they're at the bottom of the river. I shall never have such beautiful boots again as long as I live, but I'm *glad*, because it was my sacrifice, and God will forgive me. Reb' Nossen," she repeated, vehemently, "I'm *glad!*"

The rav put up his hand to hide his eyes from the little penitent. Short-sighted as he was, he had a sudden vision of spiritual vistas. After a moment, he raised his head and drew Malinke to him. Stroking her thin hair, he regarded her with grave, sad eyes. He reproached himself inwardly for his blindness on the occasion of their first interview. The signs of privation and suffering were plain in the little girl's pinched face, in the sharp angles of her figure, visible under her scanty apparel. And suddenly, across his vaguer speculations, shot a clear idea of the child's immediate want. If the chicken was rejected as unclean, what did those poor people have for dinner?

"Malinke," questioned Reb' Nossen, looking hard at the child, "what did you eat to-day?"

She returned his look with a smile of triumph.

"Nothing," she replied, with the least touch of pride in her voice. "I'm fasting, you know, for atonement."

"Fasting!" exclaimed the rav, in a tone of reproach, and rising as he spoke. "Why, you're too young to fast, my child, and too weak. Besides, it is wrong to fast on Sabbath. Your head is full of strange ideas. There are a great many things to explain to you—a great many. But there will be time enough for that when you have had something to eat."

Pushing her gently back into her chair, he went to the door and called aloud, "Deborah! Tamareh!" Once aroused, the rav was practical enough.

"You shall eat," he said again to Malinke, going back to her chair and looking down upon her. "Why, you are as thin as a skeleton. What business has such a child with fasting? You shall eat, and then we can talk. There are a great many things we can learn together, my child, but the body comes before the mind."

Malinke's eyes, that had met his so bravely at the beginning of the interview, when she expected accusation and reproof, now wavered and fell, as the old man's sympathy focused in his gaze. And then, to her own amazement, a great sob broke from her, followed by a flood of tears.

The rav strode over to the door once more, the tails of his long frock coat flying back from his white-stockinged legs. He called impatiently, "Deborah! Tamareh!"

In answer to his summons came neither his wife nor the servant, but a strange, disheveled figure, with pale eyes in a tear-blotched face. It was Breine Henne, the egg-woman, impelled by a dozen contradictory impulses to be present at what she imagined to be her child's bitter trial. At sight of Reb' Nossen's stern face, and Malinke sobbing in her chair, all her motives resolved themselves into an overpowering instinct to defend her little girl, against the rav himself, against all the world, if need be.

"Reb' Nossen, Reb' Nossen," she began to plead, "listen to me, I beg you. Don't be too hard on the child. She is so young, and so ignorant. She has no father, and I am a poor, ignorant woman, and all day long she is among strangers, because there is nobody at home to take care of her. It was a great temptation—she was so hungry, poor child. She had hardly tasted meat for weeks. We cook nothing but grits when times are so bad. She was out of her head with disappointment. May you never know what it is to be hungry for a decent meal. And it was all my fault, anyway. I should have killed the chicken last Atonement Day, and then this dreadful thing wouldn't have happened. And oh, Reb' Nossen! as I am a Jewish woman, I believe the child is out of her head this day. She stole out of the house at daybreak, will you believe me? on purpose to throw her best clothes into the river, because she imagined that would be a sacrifice in atonement for her sins! You know, Reb' Nossen, that no sane child would do such a thing. It was her only decent dress, and the boots were the best she ever had in her life. If you had seen her when she came back, blue with cold, and saying such wild things—Oh, Reb' Nossen, don't, don't be hard on my poor child!"

The rav waited patiently for Breine Henne to stop.

"Calm yourself, my good woman," he said, as soon as he could speak. "Take a seat—here—and try to be calm. I did not mean to be harsh with the child. I do not blame her for anything. On the contrary—Ah, Tamareh! yes, I called. Bring this child something to eat. She has not eaten to-day, Tamareh. Bring it in here, and be quick."

While the famished child was eating, the rav drew from the mother many details bearing on Malinke's character and education, which Breine Henne adorned with numerous comments and apologies. She was very much puzzled at the rav's benign attitude toward the child,— the very opposite of what Malinke had earned,—but she would have thought it disrespectful to question him. No doubt he knew what he was about, and if she did not understand,—why, she was only a poor, ignorant female. So she babbled on in a happy excitement, her eyes resting now and then on Malinke, feasting there in the house of the rav, and at his own invitation.

54

There was little more than crumbs left on Malinke's tray when she leaned back, with a smile of utter contentment on her face, and remarked to the friendly air, "I really can't eat any more."

The rav turned and looked at the tray.

"That's good—that's good," he said. "Now come over here. I've been talking with your mother, and I find your education has been a little defective. I have caused you—I might have saved you much trouble. I should like to make amends." He embraced them both in his look. "I shall be very glad to provide for your tuition in the future, if you will let me choose the teacher—and if you care for lessons, Malinke."

The child drew in her breath.

Breine Henne broke out in a flood of thanks and blessings, which the good man did not hear. He was waiting for Malinke to speak. At last she opened her lips.

"Shall I begin to-morrow?" she asked.

The rav smiled, pleased with her directness.

"To-morrow," he said. "It is well to hasten to a good thing. And shall I name your teacher?"

Malinke ventured on a petition.

"I hope it will be a rebbe, not a *rebbetzin* [female teacher]," she said. "The rebbetzins don't know so much."

Breine Henne broke out in reproof.

"Hush, you bold child! There you go again, talking as a child shouldn't. That's her great fault, believe me, Reb' Nossen—that tongue of hers. You ought to be more respectful, and grateful, and, whatever you do, keep your tongue quiet."

The rav uttered no direct reproof.

"If the rebbe knows more than the rebbetzin, it is because he has spent more time in study, my dear. Perhaps a rebbe would be best for you. Well, now, I cannot afford to pay much; I am not known for my riches. I must choose some one who will not ask too much tuition. What would you say to taking a few lessons with me? I have never taught girls, but I can try."

It was Breine Henne who gasped now, and Malinke who babbled excitedly.

"Oh, will you teach me everything?" she cried, "the same as a boy— the same as Yösele? I'd like to read *everything*. Yösele says a girl can't

55

understand, but I don't think that's true, do you? Do you mean you'll teach me the *Humesh*, and *Gemara*, and everything?"

The rav smiled again.

"Not all at once, my child, not all at once. We must make a beginning first. You come to-morrow before sunset prayer, and then we'll see. The Torah is inexhaustible. There are a great many things to learn—about conduct, and sacrifice, and many other things. I pray that I have the wisdom to teach you."

For the second time that day, Malinke walked home without touching the earth. But if she did not know the way she took, a third of Polotzk did. That much of the population followed her to her door, as a volunteer escort of honor.

For in the quiet of the Sabbath afternoon, the movements of the rav's messenger had been observed, and a knot of the most irrepressible gossips in Polotzk lay in wait for Malinke and her mother at Reb' Nossen's gate. Breine Henne, bursting with pride, was glad to fall upon the bosom of the first gossip with an apron who presented herself; and so the story of the great interview was out.

Before the first corner was turned, the original knot of gossips had become the indistinguishable nucleus of a rapidly growing procession, at the head of which a fairly straight version of Malinke's story was told, and at the tail of which it was rumored that Reb' Nossen was going to adopt Breine Henne's girl, and make a great scholar of her.

But Malinke heard nothing of what the people said. In the midst of the throng she was communing with herself about the mystery of divine justice. She who had sinned the most was the most blessed of all little girls in Polotzk. The Lord had accepted her atonement. In compensation for her blindness, that had led her into error, God had sent her a teacher.

The Girl Who Went Right

Edna Ferber

THERE IS A STORY—Kipling, I think—that tells of a spirited horse galloping in the dark suddenly drawing up tense, hoofs bunched, slim flanks quivering, nostrils dilated, ears pricked. Urging being of no avail the rider dismounts, strikes a match, advances a cautious step or so, and finds himself at the precipitous brink of a newly formed crevasse.

So it is with your trained editor. A miraculous sixth sense guides him. A mysterious something warns him of danger lurking within the seemingly innocent oblong white envelope. Without slitting the flap, without pausing to adjust his tortoise-rimmed glasses, without clearing his throat, without lighting his cigarette—he knows.

The deadly newspaper story he scents in the dark. Cub reporter. Crusty city editor. Cub fired. Stumbles on to a big story. Staggers into newspaper office wild-eyed. Last edition. "Hold the presses!" Crusty C. E. stands over cub's typewriter grabbing story line by line. Even foreman of pressroom moved to tears by tale. "Boys, this ain't just a story this kid's writin'. This is history!" Story finished. Cub faints. C. E. makes him star reporter.

The athletic story: "I could never marry a molly-coddle like you, Harold Hammond!" Big game of the year. Team crippled. Second half. Halfback hurt. Harold Hammond, scrub, into the game. Touchdown! Broken leg. Five to nothing. "Harold, can you ever, ever forgive me?"

57

The pseudo-psychological story: She had been sitting before the fire for a long, long time. The flame had flickered and died down to a smouldering ash. The sound of his departing footsteps echoed and re-echoed through her brain. But the little room was very, very still.

The shop-girl story: Torn boots and temptation, tears and sneers, pathos and bathos, all the way from Zola to the vice inquiry.

Having thus attempted to hide the deadly commonplaceness of this story with a thin layer of cynicism, perhaps even the wily editor may be tricked into taking the leap.

Four weeks before the completion of the new twelve-story addition the store advertised for two hundred experienced saleswomen. Rachel Wiletzky, entering the superintendent's office after a wait of three hours, was Applicant No. 179. The superintendent did not look up as Rachel came in. He scribbled busily on a pad of paper at his desk, thus observing rules one and two in the proper conduct of superintendents when interviewing applicants. Rachel Wiletzky, standing by his desk, did not cough or wriggle or rustle her skirts or sag on one hip. A sense of her quiet penetrated the superintendent's subconsciousness. He glanced up hurriedly over his left shoulder. Then he laid down his pencil and sat up slowly. His mind was working quickly enough though. In the twelve seconds that intervened between the laying down of the pencil and the sitting up in his chair he had hastily readjusted all his well-founded preconceived ideas on the appearance of shop-girl applicants.

Rachel Wiletzky had the colouring and physique of a dairymaid. It was the sort of colouring that you associate in your mind with lush green fields, and Jersey cows, and village maids, in Watteau frocks, balancing brimming pails aloft in the protecting curve of one rounded upraised arm, with perhaps a Maypole dance or so in the background. Altogether, had the superintendent been given to figures of speech, he might have said that Rachel was as much out of place among the preceding one hundred and seventy-eight bloodless, hollow-chested, stoop-shouldered applicants as a sunflower would be in a patch of dank white fungi.

He himself was one of those bleached men that you find on the office floor of department stores. Grey skin, grey eyes, greying hair, careful grey clothes—seemingly as void of pigment as one of those sunless things you disclose when you turn over a board that has long lain on the mouldy floor of a damp cellar. It was only when you looked closely that you noticed a fleck of golden brown in the cold grey of each eye, and a streak of warm brown forming an unquenchable forelock that the conquering grey had not been able to vanquish. It may have been a something within him corresponding to those outward bits of human colouring that tempted him to yield to a queer impulse. He whipped from his breast-pocket the grey-bordered handkerchief, reached up swiftly and passed one white corner of it down the length of Rachel Wiletzky's Killarney-rose left cheek. The rude path down which the handkerchief had travelled deepened to red for a moment before both rose-pink cheeks bloomed into scarlet. The superintendent gazed rather ruefully from unblemished handkerchief to cheek and back again.

"Why—it—it's real!" he stammered.

Rachel Wiletzky smiled a good-natured little smile that had in it a dash of superiority.

"If I was putting it on," she said, "I hope I'd have sense enough to leave something to the imagination. This colour out of a box would take a spiderweb veil to tone it down."

Not much more than a score of words. And yet before the half were spoken you were certain that Rachel Wiletzky's knowledge of lush green fields and bucolic scenes was that gleaned from the condensed-milk ads that glare down at one from billboards and street-car chromos. Hers was the ghetto voice—harsh, metallic, yet fraught with the resonant music of tragedy.

"H'm—name?" asked the grey superintendent. He knew that vocal quality.

A queer look stole into Rachel Wiletzky's face, a look of cunning and determination and shrewdness.

"Ray Willets," she replied composedly. "Double l."

"Clerked before, of course. Our advertisement stated——"

"Oh yes," interrupted Ray Willets hastily, eagerly. "I can sell goods. My customers like me. And I don't get tired. I don't know why, but I don't."

The superintendent glanced up again at the red that glowed higher with the girl's suppressed excitement. He took a printed slip from the little pile of paper that lay on his desk.

"Well, anyway, you're the first clerk I ever saw who had so much red blood that she could afford to use it for decorative purposes. Step into the next room, answer the questions on this card and turn it in. You'll be notified."

Ray Willets took the searching, telltale blank that put its questions so pertinently. "Where last employed?" it demanded. "Why did you leave? Do you live at home?"

Ray Willets moved slowly away toward the door opposite. The superintendent reached forward to press the button that would summon Applicant No. 180. But before his finger touched it Ray Willets turned and came back swiftly. She held the card out before his surprised eyes.

"I can't fill this out. If I do I won't get the job. I work over at the Halsted Street Bazaar. You know—the Cheap Store. I lied and sent word I was sick so I could come over here this morning. And they dock you for time off whether you're sick or not."

The superintendent drummed impatiently with his fingers. "I can't listen to all this. Haven't time. Fill out your blank, and if——"

All that latent dramatic force which is a heritage of her race came to the girl's aid now.

"The blank! How can I say on a blank that I'm leaving because I want to be where real people are? What chance has a girl got over there on the West Side? I'm different. I don't know why, but I am. Look at my face! Where should I get red cheeks from? From not having enough to eat half the time and sleeping three in a bed?"

She snatched off her shabby glove and held one hand out before the man's face.

"From where do I get such hands? Not from selling hardware over at Twelfth and Halsted. Look at it! Say, couldn't that hand sell silk and lace?"

Some one has said that to make fingers and wrists like those which Ray Willets held out for inspection it is necessary to have had at least five generations of ancestors who have sat with their hands folded in their laps. Slender, tapering, sensitive hands they were, pink-tipped, temperamental. Wistful hands they were, speaking hands, an inheritance, perhaps, from some dreamer ancestor within the old-world ghetto, some long-haired, velvet-eyed student of the Talmud dwelling within the pale with its squalor and noise, and dreaming of unseen

60

things beyond the confining gates—things rare and exquisite and fine.

"Ashamed of your folks?" snapped the superintendent.

"N-no—No! But I want to be different. I am different! Give me a chance, will you? I'm straight. And I'll work. And I can sell goods. Try me."

That all-pervading greyness seemed to have lifted from the man at the desk. The brown flecks in the eyes seemed to spread and engulf the surrounding colourlessness. His face, too, took on a glow that seemed to come from within. It was like the lifting of a thick grey mist on a foggy morning, so that the sun shines bright and clear for a brief moment before the damp curtain rolls down again and effaces it.

He leaned forward in his chair, a queer half-smile on his face.

"I'll give you your chance," he said, "for one month. At the end of that time I'll send for you. I'm not going to watch you. I'm not going to have you watched. Of course your sale slips will show the office whether you're selling goods or not. If you're not they'll discharge you. But that's routine. What do you want to sell?"

"What do I want to—— Do you mean—— Why, I want to sell the lacy things."

"The lacy——"

Ray, very red-cheeked, made the plunge. "The—the lawnjeree, you know. The things with ribbon and handwork and yards and yards of real lace. I've seen 'em in the glass case in the French Room. Seventy-nine dollars marked down from one hundred."

The superintendent scribbled on a card. "Show this Monday morning. Miss Jevne is the head of your department. You'll spend two hours a day in the store school of instruction for clerks. Here, you're forgetting your glove."

The grey look had settled down on him again as he reached out to press the desk button. Ray Willets passed out at the door opposite the one through which Rachel Wiletzky had entered.

Some one in the department nick-named her Chubbs before she had spent half a day in the underwear and imported lingerie. At the store school she listened and learned. She learned how important were things of which Halsted Street took no cognisance. She learned to make out a sale slip as complicated as an engineering blueprint. She learned that a clerk must develop suavity and patience in the same degree as a customer waxes waspish and insulting, and that the spectrum's colours do not exist in the costume of the girl-behind-the-counter. For her there are only black and white. These things she learned and many more, and remembered them, for behind the rosy cheeks and the terrier-bright eyes burned the indomitable desire to get on. And the finished embodiment of all of Ray Willets' desires and ambitions was daily before her eyes in the presence of Miss Jevne, head of the lingerie and negligées.

Of Miss Jevne it might be said that she was real where Ray was artificial, and artificial where Ray was real. Everything that Miss Jevne wore was real. She was as modish as Ray was shabby, as slim as Ray was stocky, as artificially tinted and tinctured as Ray was naturally rosy-cheeked and buxom. It takes real money to buy clothes as real as those worn by Miss Jevne. The soft charmeuse in her graceful gown was real and miraculously draped. The cobweb-lace collar that so delicately traced its pattern against the black background of her gown was real. So was the ripple of lace that cascaded down the front of her blouse. The straight, correct, hideously modern lines of her figure bespoke a real eighteen-dollar corset. Realest of all, there reposed on Miss Jevne's bosom a bar pin of platinum and diamonds—very real diamonds set in a severely plain but very real bar of precious platinum. So if you except Miss Jevne's changeless colour, her artificial smile, her glittering hair and her undulating head-of-the-department walk, you can see that everything about Miss Jevne was as real as money can make one.

Miss Jevne, when she deigned to notice Ray Willets at all, called her "girl," thus: "Girl, get down one of those Number Seventeens for me—with the pink ribbons." Ray did not resent the tone. She thought about Miss Jevne as she worked. She thought about her at night when she was washing and ironing her other shirtwaist for next day's wear. In the Halsted Street Bazaar the girls had been on terms of dreadful intimacy with those affairs in each other's lives which popularly are supposed to be private knowledge. They knew the sum which each earned per week; how much they turned in to help swell the family coffers and how much they were allowed to keep for their own use. They knew each time a girl spent a quarter for a cheap sailor collar or a pair of near-silk stockings. Ray Willets, who wanted passionately to be different, whose hands so loved the touch of the lacy, silky garments that made up the lingerie and negligee departments, recognised the perfection of Miss Jevne's faultless realness—recognised it, appreciated it, envied it. It worried her too. How did she do it? How did one go about attaining the same degree of realness?

Meanwhile she worked. She learned quickly. She took care always to be cheerful, interested, polite. After a short week's handling of lacy silken garments she ceased to feel a shock when she saw Miss Jevne displaying a *robe-de-nuit* made up of white cloud and sea-foam and languidly assuring the customer that of course it wasn't to be expected that you could get a fine handmade lace at that price—only twenty-seven-fifty. Now if she cared to look at something really fine—made entirely by hand—why——

The end of the first ten days found so much knowledge crammed into Ray Willets' clever, ambitious little head that the pink of her cheeks had deepened to carmine, as a child grows flushed and too bright-eyed when overstimulated and overtired.

Miss Myrtle, the store beauty, strolled up to Ray, who was straightening a pile of corset covers and *brassieres*. Miss Myrtle was the store's star cloak-and-suit model. Tall, svelte, graceful, lovely in line and contour, she was remarkably like one of those exquisite imbeciles that Rossetti used to love to paint. Hers were the great cowlike eyes, the wonderful oval face, the marvellous little nose, the perfect lips and chin. Miss Myrtle could don a forty-dollar gown, parade it before a possible purchaser, and make it look like an imported model at one hundred and twenty-five. When Miss Myrtle opened those exquisite lips and spoke you got a shock that hurt. She laid one cool slim finger on Ray's ruddy cheek.

"Sure enough!" she drawled nasally. "Whereja get it anyway, kid? You must of been brought up on peaches 'n' cream and slept in a pink cloud somewheres."

"Me!" laughed Ray, her deft fingers busy straightening a bow here, a ruffle of lace there. "Me! The L-train runs so near my bed that if it was ever to get a notion to take a short cut it would slice off my legs to the knees."

"Live at home?" Miss Myrtle's grasshopper mind never dwelt long on one subject.

"Well, sure," replied Ray. "Did you think I had a flat up on the Drive?"

"I live at home too," Miss Myrtle announced impressively. She was leaning indolently against the table. Her eyes followed the deft, quick movements of Ray's slender, capable hands. Miss Myrtle always leaned when there was anything to lean on. Involuntarily she fell into melting poses. One shoulder always drooped slightly, one toe always trailed a bit like the picture on the cover of the fashion magazines, one hand and arm always followed the line of her draperies while the other was raised to hip or breast or head.

Ray's busy hands paused a moment. She looked up at the picturesque Myrtle. "All the girls do, don't they?"

"Huh?" said Myrtle blankly.

"Live at home, I mean? The application blank says——"

"Say, you've got clever hands, ain't you?" put in Miss Myrtle irrelevantly. She looked ruefully at her own short, stubby, unintelligent hands, that so perfectly reflected her character in that marvellous way hands have. "Mine are stupid-looking. I'll bet you'll get on." She sagged to the other hip with a weary gracefulness. "I ain't got no brains," she complained.

"Where do they live then?" persisted Ray.

"Who? Oh, I live at home"—again virtuously—"but I've got some heart if I am dumb. My folks couldn't get along without what I bring home every week. A lot of the girls have flats. But that don't last. Now Jevne——"

"Yes?" said Ray eagerly. Her plump face with its intelligent eyes was all aglow.

Miss Myrtle lowered her voice discreetly. "Her own folks don't know where she lives. They says she sends 'em money every month, but with the understanding that they don't try to come to see her. They live way over on the West Side somewhere. She makes her buying trip to Europe every year. Speaks French and everything. They say when she started to earn real money she just cut loose from her folks. They was a drag on her and she wanted to get to the top."

"Say, that pin's real, ain't it?"

"Real? Well, I should say it is! Catch Jevne wearing anything that's phony. I saw her at the theatre one night. Dressed! Well, you'd have thought that birds of paradise were national pests, like English sparrows. Not that she looked loud. But that quiet, rich elegance, you know, that just smells of money. Say, but I'll bet she has her lonesome evenings!"

Ray Willets' eyes darted across the long room and rested upon the shining black-clad figure of Miss Jevne moving about against the luxurious ivory-and-rose background of the French Room.

"She—she left her folks, h'm?" she mused aloud.

Miss Myrtle, the brainless, regarded the tips of her shabby boots.

"What did it get her?" she asked as though to herself. "I know what it does to a girl, seeing and handling stuff that's made for millionaires, you get a taste for it yourself. Take it from me, it ain't the six-dollar girl that needs looking after. She's taking her little pay envelope home to her mother that's a widow and it goes to buy milk for the kids. Sometimes I think the more you get the more you want. Somebody ought to turn that vice inquiry on to the tracks of that thirty-dollar-a-week girl in the Irish crochet waist and the diamond bar pin. She'd make swell readin'."

There fell a little silence between the two—a silence of which neither was conscious. Both were thinking, Myrtle disjointedly, purposelessly, all unconscious that her slow, untrained mind had groped for a great and vital truth and found it; Ray quickly, eagerly, connectedly, a new and daring resolve growing with lightning rapidity.

"There's another new baby at our house," she said aloud suddenly. "It cries all night pretty near."

"Ain't they fierce?" laughed Myrtle. "And yet I dunno——"

She fell silent again. Then with the half-sign with which we waken from day dreams she moved away in response to the beckoning finger of a saleswoman in the evening-coat section. Ten minutes later her exquisite face rose above the soft folds of a black charmeuse coat that rippled away from her slender, supple body in lines that a sculptor dreams of and never achieves.

Ray Willets finished straightening her counter. Trade was slow. She moved idly in the direction of the black-garbed figure that flitted about in the costly atmosphere of the French section. It must be a very special customer to claim Miss Jevne's expert services. Ray glanced in through the half-opened glass and ivory-enamel doors.

65

"Here, girl," called Miss Jevne. Ray paused and entered. Miss Jevne was frowning. "Miss Myrtle's busy. Just slip this on. Careful now. Keep your arms close to your head."

She slipped a marvellously wrought garment over Ray's sleek head. Fluffy drifts of equally exquisite lingerie lay scattered about on chairs, over mirrors, across showtables. On one of the fragile little ivory-and-rose chairs, in the centre of the costly little room, sat a large, blonde, perfumed woman who clanked and rustled and swished as she moved. Her eyes were white-lidded and heavy, but strangely bright. One un-gloved hand was very white too, but pudgy and covered so thickly with gems that your eye could get no clear picture of any single stone or setting.

Ray, clad in the diaphanous folds of the *robe-de-nuit* that was so beautifully adorned with delicate embroideries wrought by the patient, needle-scarred fingers of some silent, white-faced nun in a far-away convent, paced slowly up and down the short length of the room that the critical eye of this coarse, unlettered creature might behold the wonders woven by this weary French nun, and, beholding, approve.

"It ain't bad," spake the blonde woman grudgingly. "How much did you say?"

"Ninety-five," Miss Jevne made answer smoothly. "I selected it myself when I was in France my last trip. A bargain."

She slid the robe carefully over Ray's head. The frown came once more to her brow. She bent close to Ray's ear. "Your waist's ripped under the left arm. Disgraceful!"

The blonde woman moved and jangled a bit in her chair. "Well, I'll take it," she sighed. "Look at the colour on that girl! And it's real too." She rose heavily and came over to Ray, reached up and pinched her cheek appraisingly with perfumed white thumb and forefinger.

"That'll do, girl," said Miss Jevne sweetly. "Take this along and change these ribbons from blue to pink."

Ray Willets bore the fairy garment away with her. She bore it tenderly, almost reverently. It was more than a garment. It represented in her mind a new standard of all that was beautiful and exquisite and desirable.

Ten days before the formal opening of the new twelve-story addition there was issued from the superintendent's office an order that made a little flurry among the clerks in the sections devoted to women's dress. The new store when thrown open would mark an epoch in the retail drygoods business of the city, the order began. Thousands were to be spent on perishable decorations alone. The highest type of patronage was to be catered to. Therefore the women in the lingerie, negligée, millinery, dress, suit and corset sections were requested to wear during opening week a modest but modish black one-piece gown that would blend with the air of elegance which those departments were to maintain.

Ray Willets of the lingerie and negligée sections read her order slip slowly. Then she reread it. Then she did a mental sum in simple arithmetic. A childish sum it was. And yet before she got her answer the solving of it had stamped on her face a certain hard, set, resolute look.

The store management had chosen Wednesday to be the opening day. By eight-thirty o'clock Wednesday morning the French lingerie, millinery and dress sections, with their women clerks garbed in modest but modish black one-piece gowns, looked like a levee at Buckingham when the court is in mourning. But the ladies-in-waiting, grouped about here and there, fell back in respectful silence when there paced down the aisle the queen royal in the person of Miss Jevne. There is a certain sort of black gown that is more startling and daring than scarlet. Miss Jevne's was that style. Fast black you might term it. Miss Jevne was aware of the flurry and flutter that followed her majestic progress down the aisle to her own section. She knew that each eye was caught in the tip of the little dog-eared train that slipped and slunk and wriggled along the ground, thence up to the soft drapery caught so cunningly just below the knee, up higher to the marvelously simple sash that swayed with each step, to the soft folds of black against which rested the very real diamond and platinum bar pin, up to the lace at her throat, and then stopping, blinking and staring again gazed fixedly at the string of pearls that lay about her throat, pearls rosily pink, mistily grey. An aura of self-satisfaction enveloping her, Miss Jevne disappeared behind the rose-garlanded portals of the new cream-and-mauve French section. And there the aura vanished, quivering. For standing before one of the plate-glass cases and patting into place with deft fingers the satin bow of a hand-wrought chemise was Ray Willets, in her shiny little black serge skirt and the braver of her two white shirtwaists.

Miss Jevne quickened her pace. Ray turned. Her bright brown eyes grew brighter at sight of Miss Jevne's wondrous black. Miss Jevne, her train wound round her feet like an actress' photograph, lifted her eyebrows to an unbelievable height.

"Explain that costume!" she said.

"Costume?" repeated Ray, fencing.

Miss Jevne's thin lips grew thinner. "You understood that women in this department were to wear black one-piece gowns this week!"

Ray smiled a little twisted smile. "Yes, I understood."

"Then what——"

Ray's little smile grew a trifle more uncertain. "—I had the money—last week—I was going to—— The baby took sick—the heat I guess, coming so sudden. We had the doctor—and medicine—I—— Say, your own folks come before black one-piece dresses!"

Miss Jevne's cold eyes saw the careful patch under Ray's left arm where a few days before the torn place had won her a reproof. It was the last straw.

"You can't stay in this department in that rig!"

"Who says so?" snapped Ray with a flash of Halsted Street bravado. "If my customers want a peek at Paquin I'll send 'em to you."

"I'll show you who says so!" retorted Miss Jevne, quite losing sight of the queen business. The stately form of the floor manager was visible among the glass showcases beyond. Miss Jevne sought him agitatedly. All the little sagging lines about her mouth showed up sharply, defying years of careful massage.

The floor manager bent his stately head and listened. Then, led by Miss Jevne, he approached Ray Willets, whose deft fingers, trembling a very little now, were still pretending to adjust the perfect pink-satin bow.

The manager touched her on the arm not unkindly. "Report for work in the kitchen utensils, fifth floor," he said. Then at sight of the girl's face: "We can't have one disobeying orders, you know. The rest of the clerks would raise a row in no time."

Down in the kitchen utensils and household goods there was no rule demanding modest but modish one-piece gowns. In the kitch-enware one could don black sateen sleevelets to protect one's clean white waist without breaking the department's tenets of fashion. You could even pin a handkerchief across the front of your waist, if your job was that of dusting the granite ware.

At first Ray's delicate fingers, accustomed to the touch of soft, sheer white stuff and ribbon and lace and silk, shrank from contact with meat grinders, and aluminum stewpans, and egg beaters, and waffle irons, and pie tins. She handled them contemptuously. She sold them listlessly. After weeks of expatiating to customers on the beauties and excellencies of gossamer lingerie she found it difficult to work up enthusiasm over the virtues of dishpans and spice boxes. By noon she was less resentful. By two o'clock she was saying to a fellow clerk:

"Well, anyway, in this section you don't have to tell a woman how graceful and charming she's going to look while she's working the washing machine."

She was a born saleswoman. In spite of herself she became interested in the buying problems of the practical and plain-visaged housewives who patronised this section. By three o'clock she was looking thoughtful—thoughtful and contented.

Then came the summons. The lingerie section was swamped! Report to Miss Jevne at once! Almost regretfully Ray gave her customer over to an idle clerk and sought out Miss Jevne. Some of that lady's statuesqueness was gone. The bar pin on her bosom rose and fell rapidly. She espied Ray and met her halfway. In her hand she carried a soft black something which she thrust at Ray.

"Here, put that on in one of the fitting rooms. Be quick about it. It's your size. The department's swamped. Hurry now!"

Ray took from Miss Jevne the black silk gown, modest but modish. There was no joy in Ray's face. Ten minutes later she emerged in the limp and clinging little frock that toned down her colour and made her plumpness seem but rounded charm.

The big store will talk for many a day of that afternoon and the three afternoons that followed, until Sunday brought pause to the thousands of feet beating a ceaseless tattoo up and down the thronged aisles. On the Monday following thousands swarmed down upon the store again, but not in such overwhelming numbers. There were breathing spaces. It was during one of these that Miss Myrtle, the beauty, found time for a brief moment's chat with Ray Willets.

Ray was straightening her counter again. She had a passion for order. Myrtle eyed her wearily. Her slender shoulders had carried an endless number and variety of garments during those four days and her feet had paced weary miles that those garments might the better be displayed.

"Black's grand on you," observed Myrtle. "Tones you down." She glanced sharply at the gown. "Looks just like one of our eighteen-dollar models. Copy it?"

"No," said Ray, still straightening petticoats and corset covers. Myrtle reached out a weary, graceful arm and touched one of the lacy piles adorned with cunning bows of pink and blue to catch the shopping eye.

"Ain't that sweet!" she exclaimed. "I'm crazy about that shadow lace. It's swell under voiles. I wonder if I could take one of them home to copy it."

Ray glanced up. "Oh, that!" she said contemptuously. "That's just a cheap skirt. Only twelve-fifty. Machine-made lace. Imitation embroidery——"

She stopped. She stared a moment at Myrtle with the fixed and wide-eyed gaze of one who does not see.

"What'd I just say to you?"

"Huh?" ejaculated Myrtle, mystified.

"What'd I just say?" repeated Ray.

Myrtle laughed, half understanding. "You said that was a cheap junk skirt at only twelve-fifty, with machine lace and imitation——"

But Ray Willets did not wait to hear the rest. She was off down the aisle toward the elevator marked "Employées." The superintendent's office was on the ninth floor. She stopped there. The grey superintendent was writing at his desk. He did not look up as Ray entered, thus observing rules one and two in the proper conduct of superintendents when interviewing employées. Ray Willets, standing by his desk, did not cough or wriggle or rustle her skirts or sag on one hip. A consciousness of her quiet penetrated the superintendent's mind. He glanced up hurriedly over his left shoulder. Then he laid down his pencil and sat up slowly.

"Oh, it's you!" he said.

"Yes, it's me," replied Ray Willets simply. "I've been here a month to-day."

"Oh, yes." He ran his fingers through his hair so that the brown forelock stood away from the grey. "You've lost some of your roses," he said, and tapped his cheek. "What's the trouble?"

"I guess it's the dress," explained Ray, and glanced down at the folds of her gown. She hesitated a moment awkwardly. "You said you'd send for me at the end of the month. You didn't."

"That's all right," said the grey superintendent. "I was pretty sure I hadn't made a mistake. I can gauge applicants pretty fairly. Let's see— you're in the lingerie, aren't you?"

"Yes."

Then with a rush: "That's what I want to talk to you about. I've changed my mind. I don't want to stay in the lingeries. I'd like to be transferred to the kitchen utensils and household goods."

"Transferred! Well, I'll see what I can do. What was the name now? I forget."

A queer look stole into Ray Willets' face, a look of determination and shrewdness.

"Name?" she said. "My name is Rachel Wiletzky."

America and I

Anzia Yezierska

A S ONE OF THE DUMB, voiceless ones I speak. One of the millions of immigrants beating, beating out their hearts at your gates for a breath of understanding.

Ach! America! From the other end of the earth from where I came, America was a land of living hope, woven of dreams, aflame with longing and desire.

Choked for ages in the airless oppression of Russia, the Promised Land rose up—wings for my stifled spirit—sunlight burning through my darkness—freedom singing to me in my prison—deathless songs tuning prison-bars into strings of a beautiful violin.

I arrived in America. My young, strong body, my heart and soul pregnant with the unlived lives of generations clamoring for expression.

What my mother and father and their mother and father never had a chance to give out in Russia, I would give out in America. The hidden sap of centuries would find release; colors that never saw light— songs that died unvoiced—romance that never had a chance to blossom in the black life of the Old World.

In the golden land of flowing opportunity I was to find my work that was denied me in the sterile village of my forefathers. Here I was to be free from the dead drudgery for bread that held me down in Russia. For the first time in America, I'd cease to be a slave of the belly. I'd be a creator, a giver, a human being! My work would be the living joy of fullest self-expression.

72

But from my high visions, my golden hopes, I had to put my feet down on earth. I had to have food and shelter. I had to have the money to pay for it.

I was in America, among the Americans, but not of them. No speech, no common language, no way to win a smile of understanding from them, only my young, strong body and my untried faith. Only my eager, empty hands, and my full heart shining from my eyes!

God from the world! Here I was with so much richness in me, but my mind was not wanted without the language. And my body, un-skilled, untrained, was not even wanted in the factory. Only one of two chances was left open to me: the kitchen, or minding babies.

My first job was as a servant in an Americanized family. Once, long ago, they came from the same village from where I came. But they were so well-dressed, so well-fed, so successful in America, that they were ashamed to remember their mother tongue.

"What were to be my wages?" I ventured timidly, as I looked up to the well-fed, well-dressed "American" man and woman.

They looked at me with a sudden coldness. What have I said to draw away from me their warmth? Was it so low from me to talk of wages? I shrank back into myself like a low-down bargainer. Maybe they're so high up in well-being they can't any more understand my low thoughts for money.

From his rich height the man preached down to me that I must not be so grabbing for wages. Only just landed from the ship and already thinking about money when I should be thankful to associate with "Americans."

The woman, out of her smooth, smiling fatness assured me that this was my chance for a summer vacation in the country with her two lovely children. My great chance to learn to be a civilized being, to become an American by living with them.

So, made to feel that I was in the hands of American friends, invited to share with them their home, their plenty, their happiness, I pushed out from my head the worry for wages. Here was my first chance to begin my life in the sunshine, after my long darkness. My laugh was all over my face as I said to them: "I'll trust myself to you. What I'm worth you'll give me." And I entered their house like a child by the hand.

The best of me I gave them. Their house cares were my house cares. I got up early. I worked till late. All that my soul hungered to give I put into the passion with which I scrubbed floors, scoured pots, and washed clothes. I was so grateful to mingle with the American people, to hear the music of the American language, that I never knew tiredness.

There was such a freshness in my brains and such a willingness in my heart that I could go on and on—not only with the work of the house, but work with my head—learning new words from the children, the grocer, the butcher, the iceman. I was not even afraid to ask for words from the policeman on the street. And every new word made me see new American things with American eyes. I felt like a Columbus, finding new worlds through every new word.

But words alone were only for the inside of me. The outside of me still branded me for a steerage immigrant. I had to have clothes to forget myself that I'm a stranger yet. And so I had to have money to buy these clothes.

The month was up. I was so happy! Now I'd have money. *My own, earned* money. Money to buy a new shirt on my back—shoes on my feet. Maybe yet an American dress and hat!

Ach! How high rose my dreams! How plainly I saw all that I would do with my visionary wages shining like a light over my head!

In my imagination I already walked in my new American clothes. How beautiful I looked as I saw myself like a picture before my eyes! I saw how I would throw away my immigrant rags tied up in my immigrant shawl. With money to buy—free money in my hands— I'd show them that I could look like an American in a day.

Like a prisoner in his last night in prison, counting the seconds that will free him from his chains, I trembled breathlessly for the minute I'd get the wages in my hand.

Before dawn I rose.

I shined up the house like a jewel-box.

I prepared breakfast and waited with my heart in my mouth for my lady and gentleman to rise. At last I heard them stirring. My eyes were jumping out of my head to them when I saw them coming in and seating themselves by the table.

Like a hungry cat rubbing up to its boss for meat, so I edged and simpered around them as I passed them the food. Without my will, like a beggar, my hand reached out to them.

The breakfast was over. And no word yet from my wages.

"*Gottuniu!*" I thought to myself. "Maybe they're so busy with their own things they forgot it's the day for my wages. Could they who have everything know what I was to do with my first American dollars? How could they, soaking in plenty, how could they feel the longing and the fierce hunger in me, pressing up through each visionary dollar? How could they know the gnawing ache of my avid fingers for the feel of my own, earned dollars? *My* dollars that I could spend like a free person. *My* dollars that would make me feel with everybody alike."

Lunch came. Lunch past.

Oi-i weh! Not a word yet about my money.

It was near dinner. And not a word yet about my wages.

I began to set the table. But my head—it swam away from me. I broke a glass. The silver dropped from my nervous fingers. I couldn't stand it any longer. I dropped everything and rushed over to my American lady and gentleman.

"*Oi weh!* The money—my money—my wages!" I cried breathlessly.

Four cold eyes turned on me.

"Wages? Money?" The four eyes turned into hard stone as they looked me up and down. "Haven't you a comfortable bed to sleep, and three good meals a day? You're only a month here. Just came to America. And you already think about money. Wait till you're worth any money. What use are you without knowing English? You should be glad we keep you here. It's like a vacation for you. Other girls pay money yet to be in the country."

It went black for my eyes. I was so choked no words came to my lips. Even the tears went dry in my throat.

I left. Not a dollar for all my work.

For a long, long time my heart ached and ached like a sore wound. If murderers would have robbed me and killed me it wouldn't have hurt me so much. I couldn't think through my pain. The minute I'd see before me how they looked at me, the words they said to me—then everything began to bleed in me. And I was helpless.

For a long, long time the thought of ever working in an "American" family made me tremble with fear, like the fear of wild wolves. No—

never again would I trust myself to an "American" family, no matter how fine their language and how sweet their smile.

It was blotted out in me all trust in friendship from "Americans." But the life in me still burned to live. The hope in me still craved to hope. In darkness, in dirt, in hunger and want, but only to live on!

There had been no end to my day—working for the "American" family.

Now rejecting false friendships from higher-ups in America, I turned back to the Ghetto. I worked on a hard bench with my own kind on either side of me. I knew before I began what my wages were to be. I knew what my hours were to be. And I knew the feeling of the end of the day.

From the outside my second job seemed worse than the first. It was in a sweat-shop of a Delancey Street basement, kept up by an old, wrinkled woman that looked like a black witch of greed. My work was sewing on buttons. While the morning was still dark I walked into a dark basement. And darkness met me when I turned out of the basement.

Day after day, week after week, all the contact I got with America was handling dead buttons. The money I earned was hardly enough to pay for bread and rent. I didn't have a room to myself. I didn't even have a bed. I slept on a mattress on the floor in a rat-hole of a room occupied by a dozen other immigrants. I was always hungry—oh, so hungry! The scant meals I could afford only sharpened my appetite for real food. But I felt myself better off than working in the "American" family, where I had three good meals a day and a bed to myself. With all the hunger and darkness of the sweat-shop, I had at least the evening to myself. And all night was mine. When all were asleep, I used to creep up on the roof of the tenement and talk out my heart in silence to the stars in the sky.

"Who am I? What am I? What do I want with my life? Where is America? Is there an America? What is this wilderness in which I'm lost?"

I'd hurl my questions and then think and think. And I could not tear it out of me, the feeling that America must be somewhere, some-how—only I couldn't find it—*my America*, where I would work for love and not for a living. I was like a thing following blindly after something far off in the dark!

"*Oi weh!*" I'd stretch out my hand up in the air. "My head is so lost in America! What's the use of all my working if I'm not in it? Dead buttons is not me."

Then the busy season started in the shop. The mounds of buttons grew and grew. The long day stretched out longer. I had to begin with the buttons earlier and stay with them till later in the night. The old witch turned into a huge greedy maw for wanting more and more buttons.

For a glass of tea, for a slice of herring over black bread, she would buy us up to stay another and another hour, till there seemed no end to her demands.

One day, the light of self-assertion broke into my cellar darkness.

"I don't want the tea. I don't want your herring," I said with terrible boldness. "I only want to go home. I only want the evening to myself!"

"You fresh mouth, you!" cried the old witch. "You learned already too much in America. I want no clockwatchers in my shop. Out you go!"

I was driven out to cold and hunger. I could no longer pay for my mattress on the floor. I no longer could buy the bite in my mouth. I walked the streets. I knew what it is to be alone in a strange city, among strangers.

But I laughed through my tears. So I learned too much already in America because I wanted the whole evening to myself? Well America has yet to teach me still more: how to get not only the whole evening to myself, but a whole day a week like the American workers.

That sweat-shop was a bitter memory but a good school. It fitted me for a regular factory. I could walk in boldly and say I could work at something, even if it was only sewing on buttons.

Gradually, I became a trained worker. I worked in a light, airy factory, only eight hours a day. My boss was no longer a sweater and a blood-squeezer. The first freshness of the morning was mine. And the whole evening was mine. All day Sunday was mine.

Now I had better food to eat. I slept on a better bed. Now, I even looked dressed up like the American-born. But inside of me I knew that I was not yet an American. I choked with longing when I met an American-born, and I could say nothing.

Something cried dumb in me. I couldn't help it. I didn't know what it was I wanted. I only knew I wanted. I wanted. Like the hunger in the heart that never gets food.

An English class for foreigners started in our factory. The teacher had such a good, friendly face, her eyes looked so understanding, as if she could see right into my heart. So I went to her one day for an advice:

"I don't know what is with me the matter," I began. "I have no rest in me. I never yet done what I want."

"What is it you want to do, child?" she asked me.

"I want to do something with my head, my feelings. All day long, only with my hands I work."

"First you must learn English." She patted me as if I was not yet grown up. "Put your mind on that, and then we'll see."

So for a time I learned the language. I could almost begin to think with English words in my head. But in my heart the emptiness still hurt. I burned to give, to give something, to do something, to be something. The dead work with my hands was killing me. My work left only hard stones on my heart.

Again I went to our factory teacher and cried out to her: "I know already to read and write the English language, but I can't put it into words what I want. What is it in me so different that can't come out?"

She smiled at me down from her calmness as if I were a little bit out of my head. "What *do you want* to do?"

"I feel. I see. I hear. And I want to think it out. But I'm like dumb in me. I only feel I'm different—different from everybody."

She looked at me close and said nothing for a minute. "You ought to join one of the social clubs of the Women's Association," she advised.

"What's the Women's Association?" I implored greedily.

"A group of American women who are trying to help the working-girl find herself. They have a special department for immigrant girls like you."

I joined the Women's Association. On my first evening there they announced a lecture: "The Happy Worker and His Work," by the Welfare director of the United Mills Corporation.

"Is there such a thing as a happy worker at his work?" I wondered. "Happiness is only by working at what you love. And what poor girl can ever find it to work at what she loves? My old dreams about my

America rushed through my mind. Once I thought that in America everybody works for love. Nobody has to worry for a living. Maybe this welfare man came to show me the *real* America that till now I sought in vain."

With a lot of polite words the head lady of the Women's Association introduced a higher-up that looked like the king of kings of business. Never before in my life did I ever see a man with such a sureness in his step, such power in his face, such friendly positiveness in his eye as when he smiled upon us.

"Efficiency is the new religion of business," he began. "In big business houses, even in up-to-date factories, they no longer take the first comer and give him any job that happens to stand empty. Efficiency begins at the employment office. Experts are hired for the one purpose, to find out how best to fit the worker to his work. It's economy for the boss to make the worker happy." And then he talked a lot more on efficiency in educated language that was over my head.

I didn't know exactly what it meant—efficiency—but if it was to make the worker happy at his work, then that's what I had been looking for since I came to America. I only felt from watching him that he was happy by his job. And as I looked on this clean, well-dressed, successful one, who wasn't ashamed to say he rose from an office-boy, it made me feel that I, too, could lift myself up for a person.

He finished his lecture, telling us about the Vocational-Guidance Center that the Women's Association started.

The very next evening I was at the Vocational-Guidance Center. There I found a young, college-looking woman. Smartness and health shining from her eyes! She, too, looked as if she knew her way in America. I could tell at the first glance: here is a person that is happy by what she does.

"I feel you'll understand me," I said right away.

She leaned over with pleasure in her face: "I hope I can."

"I want to work by what's in me. Only, I don't know what's in me. I only feel I'm different."

She gave me a quick, puzzled look from the corner of her eyes. "What are you doing now?"

"I'm the quickest shirtwaist hand on the floor. But my heart wastes away by such work. I think and think, and my thoughts can't come out."

"Why don't you think out your thoughts in shirtwaists? You could learn to be a designer. Earn more money."

"I don't want to look on waists. If my hands are sick from waists, how could my head learn to put beauty into them?"

"But you must earn your living at what you know, and rise slowly from job to job."

I looked at her office sign: "Vocational Guidance." "What's your vocational guidance?" I asked. "How to rise from job to job—how to earn more money?"

The smile went out from her eyes. But she tried to be kind yet. "What *do* you want?" she asked, with a sigh of last patience.

"I want America to want me."

She fell back in her chair, thunderstruck with my boldness. But yet, in a low voice of educated self-control, she tried to reason with me:

"You have to *show* that you have something special for America before America has need of you."

"But I never had a chance to find out what's in me, because I always had to work for a living. Only, I feel it's efficiency for America to find out what's in me so different, so I could give it out by my work."

Her eyes half closed as they bored through me. Her mouth opened to speak, but no words came from her lips. So I flamed up with all that was choking in me like a house on fire:

"America gives free bread and rent to criminals in prison. They got grand houses with sunshine, fresh air, doctors and teachers, even for the crazy ones. Why don't they have free boarding-schools for immigrants—strong people—willing people? Here you see us burning up with something different, and America turns her head away from us."

Her brows lifted and dropped down. She shrugged her shoulders away from me with the look of pity we give to cripples and hopeless lunatics.

"America is no Utopia. First you must become efficient in earning a living before you can indulge in your poetic dreams."

I went away from the vocational-guidance office with all the air out of my lungs. All the light out of my eyes. My feet dragged after me like dead wood.

Till now there had always lingered a rosy veil of hope over my emptiness, a hope that a miracle would happen. I would open up my eyes some day and suddenly find the America of my dreams. As a young girl hungry for love sees always before her eyes the picture of lover's arms around her, so I saw always in my heart the vision of Utopian America.

But now I felt that the America of my dreams never was and never could be. Reality had hit me on the head as with a club. I felt that the America that I sought was nothing but a shadow—an echo—a chimera of lunatics and crazy immigrants.

Stripped of all illusion, I looked about me. The long desert of wasting days of drudgery stared me in the face. The drudgery that I had lived through, and the endless drudgery still ahead of me rose over me like a withering wilderness of sand. In vain were all my cryings, in vain were all frantic efforts of my spirit to find the living waters of understanding for my perishing lips. Sand, sand was everywhere. With every seeking, every reaching out I only lost myself deeper and deeper in a vast sea of sand.

I knew now the American language. And I knew now, if I talked to the Americans from morning till night, they could not understand what the Russian soul of me wanted. They could not understand *me* any more than if I talked to them in Chinese. Between my soul and the American soul were worlds of difference that no words could bridge over. What was that difference? What made the Americans so far apart from me?

I began to read the American history. I found from the first pages that America started with a band of Courageous Pilgrims. They had left their native country as I had left mine. They had crossed an unknown ocean and landed in an unknown country, as I.

But the great difference between the first Pilgrims and me was that they expected to make America, build America, create their own world of liberty. I wanted to find it ready made.

I read on. I delved deeper down into the American history. I saw how the Pilgrim Fathers came to a rocky desert country, surrounded by Indian savages on all sides. But undaunted, they pressed on— through danger—through famine, pestilence, and want—they pressed on. They did not ask the Indians for sympathy, for understanding. They made no demands on anybody, but on their own indomitable spirit of persistence.

And I—I was forever begging a crumb of sympathy, a gleam of understanding from strangers who could not understand.

I, when I encountered a few savage Indian scalpers, like the old witch of the sweat-shop, like my "Americanized" countryman, who cheated me of my wages—I, when I found myself on the lonely, untrodden path through which all seekers of the new world must pass, I lost heart and said: "There is no America!"

Then came a light—a great revelation! I saw America—a big idea— a deathless hope—a world still in the making. I saw that it was the glory of America that it was not yet finished. And I, the last comer, had her share to give, small or great, to the making of America, like those Pilgrims who came in the *Mayflower*.

Fired up by this revealing light, I began to build a bridge of understanding between the American-born and myself. Since their life was shut out from such as me, I began to open up my life and the lives of my people to them. And life draws life. In only writing about the Ghetto I found America.

Great chances have come to me. But in my heart is always a deep sadness. I feel like a man who is sitting down to a secret table of plenty, while his near ones and dear ones are perishing before his eyes. My very joy in doing the work I love hurts me like secret guilt, because all about me I see so many with my longings, my burning eagerness, to do and to be, wasting their days in drudgery they hate, merely to buy bread and pay rent. And America is losing all that richness of the soul.

The Americans of tomorrow, the America that is every day nearer coming to be, will be too wise, too open-hearted, too friendly-handed, to let the least last-comer at their gates knock in vain with his gifts unwanted.

Seven Candles

Fannie Hurst

THE WIND HAD a long whizz to it. *Zeouw!* It raced around corners so that it struck Molla Ivanü broadside and jerked her breath away. It rose up under her hat and set it on end like a plate on a juggler's brow. It sent up spiral snow ghosts in front of her and blew flurries of them into her mouth. It caught at her skirts and tore up under, chapping her knees. It tweaked her ears until the lobes were red and swollen and shiny. *Zeouw!*

She was winded and twisted and her carpet bag hooked into burningly cold fingers when she finally staggered into a drug store. There was a pot-bellied stove with an iron fence around it. Her flesh began to sing. She cupped her hands against the warm sheet iron fence. All ten of her fingers, little bells ringing.

The chemist glanced up and shrugged softly.

"Worst blizzard in ten years."

"Yes," she said, with her mouth full of the chattering dice of her teeth.

"Where you going? Traveling? You won't get a train out of this town today. Worst tie-up in ten years."

"No. No. I got to go down to Front Street, where I got a aunt."

"Front Street? Docks, huh? You have as much chance getting down to Front Street as a duck has of swimming through snowdrifts."

"I got to go," she said.

He looked at her over his glasses. He had a Yankee face with a kick-up of beard.

"Where are you going, back to the old country?"

"Back? I've never been."

"Ain't you a Finn or something? You look about as foreign to me as a samovar. Got some foreign streaks in you, I'll wager."

"Many—but I don't know—all mixed up——"

"Melting pot—eh? Well, it's a bad morning to have going anywhere on your mind. Worst in ten years."

"I'm yoost changing places."

"Oh—housework?"

"Cook, mostly."

"Who's firing a good hefty girl like you on such a morning?"

"Not fired. I got references."

"Say, I have a customer over on Fifty-eighth Street needs a cook—worst way! Small family. Good wages. I'm putting up these aromatic spirits now for the old woman. You might take it over for me and size up the place. Want the address? Good folks——"

"If you will please be so good——"

He ran his tongue over a label, smacking it on to the bottle. "No slip-ups on the way over. I'm taking a chance on you. My delivery boy wouldn't miss the chance of staying away for a snowstorm like this if he lived upstairs. Here's the name and address."

She took the slip with her thick, numbed fingers.

"Pal-es-tine——"

"Just around the corner. Tell them I sent you. He's the owner of the Sample Shoe Store on Thirty-fourth Street. You're a nice girl. They'll be lucky to get you. Wish I could afford you for the wife. Don't forget the package. It's spirits of ammonia for the old mother."

She picked up her bag and went out.

The wind met her with a swoop and a yell—standing her hat again up on end.

She bent into it, baring her teeth with the effort.

The Palestines lived on the fifth floor. Their living room overlooked the heads of the buildings opposite and took in a fleeting view of Central Park. A showy room of velour hangings with tassels. A handsome baby grand piano and a lamp with an openwork brass shade.

Paintings in shadow boxes, and incongruously enough, to fill in the narrow panel of wall between the mantelpiece and door, a few Japanese prints which Mr. Palestine had once been obliged to take over as part payment of a bad account. Cool and thin with the fine calligraphy of a minute and apparently emotionless art. Molla Ivanü liked to dust their impassiveness.

Evenings, when there was not a poker party around the dining room table, the Palestines lounged about this room in loose unexcited attitudes. Mr. Palestine reading the paper and yawning enormously with protracted shudderings as he turned the pages. He was a tall, heavy-set fellow with very black hair parted down the center and set on to his head squarely, like a toupee. His small straight mustache with the ends waxed up enhanced this squareness.

Mrs. Palestine, on these evenings when there was no poker game, uncorseted herself immediately after the evening meal, the soft white flesh running down the hill of her body. She was very blonde and wore her hair in elaborate tier upon tier of puffs. These puffs, made in rows of three, four and five, like hot buns, littered the house.

Whenever old Mrs. Palestine found one she picked it up gingerly as if it were a mouse by the tail and handed it in a scathing kind of silence to her daughter-in-law. *"Pfui!"* was how she felt about most things pertaining to her son's wife. But she sat, too, in the living room with the pair of them after dinner. There was an arch of shadow where the lamplight did not reach. Old Mrs. Palestine liked to sit back in that, idle and brooding and with dry old eyes like prunes.

She had to have a hassock because her feet did not touch the floor. Young Mrs. Palestine had a way of kicking the hassock savagely when her mother-in-law was not about, gritting her teeth with pain at her stubbed toes and taking a fierce kind of delight in that pain, and then kicking it again and again with her fancy tipped shoes.

Young Mrs. Palestine's shoes were eloquent. They were short-vamped, florid, and even after one wearing apt to tipple a little of run-over heels. Old Mrs. Palestine wore square-toed black bluchers with rubber insets, which she polished herself every morning and set out on the fire escape outside Molla's window to dry. Her son, who was inclined to bunions, wore square toes too, but with the additional flourish of spats with the green or ruby of vivid hose above them.

85

Underneath the dining room table, their respective feet spoke volumes. The polished orthodox ones of old Mrs. Palestine on their hassock. The short-vamp champagne ones with the run-down heels. Palestine's rather stolid ones between the two.

Difficult, nervous meals of three kinds of silences. An old lady's aching one. A young woman's high-tensioned one. Palestine's tired one.

Sometimes it seemed to Molla Ivanü that the dining room of golden oak and swell of elaborate sideboard was filled with a gale of this silence, like one of those terrific arctic windstorms that old sea dogs dread because the water, in horrible phenomena, lies like glass under the gale, too windbeaten to lift a wave.

"Pass me the butter, Pal." Scarcely the phraseology to rock empires. "Pass me the butter, Pal"; and yet when May Palestine said it, old Mrs. Palestine, whose skin was sapless at best, could seem to shrivel into the ancient parchment of the Torah.

She kept kosher. Valiantly. The forbidden combination of meat and butter might desecrate her daughter-in-law's board, but not the spirit nor the palate of the old lady. At her end of the table the sacred rituals of the "meat dishes" and "milk dishes" remained unviolated. There was a shelf in the kitchen, especially contrived by her son, for the kosher utensils, and a two burner gas stove in the corner for the personal and private preparation of her orthodox foods.

May hated that stove and the little whisper of garlic that hung over it. "Makes me sick to my stummick to walk into my own kitchen," was one of her *sotto voces*. "I'm Episcopalian, but I'd like to see myself frying myself Episcopalian pork chops. Good to their stummicks! Oh Lord! *Kosher* is another word for stummick love."

And Molla, hearing, would clatter pans and turn on the spigot for the plunge of water into the sink, because sometimes the undertones percolated to the old woman's dim ears and then she would have one of her smothering spells or sinking fits, and spirits of ammonia would have to be administered. On one occasion Mr. Palestine, in the midst of a Monday marked-down sale of Oxford ties, had to be sent for, and all through the rush hours was obliged to sit alternating between holding his mother's hand in her darkened bedroom or pacifying his wife, who invariably expressed her frenzy by throwing articles of clothing into a traveling bag and then strewing them all out again.

"No. I won't be the one to go. Why should I? That's just what she's laying for, to break up this house. But she won't! She won't! Not while my dress buttons up the back with tiddlewinks!"

The last was a favorite aphorism of Mrs. Palestine. You could hear it from the poker table.

"I'll raise you two bones. You can't bluff me. Not while my dress buttons up the back with tiddlewinks."

A festive, painted phrase like the little pagoda all lantern-hung in one of the Japanese prints. Molla Ivanü liked it. Button up the back like tiddlewinks! It made Molla feel gay somehow just to repeat it to herself.

But generally there was little enough to feel gay about at the Palestines' with May and her tantrums so quick on the trigger or the broody old woman who on Friday evenings would light the candles in her room and keep open her door so that the sound of her weeping came in little bleatings down the hallway.

"She's putting on, putting on," May would singsong as she lolled *en déshabille* in the living room. She had a perpetually hoarse voice, full of fog. "When *I* feel like having a good cry, I go in my room and shut the door, and Lord knows there's enough reasons around here for having a good cry. Evening's diversion. Lord, how they love to cry! It's a wonder there's not an Atlantic Ocean somewheres made up of noisy kosher tears."

"I wish you'd leave my mother out of your gab, May."

"Oh, you do, do you? Well then, I wish she'd leave her gab out of my business!"

"Between you and your rows, you two women are driving me plumb raving crazy. At least if I was the youngest I'd give in to an old woman— an old tired woman like my mother with only a few years left to live. I'd humor her, May. Honest I would."

"Few years! Long enough to ruin my home for six years! Few years! With her digestion for the greasy meals she eats, she stands a good chance of ruining it for many years to come."

"May, you can't change a leopard's spots. My mother's old and she's grieving herself to death over things you're too young to understand. She likes you, May."

"A lot I care if she likes me or not. Nobody could live in the house with her. The dusting don't suit and the cooking don't suit and the

87

poker parties don't suit and the number of petticoats I have in the wash don't suit. Molla is the first servant we've ever been able to keep in the same house with your mother, and if that hunk is human I'll button my dress up the back with tiddlewinks . . ."

"She's the best servant we ever had."

"Yes, but nobody but a great cream-colored elephant like her would stand for the old woman's butting in. She's got a hide not even your mother can break through. That's the way to be. Tough, so that they can stick things in you and you don't feel 'em. I'm sensitive. That's me. High-strung. I can't stand no yammering old hex in my affairs, and not get the pollywog jimjams."

"You eat those words that you just called my mother!"

"Eat 'em? I'll spit 'em out, you mean! Hex—that's what she is."

"By——"

"All right, hit me! Hit me! Lot I care—go in there and cry some kosher tears with her—I can't help it because your father died—I can't help it because garlic makes me sick to my stummick—I can't help it because a penny don't look the size of a sunrise to me. Hit me—hit me—but if you do—there'll be the greatest little smash-up around here this happy home has ever known. Hit me—I'd like to see you try it, sheenie!"

"You——"

"Ah—ow——"

Then to Molla, shuddering in the kitchen, the tormented frenzied tumble of him down the hallway, the slam into his room, and presently the violent sickness which these scenes never failed to induce in him.

Silence, with May lying swollen and wet-mouthed on the couch and the bleating from the old woman's room whimpering down into sobs.

Virtually, it was Molla who put the family to bed—additional blankets to be laid out, pillows fluffed. The hot water bag for the old woman's chilled spine. Ice for Palestine to suck. Spirits of camphor for the threat of fever sore on May's lips.

Yes, generally there was little enough to be glad about at the Palestines'.

In spring Molla wheeled the old lady out in her rolling chair. She had a hip bone complaint, and except in the house she seldom walked.

Molla liked wheeling her out in the spring. Usually she trundled her directly to the Park.

There was a tree there beside the lake with the swan boats on it that in April popped out in a delicate rash of leaves. It was down eight steps hewn out of natural rock and there was a bench beside the water.

Long, sedative afternoons with the old woman droning into them, and Molla, her hand joggling the chair as if it were a perambulator, watching the light bend around the lake. In repose, the look of tightness would seem to ease up in Mrs. Palestine's face like the flesh of a prune that has been dropped in water. The flesh softened up a bit and smooth little areas in her cheeks sprang out that usually looked sucked in.

Faces like hers, strong-skinned, high-boned, and the eyes a little fanatical with love, had kept the storm-blown flames of the seven-branch candlestick burning down through the ages.

When Mrs. Palestine wept for her son she wept for Israel, and that is why her eyes could sometimes seem dry as salt beds with bitter residuum.

Often, talking through the quiet afternoon, her lips would try to shape themselves for words too heart-twisting for her to speak, and so she would cry them, her mouth writhing back from the gums. "My boy. I don't care, Molla, so much that she has stolen him from me—every mother who loses a son to a wife must learn such pain—but, Molla—she's stolen him from his faith. Ain't that an awful pain, Molla, to have a son stolen like a baby from his cradle out of his religion? Away from his God to hers."

Here was that God business again. Why was Mrs. Palestine's God a better God than May's God? Why was not the God who made May the same God who made Mrs. Palestine? All this wrangling over your God and my God. May Palestine went out on Saint days to visit hers. Mrs. Palestine burned candles and kept her tongue free of the salt of swine in His name. One God, and yet all struggling over Him. Tearing Him to pieces and setting up each his shred. Mrs. Palestine refuting May's Shred for her Shred. Your Shred. My Shred. Yet all torn off the divinely bleeding and omnipotent form.

"A boy who was raised in such a home like his should go out of it to another religion! Not a Friday night in his life that he didn't see his papa and me light the candles for our *Shabbas*. I'm afraid to die. I'm afraid to die and leave him to face her God. I—Molla—Molla—

89

an old woman like me—tired—tired—my husband waiting—my home broke up—my life a misery—so ready to go—afraid to die—afraid to leave my boy and go meet my husband."

Silently then Molla would jounce the handle of the chair.

"She's not right for him, Molla. How I prayed with him that night he came home from the dance hall where he met her, he should not go to such places—even before I knew where it would lead to. She ain't a helpful wife, Molla—like I was to mine. I stinted. She spends. I mended and washed and ironed. She plays poker and eats all day, chocolates. My boy works on his feet fifteen hours and she spends it faster as he can earn it. I can't stand to see it she should spend for manicures, money what it has hurt my boy to stand all day on his bunions to earn. He don't know it yet—he's in love. It ain't nice to say it—he's in love with her body. No man can change his God for a woman's body—and have it last. She ain't the wife for him. I can't sit by and see it—can't—can't——"

Talk—talk—talk—through the long, sedative afternoons. Sometimes Molla dozed a little, coming up to consciousness for snatches of it and then slipping off again, her head over toward one shoulder and her hand automatically at the sedative jouncing motion.

"You should have seen, Molla—such a new suit as his papa bought him for *bar mizvah*—to get *bar mizvah* by us is the holy time when boy becomes a little man in his religion. His papa—how every night after supper, in the back of the store so sometimes the customers had to wait, my husband heard that child his *bar mizvah* lesson. A rabbi—that was what his papa wanted for him to be—a rabbi. But he didn't want it—he wanted to sell shoes—like his papa. All right, he should sell shoes! How his papa learned him from the ground up the shoe business. How we lived our whole lives for that boy. None but the nicest girls at our house for Friday night supper—maybe he should fall in love with one. There was one—Selma Rabinovitch—a wife we could have been proud of for him—four of her own beautiful children now and a husband in the mattress business.

"My boy should have missed that! And for what?—such a blonde *shickser* what don't do nothing except set him against his mother and his religion and throw out his money for him faster as he can make it. Blonde—*shickser*—Pal—my boy—gone! Thank God his papa didn't live to see it—maybe he blames me when we meet again. I couldn't help it, Julius. I tried—I prayed—she got him with her white flesh, Julius—blonde flesh like he wasn't used to. When a woman gets a boy that way—not even his God, Julius—can hold him back."

And so on and on through the whimpering lips, until the copper band of light around the lake snapped out, and with a great pulling and tugging and sometimes the help of a passer-by Molla began to yank the wheel chair up the steps that were hewn out of natural rock.

That summer Palestine and his wife took a two weeks' holiday at a small lake resort upstate known as Becker's Point. May's second brother ran what they called "the pickle boat" around the lake there. A small provision tug which puffed about all day, dispensing from landing to landing the tinned, tabloid and the compressed foods of the summer colony.

"You would rather have your vacation, Pal, by Fleishmans in the Catskills where you're used to it, but lots she cares where you get your vacation just so she gets hers. Her brother with his store on a boat. We're plain but substantial people. In our family we got our stores on streets like it is legitimate. I pretend like I don't know it, but just the same I do know it that it is your hard earned money, son, put him in that business on a boat. And now my boy has got to go and see her brother lose his money in such a business what ain't even on land to pay taxes."

Palestine took his mother by the wrists and pressed his fingers into them until white areas sprang. "Mama, don't start anything with May now. I *do* want to go to Becker's Point. I need a rest. I'm nervous. Terribly nervous."

"I won't say anything, son, to her if I bust with it. I'm only saying it to you—I know how you like it at Fleishmans in the Catskills."

"I'll send you there, ma—Molla can take you."

"Me? I don't think on myself. I'm satisfied to stay home and do a little saving—but that you should have to lay around such a *goy* place!"

"Ma, if I hear that hateful word from you one more time! I'm worn out—I can't stand it—I'm nervous—you hear——"

"All right, son. Don't holler. Maybe I won't be here so much longer you should holler at me like that—if only I wasn't afraid to die and meet papa——"

91

He dropped to one knee, kissing her hand.

"Mama, mama, don't torment me, I love her, mama, and I—I hate her! That's torment for you—torment of Hell on earth. To love a woman at the same time you hate her!"

So for two weeks of an August that glared down upon the city until it was as bleached and polished as old bone, Molla and Mrs. Palestine had the flat to themselves.

Hot, motionless days and nights that seemed to sit still and brood like pyramids! For the time, Molla slept on a cot at the foot of the old woman's bed. She tossed a great deal and a little moan ran through her light snores, and sometimes she started up with short sharp cries.

"Son! Don't let her! Julius! It's *Pesach*. Son—don't eat that bread! *Shickser!* A *shickser* wife! No, no, papa—I tried—I begged. I prayed. The dance halls—don't be mad with me, papa . . ."

Often Molla had to get up and turn on the light.

"You bane dreaming, Mrs. Palestine. See. It's Molla. Here, let me fix your pillows—take a sip of water—so—there's nobody here but Molla."

"I thought it was *Pesach*, Molla—when my people must eat only matzoth—the unleaven bread of God—and she wouldn't let me. She stepped on them once," and up went the voice to the peak of hysteria that was so hard to quell. "She stepped on them once with her heels—matzoth—God's bread. I can't ever forgive her that . . ."

And so on and so on and so on through the burning deserts of these motionless August nights, and sometimes, of sheer exhaustion, Molla slept. Vastly.

One dawn a withered leaf fluttered down upon the heavy torpor of Molla. It was Mrs. Palestine's hand, plucking at her from across the footboard of her bed. "Molla!"

"Oh—what—yes, Mrs. Palestine."

"Molla, I been called home. I want to go, Molla. It ain't long now before I won't be here no more, and before I go—I want to go back down there. It won't be so hard I should have to face Julius if first I can only go home."

"Why, Mrs. Palestine, you bane home—here."

"Here is not home for me. Get me my foulard dress and my bonnet. I want we should start before the heat of the day."

"But your son will not like it."

A sudden slyness came curling out in the old woman's face.

"No, he don't like it if I go, Molla. It ain't stylish that his old mother should remember old days, but, Molla, please, take me home. I want more as anything to go. Only down by Division Street."

"Mrs. Palestine—you can't walk——"

"Who says I can't walk? It is only when I ain't got no ambition that I can't walk. Take me home, Molla. I can walk there. I got to go. I can't stand it no more. The ache to go home. If you don't take me I crawl by myself on my hands and my knees. I ain't here long no more. I know it by my dreams. And I got to go home first. Look, Molla, when I got ambition, see how I can walk—see, Molla—please——"

And sure enough she began to limp about, outlandish in her night-dress with the rack of her old body shaking through, but her face thrust out ahead of herself like a lantern.

"Mrs. Palestine—your son—I promised to take good care——"

She was slyer and slyer, her eyebrows running up into little peaks and her cheek bones and chin jutting out into points.

"He don't got to know, Molla. Take me home, Molla, before I die. I'm going to die—soon. I hear it at nights underneath my sleep. And you know what it is, Molla, to hear things—that way. Because always you too are listening to something. I heard it again last night. Take me home, Molla, so I can get strength back to meet papa—I want my old home where we lived twenty years and where my boy learned his *bar mizvah* lessons behind the counter—I want to go back——"

And Molla washed the old face of its tear traces, brushed back the old hair into thin streaks that scarcely covered the scalp and fastened around her the decent silk foulard dress.

The August day came out at them like a parched and coated tongue as they started for Division Street.

The wheels ran and banged and a breeze blew through the street car. A breeze as curiously alive as breath.

It stood the little invisible nap of fine hairs on Molla's forearm up on end in an electric little rash, and it rushed against her ears thick with words that could not form themselves out of the two dozen languages that the East Side exuded. A conglomerate breath, rich in nationalities, and that would one day find voice. Molla, somehow, knew that rich kind of muteness. It beat up against her so.

At Canal Street it was as if the sidewalks ran shouting to meet them. It was hard to steady Mrs. Palestine against the dizzying swirl because she was crying and through the dimness of tears wading her way eastward, her umbrella, which she carried as a steadying cane, waving out before her as if to clear the way of children and languid puffs of dirty newspaper and rinds and rinds of fruit.

"Ten years since I been home, Molla. How I worked when I was a young woman down here to get ourselves out of it, and now I got myself out of it how I eat my heart to be back in it. My boy was *bar mizvah* down here. My husband made us a living down here. My happiest days in my life I spent down here with my people—with my Shule—with my family—right over there. You see, Molla—Abraham Naftel—for twelve years every Friday morning of my life I bought pike and bass from him for my *gefüllte* fish. He remembers me, what you bet, if I go in? Hurry, Molla—I want you should see where my baby was born."

Old Mrs. Palestine, suddenly full of young little running steps, two long raspberry ovals of color out in her cheeks, the foulard dress ballooning as she hurried. Tears. Tears. Thick lenses of them.

The house in Division Street was as lean as a witch. Human bodies lax, like pillows over sills, dangling and shouting from windows. That dingy and perpetual banner of poverty, the family wash-line, kicking and writhing. There was a poultry store on the ground floor. Furious smells of chicken blood and hot fuzz, and on the high stoop, like a brooding conclave of the shawled women of the East, half a dozen old crones in white headkerchiefs, and burning back deeply in them—deeply, burningly back—tired Old Testament eyes.

Suddenly Mrs. Palestine's legs gave out under her. They would not climb that stoop. Twice with Molla's sturdy hand at her elbow she raised her foot for the first step and twice her knees doubled under, until finally she crumpled up on the first step, leaning her face against the railing to cry.

"I can't go no farther. I'm too happy. I'm home. This is my stoop. I don't know no more these faces, but this is my stoop."

And the snow of hot fuzz blew against her lips, and children gathered around, and the Biblical old women with their peering faces and dead leaf hands came down the steps. Then came an avalanche of words.

94

Words. A torrent of words that were new and alien to Molla. Down off the chute of Mrs. Palestine's tongue, tumbling in Yiddish. Coal off a chute. Clatter. Clatter. And the circle of the old women closed in. And the day grew hotter and higher and the din ground itself against the flesh like grime and Molla sat by waiting. *Oi-oi*, the thin quail voices of the old women. The dry old women, past childbearing, with the dry eyes and the dry breasts and the dry tears. The jargon of Yiddish ran in a tide. The day was on the down side before she could pry Mrs. Palestine from the hot high stoop.

Through the heat dance all the lean houses seemed to have wavy walls and it was not easy to manipulate Mrs. Palestine back again on to the street car. But finally she made the hoist and plumped down inside.

Except for the sighs which blew and blew off the twisted old crags of lips, she seemed to doze, with her fist plunged deep into Molla's palm and throbbing there.

"You seen, Molla—my people—those are my people—and his—our people, Molla. Who are your people?"

"My people?" She looked at Mrs. Palestine softly, the wide lips falling apart to smile. "My people? Why, those are my people—out there," she said. Her eyes were very blue and her lips fumbled to say more. "Those are my people. Out there. Everywhere."

It was the last time the old woman ever left the house. August roared on and Palestine and his wife returned. The old woman resumed her long motionless watches in the shadowy arch between the folding doors. Sitting there during the long merriments of the poker game, her dry eyes forever focused upon her son, they would seem to smear into a single tearless and reproachful orb in the center of her forehead.

"Gives me the jimjams—her sitting there," was a frequent *sotto voce* of May.

"Mama dear, don't you think you had better let Molla take you to bed? We're going to play a round of rudles yet and you must be tired."

"I'm all right, son."

Once a guest, a Mr. McGuire, who was a frequent visitor, swung around in his chair to her. "Come on, grandma, have one of these kosher ham sandwiches. They're kosher, ain't they, Palestine?"

Oh. Oh. Oh. The poor dried prunes of eyes in Mrs. Palestine's head. They seemed to have died there.

One January noon when there were pork chops snapping on the stove for luncheon, Mrs. Palestine was suddenly missing from her chair beside the window in her room. She left there less and less now and never without the hoist of Molla's arm.

"Mrs. Palestine—the old woman—she's not in her room! I can't find her!"

May was drying her hair in a great fan that spread in a patch of cold sunlight on the sill. "She's not far. No such luck."

Sure enough, Molla finally discovered her shivering and crying on the fire escape, where she had climbed with an agility that frenzy alone could have given her.

"Mrs. Palestine, you must come in from the cold."

"Let her stay out there, Molla. She'll soon get enough of it if she sees she can't spite me by one of her loony fits."

"Quick—come in right away. That is not nice to sit in the cold."

"I can't stand it. She should cut out my heart to get rid of me, but I can't stand it I should have to spend my days in such a household where my son's home is made every minute an insult to his religion. It's like my own heart was frying with them pork chops. She don't like pork chops, Molla. I've heard her tell it to the poker loafers how she don't like them, but has them to see how excited I can get . . . That God should find me in such a house like this. Julius—who wanted his boy to be a rabbi——"

Molla coaxed her in, dragging her a chair for the step from sill to floor, and full of little urgings—"There—now—so——"

"It would be better, Molla, if I die tomorrow. Then I don't stand any more in my son's way or my daughter-in-law's."

"No. No, Mrs. Palestine."

"It's not good, Molla, a woman should got to stand between such a good son's happiness with his wife like I do. My poor son—he don't know which he should be first. My son or her husband. I'm in the way, Molla. Nobody knows it better as I do. I'm in the way . . . Molla . . . never leave me, Molla."

She needed Molla so. Even the absurd fashion in which she pronounced her name was like a cry in the dark. A little winged sob that could beat its way and nest in Molla's heart, where it hurt. Sometimes at night, long after the lights were out, the cry would come through to her, and down she would tiptoe and curl up at the foot of the old woman's bed, ponderous as a mastiff.

Palestine was grateful. He had her come down to his retail store to be fitted for two fine strong pairs of bluchers, and as she went out with the package under her arm, he said: "Never leave my mother, Molla, and you won't regret it. She's a little peculiar in her ways and her ways aren't my wife's ways—but a better woman doesn't breathe. Never leave her, Molla."

"Yah—sure—never——"

Poor Palestine. It was as if a wire cage had curved itself somehow about him, with the egress woven cunningly into the mesh. He was in and the two women with him, making a prison of what, with either of them alone, might have been a nest.

Constantly, as that winter dragged through, there were half-moons in May's hands where the finger nails bit in, and her toes in the showy short-vamp shoes were always climbing over each other in suppression of a nervous rage.

One day she ran from the luncheon table into the clothes closet in her bedroom. It was horrible. Because she bit at the empty sleeves of gowns hanging there, tore fabrics, jerked hangers from their hooks, trampled on Palestine's dressing gown, kicked until she bruised her shoes and toes against the wall and finally half collapsed in a hurricane of garments.

It had happened trivially. Something like this.

About noon a fog had descended over the city. One of those gray smothers that roll in off the sea. There was something extremely cozy about the indoors on a day like this. Molla prepared tea and fluffed up an egg omelette with a fusty sense of that warm indoor coziness. May had been stacking chips for a poker party that night. She was playing practically every afternoon now, losing large sums which were the subject of heated controversy with Pal, and five evenings out of the week there were games at the house, too.

This day she wore a pink flannel wrapper and her hair was in curl rags that rose off her head like a shriek. She had a headache, too.

"Got it too good," was the old woman's under her breath diagnosis of the almost daily ritual of cold compress or headache powder. Lunch-

97

eon was a meal to dread, the two women alone, without the inter-
mediary influence of Palestine.

When May in the pink flannel wrapper entered the fog-swimming
dining room, she switched on the lights, seven high-power ones in
the colored glass dome over the table.

"Give me a tablet in a glass of water first, Molla. My head's splitting."

Then old Mrs. Palestine came in, stiffly, in her black calico house
dress dotted with white four leaf clovers and carrying a bowl of thick
black lentil soup which she had warmed from a specially prepared
crock of it that she kept.

"Say, May, since when have we got a stand-in with the electric light
company? If I can find my mouth in the middle of the day, you should
find yours with your younger eyes"; and with a good humor which
she valiantly tried to simulate for the trial of these noonday meals
together, the old woman clicked out the lights again just as May gulped
down the headache tablet. The almost reflex act of a woman who for
a period of thirty thrifty years had run her own home; and with that
same reflex of a woman bound in turn to run hers, May, with the
fuzz of fog in a whirlpool of anger about her, sprang to the wall,
clicking the lights back again.

"You dare," she cried with her lips lifting back dryly off her teeth,
"you dare to dictate to me when I can have light in my own house
and when I can't!"

The old woman had a way of appearing to shrivel and to yellow
under the lash of her daughter-in-law's tongue. She seemed to recede
to a point.

"Is that the way, May, a daughter-in-law should talk to her husband's
mother, nearly three times her age, and who didn't mean nothing but
a little economy?"

"Economy my hind foot! I'd like to see you or anybody like you tell
me when I can have the electric light on in my house and when I
can't. Not while my dress buttons up the back with tiddlewinks."

"Maybe, May, if you didn't know everything for yourself so well
and would let an old woman three times your age help——"

"Not you! You can't tell me nothing I don't know already."

"I can tell you that a good dutiful wife don't squander her husband's
money away on gambling debts and matinées—a good man like him
who stands on his bunions all day long earning it for you——"

"You keep your gab out of my affairs. You've done enough damage in this house as it is. My husband is my business."

"Your husband is my son!"

"More's the pity."

The shuddering, sucky, ligament-twisting cry of the mothers of sons bearing them. That was the kind of moaning noise Mrs. Palestine made as she went down into a little huddle on a dining room chair.

"Mrs. Palestine!"

"Let 'er alone, Molla. I'm used to those bluffs. I've seen her topple over into those fake faints for years now. Temper, that's all. She's tough as tripe."

"Oh, why don't I die?"

"The whine-fest will now being."

"Mrs. Palestine—she bane old———"

"Let her alone, Molla, I said. Hands off! That's the trouble now. Her out there in the kitchen with you all day crying for sympathy. I'm sick of it. Pal's got to decide between her and me and pretty quick too. I wish to Heaven I could go off somewhere and live in one room and never have to clap eyes on the whole shebang again. He'll have to settle good and heavy on me, too—mind you that. Matzoth house, that's what I call this. Well, thank God, I wasn't raised no matzoth eater!"

"No, no. Belittle me. Belittle even my boy—but don't make little my religion—don't make little my God because he is not your God."

"God! Who said anything about your God? Matzoth is what I said, and I say it again. *Matzoth house.* Two stoves. Two sets of dishes. Matzoth crumbs all over the house so I have to be ashamed to have company at my own table for matzoth. Matzoth. He likes 'em too—dips 'em in coffee like—slop. Once a matzoth dunker always a matzoth dunker."

"Julius, my husband! Junior, my son! My men! I can't keep it shut up in me no more. I can't live here no more. To have to see with every hour I live everything what is sacred to me and to mine made little. Papa, where are you up there? Let me come to you. Help me, Julius!"

May swung heavily into her chair. She was like a storm, her eyebrows seeming to meet and click in a furrow above her nose.

"Well," she said, flopping the omelette, which had fallen, on to her plate and jabbing into it with her fork, "here is where I am let in for another pleasant lunch hour. It's a wonder I don't croak of indigestion."

"Oh—oh—if only my son would let me rent somewhere a little room off by myself where I can live alone and die alone!"

"Well, he won't, so what you going to do about it? Dutiful son! I wish he'd try a little dutiful husband on me."

"You say that! The woman for whose extravagances my son works day and night his fingers to the bone—a boy what never in his life played a card or took more as a drink of sassaparilla before."

"My ways suit my husband when you ain't around to poison him."

"Mark my word, May, the kind of love my boy has for you—it ain't the kind that lasts. The woman who puts by something of herself for the day when her husband gets tired of the flesh and has a big fine companionship waiting for him is the smart woman. I won't do nothing to come between you—but——"

"Oh no! Oh no! You only started by doing everything in the world to keep him from marrying me."

"Yes, maybe, because he was all mine then and I had the right to fight for what I thought was his happiness, but after he did it, never one word——"

"Hah—you make me laugh! You got the nerve to say that when you can cut the hate in this house with a knife! Who do you think your son is, anyhow? When I married him there was fellas wanting to buy my meal ticket that could buy and sell him six ways for Sunday. And they wasn't kosher meals, neither."

"I can't hear that word no more so abused! It's like salt in a sore. Oh—oh—oh—if not for my son, I would right away pack my things. Why did he pull me up away from my people down there? These ways ain't my ways—those are my people—he should let me go back."

"Well, no insinuations, but you can take it from me if he didn't always have you nagging him over to your ways I could make him a darn sight happier than he's ever been in his life before. He'd be a live one, that son of yours—if he dared."

"That just goes to show! A woman with her thoughts on her home and her husband's interest and—and children—don't got time for such shennanigan talk like her husband should be a—a *live* one."

"You're going to ram that children talk down my throat once too often. I'll have children when I get good and ready to have children and not before."

"A woman shouldn't put her time for it before God's time for it."

"If—if you weren't his mother and—old—I'd drive you out of the house for less than that."

"Why don't you? It would make it easier than I should walk out from my son's house on my own——"

"Well then—I do! You can't stay here day after day to devil the life and soul out of me. I won't stand it! I—now—you—go!"

"God—papa—God—son—no—no—it ain't possible I should live to see it—out from my own son's home——"

"Yes—yes—out of your own son's home—driven out by the devil in you——"

"Oh, Mrs. Palestine—she bane old—oh—oh—oh, Mrs. Palestine——"

"And you! Square-head! You! Lump! Who are you, anyhow? There's something about you gives me the jimjams. For all I know you're one of those still ones that run deep. How do I know you're not taking sides with the old woman and running to my husband with lies? Go—the two of you—the quicker the better—go—go—go——"

It was then, because the words in her throat were a mere strangle and her hands were curved and spread out like claws, that May ran screaming to the clothes closet, dragging the garments in their avalanche of fury down about her, and gasping, choking, spluttering.

Toward dusk Molla began to try to feed the old woman soup out of a spoon.

"Can't swallow. Leave me alone, Molla. I'm an old woman put out from my own son's house. Where shall I go, Molla? No. No. I won't go. Nobody can drive me out from my son who needs me and who has lost his God."

There was no suppressing the mother of Palestine. Oppress her, yes, but the light of the children of Israel was like a campfire in her eyes and would not be ground out.

It was bitter to stay, and the lips of the mother of Palestine were twisted as old paint tubes with that bitterness.

101

The old woman slept finally. At seven Palestine would come. There was dinner to be prepared. Molla had a sly little procedure before dinner. It was to draw together two of the most comfortable chairs in the living room, chummily, as if two women had been sewing and gossiping there during the long quiet of an afternoon. The look of strain and of drain would run out of his face when he walked in on evidences of what might indicate that a day of rare tranquility had rolled over the household.

Molla dragged the two chairs together and they squealed on their castors. May was stretched asleep on the sitting room couch, her cheeks still wet and her lips flat and heavy, and always with the sensuous look of just having been kissed very hard—slightly, rather appealingly apart. One of her hands trailed to the floor and there was a pale scatter of freckles on her arm—great isolated ones, so large and far apart that Palestine could run his lips up it as if it were a flute, kissing them one by one.

When he finally did turn his key in the lock, it was as if May, so deeply simulating sleep, had been merely lying on the edge of it waiting, so quickly she pounced at him, the castle of her yellow puffs collapsed and down over one ear, and sure enough her right eye dragged upward from lying on it.

"May! My dear——"

"Yah, 'dear'—you'd better 'dear' me—leaving me shut up here day after day with a lunatic. Well, you don't need to go no further to hear her side of the story with her lies, lies, lies! You can hear it right here from me. Either that old woman gets out of this house—here—now—tonight—or I go! You can take your choice. As God is my witness—I'm through!"

All the little wrinkles came running into his face like sand over paper, and he tried to take her in his arms.

"Oh no, you don't! Not this time. A few smooth words can't make up for the all day hell of living in this house. That old woman goes or I go! I couldn't stand another day of it. You've been a long time choosing, but you've got to choose now! I've tried. I've bit my tongue in two trying—but I'm done."

"Why, May," he said in the sedative tone that must have worn a little rut along his vocal chords from the repetition of it. "I know that ma's not easy—and there's not a day that I don't think of my girl at home under conditions that aren't just right for her—but she's old, May, and she means well and—and good heavens, May—a man's mother is a man's mother, little eccentricities and all."

"No—no—we ain't going to argue any more, not while my dress buttons up the back with tiddlewinks. I've been over it all till I'm as crazy loony as she is. You gotta decide—this time it's me or her!"

His nose was like a blade, the nostrils sort of drawn in by the sharpness of his breath, and he stood under the hall light, growing paler and paler as the fatigue lines deepened.

"May—you've never been like—this. Has anything unusual happened? My mother—how—where is she?"

"Oh no! Nothing unusual. Just the usual. That's the devil of it! Just the usual—but the camel's back broke today. There's no argument. There's just for you to decide which of us gets out."

He looked at her and at the shine of her flesh up at him through the lace of her bodice and the old familiar trembling seized him, but he dug in his nails through his palms and his words were all crowded behind his teeth, which were clinching.

"Well then, by heavens—you go!"

It was as if he had stabbed her in the upthrust of bosom she could always dazzle him with, because she threw out her arms and stood like a great open fan with the finery of her sleeve drapes falling to the floor.

"Me!"

"You," he said. "Yes—yes—you——"

"You don't mean that—Pal."

"I do," he said, still with the jam of words behind his teeth.

For the first time her body sort of unwound itself of its tight theatricalism and she looked at him with her mouth shaped to cry out, but it only quivered and formed a rhomboid.

"If anybody goes out of this house, it's not going to be my mother. Get that! I may be low—but not that low. She stays here!"

There was a pause that was full of their breathing, and then with a lightning gesture she darted out for his hand, but he was too quick for her.

"No," he said, holding it behind him. "No, none of that."

103

She darted again and he looked at her coldly and smiled, holding himself on a little oblique that eluded her.

"That don't go this time, May. I'm at the end of my rope here. You have been called upon to make certain sacrifices. I know that. And I don't say they have always been easy ones. But that's part of this game of marriage. Learning to take the hurdles. You haven't taken yours. There's no argument here. Between two women one of them young and able to take care of herself and the other seventy years old and— my mother—well, if it's a case of one of them having to go, it's not going to be my mother! Get that! Get that! Not going to be my mother! This is one of those deadlocks in marriage where there is no solution. A woman either gives in or she—don't. You don't!"

With his body thrust back from her, the words in her mouth were meal, and she knew it; and suddenly with a sinuosity that was rare with her she had her arms about his knees and her cheek to him and her sobs coming so that even through the fabric her warm breath reached him.

"Pal!"

He wrenched himself, but the vise of her arms was relentless, and so with his head held up and his body still tense he stood taut, feeling the tremor of her body and finally the wet of her tears—warm—warm— against his knee.

"Get up," he said, with his head back and his body away from her.

"Pal—Pal—don't—don't throw me off for her—Pal——"

"Off! Good heavens, what's a man to do—murder an old woman to get her out of the way of a young one? God—God—what mess have I let myself into! May—don't——"

"Pal"—her hands were up now against his waistcoat so that the shape of them burned through, and his face, which he kept averted, was reddening, a slow red that ran down into his collar.

"You can't get me that—way—any—more," he said and caught her two hands by the wrists and flung her backward; but she was too quick for him again, and as if from the momentum of the shove she was back again, with her arms about his neck this time, and her lips which were shining with tears straight and pat against his.

"No—no—May—none of that—no—I say—oh——"

Suddenly it was quiet, and when he lifted his head she was crouched in a cradle his arms made for her, and the tears were running heavily down his cheeks.

"I'm tired," he said, crying frankly and daubing his eyes with the back of her hand, "dog—dog tired," and sank down on a chair in the hallway. She dragged up a stool, an outlandish one on the four curved horns of a bull, and her arms were about his knees again and her shining lips always close enough for him to feel the breath.

"You love me, Pal—I love you. What's the use—you can't give me up——"

He beat his knees.

"God! God! Was ever a man in my plight? I can't give you up. Well, where does that get me? I can't give her up. My home a hades. I'm cursed with you and I'm cursed without you. Was ever a man in such torment? I can't come home—I'll be the one to get out—I'll end it—I'll be the one to get out——"

"Pal—Pal, that won't solve anything—that will bust it up for all three. I've got a way out for us, Pal—it's the old woman. I tell you— she's got to go!"

"And I tell you, no! My mother doesn't pine out her days alone in a rooming house——"

"No—no, Pal—you don't understand. Why, the old woman's sick, Pal—her mind's sick—the old woman needs a hospital—a fine, sunny, big hospital where they can take care of her——"

Her eyes were very round and glossed over with tears and her ten fingers very soft against his cheeks, and always her breathing so he could feel its fanning warmth.

"My mother's not sick. She's—she's old. She's orthodox and she believes so strong it makes her eccentric. She's not sick——"

"She is, Pal. Any doctor would say so. You don't see her all day in the house like I do. You're making me live with—with a lunatic, Pal."

"You—take that back!"

"You don't know it. But I do. She sits all day talking to herself. I'm afraid of her. I wouldn't ask you to throw her out, Pal—I'm telling you she's got screws loose—she can get violent any time and then you *will* have trouble. There's institutions—fine, sunny, clean ones. She ought to be committed. It's the only way, Pal—to save her—and to save us. You want us to go to hell over a—a loon. Lots of people go crazy on religion. The old woman, Pal—has screws loose. It's against the law not to give her medical treatment.

"There's plenty places, Pal—fine, clean places where they don't even know they're in that kind of a place where she can live in peace and we can stay here in peace. Pal, are you going to throw me over for a poor old woman that's lost her mind? I tell you she's crazy, Pal. What'll you have out of it if I get out and leave you here with a loon? You got to support me—no man can get away without doing his duty to me—you got her and you got me any way you look at it. If one of us got to go—the poor crazy old lady ought to be the one. Get her in a—a hospital, Pal—and that'll leave us here—in our home—together. Pal—poor, tired Pal—home alone—here with his May."

His head fell down against the little cove of her shoulder and he could feel her warm kisses through his hair, and finally when he looked up with the stricken eyes of a St. Bernard dog, the tears ran down over his words.

"I can't give you up, May. My poor mother—she's sick—she needs the best of care—best—institution. She's sick—and she's got—to—go——"

Tears. Tears. The dining room looked crazy through the blur of them, and setting out the salt cellars and the vinegar cruet, Molla Ivanü could scarcely find the table. It waved up at her. Tilted. Ran in little ripples that the tears made. Tears. Tears. The old woman——

She ran down the hall. It shot off in a little ell and on the slant of wall was the door—the door that was between the old woman and the knowing. The bitter knowing that must presently creep toward it and under it like a terrible tide. Molla crashed through the door and stood trembling in the center of the room.

The night light was burning and the old woman flew up in her vast walnut bed with a cry.

"Son—who—*ach*, Molla, how you frightened me! I must have been dreaming. My son! my Julius—Molla—it ain't nice you should rush in so on me—you've made me a pain—here. What is it, Molla— nothing ain't wrong? Pal—home yet? Nothing ain't wrong?"

"Why—no—Mrs. Palestine—nothing—I yoost looked in a minute. Maybe you want something?"

"No—I—Molla—you shouldn't rush in so—a pain here—from the

fright you gave me—such a pain—my heart—*ach*, no—Molla—I can't lay down. It's a knife in me. You frightened me so—my heart——"

Her face was so little, and back in the frill of her cap a pointed sort of receding look had set in, and she writhed up from the support of Molla's arm.

"My drops—quick, Molla—my drops—I—you shouldn't have frightened me—quick—my drops from the doctor."

There they stood, the little colorless phial of them on the table beside the bed. Five of them—Molla knew how—drop-drop-drop-drop-drop—in a tumbler.

"Molla—please——"

"No, Mrs. Palestine—no—yoost—lay still. No—no—drops this time—sleep—sh-h-h—no drops—sleep."

"I—my drops—pain—I—I'm so tired, Molla—hold me—you frightened me so. I was dreaming—my boy—she didn't get him—away from me. She tried, Molla—I dreamed—but she didn't—he wouldn't—my boy—he stuck to his mama. She's old—she's in the way—but he stuck. Why don't you give me my drops, Molla? I—he stuck by his mama, Molla——"

"Yes, Mrs. Palestine—he stuck——"

"I—I was never so tired. My drops—you should give me my drops. Dark—Molla—yes, Julius—tired—he stuck—my boy—to his mama—not, Molla?"

"Yes, Mrs. Palestine—yes——"

"Tired—my drops—son—oh—God—ouch—oh—oh—ah——"

A sudden lurch forward in Molla's arms so that her torso rounded up and left an arch of space between it and the bed.

It was so hard to unbend it because the body had stiffened so, and with her cheek to Mrs. Palestine's heart Molla pressed gently until the little attitude of convulsion had straightened. It was so quiet there with her cheek to Mrs. Palestine's dead heart.

A doctor folded the brittle hands. Little gulls skimming the placid old breast. The preliminaries of death were set in motion. A soul had been set free and mortals were solemn. Almost immediately the shades somehow were down and there was a new odor. The odor of death. May had gone out like a flame. Her face seemed suddenly very small between the two enormous blobs of pearl earrings, and she had pinned up the flowing sleeves so that she had the plucked, necky look of a fine bird that has lost its feathers revealing the long pores of dingy flesh.

"Poor Pal! Poor Pal!"

He looked at her through tear-scalded eyes that did not see her at all.

"My mother—my poor little mother—gone without a word——"

"Lots of them go that way, Pal. My old woman died in her sleep——"

"What her poor little life must have been here alone in this room—nights. Mama, forgive me. Mama, forgive me."

"She was a good sleeper, Pal. I used to hear her snoring and always tiptoe by the door—I was always careful not to wake her."

May, craven with death.

He looked at her with his eyes twisted out of focus and kept repeating over and over again his phrases. "Mama, forgive me—poor little life—I knew what you suffered, mama—there wasn't an hour of the day or night it wasn't over me—I did it—I did it—mama, mama, forgive—why did you leave me?"

"Pal—you've got your May—poor, poor Pal—don't cry—ain't you got your May?"

He kissed her then wildly, his wet lips smearing over her cheeks, the twisted, crazy look in his eyes.

"Help me—help me to bear my remorse. I used to snap her off. I never had patience with her. We left her alone when we went to the country—alone here. She might have died like a dog. She did die alone—like a dog—alone——"

"No, Pal. No. Molla was with her!"

"Molla! Then why didn't she give my mother her drops? She let her die like a dog. That's what the doctor asked—why didn't the person in whose arms she died—give her the drops? Murderer—where is she? Get out—where is she? I want her to get out!"

And Molla, carrying, down the gloom of the hallway, the seven-branch candlestick for the foot of old lady Palestine's bed, stood hearing, her face picked out in light above the pointing flames. A white face, floating in shadow and shining out of the darkness that poured around it.

A clear, prophetic face above the seven lights.

It was then, gazing upon her, that Palestine turned on his wife and struck her three times on the very cheek that his lips had smeared.

"Mama," he screamed, "forgive me!" and smoking hot off his lips and trembling with fervor for them came words that had long since lain dead like dried rose leaves in his memory:

ברוך אלהינו שבראנו לכבודן [Blessed is our God who created us for his glory.]

Then he turned around on May. He was laughing now, and she bent from that laughter in terror.

"You go," he said with his hands held out in talons and his fingers curling inward to form little cages. "Go—go—while God gives me strength not to kill you! My mama—my God—my darling, heartbroken mama. You made me a traitor to her—you—you—you! My little mama—go—go—or so help me God—if ever I see you again—God strike me dead if I don't kill you!"

"Pal—don't—don't—let me loose—I'll go, Pal—leave me go, Pal—for God's sake—I'll go—Pal."

After a while it was quiet in the house. There was still the little frangipani scent of May in her room where she had fussed about in the hysteria of packing; it followed her trail along the hallway as she backed down it in terror, her little valise, with the twist of lace caught in the fastening, held out before her. Then the outer door—and out.

Quiet. With the light from the seven candles burning against the transom and out into the hall so palely and Palestine silent in there hour after hour, cramped up there against the bedside of his dead.

At midnight the first mourner sprang up—one of the Old Testament women off the stoop in Division Street; and from behind the closed door, when she slid in to join Palestine, her cry went down like a rapier into the heart of the silence.

A cry that stuck there to the hilt, and throbbed.

Toward morning the mourner slept on in a rocker at the foot of the old woman's bed. Palestine, who had never moved from his couch at the headboard, sprang up suddenly. His hair torn down over his face but his eyes clear.

"Molla!" he called and ran out into the hallway and into her room.

"Molla—you—you knew—Molla—you cook! Who are you? Molla—Molla—come back—Molla—Molla . . ."

At that moment, in a dawn that ran thinly along the edge of the roofs, Molla Ivanü with her carpet bag hooked to her fingers was walking. East. A wettish wind, the wind before the dawn, blew her all forward. Her skirts. Some strands of her paling yellow hair and the terribly dilapidated old rose on her hat.

There were no pedestrians. Not even milk carts yet. Only Molla, walking before the wind.

PART 2

Troubles in the New World: 1930–1959

Missis Flinders

Tess Slesinger

"HOME YOU GO!" Miss Kane, nodding, in her white nurse's dress, stood for a moment—she would catch a breath of air—in the hospital door; "and thank you again for the stockings, you needn't have bothered"—drew a sharp breath and turning, dismissed Missis Flinders from the hospital, smiling, dismissed her forever from her mind.

So Margaret Flinders stood next to her basket of fruit on the hospital steps; both of them waiting, a little shame-faced in the sudden sunshine, and in no hurry to leave the hospital—no hurry at all. It would be nicer to be alone, Margaret thought, glancing at the basket of fruit which stood respectable and a little silly on the stone step (the candy-bright apples were blushing caricatures of Miles: Miles' comfort, not hers). Flowers she could have left behind (for the nurses, in the room across the hall where they made tea at night); books she could have slipped into her suit-case; but fruit—Miles' gift, Miles' guilt, man's tribute to the Missis in the hospital—must be eaten; a half-eaten basket of fruit (she had tried to leave it: Missis Butter won't you . . . Missis Wiggam wouldn't you like . . . But Missis Butter had aplenty of her own thank you, and Missis Wiggam said she couldn't hold acids after a baby)—a half-eaten basket of fruit, in times like these, cannot be left to rot.

Down the street Miles was running, running, after a taxi. He was going after the taxi for her; it was for her sake he ran; yet this minute

113

that his back was turned he stole for his relief and spent in running away, his shoulders crying guilt. And don't hurry, don't hurry, she said to them; I too am better off alone.

The street stretched in a long white line very finally away from the hospital, the hospital where Margaret Flinders (called there so solemnly Missis) had been lucky enough to spend only three nights. It would be four days before Missis Wiggam would be going home to Mister Wiggam with a baby; and ten possibly—the doctors were uncertain, Miss Kane prevaricated—before Missis Butter would be going home to Mister Butter without one. Zigzagging the street went the children; their cries and the sudden grinding of their skates she had listened to upstairs beside Missis Butter for three days. Some such child had she been—for the styles in children had not changed—a lean child gliding solemnly on skates and grinding them viciously at the nervous feet of grown-ups. Smile at these children she would not or could not; yet she felt on her face that smile, fixed, painful and frozen, that she had put there, on waking from ether three days back, to greet Miles. The smile spoke to the retreating shoulders of Miles: I don't need you; the smile spoke formally to life: thanks, I'm not having any. Not so the child putting the heels of his skates together Charlie Chaplin-wise and describing a scornful circle on the widest part of the sidewalk. Not so a certain little girl (twenty years back) skating past the wheels of autos, pursuing life in the form of a ball so red! so gay! better death than to turn one's back and smile over one's shoulder at life!

Upstairs Missis Butter must still be writhing with her poor caked breasts. The bed that had been hers beside Missis Butter's was empty now; Miss Kane would be stripping it and Joe would come in bringing fresh sheets. Whom would they put in beside Missis Butter, to whom would she moan and boast all night about the milk in her breasts that was turning, she said, into cheese?

Now Miles was coming back, jogging sheepishly on the running-board of a taxi, he had run away to the end of his rope and now was returning penitent, his eyes dog-like searching her out where she stood on the hospital steps (did they rest with complacence on the basket of fruit, his gift?), pleading with her, Didn't I get the taxi fast? like an anxious little boy. She stood with that smile on her face that hurt like too much ice-cream. Smile and smile; for she felt like a fool, she had walked open-eyed smiling into the trap (*Don't wriggle, Missis, I might injure you for life, Miss Kane had said cheerfully*) and felt the spring only when it was too late, when she waked from ether and knew like the thrust of a knife what she had ignored before. *Whatever did you do it for, Missis Flinders, Missis Butter was always saying; if there's nothing the matter with your insides—doesn't your husband . . . and Won't you have some fruit, Missis Butter, her calm reply: meaning, My husband gave me this fruit so what right have you to doubt that my husband. . .* Her husband who now stumbled up the steps to meet her; his eyes he had sent ahead, but something in him wanted not to come, tripped his foot as he hurried up the steps.

"Take my arm, Margaret," he said. "Walk slowly," he said. The bitter pill of taking help, of feeling weakly grateful, stuck in her throat. Miles' face behind his glasses was tense like the face of an amateur actor in the rôle of a strike-leader. That he was inadequate for the part he seemed to know. And if he felt shame, shame in his own eyes, she could forgive him; but if it was only guilt felt man-like in her presence, a guilt which he could drop off like a damp shirt, if he was putting it all off on her for being a woman! "The fruit, Miles!" she said; "you've forgotten the fruit." "The fruit can wait," he said bitterly.

He handed her into the taxi as though she were a package marked glass—something, she thought, not merely troublesomely womanly, but ladylike. "Put your legs up on the seat," he said. "I don't want to, Miles." *Goodbye Missis Butter* Put your legs up on the seat. I don't want to—*Better luck next time Missis Butter* Put your legs *I can't make out our window, Missis Butter* Put your "All right, it will be nice and uncomfortable." (She put her legs up on the seat.) *Goodbye Missis But. . .* "Nothing I say is right," he said. "It's good with the legs up," she said brightly.

Then he was up the steps agile and sure after the fruit. And down again, the basket swinging with affected carelessness, arming him, till he relinquished it modestly to her outstretched hands. Then he seated himself on the little seat, the better to watch his woman and his woman's fruit; and screwing his head round on his neck said irritably to the man who had been all his life on the wrong side of the glass pane: "Charles street!"

"Hadn't you better ask him to please drive slowly?" Margaret said.

"I was just going to," he said bitterly.

"And drive slowly," he shouted over his shoulder.

The driver's name was Carl C. Strite. She could see Carl Strite glance cannily back at the hospital: Greenway Maternity Home; pull his lever with extreme delicacy as though he were stroking the neck of a horse. There was a small roar—and the hospital glided backward: its windows ran together like the windows of a moving train; a spurt—watch out for those children on skates!—and the car was fairly started down the street.

Goodbye Missis Butter I hope you get a nice roommate in my place, I hope you won't find that Mister B let the ice-pan flow over again—and give my love to the babies when Miss Kane stops them in the door for you to wave at—goodbye Missis Butter, really goodbye.

Carl Strite (was he thinking maybe of his mother; an immigrant German woman she would have been, come over with a shawl on her head and worked herself to skin and bone so the kids could go to school and turn out good Americans—and what had it come to, here he was a taxi-driver, and what taxi-drivers didn't know! what in the course of their lackeys' lives they didn't put up with, fall in with! well, there was one decent thing left in Carl Strite, he knew how to carry a woman home from a maternity hospital) drove softly along the curb . . . and the eyes of his honest puzzled gangster's snout photographed as "Your Driver" looked dimmed as though the glory of woman were too much for them, in a moment the weak cruel baby's mouth might blubber. Awful to lean forward and tell Mr Strite he was laboring under a mistake. *Missis Wiggam's freckled face when she heard that Missis Butter's roommate . . . maybe Missis Butter's baby had been born dead but anyway she had had a baby . . . whatever did you do it for Missis Flind. . .*

"Well, patient," Miles began, tentative, nervous (bored? perturbed? behind his glasses?).

"How does it feel, Maggie?" he said in a new, small voice.

Hurt and hurt this man, a feeling told her. He is a man, he could have made you a woman. "What's a D and C between friends?" she said. "Nobody at the hospital gave a damn about my little illegality."

"Well, but I do," he protested like a short man trying to be tall.

She turned on her smile; the bright silly smile that was eating up her face.

116

Missis Butter would be alone now with no one to boast to about her pains except Joe who cleaned the corridors and emptied bed-pans— and thought Missis Butter was better than an angel because although she had incredible golden hair she could wise-crack like any brunette. Later in the day the eight-day mothers wobbling down the corridors for their pre-nursing constitutional would look in and talk to her; for wasn't Missis Butter their symbol and their pride, the one who had given up her baby that they might have theirs (for a little superstition is inevitable in new mothers, and it was generally felt that there must be one dead baby in a week's batch at any decent hospital) for whom they demanded homage from their visiting husbands? for whose health they asked the nurses each morning second only to asking for their own babies? That roommate of yours was a funny one, Missis Wiggam would say. Missis Wiggam was the woman who said big breasts weren't any good: here she was with a seven-pound baby and not a drop for it (here she would open the negligée Mister Wiggam had given her not to shame them before the nurses, and poke contemptuously at the floppy parts of herself within) while there was Missis Butter with no baby but a dead baby and her small breasts caking because there was so much milk in them for nothing but a . . . Yes, that Missis Flinders was sure a funny one, Missis Butter would agree.

"Funny ones", she and Miles, riding home with numb faces and a basket of fruit between them—past a park, past a museum, past elevated pillars—intellectuals they were, bastards, changelings . . . giving up a baby for economic freedom which meant that two of them would work in offices instead of one of them only, giving up a baby for intellectual freedom which meant that they smoked their cigarettes bitterly and looked out of the windows of a taxi onto streets and people and stores and hated them all. "We'd go soft," Miles had finally said, "we'd go bourgeois." Yes, with diapers drying on the radiators, bottles wrapped in flannel, the grocer getting to know one too well—yes, they would go soft, they might slump and start liking people, they might weaken and forgive stupidity, they might yawn and forget to hate. "Funny ones," class-straddlers, intellectuals, tight-rope-walking some- where in the middle (how long could they hang on without falling to one side or the other? one more war? one more depression?); intel- lectuals, with habits generated from the right and tastes inclined to the left. Afraid to perpetuate themselves, were they? Afraid of anything that might loom so large in their personal lives as to outweigh other considerations? Afraid, maybe, of a personal life?

"Oh give me another cigarette," she said.

And still the taxi, with its burden of intellectuals and their inarticulate fruit-basket, its motherly, gangsterly, inarticulate driver, its license plates and its photographs all so very official, jogged on; past Harlem now; past fire-escapes loaded with flowerpots and flapping clothes; dingy windows opening to the soot-laden air blown in by the elevated roaring down its tracks. Past Harlem and through 125th street: stores and wise-cracks, Painless Dentists, cheap florists; Eighth Avenue, boarded and plastered, concealing the subway that was reaching its laborious birth beneath. But Eighth Avenue was too jouncy for Mr Strite's precious burden of womanhood (who was reaching passionately for a cigarette); he cut through the park, and they drove past quiet walks on which the sun had brought out babies as the Fall rains give birth to worms.

"But ought you to smoke so much, so soon after—so soon?" Miles said, not liking to say so soon after what. His hand held the cigarettes out to her, back from her.

"They do say smoking's bad for child-birth," she said calmly, and with her finger-tips drew a cigarette from his reluctant hand.

And tapping down the tobacco on the handle of the fruit-basket she said, "But we've got the joke on them there, we have." (Hurt and hurt this man, her feeling told her; he is a man and could have made you a woman.)

"It was your own decision too," he said harshly, striking and striking at the box with his match.

"This damn taxi's shaking you too much," he said suddenly, bitter and contrite.

But Mr Strite was driving like an angel. He handled his car as though it were a baby-carriage. Did he think maybe it had turned out with her the way it had with Missis Butter? I could have stood it better, Missis Butter said, if they hadn't told me it was a boy. And me with my fourth little girl, Missis Wiggam had groaned (but proudly, proudly); why I didn't even want to see it when they told me. But Missis Butter stood it very well, and so did Missis Wiggam. They were a couple of good bitches; and what if Missis Butter had produced nothing but a dead baby this year, and what if Missis Wiggam would bring nothing to Mister Wiggam but a fourth little girl this year—why there was next year and the year after, there was the certain little world from grocery-store to kitchen, there were still Mister Butter and Mister Wiggam who were both (Missis Wiggam and Missis Butter vied with each other) just *crazy* about babies. Well, Mister Flinders is different, she had lain there thinking (he cares as much for his unborn gods as I for my unborn babies); and wished she could have the firm assurance they had in "husbands," coming as they did year after year away from them for a couple of weeks, just long enough to bear them babies either dead-ones or girl-ones . . . good bitches they were: there was something lustful besides smug in their pride in being "Missis." Let Missis Flinders so much as let out a groan because a sudden pain grew too big for her groins, let her so much as murmur because the sheets were hot beneath her—and Missis Butter and Missis Wiggam in the security of their maternity-fraternity exchanged glances of amusement: SHE don't know what pain is, look at what's talking about PAIN. . . .

"Mr Strite flatters us," she whispered, her eyes smiling straight and hard at Miles. (Hurt and hurt . . .)

"And why does that give you so much pleasure?" He dragged the words as though he were pounding them out with two fingers on the typewriter.

The name without the pain—she thought to say; and did not say. All at once she lost her desire to punish him; she no more wanted to "hurt this man" for he was no more man than she was woman. She would not do him the honor of hurting him. She must reduce him as she felt herself reduced. She must cut out from him what made him a man, as she had let be cut out from her what would have made her a woman. He was no man: he was a dried-up intellectual husk; he was sterile; empty and hollow as she was.

Missis Butter lying up on her pillow would count over to Missis Wiggam the fine points of her tragedy: how she had waited two days to be delivered of a dead baby; how it wouldn't have been so bad if the doctor hadn't said it was a beautiful baby with platinum-blond hair exactly like hers (and hers bleached unbelievably, but never mind, Missis Wiggam had come to believe in it like Joe and Mister Butter, another day and Missis Flinders herself, intellectual sceptic though

119

she was, might have been convinced); and how they would pay the last instalment on—what a baby-carriage, Missis Wiggam, you'd never believe me!—and sell it second-hand for half its worth. I know when I was caught with my first, Missis Wiggam would take up the story her mouth had been open for. And that Missis Flinders was sure a funny one. . . .

But I am not such a funny one, Margaret wanted, beneath her bright and silly smile, behind her cloud of cigarette smoke (for Miles had given in; the whole package sat gloomily on Margaret's lap) to say to them; even though in my "crowd" the girls keep the names they were born with, even though some of us sleep for a little variety with one another's husbands, even though I forget as often as Miles—Mister Flinders to you—to empty the pan under the ice-box. Still I too have known my breasts to swell and harden, I too have been unable to sleep on them for their tenderness to weight and touch, I too have known what it is to undress slowly and imagine myself growing night to night . . . I knew this for two months, my dear Missis Wiggam; I had this strange joy for two months, my dear Missis Butter. But there was a night last week, my good ladies, on coming home from a party, which Mister Flinders and I spent in talk—and damn fine talk, if you want to know, talk of which I am proud, and talk not one word of which you, with your grocery-and-baby minds, could have understood; in a régime like this, Miles said, it is a terrible thing to have a baby— it means the end of independent thought and the turning of everything into a scheme for making money; and there must be institutions such as there are in Russia, I said, for taking care of the babies and their mothers; why in a time like this, we both said, to have a baby would be suicide—goodbye to our plans, goodbye to our working out schemes for each other and the world—our courage would die, our hopes concentrate on the sordid business of keeping three people alive, one of whom would be a burden and an expense for twenty years. . . . And then we grew drunk for a minute making up the silliest names that we could call it if we had it, we would call it Daniel if it were a boy, call it for my mother if it were a girl—and what a tough little thing it is, I said, look, look, how it hangs on in spite of its loving mother jumping off tables and broiling herself in hot water . . . until Miles, frightened at himself, washed his hands of it: we mustn't waste any more time, the sooner these things are done the better. And I as though the ether cap had already been clapped to my nose, agreed off-handedly. That night I did not pass my hands contentedly over my hard breasts; that night I gave no thought to the nipples grown suddenly brown and competent; I packed, instead, my suit-case: I filled it with all the white clothes I own. Why are you taking white clothes to the hospital? Miles said to me. I laughed. Why did I? White, for a bride; white, for a corpse; white, for a woman who refuses to be a woman. . . .

"Are you all right, Margaret?" (They were out now, safely out on Fifth Avenue, driving placidly past the Plaza where ancient coachmen dozed on the high seats of the last hansoms left in New York.)

"Yes, dear," she said mechanically, and forgot to turn on her smile. Pity for him sitting there in stolid New England inadequacy filled her. He was a man, and he could have made her a woman. She was a woman, and could have made him a man. He was not a man; she was not a woman. In each of them the life-stream flowed to a dead-end.

And all this time that the blood, which Missis Wiggam and Missis Butter stored up preciously in themselves every year to make a baby for their husbands, was flowing freely and wastefully out of Missis Flinders—toward what? would it pile up some day and bear a book? would it congeal within her and make a crazy woman?—all this time Mr Strite, remembering, with his pudgy face, his mother, drove his taxi softly along the curb; no weaving in and out of traffic for Mr Strite, no spurting at the corners and cheating the side-street traffic, no fine heedless rounding of rival cars for Mr Strite; he kept his car going at a slow and steady roll, its nose poked blunt ahead, following the straight and narrow—Mr Strite knew what it was to carry a woman home from the hospital.

But what in their past had warranted this? She could remember a small girl going from dolls to books, from books with colored pictures to books with frequent conversations; from such books to the books at last that one borrowed from libraries, books built up of solemn text from which you took notes; books which were gray to begin with, but which opened out to your eyes subtle layers of gently shaded colors. (And where in these texts did it say that one should turn one's back on life? Had the coolness of the stone library at college made one

121

afraid? Had the ivy nodding in at the open dormitory windows taught one too much to curl and squat looking out?) And Miles? What book, what professor, what strange idea, had taught him to hunch his shoulders and stay indoors, had taught him to hide behind his glasses? Whence the fear that made him put, in cold block letters, implacably above his desk, the sign announcing him "Not at Home" to life?

Missis Flinders, my husband scaled the hospital wall at four o'clock in the morning, frantic I tell you. . . . But I just don't understand you, Missis Flinders (if there's really nothing the matter with your insides), do you understand her, Missis Wiggam, would your husband? . . . Why goodness, no, Mister Wiggam would sooner . . . ! And there he was, and they asked him, Shall we try an operation, Mister Butter? scaled the wall . . . shall we try an operation? (Well, you see, we are making some sort of protest, my husband Miles and I; sometimes I forget just what.) If there's any risk to Shirley, he said, there mustn't be any risk to Shirley. . . . Missis Wiggam's petulant, childish face, with its sly contentment veiled by what she must have thought a grown-up expression: Mister Wiggam bought me this negligée new, surprised me with it, you know—and generally a saving man, Mister Wiggam, not tight, but with three children—four now! Hetty, he says, I'm not going to have you disgracing us at the hospital this year, he says. Why the nurses will all remember that flannel thing you had Mabel and Suzy and Antoinette in, they'll talk about us behind our backs. (It wasn't that I couldn't make the flannel do again, Missis Butter, it wasn't that at all.) But he says, Hetty, you'll just have a new one this year, he says, and maybe it'll bring us luck, he says—you know, he was thinking maybe this time we'd have a boy. . . . Well, I just have to laugh at you, Missis Flinders, not *wanting* one, why my sister went to doctors for five years and spent her good money just *trying* to have one. . . . Well, poor Mister Wiggam, so the negligée didn't work, I brought him another little girl—but he didn't say boo to me, though I could see he was disappointed. Hetty, he says, we'll just have another try! oh I thought I'd die, with Miss Kane standing right there you know (though they do say these nurses . . .); but that's Mister Wiggam all over, he wouldn't stop a joke for a policeman. . . . No, I just can't get over you, Missis Flinders, if Gawd was willing to let you have a baby—and there really isn't anything wrong with your insides?

Miles' basket of fruit standing on the bed-table, trying its level inadequate best, poor pathetic inarticulate intellectual basket of fruit, to comfort, to bloom, to take the place of Miles himself who would come in later with Sam Butter for visiting hour. Miles' too-big basket of fruit standing there, embarrassed. Won't you have a peach, Missis Wiggam (I'm sure they have less acid)? Just try an apple, Missis Butter? Weigh Miles' basket of fruit against Mister Wiggam's negligée for luck, against Mister Butter scaling the wall at four in the morning for the mother of his dead baby. *Please* have a pear, Miss Kane; a banana, Joe? How they spat the seeds from Miles' fruit! How it hurt her when, unknowing, Missis Butter cut away the brown bruised cheek of Miles' bright-eyed, weeping apple! Miles! they scorn me, these ladies. They laugh at me, dear, almost as though I had no "husband," as though I were a "fallen woman". Miles, would you buy me a new negligée if I bore you three daughters? Miles, would you scale the wall if I bore you a dead baby? . . . Miles, I have an inferiority complex because I am an intellectual. . . . But a peach, Missis Wiggam! can't I possibly tempt you?

To be driving like this at mid-day through New York; with Miles bobbing like an empty ghost (for she could see he was unhappy, as miserable as she, he too had had an abortion) on the side-seat; with a taxi-driver, solicitous, respectful to an ideal, in front; was this the logical end of that little girl she remembered, of that girl swinging hatless across a campus as though that campus were the top of the earth? And was this all they could give birth to, she and Miles, who had closed up their books one day and kissed each other on the lips and decided to marry?

And now Mr Strite, with his hand out, was making a gentle right-hand turn. Back to Fifth Avenue they would go, gently rolling, in Mr Strite's considerate charge. Down Fourteenth Street they would go, past the stores unlike any stores in the world: packed to the windows with imitation gold and imitation embroidery, with imitation men and women coming to stand in the doorways and beckon with imitation smiles; while on the sidewalks streamed the people unlike any other people in the world, drawn from every country, from every stratum, carrying babies (the real thing, with pinched anaemic faces) and parcels (imitation finery priced low in the glittering stores). There goes a woman, with a flat fat face, will produce five others just like herself, to dine off one-fifth the inadequate quantity her Mister earns today. These are the people not afraid to perpetuate themselves (forbidden to stop, indeed) and they will go on and on until the bottom of the world is filled with them; and suddenly there will be enough of them to combine their wild-eyed notions and take over the world to suit themselves. While I, while I and my Miles, with out good clear heads will one day go spinning out of the world and leave nothing behind . . . only diplomas crumbling in the museums. . . .

The mad street ended with Fifth Avenue; was left behind.

They were nearing home. Mr Strite, who had never seen them before (who would never again, in all likelihood, for his territory was far uptown) was seeing them politely to the door. As they came near home all of Margaret's fear and pain gathered in a knot in her stomach. There would be nothing new in their house; there was nothing to expect; yet she wanted to find something there that she knew she could not find, and surely the house (once so gay, with copies of old paintings, with books which lined the walls from floor to ceiling, with papers and cushions and typewriters) would be suddenly empty and dead, suddenly, for the first time, a group of rooms unalive as rooms with "For Rent" still pasted on the windows. And Miles? did he know he was coming home to a place which had suffered no change, but which would be different forever afterward? Miles had taken off his glasses; passed his hand tiredly across his eyes; was sucking now as though he expected relief, some answer, on the tortoise-shell curve which wound around his ear.

Mr Strite would not allow his cab to cease motion with a jerk. Mr Strite allowed his cab to slow down even at the corner (where was the delicatessen that sold the only loose ripe olives in the Village), so they rolled softly past No. 14; on past the tenement which would eventually be razed to give place to modern three-room apartments with In-a-Dor beds; and then slowly, so slowly that Mr Strite must surely be an artist as well as a man who had had a mother, drew up and slid to a full stop before No. 60, where two people named Mister and Missis Flinders rented themselves a place to hide from life (both life of the Fifth Avenue variety, and life of the common, or Fourteenth Street, variety: in short, life).

So Miles, with his glasses on his nose once more, descended; held out his hand; Mr Strite held the door open and his face most modestly averted; and Margaret Flinders painfully and carefully swung her legs down again from the seat and alighted, step by step, with care and confusion. The house was before them; it must be entered. Into the house they must go, say farewell to the streets, to Mr Strite who had guided them through a tour of the city, to life itself; into the house they must go and hide. It was a fact that Mister Flinders (was he reluctant to come home?) had forgotten his key; that Missis Flinders must delve under the white clothes in her suit-case and find hers; that Mr Strite, not yet satisfied that his charges were safe, sat watchful and waiting in the front seat of his cab. Then the door gave. Then Miles, bracing it with his foot, held out his hand to Margaret. Then Mr Strite came rushing up the steps (something had told him his help would be needed again!), rushing up the steps with the basket of fruit hanging on his arm, held out from his body as though what was the likes of him doing holding a woman's basket just home from the hospital.

"You've forgotten your fruit, Missis!"

Weakly they glared at the fruit come to pursue them; come to follow them up the stairs to their empty rooms; but that was not fair: come, after all, to comfort them. "You must have a peach," Margaret said.

No, Mr Strite had never cared for peaches; the skin got in his teeth.

"You must have an apple," Margaret said.

Well, no, he must be getting on uptown. A cigarette (he waved it, deprecated the smoke it blew in the lady's face) was good enough for him.

"But a pear, just a pear," said Margaret passionately.

Mr Strite wavered, standing on one foot. "Maybe he doesn't want any fruit," said Miles harshly.

"Not want any *fruit!*" cried Margaret gayly, indignantly. Not want any fruit?—ridiculous! Not want the fruit my poor Miles bought for his wife in the hospital? Three days I spent in the hospital, in a Maternity Home, and I produced, with the help of my husband, one basket of fruit (tied with ribbon, pink—for boys). Not want any of our fruit? I couldn't bear it, I couldn't bear it. . . .

Mr Strite leaned over; put out a hand and gingerly selected a pear— "For luck," he said, managing an excellent American smile. They watched him trot down the steps to his cab, all the time holding his

pear as though it were something he would put in a memory book.
And still they stayed, because Margaret said foolishly, "Let's see him
off"; because she was ashamed, suddenly, before Miles; as though she
had cut her hair unbecomingly, as though she had wounded herself
in some unsightly way—as though (summing up her thoughts as precisely, as decisively as though it had been done on an adding-machine)
she had stripped and revealed herself not as a woman at all, but as a
creature who would not be a woman and could not be a man. And
then they turned (for there was nothing else to stay for, and on the
street and in the sun before Missis Salvemini's fluttering window-
curtains they were ashamed as though they had been naked or dead)—
and went in the door and heard it swing to, pause on its rubbery hinge,
and finally click behind them.

Room in the World

Leane Zugsmith

WHEN SHE HEARD Ab's footsteps approaching the door, she knew, without having to see or to hear him, that it had been the same as yesterday and all the days before, since he had been fired from the job he had held as watchman for the office building. He couldn't do anything but talk about it all night long, and every day he went back trying to get to someone higher up who would tell the new superintendent "Ab's been with us nine years, there ain't no reason to let him go." If she was him, Pauline thought, she'd give it up and if, like he said, there wasn't no job for him no place, she'd go on Relief. With a five-months-old baby and a three-year-old boy growing so fast that the Lord only knew how she was going to make this suit of his any bigger, and a girl of eight, already in the second grade, she'd give it up. But Ab was bull-headed, always had been, and maybe he'd get back, like he said.

As Ab came in, she hastened to close the door leading off the kitchen into the room where Jappy was taking his nap. Even when Ab raised his voice, it wouldn't wake the baby in the market basket near the stove. She was a dandy sleeper, better than Jappy, much better than Frances ever had been.

She thrust the needle into the material, waiting to see if Ab was going to speak first. If he kept on staring at her, it was up to her and it meant he was good and sore. After a while, she knew it was up to her.

"Either the clock's fast," she said in the casual, conversational tone she had lately learned to use, "or Frances must of been kept in."

Gloomily he stared at her.

"She done her homework, I know." Pauline turned Jappy's drawers inside out and studied the problem of enlarging them.

"I tried every God-damned one of them," he said between his teeth. "I seen all their chippy secretaries. They're all too God-damned busy to see me. I'm only working there *nine* years. Maybe that ain't long enough."

"No one can say you ain't tried," she said.

"Tried? I done everything but crawl along the corridors on my belly. It's 'see the super. It's up to the super.' Nuts!"

"Them real-estate people are over the super," she said sympathetically and she thought: he won't give it up yet. No use telling him about the gas or how they wouldn't give her credit at the other grocery store she tried out.

"They won't even see me. You seen what they written me."

"It was a sin the old super had to die," she said.

"The new one will take me back," he said ominously. "I ain't saying how, but I'm gonta get back on the job."

Hooding her anxious eyes as she watched him to read what was in his mind, she heard Frances at the door. She hurried to open it, her mind still on her husband's words. The kid was all excited about something, the way she got sometimes, dancing around the room. She sure was high-strung; good thing the baby didn't seem to take after her. Pauline was afraid she'd begin to bother her pa, but he didn't seem to take notice, banging his hand down on the kitchen table, crying out:

"I ain't going back crawling to them, neither, to get it!"

She cast a swift look at the baby to see if she had been disturbed by the noise. "Maybe—" Pauline began.

"Maybe, nothing! I'll be back on the job, wait and see."

Frances kept tugging at her arm. "*Ma*, I been telling you."

Ab glared at his daughter.

"We're talking now, Pa and me," Pauline said quickly.

"Only, Ma, let me tell about the new little girl, she come today. She's got curls just like Shirley Temple." Frances's voice went up high.

"Shut up!" said Ab.

"The new little girl, she looks just like Shirley Temple."

"Play in the other room." Her mother pinched her cheek. "Jappy's asleep in yours and his."

"No, I don't wanta. I wanta tell you about the new little girl, Ma, she's got red paint on her fingernails. Can't I have—"

Her mother interrupted her. "You're getting your Pa worked up, not minding." She reached for a tin pail. "Go on down and get me five cents' worth of milk, hear me. Tell him your Ma said she'd stop in and pay up tomorrow."

Ab breathed heavily after the little girl had left the room. Without looking up from her sewing, his wife said calmly: "She's only eight." And she thought: in a while, when we can't get no credit no place, there won't be that much spirit in any of them.

"I'm trying to think out what to do, and she comes in babbling till she gets me all mixed up."

"Try to think what you was thinking before."

"What do you think I'm trying to do?"

The tick of the clock sounded loud now. The baby's occasional soft snores could be heard. Pauline kept her head bent over her sewing until Ab spoke up.

"You know how they do when a lot of them go out on strike," he said.

"Well?"

"Like I read once in a newspaper, see, a fellow and his whole family, they go out with signs, asking for his job back."

Her face became thoughtful. "Like them pickets is what you mean?"

"You got me."

She ceased to sew. "I couldn't leave Frances take care of the baby."

"No. She'd let it smother or something." He looked down at his hands for a while. Presently he said: "I could take the two kids, see, all of us wearing signs asking for my job back."

"I could make the signs O. K., if we had some kind of stiff paper," she said. "You wouldn't walk Jappy too long, would you, Ab? He don't stand much walking."

Ab stood up, his face lighted. "That would get them, all right, you bet! Maybe them newspaper guys will come around and take our

129

pictures." He pulled a pencil from his vest pocket and smoothed the wrinkles from a brown paper bag.

"Maybe down at the corner, they'd give you some stiff paper," said Pauline.

He wet the pencil, leaning over the kitchen table, too elated to sit down. "Now, we'll say—" He wet the pencil once more. "What'll we say?"

"If the sign's for the kids it had oughta say something about 'my Pa' and so on."

"You got brains, Pauline," he said. " 'Please get my Pa back his job.' How's that?"

"O. K."

"We'll make Jappy's and Frances's alike. Now mine." He wet the pencil. "What would you say?"

" 'Get me back my job at the Stark Building,' how about that?"

"No," he said. He started to print letters. "How's this? 'Fired for no reason after nine years being watchman at the Stark Building.' "

"That's O. K.," she said.

"O. K.? It's the nuts!" he cried out gleefully. "Wait till I see the faces of them birds who think they ain't gonta take me back!"

It was getting past the baby's feeding time; Pauline thanked her stars that she was so good she wouldn't start bawling right off. She couldn't pick her up with Jappy goose-stepping around, already dressed to go out, the sign flapping as he thrust each leg straight out before him, Frances trying to see how the sign looked on her before the little mirror over the dresser, and Ab yelling: "Let's go to town. Come on, you kids."

Jappy couldn't be held down. He kept singing: "I'm a picket, I'm a picket, I'm a picket," until they couldn't help laughing.

"Them signs are going to blow all around on them," Pauline said.

"Don't worry about them signs," Ab cried out. "Come on, you kids."

"I'm a picket," shouted Jappy. In a fit of wildness, he dug his forefinger into the top of his cap and began whirling around.

"You'll get dizzy. Stop it!" his mother called out.

Frances ran in. "I can't see what I look like, Ma," she complained.

Jappy started going round too fast and fell down.

130

"You bent the sign," his father said crossly, picking him up.

Jappy smiled when he saw that he didn't have to cry.

"It'll only take a minute." Pauline threaded a needle and began to sew the bottom corners of the sign on to Jappy's little coat. "I'll sew on yours, too," she told Frances.

"Lift me up, Pa, in by the looking-glass, so's I can see," Frances begged.

As Ab took her into the other room, Pauline said to her son with exasperation: "Keep still, will you!"

"I'm gonta be a picket," he screamed joyfully. "I'm gonta go up to them dopes—"

"Where did you learn that?" She bit off the thread.

"I'm gonta be a dope, I'm gonta be a picket."

Frances came back, saying sulkily: "I can't read what it says in the looking-glass."

"You know what it says. I told her." Ab followed her.

"What's mine say?" cried Jappy.

"It says 'Give my Pa back his job,' " said Frances, holding still while her mother sewed the bottom corners of her sign on to her jacket.

"Give my Pa back his job," Jappy chanted, starting once more to goose-step.

Ab grabbed his hand. "Come on. I ain't gonta wait another minute."

Picking up the baby, Pauline followed them to the door. As soon as she had closed it, she heard sounds of bawling outside. It was Jappy, all right. She opened the door. Ab called angrily to her from the stairs. "He wantsta take his Popeye doll along with him. He ain't gonta."

Jappy's cries were louder now that he knew his mother was listening. "Let him," she said. "It won't do no harm." Might do good, she thought, them seeing a little kid with a doll. "I'll get it."

"Make it snappy," Ab called back.

She found the wooden figure from which all the paint had streaked. Jappy was back at the door with Frances just behind. The little boy smirked. "Popeye the Sailor's gonta be a picket," he said.

"Hurry up!" Ab called out.

"Popeye wants a sign." Jappy held the doll up to his mother. "Make him a sign." His chin was beginning to tremble.

She snatched a fragment of paper from the table, scribbled on it

131

and attached it precariously to the doll. "Hurry." She gave both children little pushes and then stood with her ear to the crack of the door where she could hear them talking as they went toward the stairs.

"Popeye's sign says, 'Give my Pa back his job,' " said Jappy.

"It don't say nothing," said Frances. "It's only scribble."

"It do, too," he said.

Then their voices became fainter. She wished she could see the street from their windows to watch them walking away. Hope Ab don't forget he shouldn't keep them out too long. The baby began to whimper, and she patted its back as she unbuttoned her blouse. It don't do no good for me to skimp on eating, she thought, or I'll only take it away from the baby.

When they came back, Ab couldn't talk of anything but the expression on the new super's face and how people had stopped them and they almost had their pictures taken. As Pauline ripped the stitches off Jappy's sign, she noticed that he was almost asleep on his feet. When she started to rip the stitches off Frances' sign, she saw that her skinny legs were trembling. She looked up into the little girl's miserable face. "Why, what's the matter, honey?"

Before Frances could get out a word, she began to bawl. She bawled just like she did when she was a baby.

"What happened to her?" Pauline turned to Ab.

"I don't know." He was beginning to be gloomy again.

Pauline put her arms around Frances. "Tell Ma," she said.

Her breath catching, the tears streaming down the monkey face she was making, Frances said: "The new little girl seen me."

"A lot of people seen you," said Pauline. "That don't make no difference." She was trying to keep her voice steady.

Frances struggled out of her mother's reach. "The new little girl seen me," she got out between sobs and ran from the room.

"I try to get back my job," said Ab heavily, "and that's the thanks I get."

Before she spoke, she looked around for Jappy and, finding him asleep on the floor, she said, trying to pick her words:

"She got a crush on some little girl at school she says looks like Shirley Temple."

132

"That ain't gonta get my job back." Ab bent his head over the table where his sign and Jappy's lay.

Both of them could hear, through the closed door, Frances's frenzy of weeping.

Pauline swallowed. "Other people seeing her don't make no difference, on account of she's at the age, see what I mean?"

"No," he said, but his lowered voice had in it a curious strain.

"She's highstrung, Ab. To some other kid it mightn't mean nothing, only with her it might set her back, you know how kids are."

She waited for him to reply, watching him make marks on the back of his sign with his pencil. It was the truth, he might as well admit it. Other people didn't have to take out their kids with signs on them begging for their Pa's job. The weeping in the next room had subsided into long sighs and occasional hiccoughs.

Presently, without looking up, he said: "I shouldn't oughta take her tomorrow."

"Jappy likes it," Pauline said hopefully.

He made more marks on the back of the sign. Still without looking up, he said: "We could change the words tomorrow." He pushed the lettering toward her, keeping his eyes averted.

The crooked printing said: "Ain't there room in the world for us?" Now it's gonta bust out, she thought. Only you can't let it go, not with the kid bawling in the other room and him so down in the mouth. She swallowed the thing in her throat. And, searching for it, she found the tone she had lately learned to use.

"It don't seem like 'ain't' is the right word there," she said in a casual, conversational voice.

Second Blood:
A Rosh Hashonoh Story

Jo Sinclair

T HE SECOND TRIP Dave made to the Red Cross blood donor head-quarters was different from the first. It was a little over six months after his first contribution, and he made the appointment by telephone for Saturday.

When the woman on the phone said she could not take him because of a full schedule, he gently insisted.

"It's the only time I can come," he lied. "Squeeze me in, will you? I'm anxious to give my second pint, but I'm afraid I couldn't do it for another six months if I don't get down this Saturday. I'm working overtime a lot. War work, you know."

It was a lie about the overtime, but it worked. She'd finally said yes, Saturday at three o'clock, and when he hung up he felt such a full little throb of satisfaction that it made him smile, just thinking of it. Saturday was the first day of *Rosh Hashonoh*, and for some stubborn, fierce reason he wanted to contribute his blood on that day.

It was an odd notion. He had not been in a synagogue for years, not since his mother had died. There was one other Jew at the National Chemical Company, where he did research chemistry in anesthetics. He was as friendly with the other Jew, Martin Lieberman, as he was with the other fellows, but certainly not friendlier. Lieberman was a lot like himself, thirtyish, fond of bridge and musical comedies, and married, with two kids, too. Certainly he and Lieberman had sat over enough ham sandwiches in the company lunchroom not to be bothered about orthodox Judaism. Neither of them looked Jewish either, being sandy blond, with regular—what Dave always called American—features.

He just wasn't a *kosher yid*, Dave thought with a little smile. Now what the heck was this *Rosh Hashonoh* anyway? He had not fully understood it when the impulse cropped up in him, and he did not really understand it even now, after the appointment had been made. He had not thought of being a Jew for such a long time that this business now was a little scarey. He felt so determined about it, that was the scarey angle.

At five o'clock he rang out, got into his car and drove home at thirty miles an hour. He had been keeping the car at thirty ever since the rubber business had begun to stew all over the nation.

It was enough to be an American, wasn't it? he asked himself soberly. Without a fellow having to stress the fact that he was a Jew? He thought for a moment of his mother. She had wanted him to go to Temple, and sometimes he had gone. Ten years now since she had died. And Dad dead four years before that. Eight years married. His mother had never even seen Cathy.

He had always thought it was enough to be an American. He was working on that principle now; conserving tires, gas, warden duty and advanced first aid, careful about things like sugar rationing and charge accounts and picking up groceries himself instead of asking for delivery. He and Cathy had rigged up a blackout room in the basement when the first excitement came, and the kids were primed for it; for more than a year, they had even practiced once a week going down and playing there for an hour while he and Cathy read in the room. Chuck and Edie; they were good, sensible kids who had taken the war in their stride from the very first.

He drove thoughtfully. Halfway home he knew he was not going to tell Cathy about *Rosh Hashonoh*. After all, a fellow's wife didn't have to know everything he did. It was enough that a man and his wife loved one another and shared in the most important things. A little thing like this; Cathy didn't have to know about it.

Saturday, at two o'clock, he phoned home. "Dearest? I'm working until five. Special rush job. Sorry, darling. I'll pick up the groceries on my way home. See you later."

He was at the Red Cross by ten of three. Everything was familiar, the same as last time. The same smiling, joking assistants in their cerise uniforms. He handed one of them his blood donor card and went to hang his coat in the men's room.

In the outer room again, he sat in one of the chairs and the assistant stuck a thermometer in his mouth. "Let's see what a raging fever you have," she joked, and he exchanged a smile with several of the others who sat there with thermometers in their mouths.

People came in and were immediately made ready. He liked the looks of the people in the room; most of them were smiling, their eyes eager. There were about three women to each man.

He signed the big white record card for the clerk at the desk, then went into the hallway to the small desk, where a jolly nurse pricked his finger for the hemoglobin test and asked him the rapid questions about serious operations, recent colds, and all the rest of the no's. Then came the blood pressure examination.

It was all the same as last time, even to the little jokes and smiles from the nurses and volunteer workers. But somehow it was different, too. He sat in the narrow hallway, his record card in his hand, his shirt sleeves rolled up, and waited for an empty cot. He could see into the outer room, the constant flow and ebb of donors through the door, hear the nurses saying, "How do you do," and "Goodbye. Come again!" There he sat, feeling like—by God, like he was in *shule*, praying!

Then a nurse beckoned to him; a cot was empty. He walked into the inner room and got up on the high cot, and she took his card. He glanced swiftly about him. Yes, it was the same. People were lying on the other cots, stretched out flat, their eyes closed, the thin rubber pipes extending from their arms into glass flasks. Women and men; but I'll bet I'm the only Jew here, he thought, all the others are in *shule*.

His lips tightened. This was his way of praying, wasn't it?

The nurse swabbed his arm with antiseptic. "Doctor," she called, "will you find a vein, please?"

Dave watched intently. Last time there had been a woman doctor; this time the doctor was a dark, oldish man with deft hands. He found a vein quickly, then there was the almost painless plunge of the needle, and, looking down out of the corner of his eye, Dave could see the thin rubber leading from his arm down into the flask.

"Keep clenching and opening your hand," the nurse said, smiling down at him. "You'll be pumping your own blood that way."

It took almost ten minutes. As he lay there, the blood flowing slowly out of him into the bright glass flask with his name on the tag, Dave thought hard of why he had felt compelled to come here today.

Looking at the tag with "David Gordon" written on it, Dave remembered that Sunday night. He and Cathy had gone to a neighborhood movie. They had had Mrs. Lowell's daughter stay in the house with the kids, and they had just made the eight-ten show.

After the feature one of those news shorts flashed on. It was made up of captured film which had been put together into some kind of sequence. The shots concerned Jews in occupied countries and their treatment at the hands of the Nazis.

He sat there watching the rather blurred pictures of bearded men, narrow twisting ghetto streets filled with crouched people and uniforms, old women being forced to clean streets, huddled crowds of men and women with starving eyes. And there were kids everywhere, kids with little, pinched, dark faces and terrible eyes. When he saw their eyes he felt himself squeezing together inside, and his chest hurt.

Then, in one of the large ghettos, he suddenly thought he saw his mother. In a group of Jews outside a synagogue, she stood out in almost an isolated way because of the expression on her face. Next to the haunted faces of the group, hers seemed strong and determined. A tall, grave woman, dark hair pulled straight back from her face and tied in a knob behind her head, her eyes looked out at him the way his mother's often had looked when she was sad or troubled.

He trembled, sitting there, the shiver going through him so strongly that Cathy whispered, "David, what's the matter? Are you feeling ill?"

He squeezed her arm. "It's nothing," he whispered.

It was impossible, but that woman was exactly like his mother. A soldier was pushing her around, but she wasn't being pushed; her rigid body and held-high head were insisting on her right to walk by herself.

The voice of the commentator in the picture said, "Jews in this barricaded ghetto are being kept from worship on the eve of one of their holidays."

The woman who looked like his mother stared at Dave from in front of that huddled group. Her eyes were stern, troubled, accusing—and unafraid. And, watching her, he remembered his mother so vividly it was almost a pain.

She had had a favorite saying. "Davey, what one Jew does anywhere in the world is the business of all Jews. If a Jew in Europe is whipped, I'll feel the whip, too." That had been at the very beginning of all the awful mess in Europe. How she would suffer now if she were alive to feel the many new whips.

The short was over. The woman who looked like his mother flashed off the screen, and the feature came on. When Cathy got up to go, he stumbled after her.

Outside, walking toward the car, she said casually, "Weren't those European pictures awful, David? But it's unbelievable. That just couldn't happen, could it?"

She was a good woman and sensitive, and he loved her very much. he respected her mind, too. She read a lot and she was cynical about a lot of things most women took for granted. But she didn't understand. That woman—why, that woman was practically his mother! It was almost as if she'd opened her mouth and talked to him. Those accusing eyes! "Any Jew, anywhere in the world, Davey." Well, but of course he didn't expect Cathy to feel it as strongly as he did.

He kept himself from shouting. "Don't be absurd, Cathy?" he said quietly. "Those pictures were the real thing."

He hadn't slept well. In the night he had asked himself, Well, what *can* I do? I'm doing something in the lab that's as essential as marching and shooting. Any Jew, anywhere in the world. By God, she was right; that's exactly the way I felt.

Then he thought wryly, So, after all these years, a guy turns out to be not only an American but a Jewish American. Very interesting!

The next day, during his lunch hour, he had phoned the library reference division. "I want to know when the next Jewish holiday occurs," he said firmly.

The information had been told him in the usual monotone; full details, as if he were a gentile asking for mysterious information, he thought with a shaky grin.

"The next holiday is the one called *Rosh Hashonoh* (the voice spelled it out for him), which is the Jewish New Year (the voice had then told him the exact Jewish year). It occurs this coming Saturday, starting, as is customary in Jewish law, sundown the preceding evening."

And as the voice talked, he remembered *Rosh Hashonoh* all through his boyhood. New clothes, and the house so clean, and cake baked so that the house was fragrant with it, holiday food cooked; and all of them had gone to *shule,* and on the way there and on the way home again, one met relatives and friends in the street, and one cried gaily: "Happy New Year!" and the glad cries came back from other people, and everybody smiled, everybody was all dressed up and clean and happy for the new year.

The telephone voice stopped talking. "Thank you very much," he had said mechanically, and hung up.

On the cot now, in the Red Cross room, Dave thought grimly: All right. This is from one Jew to all Jews, wherever they are. I give my pint of blood on a Jewish holiday, on the first day of *Rosh Hashonoh,* to make up for all of them getting kicked out of that ghetto *shule* on a holiday (if you'll excuse my melodrama!).

But he did not feel dramatic. Looking at the almost full flask, he felt grimmer than ever.

All right, Ma, he thought, and the tears bit back of his eyes.

"That's that," the nurse said, smiling down at him. "You hold this pad against your arm now."

She sniped the rubber tube and put the last touches on the flask as he lay watching, holding the small bandage against his arm.

Then she fixed the bandage, pressing the adhesive down gently, and he was through.

"Sit up," she said cheerfully. "But don't jump right down. Sit quiet for a while."

He sat there feeling fine, not a thing the matter with him. The other cots were still occupied; but with new donors, he thought with satisfaction. And he felt a momentary surge of gladness as he thought of the front door opening so steadily and the donors coming so steadily, a never-stopping march of them into this building and into this roomful of cots. A never-ending march of shining glass flasks full of blood across the world.

After a few moments he jumped down and went into the canteen.

139

It looked the same, the easy chairs covered with bright cretonne, the sandwich bar, the smiling assistants carrying the trays.

He drank down the glass of water one of them gave him, then ate a peanut butter sandwich and drank two cups of coffee.

"Is this your first time?" the woman asked.

"No, second."

"Well, you don't get a button this time," she explained. "You wear the button you received the first time." She stamped the date on his card. "You get a silver button at the third contribution, you know."

I don't need a button, he thought. "That's fine," he said automatically. He looked down at the lump of bandage on his arm. Over there they wore a button with the word *Jude* on it!

He got his jacket from the dressing room, and left. "Goodbye," the nurse in the outer room called. "Thank you, and do come again!"

"I will," he said as he went out. As he walked down the steps three others came up, two women and a man. Again he felt that throb of gladness.

He started to drive home. No, he would not tell Cathy. Maybe she would understand, but it was quite all right not to tell her; this was something she did not have to understand.

He drove slowly, a soft and tender feeling like a bruise in his chest. Yes, his mother would have understood why he had gone today, yes and why he was not going to tell Cathy. She would have nodded— he could see her eyes now—and smiled.

The tender, bruised feeling deepened. And this thing he had just done, yes, his mother would have understood it very well. How, in this second giving of his blood, he had given not only as an American but as a Jew.

As the light began to change, the feeling inside of him suddenly became clarified. With a jerk, he turned the car toward the right, and drove up Kinsman Road. His lips were tight, but the tears had broken through at last, and he let them slide down his cheeks as he stepped on the gas pedal.

All right, ma, he thought tenderly.

He was driving through the Jewish district now, the streets he had not seen for ten years. When he passed the Imperial Theatre, where he had gone to the movies in his childhood, he relaxed, his lips shaky in a smile. He wiped his eyes, slowing down.

In another five minutes he would be at the *shule* his parents attended all their years in America. They had moved with it up from the narrow, cluttered street which was now slums, the street where he'd been born; when the Jews had started to move they had moved too, and the first thing all the Jews had done on Kinsman was to build a new place for their beloved *shule*. How many times his mother had told him the story.

He could see the big, sprawling building now, and a feeling of quiet elation began to hum in his chest. He had come home, at last.

Old Stock

Hortense Calisher

THE TRAIN CREAKED through the soft, heat-promising morning like an elderly, ambulatory sofa. Nosing along, it pushed its corridor of paper-spattered floors and old plush seats through towns whose names—Crystal Run, Mamakating—were as soft as the morning, and whose dusty little central hearts—all livery stable, freight depot, and yard buildings with bricked-up windows and faded sides that said "Purina Chows"—were as down-at-the-heel as the train that strung them together.

Hester, feeling the rocking stir of the journey between her thighs, hanging her head out of the window with her face snubbed against the hot breeze, tried to seize and fix each picture as it passed. At fifteen, everything she watched and heard seemed like a footprint on the trail of some eventuality she rode to meet, which never resolved but filled her world with a verve of waiting.

Opposite her, her mother sat with the shuttered, conscious look she always assumed in public places. Today there was that added look Hester also knew well, that prim display of extra restraint her mother always wore in the presence of other Jews whose grosser features, voices, manners offended her sense of gentility all the more out of her resentful fear that she might be identified with them. Today the train rang with their mobile gestures, and at each station crowds of them got off— great-breasted, starched mothers trailing mincing children and shopping bags stuffed with food, gawky couples digging each other in the side with their elbows, girls in beach pajamas, already making the farthest use of their smiles and great, effulgent eyes. At each station, they were met by the battered Fords and wagons that serviced the farms which would accommodate them, where for a week or two they would litter the tight Catskill towns with their swooping gaiety and their weary, rapacious hope.

"Wild!" said Mrs. Elkin, sotto voce, pursing her mouth and tucking her chin in her neck. "Your hair and that getup! Always so wild." Hester, injured, understood that the indictment was as much for the rest of the train as for herself. Each summer for the past three years, ever since Mr. Elkin's business had been doing poorly and the family had been unable to afford the summer rental in Westchester, Mrs. Elkin had resisted the idea of Old Corner Farm, and each year she had given in, for they were still of a status which made it unthinkable that they would not leave New York for some part of the season. This year and last, they had not been able to manage it until September, with its lowered rates, but it would have been a confession of defeat for Mr. Elkin had he not been able to say during the week to casual business acquaintances, "Family's up in the country. I go up weekends." Once at the farm—although the guests there were of a somewhat different class from the people in this train, most of them arriving in their own cars and one or two with nursegirls for the children—Mrs. Elkin would hold herself aloof at first, bending over her embroidery hoop on the veranda, receiving the complimentary "What gorgeous work you do!" with a *moue* of distaste for the flamboyant word that was a hallmark of what she hated in her own race, politely refusing proffered rides to the village, finally settling the delicate choice of summer intimacy on some cowed spinster or recessive widow whom life had dampened to the necessary refinement. For Mrs. Elkin walked through the world swinging the twangy words "refined," "refinement," like a purifying censer before her.

Hester, roused momentarily from her dream of the towns, looked idly across at her mother's neat navy-and-white version of the late-summer uniform of the unadventurous and the well bred. Under any hat, in any setting, her mother always looked enviably right, and her face, purged of those youthful exoticisms it once might well have had, had at last attained a welcomed anonymity, so that now it was like a medallion whose blurred handsomeness bore no denomination other than the patent, accessible one of "lady." Recently, Hester had begun to doubt the very gentility of her mother's exorcistic term itself, but she was still afraid to say so, to put a finger on this one of the many ambiguities that confronted her on every side. For nowadays it seemed to her that she was like someone forming a piece of crude statuary which had to be reshaped each day—that it was not her own character which was being formed but that she was putting together, from whatever clues people would let her have, the shifty, elusive character of the world.

"Summitville!" the conductor called, poking his head into the car.

Hester and her mother got off the train with a crowd of others. Their feet crunched in the cinders of the path. The shabby snake of the train moved forward through its rut in the checkerboard hills. Several men who had been leaning on battered Chevvies ran forward, hawking persistently, but Mrs. Elkin shook her head. "There's Mr. Smith!" She waved daintily at an old man standing beside a truck. They were repeat visitors. They were being met.

Mrs. Elkin climbed into the high seat and sat tight-elbowed between Mr. Smith and Hester, denying the dusty indignity of the truck. The Smiths, people with hard faces the color of snuff, made no concession to boarders other than clean lodging and massive food. Mr. Smith, whose conversation and clothing were equally gnarled, drove silently on. At the first sight of him, of old Mr. Smith, with his drooping scythe of mustache, Hester, in one jolt, had remembered everything from the summers before.

The farm they travelled toward lay in a valley off the road from Kerhonkson to Accord. The house, of weather-beaten stone, was low and thick, like a blockhouse still retreating suspiciously behind a stockade long since gone; upstairs, beaverboard had partitioned it into many molasses-tinted rooms. In front of it would be the covered well, where the summer people made a ceremony of their dilettante thirst, the children forever sawing on the pulley, the grown-ups smacking their lips over the tonic water not drawn from pipes. Mornings, after breakfast, the city children gravitated to the barn with the indecipherable date over its lintel and stood silent watching the cows, hearing their soft droppings, smelling the fecund smell that was like the perspiration

144

the earth made in moving. Afterward, Hester, usually alone, followed the path down to the point where the brown waters of Schoharie Creek, which featherstitched the countryside for miles, ran, darkly overhung, across a great fan of ledges holding in their center one deep, minnow-flecked pool, like a large hazel eye.

"There's Miss Onderdonk's!" Hester said suddenly. They were passing a small, square house that still preserved the printlike, economical look of order of old red brick houses, although its once-white window frames were weathered and shutterless, and berry bushes, advancing from the great thorny bower of them at the back, scraggled at the first-floor windows and scratched at the three stone steps that brinked the rough-cut patch of lawn. A collie, red-gold and white, lay on the top step. "There's Margaret!" she added. "Oh, let's go see them after lunch!"

A minute before, if asked, Hester could not have told the name of the dog, but now she remembered everything: Miss Onderdonk, deaf as her two white cats, which she seemed to prize for their affliction (saying often how it was related in some way to their blue eyes and stainless fur), and Miss Onderdonk's parlor, with a peculiar, sooty darkness in its air that Hester had never seen anywhere else, as if shoe blacking had been mixed with it, or as if the only sources of light in it were the luminous reflections from the horsehair chairs. Two portraits faced you as you entered from the bare, poor wood of the kitchen; in fact, you had only to turn on your heel from the splintered drainboard or the match-cluttered oilstove to see them—Miss Onderdonk's "great-greats"—staring nastily from their unlashed eyes, their pale faces and hands emerging from their needle-fine ruffles. The left one, the man, with a face so wide and full it must surely have been redder in life, kept his sneer directly on you, but the woman, her long chin resting in the ruffle, one forefinger and thumb pinching at the lush green velvet of her dress as if to draw it away, stared past you into the kitchen, at the bare drainboard and the broken-paned window above it.

Last year, Hester had spent much of her time "helping Miss Onderdonk," partly because there was no one her own age at the farm with whom to while away the long afternoons, partly because Miss Onderdonk's tasks were so different from anyone else's, since she lived,

145

as she said, "offen the land." Miss Onderdonk was one of those deaf persons who do not chatter; her remarks hung singly, like aphorisms, in Hester's mind. "All white cats are deaf." "Sugar, salt, lard—bacon, flour, tea. The rest is offen the land." The articles thus enumerated lodged firmly in Hester's memory, shaped like the canisters so marked that contained the only groceries Miss Onderdonk seemed to have. Most of the time, when Hester appeared, Miss Onderdonk did not spare a greeting but drew her by an ignoring silence into the task at hand—setting out pans of berries to ferment in the hot sun, culling the warty carrots and spotted tomatoes from her dry garden. Once, when she and Hester were picking blackberries from bushes so laden that, turning slowly, they could pick a quart in one spot, Hester, plucking a fat berry, had also plucked a bee on its other side.

"Best go home. Best go home and mud it," Miss Onderdonk had said, and had turned back to the tinny plop of berries in her greedy pail. She had not offered mud. Hester, returning the next day, had not even felt resentment, for there was something about Miss Onderdonk, even if one did not quite like her, that compelled. As she worked at her endless ministrations to herself in her faded kitchen and garden, she was just like any other old maid, city or country, whose cottony hair was prigged tight from nightly crimpings never brushed free, whose figure, boarded up in an arid dress, made Hester gratefully, uneasily aware of her own body, fresh and moist. But when Miss Onderdonk stepped into her parlor, when she sat with her hands at rest on the carved knurls of the rocker or, standing near the open calf-bound book that chronicled the Onderdonk descent from De Witt Clinton, clasped her hands before her on some invisible pommel—then her role changed. When she stepped into her parlor, Miss Onderdonk swelled.

"How *is* Miss Onderdonk, Mr. Smith?" Mrs. Elkin asked lightly.

"The same." Mr. Smith kept his eyes on the road.

They turned in to the narrow dirt road that led off the highway down to the farm. Hester recognized a familiar curve in the sweep of surrounding hills, patch-quilted with crops. "There are hardly any white patches this year," she said.

Mr. Smith flicked a look at her, almost as if she had said something sensible. "People don't eat much buckwheat any more," he said, and brought the truck to a bumpy stop in front of the covered well.

Hester and her mother ran the gauntlet of interested glances on the porch and went up to their room. The room had a mail-order austerity, with nothing in it that was not neutralized for the transient except the dim cross-stitch doily on the dresser. Hester was glad to see their clothing shut away in the tar-paper wardrobe, sorry to see their toilet articles, the beginning of clutter, ranged on the dresser. This was the most exciting moment of all, before the room settled down with your own coloration, before the people you would get to know were explored.

"I saw that Mrs. Garfunkel on the porch," she said.

Her mother said "Yes" as if she had pins in her mouth, and went on putting things in drawers.

Mrs. Garfunkel was one of the ones who said "gorgeous"; it was perhaps her favorite word. A young matron with reddish hair, chunky, snub features, and skin tawnied over with freckles, she had the look of a Teddy bear fresh from the shop. Up here, she dressed very quietly, with an absence of heels and floppy sunwear that, with her pug features, might have satisfied certain requirements in Mrs. Elkin's category of refinement. Neither did she talk with her hands, touch your clothing with them, or openly give the prices of things. But it was with her eyes that she estimated, with her tongue that she preened, and it was not long before you discovered that her admiring comment on some detail of your equipment was really only a springboard for the description of one or the other of her own incomparable possessions. Her satisfaction in these rested in their being not only the best but the best acquired for the least: the furs bought in August, the West Indian nursegirl who would work a year or so before realizing that the passage money Mrs. Garfunkel had advanced was more than underwritten by her inequitable salary, the compliant, self-effacing Mr. Garfunkel, who would probably go on working forever without realizing anything—even the languid, six-year-old Arline, who was so exactly suitable that she might have been acquired, after the canniest negotiation, from someone in that line to whom Mrs. Garfunkel had had a card of introduction. Perhaps, Hester thought now, her mother could better have borne Mrs. Garfunkel and her bargains if all of them had not been so successful.

When Hester and her mother, freshly washed and diffidently late, entered the dining room for dinner, which was in the middle of the day here, Mrs. Garfunkel hailed them, called them over to her table, pressed them to sit there, and introduced them to the others already seated. "Mrs. Elkin's an old-timer, like Mel and me. Meet Mr. and Mrs. Brod, and Mr. Brod's mother. And my brother Wally, Mrs. Elkin and daughter. What's your name again, dear?" She paid no heed to Hester's muttered response but dug her arm affectionately against the side of the rickety young man with slick hair who sat next to her, doggedly accumulating food on his plate. "Wally ran up here to get away from half the girls in Brooklyn."

The young man gave her a look of brotherly distaste. "Couldn't have come to a better place," he said, and returned to his plate. Great platters of sliced beefsteak tomatoes and fricasseed chicken were passed, nubs of Country Gentleman corn were snatched and snatched again; the table was one flashing activity of reaching arms, although there was much more food upon it than the few of them could possibly eat. This amplitude was what one came for, after all, and this was its high point, after which there would be nothing much to look forward to through the afternoon daze of heat but supper, which was good, though not like this.

Eating busily, Hester, from under the wing of her mother's monosyllabic chilliness, watched Mr. and Mrs. Brod. They were newly married, it developed, but this was not the honeymoon. The honeymoon, as almost every turn in the conversation indicated, had been in California; they were at the farm to visit old Mrs. Brod, a little leathery grandmother of a woman, dressed in a jaunty Roman-stripe jumper and wearing a ribbon tied around hair that had been bobbed and blued. The young Mrs. Brod had a sleepy melon face with a fat mouth, dark-red nails, and black hair cut Buster Brown. Mr. Brod, a bald young man in fawn-colored jacket and knickers, said almost nothing, but every so often he did an extraordinary thing. At intervals, his wife, talking busily, would extend her hand sidewise, palm upward, without even looking at him, and in one convulsive movement that seemed to start somewhere outside him and end at his extremities, as if he were the tip of a smartly cracked whip, a gold case would be miraculously there in his hand, and he would place a cigarette tenderly in her palm. A second but lesser convulsion produced a lighter for the negligently held cigarette. He did not smoke.

The two Mrs. Brods were discussing the dress worn by the younger, evidently a California purchase. "Right away, I said, 'This one I take!' " said the bride. "Definitely a knockout!"

"Vunt vash," said her mother-in-law, munching on an ear of corn. The bride shrugged. "So I'll give to cleaners."

"Give to clean, give to ket." The mother put down her ear of corn, rolling it over reflectively.

"Don't have a cat, Ma."

Mrs. Brod the elder turned away momentarily from her plate. "Sah yull *buy* ah ket!" she said, and one lean brown arm whipped out and took another ear of corn.

The bride looked miffed, then put out the cigarette-seeking hand. Flex, flash from the solicitous Mr. Brod and the cigarette, lit, was between her lips, smoke curling from her scornful nostrils.

"Sweet, isn't it, the way he does that? And not a smoke for himself," said Mrs. Garfunkel in an aside to Hester's mother. "You better watch out, Syl," she called across the table to the bride. "He forgets to do that, then the honeymoon is over."

Mrs. Elkin smiled, a little rigid but perfectly cordial, unless you knew the signs, and stood up, reaching around for her big knitting bag, which was hung on the back of her chair. "Come, dear," she said to Hester, in accents at which no purist could cavil. "Suppose you and I go out on the porch."

On the empty porch, Mrs. Elkin selected a chair far down at the end. "Those people!" she said, and blew her breath sharply between set teeth. "I told your father this place was getting rundown."

"Sah yull *buy* ah ket," said Hester dreamily, and chuckled. It was the illogic of the remark that charmed.

"Must you *imitate?*" said her mother.

"But it's funny, Mother."

"Oh, you're just like your father. Absolutely without discrimination."

Hester found nothing to answer. "I think I'll walk down to the creek," she said.

"Take a towel."

Hester ran upstairs. Suddenly it was urgent that she get down to the creek alone, before the others, digestion accomplished, went there to bathe. Upstairs, she shed her clothes swiftly and crammed herself into last year's bathing suit—tight and faded, but it would not matter here. She ran downstairs, crossed the porch without looking at her mother, and ran across the lawn into the safety of the path, which had a wall of weeds on either side. Once there, she walked on, slow and happy. The wire tangle of weeds was alive with stalks and pods and beadlets of bright green whose shapes she knew well but could not, need not, name. Above all, it was the same.

She pushed through the bushes that fringed the creek. It, too, was the same. In the past year, it must have gone through all the calendar changes. She imagined each of them—the freeze, the thaw, the spring running, like conventionalized paper pictures torn off one by one— but they were as unreal as the imagined private dishabille of a friend. Even the bushes that ran for miles along its edge were at the same stage of their bloom, their small, cone-shaped orange flowers dotted along the leaves for as far as she could see. The people around the farm called them "scarlet runners," although their flowers were as orange as a color could be.

She trod carefully across the slippery ledges out to the wide, flat slab that rose in the middle of the stream, and stretched out on her stomach on its broad, moss-slimed back. She lay there for a long time looking into the eye of the pool. One need not have an appointment with minnows, she thought. They are always the same, too.

At a crackling sound in the brush, she looked up. Mrs. Garfunkel's head appeared above the greenery, which ended in a ruff at her neck, like the painted backdrops behind which people pose at amusement parks. "Your mother says to tell you she's gone on down to Miss Onderdonk's." She waited while Hester picked her way back to shore. Until Hester gained the high weeds of the path, she felt the Teddy-bear eyes watching idly, calculating and squint.

In her room once more, Hester changed to a paper-dry cotton dress, then hurried out again, down the dirt road this time, and onto the state highway, slowing down only when she was in sight of Miss Onderdonk's house, and saw her mother and Miss Onderdonk sitting facing one another, one on each of the two butterfly-winged wooden benches built on the top step at either side of the door, forming the only porch there was.

"Why that dress?" asked her mother, with fair reason, for it was

Hester's best. "You remember Hester, Miss Onderdonk?" she added.

Miss Onderdonk looked briefly at Hester with her watery, time-eclipsing stare. There was no indication that she knew Hester's name, or ever had. One of the white cats lay resiliently on her lap, with the warning look of toleration common to cats when held. Miss Onderdonk, like the creek, might have lived suspended from last September to this, untouched by the flowing year, every crimp in her hair the same. And the parlor? It would have to be seen, for certain.

Hester sat down quietly next to her mother, whose sewing went on and on, a mild substitute for conversation. For a while, Hester watched the long, important-looking shadows that encroached upon the hills, like enigmas stated every afternoon but never fully solved. Then she leaned carefully toward Miss Onderdonk. "May I go see your parlor?" she asked.

Miss Onderdonk gave no sign that she had heard. It might have been merely the uncanny luck of the partly deaf that prompted her remark. "People come by here this morning," she said. "From down to your place. Walk right into the parlor, no by-your-leave. Want to buy my antiques!"

Mrs. Elkin, needle uplifted, shook her head, commiserating, gave a quick, consolatory mew of understanding, and plunged the needle into the next stitch.

"Two women—and a man all ninnied out for town," said Miss Onderdonk. "Old woman had doctored hair. Grape-colored! Hollers at me as if I'm the foreign one. Picks up my Leather-Bound Onderdonk History!" Her explosive breath capitalized the words. The cat, squirting suddenly from her twitching hand, settled itself, an aggrieved white tippet, at a safe distance on the lawn. " 'Put that down,' I said," said Miss Onderdonk, her eyes as narrow as the cat's. " 'I don't have no antiques,' I said. 'These here are my belongings.' "

Mrs. Elkin put down her sewing. Her broad hands, with the silver-and-gold thimble on one middle finger, moved uncertainly, unlike Miss Onderdonk's hands, which were pressed flat, in triumph, on her faded flour-sack lap.

"I told Elizabeth Smith," Miss Onderdonk said. "I told her she'd rue the day she ever started taking in Jews."

The short word soared in an arc across Hester's vision and hit the

151

remembered, stereopticon picture of the parlor. The parlor sank and disappeared, a view in an album snapped shut. Now her stare was for her mother's face, which was pink but inconclusive.

Mrs. Elkin, raising her brows, made a helpless face at Hester, as if to say, "After all, the vagaries of the deaf . . ." She permitted herself a minimal shrug, even a slight spreading of palms. Under Hester's stare, she lowered her eyes and turned toward Miss Onderdonk again.

"I thought you knew, Miss Onderdonk," said her mother. "I thought you knew that we were—Hebrews." The word, the ultimate refinement, slid out of her mother's soft voice as if it were on runners.

"Eh?" said Miss Onderdonk.

Say it, Hester prayed. She had never before felt the sensation of prayer. Please say it, Mother. *Say "Jew."* She heard the word in her own mind, double-voiced, like the ram's horn at Yom Kippur, with an ugly present bray but with a long, urgent echo as time-spanning as Roland's horn.

Her mother leaned forward. Perhaps she had heard it, too—the echo. "But we are Jewish," she said in a stronger voice. "Mr. Elkin and I are Jewish."

Miss Onderdonk shook her head, with the smirk of one who knew better. "Never seen the Mister. The girl here has the look, maybe. But not you."

"But—" Mrs. Elkin, her lower lip caught by her teeth, made a sound like a stifled, chiding sigh. "Oh, yes," she said, and nodded, smiling, as if she had been caught out in a fault.

"Does you credit," said Miss Onderdonk. "Don't say it don't. Make your bed, lie on it. Don't have to pretend with me, though."

With another baffled sigh, Mrs. Elkin gave up, flumping her hands down on her sewing. She was pinker, not with anger but, somehow, as if she had been cajoled.

"Had your reasons, maybe." Miss Onderdonk tittered, high and henlike. "Ain't no Jew, though. Good blood shows, any day."

Hester stood up. "We're in a book at home, too," she said loudly. " 'The History of the Jews of Richmond, 1769–1917.' " Then she turned her back on Miss Onderdonk, who might or might not have heard, on her mother, who had, and stomped down the steps.

At the foot of the lawn, she stopped behind a bush that hid her from the steps, feeling sick and let-down. She had somehow used Miss Onderdonk's language. She hadn't said what she meant at all. She heard her father's words, amused and sad, as she had heard them once, over her shoulder, when he had come upon her poring over the red-bound book, counting up the references to her grandfather. "That Herbert Ezekiel's book?" He had looked over her shoulder, twirling the gold cigar-clipper on his watch chain. "Well, guess it won't hurt the sons of Moses any if they want to tally up some newer ancestors now and then."

Miss Onderdonk's voice, with its little, cut-off chicken laugh, travelled down to her from the steps. "Can't say it didn't cross my mind, though, that the girl does have the look."

Hester went out onto the highway and walked quickly back to the farmhouse. Skirting the porch, she tiptoed around to one side, over to an old fringed hammock slung between two trees whose broad bottom fronds almost hid it. She swung herself into it, covered herself over with the side flaps, and held herself stiff until the hammock was almost motionless.

Mrs. Garfunkel and Arline could be heard on the porch, evidently alone, for now and then Mrs. Garfunkel made one of the fretful, absent remarks mothers make to children when no one else is around. Arline had some kind of wooden toy that rumbled back and forth across the porch. Now and then, a bell on it went "ping."

After a while, someone came along the path and up on the porch. Hester lay still, the hammock fringe tickling her face. "Almost time for supper," she heard Mrs. Garfunkel say.

"Yes," said her mother's voice. "Did Hester come back this way?"

"I was laying down for a while. Arline, dear, did you see Hester?"

"No, Mummy." "Ping, ping" went Arline's voice.

" 'Mummy'!" said Mrs. Garfunkel. "That's that school she goes to—you know the Kemp-Willard School, on Eighty-sixth?"

"Oh, yes," said Mrs. Elkin. "Quite good, I've heard."

"Good!" Mrs. Garfunkel sighed, on a sleek note of outrage. "What they soak you, they ought to be."

Arline's toy rumbled across the porch again and was still.

"She'll come back when she's hungry, I suppose," said Mrs. Elkin. "There was a rather unfortunate little—incident, down the road."

153

"Shush, Arline. You don't say?"

Chairs scraped confidentially closer. Mrs. Elkin's voice dropped to the low, *gemütlich* whisper reserved for obstetrics, cancer, and the peculations of servant girls. Once or twice, the whisper, flurrying higher, shook out a gaily audible phrase. "Absolutely wouldn't believe—" "Can you imagine anything so silly?" Then, in her normal voice, "Of course, she's part deaf, and probably a little crazy from being alone so much."

"Scratch any of them and you're sure to find it," said Mrs. Garfunkel.

"Ah, well," said Mrs. Elkin. "But it certainly was funny," she added, in a voice velveted over now with a certain savor of reminiscence, "the way she kept *insisting*."

"Uh-huh," said Mrs. Garfunkel rather flatly. "Yeah. Sure."

Someone came out on the back porch and vigorously swung the big bell that meant supper in fifteen minutes.

"Care for a little drive in the Buick after supper?" asked Mrs. Garfunkel.

"Why—why, yes," said Mrs. Elkin, her tones warmer now with the generosity of one whose equipment went beyond the realm of bargains. "Why, I think that would be very nice."

"Any time," said Mrs. Garfunkel. "Any time you want stamps or anything. Thought you might enjoy a little ride. Not having the use of a car."

The chairs scraped back, the screen door creaked, and the two voices, linked in their sudden, dubious rapprochement, went inside. The scuffling toy followed them.

Hester rolled herself out of the hammock and stood up. She looked for comfort at the reasonable hills, whose pattern changed only according to what people ate; at the path, down which there was nothing more ambiguous than the hazel-eyed water or the flower that should be scarlet but was orange. While she had been in the hammock, the dusk had covered them over. It had settled over everything with its rapt, misleading veil.

She walked around to the foot of the front steps. A thin, emery edge of autumn was in the air now. Inside, they must all be at supper; no one else had come by. When she walked into the dining room, they would all lift their heads for a moment, the way they always did when someone walked in late, all of them regarding her for just a minute with their equivocal adult eyes. Something would rise from them all like a warning odor, confusing and corrupt, and she knew now what it was. Miss Onderdonk sat at their table, too. Wherever any of them sat publicly at table, Miss Onderdonk sat at his side. Only, some of them set a place for her and some of them did not.

I Stand Here Ironing

Tillie Olsen

I STAND HERE IRONING, and what you asked me moves tormented back and forth with the iron.

"I wish you would manage the time to come in and talk with me about your daughter. I'm sure you can help me understand her. She's a youngster who needs help and whom I'm deeply interested in helping."

"Who needs help." . . . Even if I came, what good would it do? You think because I am her mother I have a key, or that in some way you could use me as a key? She has lived for nineteen years. There is all that life that has happened outside of me, beyond me.

And when is there time to remember, to sift, to weigh, to estimate, to total? I will start and there will be an interruption and I will have to gather it all together again. Or I will become engulfed with all I did or did not do, with what should have been and what cannot be helped.

She was a beautiful baby. The first and only one of our five that was beautiful at birth. You do not guess how new and uneasy her tenancy in her now-loveliness. You did not know her all those years she was thought homely, or see her poring over her baby pictures, making me tell her over and over how beautiful she had been—and would be, I would tell her—and was now, to the seeing eye. But the seeing eyes were few or non-existent. Including mine.

I nursed her. They feel that's important nowadays. I nursed all the children, but with her, with all the fierce rigidity of first motherhood, I did like the books then said. Though her cries battered me to trembling and my breasts ached with swollenness, I waited till the clock decreed.

Why do I put that first? I do not even know if it matters, or if it explains anything.

She was a beautiful baby. She blew shining bubbles of sound. She loved motion, loved light, loved color and music and textures. She would lie on the floor in her blue overalls patting the surface so hard in ecstasy her hands and feet would blur. She was a miracle to me, but when she was eight months old I had to leave her daytimes with the woman downstairs to whom she was no miracle at all, for I worked or looked for work and for Emily's father, who "could no longer endure" (he wrote in his good-bye note) "sharing want with us."

I was nineteen. It was the pre-relief, pre-WPA world of the depression. I would start running as soon as I got off the streetcar, running up the stairs, the place smelling sour, and awake or asleep to startle awake, when she saw me she would break into a clogged weeping that could not be comforted, a weeping I can hear yet.

After a while I found a job hashing at night so I could be with her days, and it was better. But it came to where I had to bring her to his family and leave her.

It took a long time to raise the money for her fare back. Then she got chicken pox and I had to wait longer. When she finally came, I hardly knew her, walking quick and nervous like her father, looking like her father, thin, and dressed in a shoddy red that yellowed her skin and glared at the pockmarks. All the baby loveliness gone.

She was two. Old enough for nursery school they said, and I did not know then what I know now—the fatigue of the long day, and the lacerations of group life in the kinds of nurseries that are only parking places for children.

Except that it would have made no difference if I had known. It was the only place there was. It was the only way we could be together, the only way I could hold a job.

And even without knowing, I knew. I knew the teacher that was evil because all these years it has curdled into my memory, the little boy hunched in the corner, her rasp, "why aren't you outside, because

Alvin hits you? that's no reason, go out, scaredy." I knew Emily hated it even if she did not clutch and implore "don't go Mommy" like the other children, mornings.

She always had a reason why we should stay home. Momma, you look sick, Momma. I feel sick. Momma, the teachers aren't there today, they're sick. Momma, we can't go, there was a fire there last night. Momma, it's a holiday today, no school, they told me.

But never a direct protest, never rebellion. I think of our others in their three-, four-year-oldness—the explosions, the tempers, the denunciations, the demands—and I feel suddenly ill. I put the iron down. What in me demanded that goodness in her? And what was the cost, the cost to her of such goodness?

The old man living in the back once said in his gentle way: "You should smile at Emily more when you look at her." What *was* in my face when I looked at her? I loved her. There were all the acts of love.

It was only with the others I remembered what he said, and it was the face of joy, and not of care or tightness or worry I turned to them— too late for Emily. She does not smile easily, let alone almost always as her brothers and sisters do. Her face is closed and sombre, but when she wants, how fluid. You must have seen it in her pantomimes, you spoke of her rare gift for comedy on the stage that rouses a laughter out of the audience so dear they applaud and applaud and do not want to let her go.

Where does it come from, that comedy? There was none of it in her when she came back to me that second time, after I had had to send her away again. She had a new daddy now to learn to love, and I think perhaps it was a better time.

Except when we left her alone nights, telling ourselves she was old enough.

"Can't you go some other time, Mommy, like tomorrow?" she would ask. "Will it be just a little while you'll be gone? Do you promise?"

The time we came back, the front door open, the clock on the floor in the hall. She rigid awake. "It wasn't just a little while. I didn't cry. Three times I called you, just three times, and then I ran downstairs to open the door so you could come faster. The clock talked loud. I threw it away, it scared me what it talked."

She said the clock talked loud again that night I went to the hospital to have Susan. She was delirious with the fever that comes before red

158

measles, but she was fully conscious all the week I was gone and the week after we were home when she could not come near the new baby or me.

She did not get well. She stayed skeleton thin, not wanting to eat, and night after night she had nightmares. She would call for me, and I would rouse from exhaustion to sleepily call back: "You're all right, darling, go to sleep, it's just a dream," and if she still called, in a sterner voice, "now go to sleep, Emily, there's nothing to hurt you." Twice, only twice, when I had to get up for Susan anyhow, I went in to sit with her.

Now when it is too late (as if she would let me hold and comfort her like I do the others) I get up and go to her at once at her moan or restless stirring. "Are you awake, Emily? Can I get you something?" And the answer is always the same: "No, I'm all right, go back to sleep, Mother."

They persuaded me at the clinic to send her away to a convalescent home in the country where "she can have the kind of food and care you can't manage for her, and you'll be free to concentrate on the new baby." They still send children to that place. I see pictures on the society page of sleek young women planning affairs to raise money for it, or dancing at the affairs, or decorating Easter eggs or filling Christmas stockings for the children.

They never have a picture of the children so I do not know if the girls still wear those gigantic red bows and the ravaged looks on the every other Sunday when parents can come to visit "unless otherwise notified"—as we were notified the first six weeks.

Oh it is a handsome place, green lawns and tall trees and fluted flower beds. High up on the balconies of each cottage the children stand, the girls in their red bows and white dresses, the boys in white suits and giant red ties. The parents stand below shrieking up to be heard and the children shriek down to be heard, and between them the invisible wall "Not To Be Contaminated by Parental Germs or Physical Affection."

There was a tiny girl who always stood hand in hand with Emily. Her parents never came. One visit she was gone. "They moved her to Rose Cottage" Emily shouted in explanation. "They don't like you to love anybody here."

She wrote once a week, the labored writing of a seven-year-old. "I am fine. How is the baby. If I write my leter nicly I will have a star. Love." There never was a star. We wrote every other day, letters she could never hold or keep but only hear read—once. "We simply do not have room for children to keep any personal possessions," they patiently explained when we pieced one Sunday's shrieking together to plead how much it would mean to Emily, who loved so to keep things, to be allowed to keep her letters and cards.

Each visit she looked frailer. "She isn't eating," they told us.

(They had runny eggs for breakfast or mush with lumps, Emily said later, I'd hold it in my mouth and not swallow. Nothing ever tasted good, just when they had chicken.)

It took us eight months to get her released home, and only the fact that she gained back so little of her seven lost pounds convinced the social worker.

I used to try to hold and love her after she came back, but her body would stay stiff, and after a while she'd push away. She ate little. Food sickened her, and I think much of life too. Oh she had physical lightness and brightness, twinkling by on skates, bouncing like a ball up and down up and down over the jump rope, skimming over the hill; but these were momentary.

She fretted about her appearance, thin and dark and foreign-looking at a time when every little girl was supposed to look or thought she should look a chubby blonde replica of Shirley Temple. The doorbell sometimes rang for her, but no one seemed to come and play in the house or be a best friend. Maybe because we moved so much.

There was a boy she loved painfully through two school semesters. Months later she told me how she had taken pennies from my purse to buy him candy. "Licorice was his favorite and I brought him some every day, but he still liked Jennifer better'n me. Why, Mommy?" The kind of question for which there is no answer.

School was a worry to her. She was not glib or quick in a world where glibness and quickness were easily confused with ability to learn. To her overworked and exasperated teachers she was an overconscientious "slow learner" who kept trying to catch up and was absent entirely too often.

I let her be absent, though sometimes the illness was imaginary. How different from my now-strictness about attendance with the others. I wasn't working. We had a new baby, I was home anyhow. Sometimes, after Susan grew old enough, I would keep her home from school, too, to have them all together.

Mostly Emily had asthma, and her breathing, harsh and labored, would fill the house with a curiously tranquil sound. I would bring the two old dresser mirrors and her boxes of collections to her bed. She would select beads and single earrings, bottle tops and shells, dried flowers and pebbles, old postcards and scraps, all sorts of oddments; then she and Susan would play Kingdom, setting up landscapes and furniture, peopling them with action.

Those were the only times of peaceful companionship between her and Susan. I have edged away from it, that poisonous feeling between them, that terrible balancing of hurts and needs I had to do between the two, and did so badly, those earlier years.

Oh there are conflicts between the others too, each one human, needing, demanding, hurting, taking—but only between Emily and Susan, no, Emily toward Susan that corroding resentment. It seems so obvious on the surface, yet it is not obvious. Susan, the second child, Susan, golden- and curly-haired and chubby, quick and articulate and assured, everything in appearance and manner Emily was not; Susan, not able to resist Emily's precious things, losing or sometimes clumsily breaking them; Susan telling jokes and riddles to company for applause while Emily sat silent (to say to me later: that was *my* riddle, Mother, I told it to Susan); Susan, who for all the five years' difference in age was just a year behind Emily in developing physically.

I am glad for that slow physical development that widened the difference between her and her contemporaries, though she suffered over it. She was too vulnerable for that terrible world of youthful competition, of preening and parading, of constant measuring of yourself against every other, of envy, "If I had that copper hair," "If I had that skin. . . ." She tormented herself enough about not looking like the others, there was enough of the unsureness, the having to be conscious of words before you speak, the constant caring—what are they thinking of me? without having it all magnified by the merciless physical drives.

Ronnie is calling. He is wet and I change him. It is rare there is such a cry now. That time of motherhood is almost behind me when

161

the ear is not one's own but must always be racked and listening for the child cry, the child call. We sit for a while and I hold him, looking out over the city spread in charcoal with its soft aisles of light. "*Shoogily*," he breathes and curls closer. I carry him back to bed, asleep. *Shoogily*. A funny word, a family word, inherited from Emily, invented by her to say: *comfort*.

In this and other ways she leaves her seal, I say aloud. And startle at my saying it. What do I mean? What did I start to gather together, to try and make coherent? I was at the terrible, growing years. War years. I do not remember them well. I was working, there were four smaller ones now, there was not time for her. She had to help be a mother, and housekeeper, and shopper. She had to set her seal. Mornings of crisis and near hysteria trying to get lunches packed, hair combed, coats and shoes found, everyone to school or Child Care on time, the baby ready for transportation. And always the paper scribbled on by a smaller one, the book looked at by Susan then mislaid, the homework not done. Running out to that huge school where she was one, she was lost, she was a drop; suffering over the unpreparedness, stammering and unsure in her classes.

There was so little time left at night after the kids were bedded down. She would struggle over books, always eating (it was in those years she developed her enormous appetite that is legendary in our family) and I would be ironing, or preparing food for the next day, or writing V-mail to Bill, or tending the baby. Sometimes, to make me laugh, or out of her despair, she would imitate happenings or types at school.

I think I said once: "Why don't you do something like this in the school amateur show?" One morning she phoned me at work, hardly understandable through the weeping: "Mother, I did it. I won, I won; they gave me first prize; they clapped and clapped and wouldn't let me go."

Now suddenly she was Somebody, and as imprisoned in her difference as she had been in anonymity.

She began to be asked to perform at other high schools, even in colleges, than at city and statewide affairs. The first one we went to, I only recognized her that first moment when thin, shy, she almost drowned herself into the curtains. Then: Was this Emily? The control, the command, the convulsing and deadly clowning, the spell, then

162

the roaring, stamping audience, unwilling to let this rare and precious laughter out of their lives.

Afterwards: You ought to do something about her with a gift like that—but without money or knowing how, what does one do? We have left it all to her, and the gift has as often eddied inside, clogged and clotted, as been used and growing.

She is coming. She runs up the stairs two at a time with her light graceful step, and I know she is happy tonight. Whatever it was that occasioned your call did not happen today.

"Aren't you ever going to finish the ironing, Mother? Whistler painted his mother in a rocker. I'd have to paint mine standing over an ironing board." This is one of her communicative nights and she tells me everything and nothing as she fixes herself a plate of food out of the icebox.

She is so lovely. Why did you want me to come in at all? Why were you concerned? She will find her way.

She starts up the stairs to bed. "Don't get me up with the rest in the morning." "But I thought you were having midterms." "Oh, those," she comes back in, kisses me, and says quite lightly, "in a couple of years when we'll all be atom-dead they won't matter a bit."

She has said it before. She *believes* it. But because I have been dredging the past, and all that compounds a human being is so heavy and meaningful in me, I cannot endure it tonight.

I will never total it all. I will never come in to say: She was a child seldom smiled at. Her father left me before she was a year old. I had to work her first six years when there was work, or I sent her home and to his relatives. There were years she had care she hated. She was dark and thin and foreign-looking in a world where the prestige went to blondeness and curly hair and dimples, she was slow where glibness was prized. She was a child of anxious, not proud, love. We were poor and could not afford for her the soil of easy growth. I was a young mother, I was a distracted mother. There were the other children pushing up, demanding. Her younger sister seemed all that she was not. There were years she did not want me to touch her. She kept too much in herself, her life was such she had to keep too much in herself. My wisdom came too late. She has much to her and probably little will come of it. She is a child of her age, of depression, of war, of fear.

Let her be. So all that is in her will not bloom—but in how many does it? There is still enough left to live by. Only help her to know—help make it so there is cause for her to know—that she is more than this dress on the ironing board, helpless before the iron.

PART 3

Wider Glimpses: 1960–1979

Z'mira

Gloria Goldreich

THE FIRST WINTER I lived in Jerusalem I fell ill with a breed of amoebic dysentery unique to the Middle East. I returned from the hospital feeling marvelously healthy but when I made even vague efforts to wash the tiled floors of my flat, I collapsed with exhaustion. Friends at the Hebrew University (where I was working on a research project) finally convinced me that I should furnish myself with an *ozeret*—the Israeli equivalent of a day worker. Although I felt ridiculous and almost guilty about having someone in to clean my tiny flat, my physical condition forced me to relent and I agreed to meet Z'mira.

My friend Nona, a veteran of three years in Jerusalem, assured me that Z'mira was a "find." She only takes when you have two of something, Nona affirmed.

The morning on which I was to interview Z'mira I arose early and cleaned the house thoroughly—a habit acquired from my Brooklyn mother who never wanted her infrequent daily helpers to feel that she kept a "dirty house." I then put on a full pot of coffee, a simple black cotton dress and settled down to brace myself for the interview. Z'mira had been scheduled to appear at 10 A.M. By twelve I had drunk the entire pot of coffee, sorted out every letter I had received since my arrival in the Promised Land and was about to start studying. At one o'clock I phoned Nona who failed to understand either my irritation or my surprise.

"She'll be there—East always meets West," Nona cheerfully predicted. I silently cursed the analyst in New York who had helped Nona adjust to moving to Jerusalem with her Israeli husband and hung up. And Z'mira was there.

As I replaced the telephone I heard an incredibly soft and gentle voice say, "Ah, you have a telephone, I'll work here." And the next thing I knew a brown hand had lifted the receiver and the gentle voice was making elaborate arrangements with a Madame Levi to "do the floors" that night. "I like working at night," Z'mira explained as she hung up.

I nodded and continued to stare at her helplessly from the chair into which I had collapsed. One could easily stare at Z'mira for quite a while. For one thing she was beautiful—an adjective which no woman easily accords another but which could not be denied Z'mira. She had the darkest eyes I had ever seen and her lashes swept over cheek bones that would put Claudette Colbert to shame. A heavy rope of shining coal-black hair was twisted into a graceful braid and a bright gold and green dress clung to her delicate body. Only her hands were large and hardened—hands which seen out of context might have been attributed to the wrists of a mechanic. Z'mira neither wore nor needed makeup. Her perfect full lips were subtly red and her skin glowed with the dark sheen of a hundred generations of desert ancestors. I silently vowed that Z'mira would never do my floors at night. As a single girl I simply could not afford it.

Our first conversation was relatively uncomplicated. Z'mira conducted the interview with absolute ease. She informed me, in a Hebrew which was limited but soft and rolling, that she could allow me seven hours each week. She insisted on mopping the tile floors with a specific detergent. She did not trust electric water heaters and I probably had an electric heater. My flat was small. Her father's house was almost as large. (I later learned that her father's house was an aluminum hut in a temporary camp where the family had been transitory for almost eleven years, and these quarters were shared by numerous relations.) Z'mira also felt it was fortunate that I was an "Anglo-Saxon" (in Israel everyone who originates from an English speaking nation is Anglo-Saxon by definition) because she preferred to work for Anglo-Saxons. I was too young to wear black. She could not stay to work that day because of her sister. (On subsequent days the sister would be replaced by twin brothers, nephews, great uncles and at least seven different grandparents. Why they prevented Z'mira from working was never clear.)

As she rose to leave I managed to articulate the question which had obsessed me during the entire hour. "How much will the day's work cost?" I asked, blushing to the roots of my Anglo-Saxon hair. Discussing money fills me with discomfort but I felt I owed it to my mother. Z'mira looked hard at me and I might have imagined the spark of scorn in her eyes. "Tomorrow I will come," she answered and swept out the door.

She did come the next day and it cost me seven Israel pounds to explain American Supermarkets. I then decided that Thursdays would be dedicated exclusively to library research. I found myself rising early on Thursday mornings to escape from the flat before my dark haired *ozeret* came singing up the stairs. However, on a rare day when I happened to be home, we entered into complicated discussions of laundry problems.

The couple from whom I had sublet my flat had a small American washing machine and I had initiated Z'mira into its mysteries early in our relationship. At that time I had felt that she was singularly unenthusiastic about it considering that most laundry in Israel is done by heating a huge tub of water over a kerosene burner and laboriously scrubbing each garment, but I had not dared to ask why. Now Z'mira declared that the washing machine was unsanitary.

"The clothes go in because they are dirty—yes?"

I agreed and lit a cigarette, wishing I had a drink on hand.

"Then they make the water dirty—yes?"

I agreed, a bit less enthusiastically.

"Then dirty clothes and dirty water roll around together and you wear these clothes?"

I began to itch. The freshly ironed blouse I had put on that morning suddenly felt as though it had been laundered in a sewer not far from a leper colony. I thought of all the laundromats in America and wondered what it was worth to them to pay Z'mira not to publish this line of reasoning.

"You want to wear dirty clothes?" Z'mira asked.

"No," I replied, hoping it was the right answer.

"Our way is best," Z'mira said. "I will take the laundry home with me and my mother will wash it."

Relieved at escaping without having to burn all my clothes, I agreed. Each week Z'mira took home a sack of dirty laundry and the following week she arrived with neat piles of clean clothes. I decided that it was an ideal arrangement and forgot about it.

Jerusalem is a small city and even when its inhabitants are not on speaking terms with each other there is a general atmosphere of familiarity between them. One is aware of all manner of irrelevant information about fellow-citizens to whom not even a vague *shalom* has ever been murmured. Not too many weeks after the laundry discussion a fellow-student at the University asked if I would sell her one of my "American" shirts. I should explain that I was probably the only Jerusalem resident who dressed almost exclusively in button down man-tailored blouses and straight line skirts. I explained to Shoshanna that I was not in the habit of selling my clothes and asked why she had made such a strange request. Shoshanna was frankly embarrassed.

"But you have sold such shirts to the Moroccan girl who works for our neighbor. Or have you given them to her?"

I gave a vague answer and glanced at my watch. It was early on a Thursday afternoon and Z'mira would still be at my flat. I left the library and hurried home.

Z'mira was on the phone when I came in and she smiled a bright *shalom* at me. As she spoke she was painting the toes which shot out of her worn sandal with my Revlon polish. I put my books down and began stalking the furniture for signs of dust—a habit which I remembered from my mother's home and which I assumed would psychologically undermine any household worker. Not so Z'mira. She continued her conversation and waved her toes in the sunlight.

I put up coffee, clattering the pot, cups and saucers. Z'mira said a lingering goodbye and I looked at my watch. A full fifteen minutes had elapsed.

"Don't you feel well?" Z'mira asked.

"No," I said, "That is . . ." But it was too late. Z'mira was off on a health lecture. I smoked too much, drank too much coffee and there were so many bottles of "poison" in my tiny bar. Well, I thought, at least I don't have to worry about her stealing the liquor.

"Z'mira," I said at last, "I hear you have been wearing my blouses."

"Yes, of course," she answered in surprise. "After they are clean I wear them sometimes and then my mother makes them clean for you again. But we only make you pay for washing and ironing once."

"But Z'mira," I said weakly. "They are my blouses."

"Of course they are your blouses. I buy only with lace. But sometimes it is good to feel American. I make believe." She smiled shyly and I remembered that she was, after all, only sixteen.

"But that's not right," I said.

"To make believe is not right?" She was puzzled. I thought quickly. After all, what difference did it make if she did wear the blouses. I had never noticed until Shoshanna brought it up, so why should it trouble me now? The blouses did come back clean and it would take me a very long time to explain the concept of completely private property to Z'mira.

"But you will bring them all back?" I asked finally.

"Of course. Do you like this color?" She wagged her toe at me. I smiled mild approval and hurried back to the library praying my mother would never find out about the blouses.

Some weeks later I returned home and found Z'mira dusting my bookcase.

"Did you read all these books?" she asked me.

"Most of them," I said, wondering wistfully when I would have time to read all of them and reread those which cried out for a second or third visit.

"Then why do you keep them if you know them already?" The question was asked carefully, almost with embarrassment and I raked through my mind for an equally careful answer.

Hesitantly I tried to explain to Z'mira what books meant to me and my friends—the new lives they opened to us and how they became old friends.

"You do not give up a friend once you know him very well and you never give up a book you have come to know and love," I explained.

"I read and write," Z'mira said, and I remembered that she had once left me a note about some household matter—every word hopelessly misspelled, the letters large and sprawling. "My father cannot read but my mother learned how. It made my father angry so she stopped going to the school. He did not like it when my sisters and I went to school. We have to marry and be wives."

"But you can read and write and still be a good wife," I protested.

"Perhaps." Her voice was far from convinced. "But wherever I clean there are carpets, soft chairs, paintings and many books." A wistful hunger in her tone caused my heart to turn over in a sudden swift pang of sympathy.

I am an avid detective-story reader and I buy English paperbacks second hand by the dozen. When I am through with them, I generally string them together to be thrown away and one Thursday I placed some fifteen or twenty with my garbage. When I came home I noticed that Z'mira had placed the books in her blue plastic string shopping bag and covered them with her worn red cardigan.

"Do you want those books, Z'mira?"

"Why not?"

"But you can't read English."

"It will be good to have books in our house," she answered calmly, her dark eyes roving around my room with its book-lined walls.

I thought of the aluminum hut where Z'mira and her family made their home in the stark unrelieved boredom of poverty and wondered how much closer my pathetic unreadable Penguins would bring them to the soft chairs and carpets that dwell in other people's houses.

Shortly after this incident Nona phoned me. Z'mira cleaned for her twice a week and Nona and I, who for years had discussed Proust, Washington politics, hemlines and the peculiarities of our friends, now concentrated our conversations almost exclusively on our young helper.

"Why," Nona demanded in the tone of one trying to reason with a mental incompetent who has gone stark raving mad, "did you give Z'mira your belt?"

I should explain that the belt in question is quite unusual. It is made of wide, highly polished black leather and laces in the back with elaborate hand-tooled brass patterns in the front. When I wear it in America people ask me whether I had it made in Israel or in Europe, and in Europe everyone bemoans the fact that only Americans are capable of such originality. Actually, it was made for me by my art-teacher sister in a college leather workshop.

"But I didn't give Z'mira the belt," I protested. "You must be confused, Nona."

"*I'm* not the one who's confused. Check your closet." And Nona rang off with righteous indignation.

I checked my closet and much to my great unsurprise—no belt.

Nona's call came on a Monday and until Thursday I composed speeches. I discussed the situation endlessly with my friends who took to turning corners when they saw me coming. On Wednesday night I reported to Nona that I would assume a tone of angry shock tinged with sorrowful disappointment. "Ha!" said Nona who had been horrified when she heard of the blouse compromise. "You're weak!"

Z'mira appeared bright and early on Thursday morning. She proudly presented me with a bottle of *arak* which her father had prepared for me. She also pointed out that her mother had replaced buttons on two of my blouses. I took a deep breath.

"Z'mira," I said, fixing my eyes on my Roualt print of the Crucifixion, "Have you seen my black belt?"

"Of course," she answered without hesitating. "It is in my home." Her voice was polite but mildly surprised.

All my carefully rehearsed speeches fused into honest anger and for a moment I realized that I had more of my mother's temperament than I had supposed.

"What is my belt doing in your house?" The emphasis I placed on the possessive pronouns was unmistakable and a rich red crept into her cheeks.

"The button on my skirt broke and I could not find a safety pin. You have so many belts I did not think you would miss this one if I borrowed it for some days. Today I was to bring it back and I was already on the autobus when I realized I had forgotten it. Do you miss it so much? I will go home and get it. I know it is very beautiful and must be precious." She paused with a gasp and her dark eyes filled. I felt mine about to spill over as well and held my hand out to her.

"No, of course, I don't want you to go home. Only bring it next time. It is true I have many belts and it is not valuable but it is dear to me because it was made by my sister." Z'mira nodded and rushed into the kitchen where the sounds of clattering pots and pans over the rush of water was soon heard.

I hurried to Nona's to drown my own guilty embarrassment in a cup of Nescafe and receive my friend's congratulations. Nona, however, was singularly unenthusiastic. "You'll never see that belt again," she predicted darkly. I ignored that. Nona had been a social investigator in New York City for a few weeks and I secretly believed that her faith had been shaken forever.

The belt found its way back to my closet the next week and I wore it conspicuously on "Z'mira's day" for two consecutive weeks, and then forgot it. I thought of it again when Rachel, my next door neighbor, came in to proudly exhibit her teen-age daughter's Purim costume. Purim, in Israel, is a time of costumes and gaiety. The streets are thronged with youngsters dressed as the legendary Mordecai, Roy Rogers, Ben Gurion (a special rubber mask with tufts of white hair lovingly mocks the premier) and a variety of others. Miriam, Rachel's beautiful thirteen-year-old, was dressed as an Italian peasant girl in a flowing red skirt which her mother had worn in her native Italy and a low-cut, full-sleeved blouse.

"It is lovely," Rachel observed critically, "but something is missing. Hmm . . . a belt."

"Of course," I answered. "My black belt with the brass-work will be perfect. One second . . ."

But I returned acutely embarrassed. The belt was not in my closet. I told Rachel I had lent it to another friend but would have it for her that evening.

This time I did not mention the incident to anyone but found my way on a complicated series of buses to the section of Jerusalem where Z'mira and her multitude of relatives lived. I had driven past the area once before and had a dim idea of where the hut stood. It was a warm spring evening and each star was etched clearly into the dark sky, casting a silver light over the curving hills which surround Jerusalem. From within the aluminum huts, with their searingly ugly patches, the harsh yellow lights of unshielded electric bulbs intruded on the evening. The rough road swarmed with children, calling to each other in clear Hebrew, lightly tinged with the French and Arabic accents of their parents. The murmur of adult voices in a collage of languages rose and fell in the wind which trickled through the settlement. I felt strangely alien—no longer simply an American in Israel or a Westerner in the East—but an intruder in a different life which, with effort and pain, I might grow to understand but which I could never accept and become part of.

Then, through the veil of this new loneliness, I saw Z'mira. She was standing against the wall of a shack, the glow of light from the window catching only her profile. Large gold earrings were looped through her ears and her white blouse was intricately embroidered in a thread of rare blue which matched her skirt. My belt was clasped about her slender waist. A tall young man stood next to her dressed in dark chino pants and a whiter than white shirt open at the neck. He too leaned against the shack with one hand and with the other traced the brass-work pattern of my belt. The silent breath of a smile hovered between them. I watched for a moment and then hurried back to the city. I found another belt for Miriam.

From then on the belt appeared and disappeared at infrequent intervals. Z'mira and I did not discuss it although suddenly it had become easier for us to communicate and the complicated maze of her family life began to make some small sense to me. Although her informality persisted, she now made small deferences to me. No longer would she perch on the telephone while I was in the flat and she learned to take phone messages without inquiring extensively into the private life of the caller.

I congratulated myself secretly on the superior way in which I had coped with the situation and dismissed my lingering feeling of cowardice with a series of skillful rationalizations. I occasionally wondered, when she mentioned her *chaver* (boyfriend), if she had seen me that evening, but I carefully avoided the subject.

Several months passed and one bright afternoon I realized that I had completed my research project. Finally I was free to act on my plans for a month's holiday in Greece. I booked reservations on a freighter, accepted travel tips and proceeded to survey my wardrobe.

Z'mira accepted the news of my trip abroad with uncontained excitement. How lucky I was to be going *hutz la'aretz* (abroad)! To most

Israelis, the world which lies beyond their hostile borders is a vast dream territory, peopled with romance, excitement and shadowy dangers. Their own country is small and clearly defined. There is the Galilee, where one goes for a week in the summer, and there is the startling stretch of ever changing desert, the southland's Negev, where one usually spends a week in the winter. The more adventurous may, in the course of time, fly to Eilat on the shores of the Red Sea. But no journey ever takes more than two or three days and Israelis revel in their own cities. There are Jerusalemites who have never gone as far as Tel Aviv, and Tel Avivians and Haifaites who have not visited Jerusalem for a decade. To Z'mira, whose *maabara* (temporary immigrant camp) life did not belong even to Jerusalem and whose annual excursion to Tel Aviv, one hour and a half away, required weeks of careful packing, my projected trip across the Mediterranean was incredibly exciting.

She was distressed when I told her I would take only one small suitcase with a few skirts and blouses and indignant when I refused to pack a frilly cocktail dress.

"But there will be parties," she protested.

"I won't go to them," I answered firmly. "And, Z'mira, I'll need my black belt."

A silence fell between us. I methodically continued counting blouses.

"The belt," Z'mira repeated finally. "There is a party at Avraham's club in two weeks and I was to wear it with my blue skirt."

Another silence.

"It is my belt, you know," I finally said, resisting the annoyance slowly welling within me.

"I'll bring it to you," she said shortly.

The next week, the day before I was to sail, she came with it.

"You see, I have polished it and shined the brass," she said, mutely adding that I had never lavished such care on it. For a moment I felt ready to apologize, and then said abruptly, "Z'mira, I will look for a belt like it in Athens and bring it to you as a gift. All right?" She nodded, but her dark eyes were downcast and I knew that it was not all right.

I spent a good deal of time in Athens haunting leather shops but the only belt I could find which resembled mine was far too expensive.

Finally, on my last day, in sheer desperation I decided against two prints I had contemplated buying and purchased the belt instead. I had it gift wrapped, paying an extra five drachmae for an elaborate cardboard box and ribbon.

I had been in Jerusalem for several days when Z'mira finally appeared. By chance I was wearing my own belt and I held the carefully wrapped box out to her. She accepted it hesitantly and opened it with more self-consciousness than I had considered her capable of. "Such wrapping!" she cried, undoing the ribbon, and I considered the five drachmae well spent. She carefully folded the ribbon and shook the belt out of the tissue paper. The leather gleamed in its newness and the brass buckle shone. Z'mira passed her large hands over it, her eyes travelling from my own waist to the new belt, sniffing the fresh leather smell.

"Do you like it?" I asked at last.

She replaced the belt in its tissues and carefully rewrapped the box. Tying the ribbon, she answered. "Yours is prettier."

She never borrowed my belt again nor did she ever wear the new one. Some months later she married Avraham and when I left Israel she was three months pregnant. While in New York, I learned from a casual reference in one of Nona's letters that Z'mira was the mother of a daughter. I sent her a delicate pink sweater for the baby, wondering if the child had inherited the wonder of her mother's eyes. I received in return a photograph of the swarthy Avraham, his arm around Z'mira, who held a smiling black-eyed child, wrapped in my sweater. A sprawling thank you and a blessing covered the reverse side of the snapshot and Z'mira was wearing the belt I had brought from Greece.

L'Olam and White Shell Woman

Joanne Greenberg

I WAS BROKE and there was a Tribal Fair looming ahead, so the
Window Rock Reservation Restaurant and Coffee Shop took me on
as its first "Anglo" waitress. We started work at seven in the morning
and finished with the last coffee customer, around eight or nine at
night. We got fifty cents an hour and hypothetical tips. It wasn't bad
the first week. I got up early and walked to work in iridescent morning
light; we would serve a few customers and then sit idly and watch fat
flies fighting and making love through the siesta noons, a few more
customers and we would close up right after Mr. Coombs came in for
his eight o'clock coffee. There was time to walk in the evening cool,
enjoying the vibrating clarity of the air, feeling tired and pleasantly
philosophical in all that immense desert darkness, because of having
a job there, in a sense, belonging.

The other waitresses were Navaho girls who had learned their English sketchily, as a second language. I jumped at the chance to learn
some Navaho. (In the catalogue of accomplishments, the exceptional
ones are valued out of all proportion to their usefulness.) It would be
a wonderful tongue to "lapse into" at school. It was disappointing to
learn that Navaho is as tonal as Chinese, as inflected as Greek, as
glottal as Hottentot; a language without tenses, nouns, or verbs as
English knew them; without objective meaning as English practiced
it. In the end I had to be content just waiting table. Alas for the hope
of the scent of sagebrush blowing over the groves of academe.

By the end of the week, Navaho were beginning to drift in from the back country, and there were tourists stopping for sandwiches and coffee. The Indians would come in pairs, tall, potbellied men dressed in a Woolworth Western style, which they made theirs by wearing velveteen shirts—rust, peacock, and orchid—weighed with rows of dimes and quarters that were sewn in decorative patterns across their chests, huge turquoise belts, and long hair tied in the "butterfly" bun. They would come to us and speak their English word gravely, "Petsi." They never stopped to talk to the girls or to look around. They gave their money, drank their Pepsi's, and left, to disappear, even as I tried to follow them with my eyes, into the endless, empty landscape. Generations had lived this way in the desert, the descendants of those who had fled from the Spanish, their rich, rapacious conquerors, into the places where no one could follow them and survive. They got the horse and the sheep and the art of silver from that Spaniard and took his gifts into the desert to wed to their way. Bessie Tsosie, who had the tables by the window, told me that the People had always had these things, and this land. She couldn't imagine the People without sheep, horses, turquoise, or silver—things "ancestral."

In the early mornings, and at night after closing, I sometimes walked down the road toward Fort Defiance. It amazed me that people could live in a land where so little grew. Sheep are as rapacious as conquistadores. I soon learned that the Navaho wander by single families over hundreds of miles, moving often, to keep those sheeps' bellies full. Alice Yazzi told me that children spend the years of their childhoods alone, watching the family flocks which they drive to graze the mesas and the dry washes. "All time alone," she said. The earth and sky I saw were so overpowering that I pitied the little child who had to pass between them all alone; and I did see them occasionally, walking by in the distance, straight little figures between the great everlastings, with a stick against coyotes and their father's twenty sheep.

I'd forgotten that the idea of childhood as a separate time was not a universal idea. When a kid came in one day with his fly gaping wide and no underwear, I laughed to Alice about it, and then said half-jokingly, "Somebody should tell him to zip up before he falls out." She looked at me in wonder. "Are *his*." (His pants, his parts—if he

179

had wanted them another way he would have put them another way.)
They called themselves The People, after all.

Other Indians barely existed for them, and the Anglo was a pale
fanatic who walked around killing sheep to save the herd. But the
Anglo and his Second World War had been powerful enough to deal
a death blow to the Old Way. Husbands and sons had come back
from training camps and battlefields transformed by the white enemy-
brother, and had begun to agitate for electricity, English, and the germ
theory. I had forgotten about the Christian church.

We were clearing off the big table one afternoon when the radio
that had been blaring its standard rockabilly whine suddenly went into
syncopated, tremulous machine-gun sounds—Navaho. After some talk
there was a song, a haunting, warping, Oriental-sounding song in half-
pitches. I was sure I'd heard it somewhere before, but this was impossible. When it came to me, I burst out laughing. It was "The Old
Rugged Cross!" It sounded Oriental because in Navaho, tone dictates
meaning, whether a melody will or no. I tried to stop laughing at the
impossible sound of that hymn, to tell them that the laughter meant
no disrespect, but with every try I would get the giggles. When I finally
coughed out an apology, Alice only shrugged. "Anyway, I am not
Christian," she said.

"Not me too," Bessie echoed.

Lita and the two cooks who had come out to watch me laugh, shook
their heads. I had to laugh again.

"Well," I said, "neither am I."

"You ain' no Navaho." And the girl looked at me as though I had
stained something borrowed. The People and the Enemy, brother or
stranger.

I couldn't let things stay that simple for them. "No," I said, "and
not Tewa or Zuni. I'm something else, something called a Brooklyn
Jew."

"I never heard of that tribe," Alice answered skeptically.

I looked out the window over the dry reaches of the land. "Our two
people would have understood one another. My people once came
from a land like this, and they herded sheep too. You name everything
on your land for some event in the past, a miracle or wonder that
happened there. My fathers did that too. Navaho don't disappear into

the people of the pueblos or the white man. My fathers kept their ways too." They were quiet, still skeptical.

Then one of the cooks said, "You Anglo; you talk Anglo."

So I rared back and hit them with the "Shema," and then "Kol Nidre," which was what came to mind.

They listened in complete silence and, afterward, Bessie Tsosie said, "That sound like Tewa."

The fat cook snorted. "I speak Tewa, and that ain't Tewa."

"What did you say them people was?"

"In the beginning, Israelites, then Hebrews, then Jews."

I saw a sharp glance go between Alice and Bessie, and the two cooks were looking at one another. Having more than one name meant something to them. I was about to ask about it, but a bunch of tourists on their way to Fort Defiance came in, and we were busy all the rest of the afternoon.

When the last dinner customer left, I saw the girls whispering together, and when I walked up to them, they stopped. "What's up?" I asked. My voice sounded tired.

Alice said, "We was goin' to ask, could you an' Lita close up, cause we want to go to the Squaw Dance."

I'd wanted them to ask me to a Squaw Dance so much I had almost hinted at it. To the big Navaho socials came people from way back in the hills, the little scattered families and bands who were summering their sheep west of us. Many of them would travel for days to meet friends, eat, make love, trade horses, and dance and sing all night. The hosts laid in tremendous stores of mutton and fried bread and Anglo coffee. I knew that few Anglos had ever been invited to a Squaw Dance, and it would be ruinous to try to crash one, even though it spread out to seven acres of ground, with trucks and horses parked beyond and the courting strung out beyond that. But it was their dance, after all, so I agreed to close. As soon as I said yes, they turned and left.

Lita and I stood in the middle of the floor and looked at the nothing that was swept off, mopped up, put away. It took us until after ten to get things straight.

We left together, exhausted. Outside the air was cool, thin, and trembling, like glass. The night was black, the sky busy with all its stars; there were clouds of them—clustered, spilled, spread. There were more stars than I had ever seen before. Eastward from where we stood, and miles away, we saw the faint glow of reflected light from Gallup, and in the night wind, now faint, now clear, a series of rippled sobs: the sound of the chanting of the Squaw Dance. I tried to ask Lita why I couldn't see it; there was no light, no sign of movement over the great plain that barely rose and dipped away from us. Her English wasn't up to my question, so I finally just asked, "Where is the dance?"

"Ah," and she pointed with her lower lip, the Navaho way, out where it was, where I saw nothing but stars and the huge night overhead, brush, rock, and sand below. There wasn't even a sign of their smoke, although I knew that they would be building high fires by now. Lita could bear her separation no longer. With a quiet sound to free herself of me politely, she began to walk out into the emptiness to which she had pointed, and in a moment she had disappeared. I was alone, looking up at the crowded sky, wondering if my ancient fathers, Jacob or David, pursued in deserts and wise in the nomad way, didn't also camp so as to be invisible, lighting fires for their feast of mutton without even a wisp of betraying smoke coming between their pursuers and the friendly stars.

The next day we were up and running, the Fair gaining on us. Tourists and concessionaires and Indians from many tribes were setting up just outside the administration area. All of them wanted coffee and hot cakes and sausages and eggs cooked four minutes precisely. More coffee. More eggs.

"Hey, miss, these cakes is cold!"

"Hey, waitress, where's that order of beans and steak!"

"Hey, waitress!"

"Hey, wait-RESS!" The usual 1:30 slackening disappeared in a sea of soda, coffee, and "petsi." None of us were really good waitresses, but the girls who had spent all night at the Squaw Dance were particularly lead-footed under the pressure: endless nontipping Navaho; hot dogs: two with, three without; side of French fries; the troupe of a carnival comedy act asked for eight double orders of tomato juice with raw egg and Worcestershire. Campbell's soup calmly boiling over (cause-and-effect) to run all the way down the back counter. Five malteds. How do you make a malted? Grandma at her first Anglo restaurant and fifteen minutes of grunting and lip thrusts before I found out she wanted Alice to serve her, avoiding ritual pollution at my hand. I went and got Alice. ("I'm really Navaho or else they're really Jews, a stubborn, stiff-necked, lost tribe of Jews! Over the Bering Strait and the Mezzuzah fell in the water!")

What is graceful and natural at 7:30 in the morning and in no particular hurry, is misery at 2:00 in the afternoon with Bessie backing out, and three tables waiting, and the cook cursing the world in Navaho.

By 4:00 it's catastrophe. Alice was breaking dishes and I had gotten so far behind that customers were leaving, and the owner, working cash register during the rush, was glowering at me. The work kept building as the supper people began to come. The dinners got fancier, the table settings more elaborate, and I began to feel like the innocent bystander in an old Laurel and Hardy movie, someone suddenly caught up in a pandemonium he hadn't made and didn't understand. All this, and in the din you couldn't hear yourself think. Our customers were not city people used to living in low voices; and, of course, there was the radio. (Blood and Whiskey—eight choruses.) We closed at 10:30. Nobody said good night, and I didn't remember making it to my bed.

The next day was worse, a dish-clattering, spoon-dropping madhouse, a nightmare treadmill of noise and anger. When we got in one another's way, we growled, and the courtesy we had erected to save ourselves from one another fell away. Somebody got the idea that Bessie was taking tips off the other tables. God knows, there were few enough tippers in the crowd, and nobody had actually seen her; but the suspicion was planted; it grew and twisted in our tired minds until we found ourselves "covering" our tables against a thief, suddenly wary and unreasoning in exhaustion. The Fair was a week long and I'd wanted to see it, but we were closing late each night and I was too tired to go after work. As it was, I wondered if I could make it through the week.

And then it rained. It was a bitter thing to learn that the desert's rain was as brutal as its drought. A baked ground has no power to absorb its gift of moisture. The water rose in each little low place until it was in flood. It beat against the adobe earth; it fell sheeting solidly; exploding drops stung like shot; and I learned with my own arms and shoulders how the hard rock ridges could have been tunneled down into arroyos, the arroyos into incredible canyons. There was water flowing away to loss everywhere. The rain-eaten gullies poured water in torrents, but it was spilling away uselessly, all that needed water in the dry land, a tragic waste. We barely made it to work that morning without falling in the ruts that hadn't been there the night before. We opened late and served a couple of cowmen and a family whose car was bogged in a low spot. Later there were some Indian agents, but no one else, so after lunch hour we all went into the kitchen to see what the cooks had for us.

"Surprise for you girls," the fat cook said. "Right here."

It was "their" treat: fried bread and chili. The bread was a crisp-edged, edible platter of deep-fried dough, and the girls spread it thickly with green chili.

Alice turned to me. "You was tellin' about them people liven somewhere like us . . ."

"You mean the Hebrews?"

"Yeah, what they eat?"

"Well, they had mutton and prickly pear like yours, but more varieties of fruit . . ." And I bit with scholar's confidence into my bread covered with chili, chewed, swallowed. I had eaten fire. Fire erupted inside me. I felt my face go red, tears sprang from my eyes, searing heat traced paths into my head and down the whole track of my throat. Through tears running freely, I saw Alice and Bessie and Lita and the cooks rocking with laughter.

Then someone put a cup of hot coffee in my hand and said, "Drink."

"No," I gasped, "water."

The voice said, "Coffee, now. Hot. Water don' work."

I drank, and for a moment the heat of it only brightened the scalding pain of the chili, but then the burning leveled, then it lowered. I was still flowing tears: nose, eyes, mouth. "That was very good," I said, feeling foolish. It set us off again until we were all in tears.

"Your tribe," Alice said, "I don't know what they eat; I know what they don't eat."

I laughed wetly and held my coffee cup and looked out the window into the grim rain. There we were, enjoying my Anglo anguish while the urgent, vital, earth-feeding gift, all of it, was draining away.

I looked back at their faces, calmed and healed by the laughter, and I was wondering how I could have missed the single quality in my fathers which must have been the ground-tone of their lives: patience—with hunger and drought and such wasted plenty as this rain. We stood around quietly, eating and listening to it sound over our heads, more at peace with one another now that there was a chance to rest.

What a strange beauty the desert had. I liked it best at night. The Psalmist says God's greatness is from Everlasting to Everlasting. It was only a beautifully meaningless thought at home, because the world at home was man's creation and even time stood for a certain rate of depreciation. Here, there was Everlasting in any direction, as far as the eye could see; and through it, cutting it into east and west, north and south, a man-sized man might come, leading his sheep to where the grass was young and there was water. Abraham and Isaac knew the desert's beauty and tyranny, capriciousness and cruelty. I was learning an admiration for the strength a people must have who would wrest their lives from it. My Abraham and Isaac were American Navaho, who had never seen a Jew before.

In the late afternoon the rain stopped, and two hours later it was impossible to tell that it had fallen. Only a fresh scent hung in the air. The ground was dry; the brush was dry; the torrents that had flooded and poured downland to some distant river were gone. People were all around, putting out their heads and folding up their raincoats to go on where the rain had stopped them. There must have been a hundred people in the supper rush, and we didn't close till ten.

At quitting time I asked Alice if the Squaw Dance was still going on.

"No, they be one before end of grass here; soon people start south, away from high place, cold."

I was still hoping for that invitation, but I was afraid to press it, so I asked her what the steps looked like. She searched me for ridicule. None was there. "Here," she said, "I make it for you. . . ." And she showed me, but it wasn't much: a shuffle back and a shuffle forward, widening to the left so as to move very slowly in a circle. As she did the step she looked as embarrassed as Navaho permit themselves to look. "Step. This *step. Step* isn' *dance* . . ." Wrestling with the impossible Anglo words to try to tell me what I could never know from

185

my world of dances with *steps*. She had been forced for the first time to consider the poverty of her "step."

I said, "I can see that. I know a dance that looks like that. The joy in it is that the people are all together, stepping together and coming down with both feet on the same place as the person before them, and the dance grows in layers. The dancers make the layers together, as if they were saying: All together we make one."

"A dance of your tribe?" she asked.

"One of them."

"And you are not Indian?"

"No."

"Soun' like Indian to me."

The question of identity was put on the day before the end of the Tribal Fair. Because of overtime I would be able to get back to school in time for registration. I could leave when the Fair ended, hitch to Gallup, Gallup to Denver to New York—and no money spent staying over. As the Fair edged off, the crowds in the restaurant slackened, and on the last two nights we closed at nine.

There was a full moon. The Navaho God in charge of such things had lit my night, and I was grateful. We stood around outside and talked, waiting for the cooks to come out. There was supposed to be another Squaw Dance over near Fort Defiance but the girls were too tired to walk. The plan was to wait near the highway for a ride, and I guess I was hanging around hoping to be invited along when the car showed up. Their talk was the mixture of Navaho and English that they used when they were together. I was only half-listening.

"Who was shearing in the Fair for—" (the last lost to Navaho and to me).

"Johnny Begay an' his uncle, who—"

"Who was singin'?"

"They got—"

It reminded me of the Yiddish-English stew I spoke with my grandfather.

Lita put out her lip toward me after a while. "Her tribe—sheep— if they got song like . . ."

Navaho are a reticent people, and while the ancient Hebrews may have been reticent also, it's not noticeably present in modern Jews. I

186

was amused while I listened to them, and curious enough to speak first.

"Did you say sheep? Funny. I know a song about a lamb . . ."

They smiled, yes, in the moonlight; and I smiled, yes, took a breath and broke free. I sang "Chad Gadyo," and then translated it verse by verse, from the dog and the little lamb to God's battle with the Angel of Death. Singing got me drunk at this altitude, maybe; maybe freedom and the full moon; but I was loose-limbed and happy, and, before I knew it, we were all dancing a hora in the American desert to the very uneven strains of "El Yivneh Hagalil." They countered with two shepherd's songs.

I tried to feel them as a Navaho, but I couldn't. The trembling lifts and lowerings of their melody reminded me of a good cantor, hovering proudly, gently over his best notes. The songs were quiet, trembling, but clear; melody rising from the small voices between illimitable earth and illimitable sky might be the cry of my own people, reminding God, however gently and reverently, that One-and-Omniscient must still be instructed by man in the agonies that only man knows: mortality, imperfection, being so ceaselessly changed, and so quickly ended. I sang them a Psalm. Egypt had not yet taught us whips and slavery; Babylon had not yet made us dwellers in cities; ghettos had not yet walled us in. Afterward, we traded song for song.

Alice said, "In them songs, it's still singin' for God. You don' tell which God you singin' about."

"We were nomads," I said. "We couldn't take much with us, roaming the world. After a while we even had to leave our languages behind, and our dreams. We took our God. One God. Only One."

"Oh," she said, pitying me my poverty. "We got different song, different Spirit."

"I've heard a little about Changing Woman," I said, "and White Shell Woman, and Born of Water . . ."

"Well, White Shell Woman is Changing Woman, only change . . ."

"No," Bessie said, "White Shell Woman different. Song say," and they took the discussion away from me again.

Theology. I hoped I wasn't giving them revenge for the green chili. If I want disputations, I thought, I'll go home. Then, for no reason,

I remembered the kid with the open fly and no underwear. Blessed are the poor; they have the most stupendous pride. If you are poor and have a long history too, the pride gets perfected under the eyes of countless conquering armies.

Lita said, "Your tribe—make sand picture, like us?"

It's cold in the desert at night; I hadn't felt it before. Now I was getting dizzy looking at the stars—And I will multiply your seed as the stars in heaven . . . Well, that had been a different night and another land. I said, "My tribe wasn't like Navaho in some ways. We have one God, a spirit we believe is too great to name or picture. Names and pictures define things, limit them. He has no limit for us, no edge, no boundary. The only visible thing—is a book."

Two lights broke over the small hill to the south. It was a car on the way to Fort Defiance. It came up the road and stopped before the subtle signal of Lita's arm lifting only a degree from her side as they walked to the highway and I followed. I knew that I had been included without having to be told. I was learning. Now I could tell a silent affirmative when I heard or, rather, didn't hear one. We all got in the car and moved down the road.

I asked, "Who is giving the dance; I want to leave something."

"I take you," Bessie said.

So we went a distance, and then stopped and got out of the car in the middle of Everlasting, and we walked off the roadbed and into the desert. I stumbled over everything: white hummocks, ruts, stones. They walked easily. I was an Anglo, all right, a stranger.

In the American city of my birth I was a stranger too. I learned the city's ways until I passed, "assimilated" but for the strange intonations of my prayers, out of the ghetto. I never regretted the passage. Beyond that ghetto there are a thousand worlds to see. I was often lonely for the security of the "separated," but loneliness is a small price to pay, and the pain of it would have as much easing as I could give it. This night was such an easing. I didn't know the Navaho, not their language or beliefs. They didn't know Abraham or Isaac, but I wasn't lonely, stumbling over what they knew and expected. Why should I be; it was the biggest ghetto I had ever seen.

We went over a little rise in the land I thought was level and saw the big fires and the trucks—all of it in the downwind silence.

"Can Anglo understand Squaw Dance?" Bessie asked.

I smiled. "The tenements of the old ghetto teem with people, shriek, noise, and stench," I answered. "Washlines scar the sky between the houses. The streets shine with rotting fish skins. A man lives his swarming, impacted life without seeing one green thing growing from the ground. With such similarities, how could I miss?"

Sour or Suntanned,
It Makes No Difference

Johanna Kaplan

W HAT COULD MAKE SENSE? The Israeli playwright had such long legs it was hard to believe he was Jewish.

"Little girl," he said, coming up to Miriam with his very short pants and his heavy brown sandals that looked like they were made out of a whole rocky gang's Garrison belts, "little girl, which languages you are speaking?"

But Miriam had not been speaking to anyone: she was walking around the canteen with a milk container going gummy in her hand, and waiting by herself for all the days of camp to be over. There, in the rain, the entire room was sour from milk and muffled from rubber boots and raincoats. The sourness clung to her tongue and whined in her sinuses; locked away from rain and from mud was the whole camp. Soon, some other day, it would get sunny and Snack would be outside on long wooden picnic benches. If you made a mistake and sat down on these benches, splinters crept into your thighs, and if you sat down on the grass instead, insects roamed your whole body. For milk containers and Oreos, this was summer.

"Listen to me, please, little girl. Why you are walking away? I am asking only a simple question. Which languages you are speaking?"

"Right this minute?" Miriam said. "I wasn't speaking anything, can't you even tell?" How he could be smart enough to fix tractors or fool Arabs, let alone write plays, Miriam did not see, not that she said it.

"No, no," said the Israeli playwright. "Bring me please your counselor."

190

"She's right over there with the garbage," Miriam said, but because she was not at all sure of how words came out of his mouth or went into his head, walked over with him to Fran, who was going around with the basket.

"Amnon!" Fran screamed with her thin sparrow's voice, and immediately dropped the basket and the empty milk containers like people on TV shows who walk backward into sewers. Miriam had never seen her look so lively: Fran's flat paper face was like the front of a brand-new apartment house, and even though she was nineteen years old, did not wear lipstick. Instead, she got up very early in the morning, before any of the girls in the bunk, just to make sure that she would have enough time to stand in front of the mirror and put on all her black eye makeup. It was how Miriam woke up every morning: Fran standing at the mirror, patting and painting her eyes as if they were an Arts-and-Crafts project. Right after that, Gil Burstein, a Senior boy, went to the loudspeaker to play his bugle, and from that time on there was no way at all to stop anything that came after. Every single morning Miriam woke up in the cold light of a strange bed.

From behind all the black lines, Fran's eyes looked as if she was already set to start flirting, but even so her arm would not let go of Miriam's shoulder. It was just another thing that Miriam did not like. Simply going from one activity to another, the whole bunk walked with their arms linked around each other's waist; at flag-lowering, you joined hands and swayed in a semicircle; in swimming you had to jump for someone else's dripping hand the second the whistle blew; and at any time at all there were counselors standing with their arms around kids for no particular reason. They were all people you hardly knew and would probably never see again; there was no reason to spend a whole summer hugging them.

"Miriam," Fran said, smiling at her as if she were a new baby in somebody's carriage, "do you speak Yiddish?"

"What do you mean?" Miriam said. "Every second? I can, if I have to."

"It's all I ask you," Amnon said and, for the first time, smiled too; from way above his long legs, his face crinkled and seemed smaller, as if he wrote most of his plays right under a bulb that was going bad.

Fran said, "I don't see it. She's very quiet—her voice is much too soft."

"It's not making a difference. In America you have microphones falling from the ceiling even in a children's camp you're using only for summer."

"On that huge stage? Are you kidding? She'd fade into the woodwork. Nobody would even see her. I told you—she's very quiet."

"She is *not* quiet," Amnon said. "Not quiet, only unhappy. It's how I am choosing her. I see her face: unhappy and unhappy."

It was the last thing Miriam wanted anyone to think of. "Everything's perfect," she said, and with all the tightness inside her, quickly gave Fran a smile that tired out the corners of her mouth.

"Probably she wouldn't forget lines. But if she doesn't remember to scream when she gets up there, you're finished."

"I don't believe in screaming," Miriam said, but not so that anyone could hear her. Beneath the ceiling, there were Ping-Pong balls popping through the air like mistaken snowflakes, and behind her, some girls from her bunk were playing jacks. In the close, headachy damp, Miriam looked at Fran and hated her; in the whole canteen, that was all that there was.

It was getting to Amnon, too; the whole sour room seemed trapped in his face.

"Frances Wishinsky," he said as he watched Fran walk away with the basket. "In England are *boys* named Francis. In England, Wishinsky would already be Williams. England is a worse country, it's true. I have suffered there for eleven months."

Miriam said, "I read that it rains a lot in England," and wondered if the rainy day and gray, stuffy room were what was reminding him.

"Weathers are not so much important to me," Amnon said. "Other things I don't accustom myself so well. For me, terrible weathers I find not so bad as terrible people. For example, I think you're not liking so much your counselor Fran."

But Amnon was a stranger. "She docks us from movies a lot," Miriam said, "but with what they've got here, it doesn't even matter. The last time we went, all they had was Martians. An entire movie about a bunch of miniature green guys running around in space ships."

"You're not liking science fictions? Which kind of films you like to see?"

"All different ones. I just don't see why they can't find enough

192

movies to make up with real people's colors and sizes in them."

"Ah," said long, stretched-out Amnon. "Look here, Miriam, you have been ever in a theater?"

"A children's theater," said Miriam. "They took us once from school." The children's theater, in the auditorium of a big high school in Manhattan, was in a terrible neighborhood: in a building right across the way, a left-alone little girl was standing up completely naked, her whole dark body pressed right against the window in the cold. "She's only a little baby," Miriam had said, but there were people who giggled all the way through the play and couldn't wait to get outside again just to see if she would still be there.

"Children's theater," Amnon said, nodding. "This play we do is also children's theater. Only because it's in Yiddish, the children here will not understand. But what can I do? I am not choosing it, it's not my play, it's not my language."

It was not Miriam's language either, so she said nothing and watched Amnon stare around the room, more and more dissatisfied.

"It is not my medium. I am playwright, not director. What can I do? Many people are coming to see this play who are not interesting themselves in theater and they are not interesting themselves in the children. They are only obsessing themselves with Yiddish. For *this* they will come."

"For what?" said Miriam. "What are they all coming for?" There was a program every Friday night—nobody special came and nobody ever made a fuss about it.

"It will be performance for Parents Day," Amnon said. "In two weeks is coming Parents Day. You know about it, yes?"

But more than yes: Miriam was sure that any parents, seeing what camp was like, would be only too glad to take their children out of it. How much more than yes? It was the one day she was certain of and waited for.

Even before she got there, Miriam had a feeling that camp might not turn out to be her favorite place.

"It's terrific," was what her cousin Dina told her. But it was the same thing that Dina said about going on Ferris-wheel and roller-coaster rides in an amusement park. Coming home from school, her

193

arms full of all her heavy high-school books, she would tell Miriam, "Wait till you start doing things like that! Everybody screams and it's terrific."

"I get dizzy on the merry-go-round," Miriam said, and was very suspicious. Only a few years before, Dina used to lie around on her bed, setting her stringy strawberry-blond hair and reading love comics. With her extra baby-sitting money, she would buy different-size lipstick brushes, close the door in the bathroom, and completely mess up all her perfectly good but strange-colored brand-new lipsticks. Naturally, Dina's mother did not approve, but all she said was, "All the girls are like that. They all do it, and Miriam will be like that, too." But because she was not like Dina, who and what she would be like was in Miriam's mind very often; it was the reason she looked so closely at people's faces on the street.

"If you'd only smile once in a while," Miriam's aunt said, "you'd look like a different person." But her aunt was a liar, a person who spent her life thinking there was not much children could understand. Just to prove it once, when Miriam was in kindergarten, she gave her aunt a special lie test on purpose: on the day that Israel got started as a country, everyone had the radio on all day and many people put out little flags in their windows.

"Why do they have Jewish flags out?" Miriam asked, very pleased with herself because she had thought up the trick and knew the answer.

"What Jewish flags?" Her aunt's arms were all full of bundles and her fat, soggy face looked very annoyed. "Where? In the window? They're left over from Shabbas."

So Miriam saw she was right, but even when she got older said nothing, because she knew that for the times her mother was sick, she would still have to stick around her aunt's house, listen to some lies, and watch Dina fool around with her friends or do her home-work. Whenever her aunt bought fruit, she would say, "It's sweet as sugar," even if it was unripened grapefruit; and when she made lamb chops, she said, "Don't leave over the fat, it's delicious," even though it wasn't.

Sometimes, when Dina and her mother had fights, or when her uncle was yelling on the phone about Socialism, it would seem to Miriam very funny, so to stop them from noticing her giggles, and also to drown out the screaming, she would go into the living room and play the piano. She played from her head songs she had learned in Assembly or Hebrew School, or, even better, melodies that came into her mind like ideas: not real, official songs that people knew, but ones she made up on the spot and could change and fix up if she wanted. It was separate from things that she knew about and completely different from people; often when she played the piano, it seemed to Miriam like reading Chinese in a dream.

"I don't see what's so great about playing without piano books," Dina said. "You can't even read music. Just wait till you start taking lessons from Mrs. Landau and have to start practicing from *books*, then we'll see what a big shot you are."

"I'm not ever going to take from Mrs. Landau," Miriam said. "My mother says she's a very limited person who shouldn't be teaching anybody anything."

"Your mother tells you too much," said her aunt, but in what way this was true she had no idea. "Stalin" was what Miriam's mother called her uncle, and what she said about him was that he simply had nothing in his head and had no way of telling what was true from what wasn't. For this reason, all of his talk about Socialism was just noise-making, and all he was, she said, was a big talker who would believe anyone who was a bigger faker.

The other thing Miriam's mother most often told about was her own life when she was a child, but when she got to that, she talked only half to Miriam and half to someone who wasn't there at all.

"Who could have believed that any place could be as big as Warsaw?" is what she would say. "Streets and more streets, I couldn't understand it. I was the first girl from my town ever to be sent there to school, and I was so smart that when I got there I was the youngest in my class. But all my smartness did me no good—I looked at all the stores and the people, the streetcars and the houses, and all I did was cry constantly." This, Miriam never had any trouble believing; it was a habit her mother never got out of. Whenever the boiler broke down for a day, her mother cried all the time that she washed in cold water, and if the butcher ever sent the wrong kind of chicken, or one with too many pinfeathers on it, she cried for hours after and then started all over again when they were ready to sit down and eat it.

Still, with all the things that she did tell, when it came to camp Miriam's mother said very little.

195

"You'll meet children from all over. When Dina went, there was a girl from Winnipeg, Canada."

"Was her father a Mountie?"

"How could he be a Mountie?" her mother said. "Ask Dina, I think he was a dentist."

"Then I don't see the point."

"It isn't a question of point, Miriam. In camp you'll have grass and trees and get away. Here all you'd have is the hot city."

But it was the hot, empty city that Miriam loved. The flat, gritty sidewalks, freed of people, widened in the glassy, brilliant glare and in the distance fell away like jungle snow. Hard, strange bits of stone came bubbling up through the pavements: glazed, heated traces of another city that once drummed and droned beneath. In front of all the buildings, just where landlords had planted them, low, wiry shrubs pushed themselves out like rubber plants, and the buildings, rougher and rocklike in the ocher heat, seemed turned into brick that was brick before houses, brick that cooked up from the earth itself. From the sky, the city's summer smell sank into Miriam's skin, and walking along with the slow air, she felt her thin, naggy body skim away to the bricks and the pavement that streamed, in belonging, to the sun. What she would do with a bunch of trees, Miriam did not know.

Only dodge ball, it turned out, could have been invented by human beings: if somebody kept throwing balls at you, it was only natural to try to get away from them, and if you would just be allowed to go far enough, there wouldn't be a problem in the first place. This was what Miriam decided on for all games, so in basketball and volleyball she let other people push and scream for the ball as if there were a sale, and in badminton she watched them jump and yell, "Look at the birdie," like photographers with black cloths in an old-time movie.

Folk dancing was no improvement. "Right over left, left, step, right behind, left, step," Naamah the Yemenite folk dancer sang out instead of words in her dark Yemenite voice, while all her heavy silver jewelry sounded behind her, a rhythm as clear and alone as somebody cracking gum in an empty subway. In a way, Naamah was the most Israeli-looking person Miriam had ever seen; with her tiny, tight, dark features and black, curly hair, she flew around the room like a strange but very beautiful insect, the kind of insect a crazy scientist would let loose in a room and sit up watching till he no longer knew whether it was beautiful or ugly, human or a bug. Sometimes Naamah would pull Miriam out of the circle and sing the special right-over-left song straight into her ear as if *Miriam* were the one who couldn't speak English.

"The grapevine step," she screamed over the music. "It's necessary for all Oriental dance. Not just Israeli. Also the Greeks have it, and it's found modified with the Druse." But it seemed to Miriam like doing arithmetic with your feet, and finally Naamah let her go back into the circle, saying, "Westerners cannot do our dances. They do not have the body."

"I don't know what *she* acts so fancy about," Miriam said in a half-whisper to no one. "Everybody knows that when the Yemenites first came to Israel, they never even saw a toilet before, and when the Israelis gave them brand-new bathrooms, what they did was go all over the floor."

"Shush, Miriam," said Phyllis Axelrod, a tanned, chunky girl in Miriam's bunk. "Don't answer back. If you feel bad, just cry into your pillow. I do it every night and it works."

"What does your pillow have to do with it? That sounds like putting teeth under your pillow so that fairies will give you money."

"You get dimes that way, Miriam. Don't you even want the dimes?"

"If I want a dime, I ask my mother for it. I don't hide teeth and expect fairies, that's not something I believe in."

"My mother wouldn't just hand out dimes like that," Phyllis said, and Miriam immediately felt sorry. She liked Phyllis, though she often seemed not too brilliant; sometimes they were buddies in swimming, and once they snuck out of the water together because Phyllis heard a radio playing inside the little cabaña that was only for counselors. It was the reason that Phyllis cried into her pillow at night: she missed listening to the radio and knowing what was on the Hit Parade, and this gave Miriam the idea that when Phyllis got to be a teenager she might spend all her time hanging around cars in the street, holding up a radio and looking for boys. Sometimes Phyllis also cried because she missed her oldest brother, Ronny, who had just come back from Korea and immediately got married.

"You're not glad about being a sister-in-law?" Miriam asked her.

197

"It's not that great," Phyllis said. "I just wish I had my regular brother back again, no Army and no wedding." Still, she had a beautiful red-and-gold silk scarf that Ronny had brought back for her from Asia; once she wore it as a shawl when everyone, already in white tops and shorts, had gone out on the road to pick wild flowers for the Friday-evening table. On that road, outside camp but just behind the bunks, most of the flowers were tiger lilies, and when Phyllis bent over to pick one, she looked, with her straight black hair and broad brown face, like an Asian girl herself.

It was the closest Miriam got to "children from all over": except for a girl from Teaneck, New Jersey, everyone in her bunk was from New York, mostly from Brooklyn or Queens, both places Miriam had not been to. Still, from what they said, the only difference she could see was that they called Manhattan "going into the city," while people from the Bronx called it "going downtown." Besides Miriam, that meant only Bryna Sue Seligman, who, because she came from Riverdale, would not admit it. Everything that belonged to Bryna, her recorder included, had specially printed stickers, made up by her father who was in the printing business, that said in giant yellow letters BRYNA SUE SELIGMAN, and her favorite book in the world was the Classic Comic of *Green Mansions*. On the very first day they were in camp she asked Miriam, "Don't you wish you were Rima? Isn't *Green Mansions* the most beautiful thing you ever heard of?"

"It's OK," Miriam said; she could not see constantly going barefoot in a hot jungle and having to depend on birds when you had any trouble. But Bryna liked the whole idea so much that just in order to be like Rima, she kept her long red hair loose and hanging down her back, walked around without shoes when she wasn't supposed to, and blew into her recorder, which she couldn't really play, when she lay in bed after Lights Out. Whenever there was any free time, Bryna the bird-girl spent almost all of it either brushing her hair or dusting herself with bath powder, all in her private mirror with the yellow label, moving it constantly from side to side so that there was no part of her she would miss.

"I don't know what I'm doing here," she would say as she stared at herself and brushed all her red hair. "I'm going to be a bareback rider and my mother promised me a camp with horses."

"Jewish camps don't come with horses," Miriam said. "You should have figured that out for yourself. Besides, I thought you said you were going to be a poetess."

"Oh, I am one already," Bryna said. "Any time I feel like it, my father prints up all my poems."

"In yellow?" said Miriam.

"In any color I want. Once I wrote a poem about a rainbow and my father made every line in a different color."

This sounded like a bubble-gum wrapper and no poem, but watching Bryna trace around her suntan marks in the mirror, Miriam decided not to say it.

"I could be going horseback riding in Riverdale right now. Where I live, it's practically the country."

"Where you live is the Bronx," Miriam said. "On your letters you put Bronx, New York, and you even write in a zone number."

"It just so happens that lots of people put Riverdale-on-Hudson, and any time I wanted to, I could."

"You *could*," Miriam said, "but it would probably end up in a museum in Albany."

Because their beds were next to each other, Miriam and Bryna shared a cubby; with all Bryna's yellow labels shining through the shelves like flashbulb suns and the smell of her bath powder always hanging in the air, there was no place that Miriam felt was really hers. Her bathrobe and bathing suits hung like blind midgets in the way; they even got the Bryna bath-powder smell. It made them seem as if they were someone else's clothes and, like everything else in camp, had nothing to do with Miriam and her life.

"I could be in a special dramatics camp on a fat scholarship," Bryna said. "The only reason I told them no was that they didn't have any horseback riding, but at least *there* they would have had me starring in a million plays."

"I'm in a play here," said Miriam. It was turning out to be what she had instead of a cubby, and completely faking calmness, she waited for Bryna to faint.

Who could have believed that anyplace could be as big as Warsaw? Probably not anyone in the play: who they were, all of them, were

Jews, Nazis, and Polish partisans in the Warsaw ghetto—but where all the streets, more streets, and streetcars could be, the stage gave no idea and Amnon didn't ever say. On the stage was a tiny, crowded Warsaw filled with people who had phlegmy, sad Polish names— Dudek and Vladek, Dunya and Renya—just like in Miriam's mother's stories, and though they were always fighting and singing, there was no way for them to turn out not to be dead. Even the Yiddish song that Miriam had to sing at the end was about a girl who gets taught by her boyfriend how to shoot a gun, and who, one night in the freezing cold, goes out in her beret and shoots up a truckload of Nazis. When the girl is finished, she falls asleep, and the snow coming down makes a garland in her hair. Probably it also freezes her to death, though all it said at the end of the song was: "Exhausted from this small victory, For our new, free generation."

How could a girl who ran out all alone shooting soldiers let herself end up snowed under? And what was the point of people's running through sewers with guns if all they turned into was corpses? It was very hard to explain to Bryna, whose big question was, "Are you starring?"

"Nobody is," Miriam said. "It's not that kind of a play. Half of the time I fake being dead so that nobody finds out and they leave me."

"You mean you don't even *say* anything?"

"I do," Miriam said, "but what I say doesn't do any good. I'm a little girl in braids and I sneak out of the ghetto with my big brother."

Bryna said, "That's your big part? What do you tell him?"

"Nothing. While he's out getting guns, I hide and I hear some Nazi soldiers being so drunk that they start screaming out their plans. And that's when I immediately run back to the ghetto and warn everyone."

"Oh," Bryna said. "So the whole thing is that you copy Paul Revere."

"The only kind of Paul Revere it could be is a Jewish kind. Everyone dies and there are no horses."

Bryna said, "Some play! When we did *The Princess and the Pea*, I was the star, and then when we did *Pocahontas, Red-Skin Lady of Jamestown*, I was the heroine. In *this* moron play, I bet that there isn't even one person with a halfway decent part."

"My part's good," Miriam said. "I'm practically the only one who doesn't turn out to be killed."

200

"That's because you're a girl."

"No, it's not," Miriam said. "I don't even *know* why, that's just the way the play is."

"Listen, Miriam, I've been in a million plays. Little girls never get killed in any of them."

"Well, in this one they do. In this one the only people who don't wind up dead are me and Gil Burstein."

"You're in a play with Gil Burstein? You? Just let me come to rehearsals with you and I'll let you use my expensive bath powder any time you want."

"You can't get out of playing badminton just like that," Miriam told her. "That's only for people in the play."

But play or not, camp was still camp. At night, cold air flew in through the dark from Canada and mixed on the screens with mosquitoes; 6-12 and whispers filled up the air in the bunk and stayed there like ugly wallpaper. How could anyone sleep? Miriam played with the dark like a blind person in a foreign country: in the chilly, quiet strangeness, her bed was as black as a packed-up trunk, and her body, separate in all its sunburned parts, was suddenly as unfamiliar as someone else's toothpaste.

In the daytime, too, camp was still camp: a place dreamed up to be full of things that Miriam could not get out of. Whenever Amnon saw her face, he said, "What's the matter, Miriam?" It was how he kept starting out rehearsals.

"Look here, Mir*iam*," he would say, pronouncing her name the Hebrew way, with the accent on the last syllable. "Look here, Mir*iam*, say me what's wrong."

"Nothing," she said. "Everything's great."

"Why you are saying me 'Nothing' when I see you are crying— have been crying?"

"I wasn't, I'm not, and anyway it's not something I do."

"All girls are sometimes crying."

"Well, not me," Miriam said. "I don't believe in it." For a reason: it sometimes seemed to Miriam that if a person from a foreign country—or even a miniature green man from Mars—ever landed, by accident, in her building and by mistake walked up the six flights of stairs, all he would hear was screaming and crying: mothers screaming and children crying, fathers screaming and mothers crying, televisions screaming and vacuum cleaners crying; he could very easily get the idea that in this place there was no language, and that with all the noises there were no lives.

But crying was the last thing that Miriam thought of once she got to rehearsals. Still in camp, but not really in camp at all, it felt like a very long fire drill in school when you stayed on the street long enough to be not just a child on a line, but almost an ordinary person—someone who could walk in the street where they wanted, into stores, around corners, and maybe, if they felt like it, even disappear into buses.

As soon as Miriam put on her costume and combed her hair into braids, there was nothing on her body that felt like camp, and away from the day outside, nothing to even remind her. On the stage, Jews, Nazis, and Polish partisans were wandering through the streets of shrunken Warsaw, and in a corner, where in the real Warsaw there might have been a gas streetlight, a trolley-car stop, or even her mother's Gymnasium, Miriam and Gil Burstein played dead.

"What's the best can-opener?" Gil whispered.

"I don't know," Miriam said.

"Ex-Lax," said Gil, and laughed into his Ripley's *Believe It or Not*.

"Rest!" Amnon called out. In the middle of the stage, a Polish partisan had just kicked a Jew by mistake and suddenly the girl was crying. Nazi soldiers and Jewish resistance fighters started stampeding across the stage and charging, and Amnon, looking at no one, said, "Always they are playing Indians and Lone Rangers. It's for me completely not possible."

"Rest!" he yelled again; what he meant was "Break." Once, in one of his terrible-English times, Amnon said, "Ninety-Twoth Street Y," and Miriam, thinking suddenly of a giant tooth-building with elevators full of a thousand dentists, could not stop herself from laughing. Other times she thought of asking Amnon why she and Gil were the only ones who managed to end up not dead, but usually during breaks Amnon sat with his long legs stretched out across a whole row of chairs and just talked. He hardly even noticed who was concentrating on Cokes and who was paying attention.

"In Israel now it's not the right climate for art. You understand me?"

"It's much too hot there for people to sit around drawing pictures," Miriam said, and wished that the Arts-and-Crafts counselor could understand this too.

"No," Amnon said. "For me it means in my own country even people are not interesting themselves in my work. Here it's not my language, it's not my country, there is no place for an Israeli writer, there is nothing to do."

Gil Burstein said, "He could always take and autograph butcher-store windows or foods for Passover. I'm getting sick of this. Who wants a Coke?"

"Me," Miriam said, but knew the truth was that she didn't mind at all. From lying stretched out on the wooden stage for so long, her mind felt empty and the whole rest of her seemed dizzy in a sweet, half-sleepy way. Soon, in this dark auditorium, only the stage would be full of light and the plain wooden floor would hold up for an hour all the mistakes of a place that once had existed. A girl with braids and a too-long dress would run out into the mixed-up streets, and sitting in the audience with many other people, Miriam's mother would know what this place once was like way before and could tell how it actually looked. The girl with braids would sing the last song, and all Miriam's days of camp would finally be over.

Parents Day did not start out with Gil waking people up with his bugle; instead, from the loudspeaker in the office came records of Israeli songs—background music for the whole day, as if it were a movie. The melodies ran out quick and flying, and framed by the music, the whole camp—children, counselors, little white bunks, even trees and grass—seemed to be flying away, too, as if after all these weeks they were finally going someplace. Not exactly in the movie herself, Miriam went to the clothesline in the back, checking to make sure no bathing suit of hers was still left on it.

"Miriam, you better come in the front," Phyllis said. "There's a whole bunch of people here and they're looking for you."

Right outside the bunk, some girls in a circle were doing the dances that belonged with the melodies, and squinting there in the sun, practically trapped inside the dance, were Miriam's aunt and uncle, and with them a couple she had never seen before. The man, very short and with gray, curly hair, was dressed just like her uncle: Bermuda shorts, brown cut-out sandals with high socks, and a kind of summer hat that always looked to Miriam like a Jewish baseball cap. His wife, who was taller, had thick, dark braids all across her head, and though her skirt was very long in the sun, there was such a round, calm look in her clothes and on her face that Miriam was sure she had never had to be anybody's mother.

Miriam's aunt said, "There's my niece. Here she is. Miriam, this is Mrs. Imberman and that's Mr. Imberman, they came up with the car."

Miriam's aunt looked exactly the same: every part of her heavy face drooped like the bargain bundles she always carried, and stuck to her cheeks like decals were high pink splotches the color of eyelids—extra supplies of tears she kept up to make sure she was always ready.

"What are *you* doing here?" said Miriam. "You're not my mother. Who asked you to come?"

"Mr. and Mrs. Imberman came here to see a play," her aunt said, "and we're staying right next to them in the same little hotel, and it's not far, and they came with the car, so here we are."

"I didn't say what are *they* doing here. I said what are *you* doing here? And where's my mother?"

"Your mother couldn't come. She was going to write a letter and tell you, but I told her not to because I *know* you, Miriam, that if you knew about it you'd make a fuss, and now I see how right I was."

Turning around, Miriam stared at all the trees and grass that she had there: if they were so wonderful, the least they could do was pay attention to the music and do an Israeli dance.

"For you, your mother is your mother, but for me, she's still my little sister and there are plenty of things still that I have to tell her."

The trees, with all their millions of leaves, did not do even half a grapevine, and Miriam's uncle said, "Imberman, feel how hot it is already here and it's still early. Can you imagine what it's like a day like today in the city?"

"Hot," Mr. Imberman said. They stood there, the two of them, with their Jewish baseball caps, and Miriam thought how her uncle looked when it got too hot in his apartment: he would walk back and forth in his shorts and undershirt, fan himself with a newspaper, and say in Yiddish, "It's hot today in the city. Oh my God, it's hot!" If her uncle and midget Mr. Imberman got together, they could both walk back and forth in a little undershirt parade, fan themselves with two newspapers and, in between saying how hot it was, could have little fights about which countries were faking it with Socialism.

Miriam said, "If my mother were here, she would take me home."

"Why should she take you home? It's good for you to be outside and it's good for you to get used to it."

"Why should I get used to it if I don't like it?"

"Look how nice it is here, Miriam," her uncle said in Yiddish. "Look what you have here—a beautiful blue lake, a sky with sun and clouds that's also blue, big strong trees you can see from a mountain—with birds in them, wide, empty green fields with only grass and flowers. Look how nice."

"The lake is polluted," Miriam said. And it seemed to her that he was describing someplace else entirely—maybe a place in Poland he remembered from when he was young, maybe even a picture on a calendar, but definitely not camp on Parents Day. All the empty green fields were filling up with cars, the grass and flowers were getting covered over with blankets and beach chairs, and pretty soon the birds from the mountain would be able to come down and eat all the leftover food that people brought with them. Except that there was no sand, the whole camp could have been Orchard Beach.

"Let me tell you something," her uncle said. "First I'll tell you a little story about your cousin Dina, and then I'll give you some advice."

"I don't want any advice from you," Miriam said. "You can't even figure out which countries are faking it with Socialism, and if you're supposed to care about it so much, why don't you just write a letter to a person in the country and ask them? All they have to tell you is if they're selfish or if they share around the things they've got."

"Straight from her mother," said Miriam's aunt. "With absolutely no sense that she's talking in front of a child."

"And don't think I can't understand it either. My mother calls *him* Stalin."

Mrs. Imberman said, "Sweetheart, are you in the play?" She bent her head in the sun, and for a second her earrings, turquoise and silver, suddenly turned iridescent.

"Yes," Miriam said and looked up at her: somewhere a man with a sombrero and a mustache had gotten off his donkey and sat down in the heat to fold pieces of silver so that Mrs. Imberman could turn her head in the sun and ask questions of strange children.

"Ah hah," Mrs. Imberman said, "an *aktricekeh*. That's why she's so temperamental."

"I am *not* an actress," Miriam said. "I never was one before and I don't plan on being one again, and what I'm definitely not going to be is an explorer, so I don't see why I have to get used to so much being outside."

"Listen, Miriam," her uncle said. "Let me tell you what happened with Dina in case she was embarrassed to tell you herself. It happened that Dina didn't feel like giving in her chocolates to the counselor, so she put them under her bed and only took out the box to eat them when it was dark in the bunk at night and she was sitting up in the bed and setting her hair. She figured out that if anyone heard any noises she could tell them it was from the bobby pins and curlers."

"Such a woman's story," Mr. Imberman said in very Polish Yiddish. "I didn't know, Citrin, that you knew such women's stories."

Miriam's aunt said, "You know my Dina. She could set her hair anyplace."

"Anyway, what happened, Miriam, is that once somebody put on a light and saw her, and that's how she made some enemies, and that's why she didn't always love it here."

"I don't set my hair," Miriam said. "It's the one thing I'm lucky about—it's naturally curly, and now I have to get it put in braids for the play, so good-by."

"So quick?" her aunt said. "Good-by, Miriam, look how nice and suntanned she is. Nobody would even know she has a sour face."

Just behind the curtain, Miriam waited bunched up with everyone in their costumes on the hot, quiet stage. Sunk into the scenery, not even Gil Burstein was laughing, and all the Jews, Nazis, and Polish partisans were finally without Cokes in their hands. Amnon, still walking around in his same very short pants, gave Miriam a giant Israeli smile that she had not seen before and could not feel a part of. He said, "Now I don't worry for the play and I don't worry for the audience."

But why anyone would worry for the audience, Miriam could not see. All through the play she kept looking out at them—a little girl in braids and a too-long dress who would end up not dead—and could not tell the face of anyone. Who they were she did not know and did not want to think about: people, probably, who cried and screamed in their houses, fanned themselves with newspapers, and took along hard-boiled eggs if they went in a car for a half-hour.

The stage did not stop being hot, and lying stretched out on it with Gil Burstein, it seemed to Miriam that they were playing dead right underneath a gas streetlight from a stuffy summer night in the real Warsaw. Way above their heads hung a fat yellow bulb that was surrounded by a thousand insects. In all different shapes and sizes, they kept flying from the empty blue darkness backstage toward this one single glare, till the bulb, ugly and unshaded in the first place, seemed to be growing a beard as sweaty and uneven as a grandfather's. Back and forth, over and around, the different insects crowded and buzzed, all with each other, so that, watching them, Miriam started to wonder whether these were Socialist bugs who believed in sharing with each other what they had, or else bugs who were secretly wishing to keep the whole bulb for themselves and, by politely flying close together, just faking it.

In the woods, just outside the finished-off Warsaw ghetto, the night was bitter cold. Miriam stood up to sing the song of the girl with the velvet face who went out in the blizzard to shoot up the enemy, and knew that no matter how big the stage was, when she sang and played the piano there was nothing about her that was quiet at all. " 'Exhausted from this small victory, For our new, free generation,' " Miriam finally sang, and the curtain fell over her head like the garland of snow on the girl who could end up snowed under.

Left all by herself behind the curtain, Miriam heard crying coming from people in the audience: they were the parents of no one in the play, but were crying now because, like somebody's stupid, stupid parakeet, they had learned how to do one thing and one thing only. If anyone yelled out "Budgie!" right now, the entire audience would immediately get up and start flying. Amnon would fly out, too, and Bryna, always a bird-girl, ran up now to Miriam on the stage and right then and there began chirping.

"Guess what?" she said. "Now there are *two* people in my family with red hair. My mother got her hair dyed and I didn't even know it was her till she came over and kissed me."

"Oh," Miriam said, and because she could see that Bryna had big things on her mind—counting redheads—listened from somewhere for the sound of Amnon's voice letting out his one Israeli-parakeet line: Say-me-what's-wrong-Mir*iam*, Mir*iam*-say-me-the-matter. Standing there on the stage, a little girl in braids and a too-long dress who would end up not dead, Miriam promised herself that never again in her life would anyone look at her face and see in it what Amnon did, but just like the girl who could fake being dead, she would keep all her aliveness a secret.

The Place

Edith Konecky

THE PLACE was what we always called my father's place of business
which occupied the entire twelfth floor of a skyscraper on Seventh
Avenue and Fortieth Street. I hated going there but sometimes it was
unavoidable. Now that I was getting so tall it was even more unavoidable than usual as my father had decided that I could begin wearing
his garments instead of imposing on his friend Irving Walkowitz, who
made Dolly Dimple Preteen Frocks. I had hated going there, too, but
my mother insisted that I had to try things on to make sure they were
becoming. Becoming what, I always asked. My father's garments were
certainly not becoming. They were designed for wealthy matrons and
cost a lot of money and came in sizes all the way up to obese. No
matter how carefully these dresses were fitted to me, I always felt like
a freak in them as they were designed to have bosoms in the tops and
hips in the bottoms, items I was unable to supply.

The chief reason I hated going there, though, was that it was the
one place where I entirely lost any connection with the person I thought
I was and became someone totally different, the boss's daughter, a
complete stranger to me, an identity I bumbled around in feeling
inadequate, graceless, tongue-tied, and false. How I envied David,
whose knickers came to him in a cardboard box. It was one dumb
conversation after another with people who treated me as though I
were her royal highness, a princess with a pea-sized brain.

"GOLD-MODES, Max Goldman, Inc.," were the first words to greet

209

you when you stepped off the elevator, though there had already been a conversation with Joe, the elevator starter. Directly above these words behind a sliding-glass partition, wedged between switchboard and typewriter, was the carefully coiffed head of Millie Brodsky, receptionist, deliverer of the next words:

"Well, will you look who's here. How nice to see your fresh young face, dearie."

"Glunk," I said, trying to decide whether to enter left to the showroom or right to the shipping room. I opted for left in the hope of fewer conversations. The showroom was a big plush blue and gray room with partitioned cubicles where buyers could sit behind little glass-topped tables writing orders while models waltzed before them parading the current line and salesmen hovered, buttering them up and touting the wares. No customers today. Just Mr. Feldman and Mr. Cohen, two of the salesmen, swapping the usual dirty stories.

"Good day, Madam," Feldman said, rearranging his crotch. "What can I sell you today?"

"Glunk," I said, not breaking my stride. Through a draped opening into the models' brightly-lit cave, all mirrors at one end, racks down the other on which hung the demonstration goods. Three models, Marlene, Charlotte, and Laverne, sitting in their underwear smoking cigarettes and drinking coffee out of soggy containers, watching themselves in the mirror through glazed eyes.

"Glunk," they said to me and "Glunk," I replied.

Into the office, a dreary place full of arithmetic. Bookkeepers making entries in ledgers, making out payrolls, making deposits. Secretaries typing letters saying, "Re: your order #359685 we regret that we are unable to supply our model #0058B, size 18, of which you ordered three (3) in champagne and are therefore substituting the sauterne, a popular shade. Please let us know if this is acceptable or if you would prefer the liebfraumilch."

Off this beehive, my father's office, a narrow, windowless, no-nonsense chamber with a big leather sofa and an even bigger desk, a coat tree sprouting his hat, overcoat, suit jacket, umbrella, his rubbers neatly toed-in at the roots. I peer in. My father is going over some sketches of the upcoming line with the designer, Gus Quinzanero. Both men are in their shirtsleeves, but there the similarity ends. My father's shirts are always white, often white on white (a man who can't get enough white in his shirts, a conservative dresser), the knot of his tie loosened. Gus Quinzanero's shirt is blush-hued, his impeccable flannel trousers are held high by broad scarlet suspenders with pictures of the king, queen, and jack running up and down them.

"Crap," my father is saying. "The same warmed-over crap. Cancel that one."

"You're a real bitch today, Max," the designer says amiably. "But so what else is new?" He is the only one of my father's 150 employees allowed to talk to him that way. My mother says this is because he can go almost anywhere tomorrow and get as good a job or better and what's worse could go into business for himself and compete with my father.

My father looks up as I slide quietly into a corner of the sofa. His face rarely lights up at the sight of me; if it changes at all it is to sour even further.

"I'm busy now," he says. "Can't you see I'm busy?"

I go into the factory, first to the cutting room where the cutters, important men, are slicing around patterns through layers of costly fabrics. One false move and *disaster*. There is another huge room where the operators sit going blind over their whirring-machines and several smaller rooms for patternmakers, drapers, pressers, and etc. The factory people are mainly foreign born, Italian and Jewish, and it is they who treat me with such subservience and respect that if I were not too busy gagging I would leap onto a table and cry, "Workers of the world unite. Break the chains that bind you!" With a nod to Melanie. Though according to my father, they are already solidly united and between the crooked unions and the gangster truckers and the Mafia landlords, he is being squeezed like a blackhead out of his own business that he built with the honest manly sweat of his brow in order to give employment and livelihood to all these people who would otherwise be starving and lying around in gutters with festering sores on their eyes, to say nothing of leprosy and cholera.

"Your father makes his wealth off the backs of the honest poor," said Melanie when she learned he was a Capitalist, an employer. "Every mouthful you eat is carved from the flesh of some simple, honest, upright, noble, exploited workingman coughing his lungs out in an unsanitary shop. For shame."

Though to be perfectly honest it was not an unsanitary place and the only people I ever actually saw sweating there were my father and the pressers, and pressers would sweat anywhere, as would my father.

I am waiting for my mother who is going to select my wardrobe for the coming season. She will go through the tens in the stockroom and select what she thinks is becoming, and then Sophie, the seamstress, will appear with pins in her mouth and her hands full of chalk and rulers and together they will decide on the necessary adjustments. Meanwhile, I have nothing to do. I forage around, looking for treasures to swipe. I collect scraps of material off the cutting-room floor and stuff them into a bag. These I will take home and, in a month or two, I will throw them away as I can never think of anything to do with them. While I am browsing among the cuttings I hear my father, finished now with Gus, screaming at Agnes Mortadella. Agnes' bailiwick is a cage at one end of the cutting room. Inside the cage are shelves filled with boxes of buttons and belt buckles. This is the trimming department, and Agnes, a short stocky woman with a nervous mouth and intense eyes, is in charge of all the trimmings, a responsible position. My father is yelling at her now about some buttons.

"They break, fa chrissake. They break right in their fingers. How the hell do you expect them to sew them on, fa chrissake, they're made of matzos."

"I'm sorry, Mr. Goldman, I'll take care of it."

"Who the hell sold you these lousy buttons?"

"I'll look it up, Mr. Goldman."

"Don't you know? You're supposed to know these things, what the hell do you think I'm paying you for?"

"Here it is, Mr. Goldman, it's Superior-Rivkin. I'll call them right now."

"Goddamn sons of bitches, tell them we sew on buttons, fa chrissake, not crackers. Don't you feel the goddamn buttons before you buy them?"

"I can't feel all the buttons, Mr. Goldman, be reasonable."

"Don't stand there and tell me to be reasonable, fa chrissake, I'll throw you right out in the street where you came from."

By this time Agnes Mortadella was crying hard enough to make my father feel better so he stormed off to some greener pasture. I sidled up to Agnes' cage.

212

"Oh, hello, Allegra," she said, blowing her nose.

"Why don't you quit?" I said. "How can you let anyone talk to you that way?"

She was on the telephone. "Just a minute," she said to me. "Hello, Superior-Rivkin? Let me talk to Bernie." She put her hand over the mouthpiece, waiting. "Your father can kiss my ass on forty-second street. Hello, Bernie, you shit. That lot number WJZ127936. No, not that one. Yeah, those. Oh, you know about it, whadderyou some kind of jokers up there? You better haul your ass right over here. Not four o'clock, right now, or I'll throw the whole entire order back at you and good-bye Superior-Rivkin where Gold-Modes is concerned." She banged the two halves of the phone back together.

"Now, what were you saying, darling?"

"Why do you stand for it? Why don't you work for someone else? There must be lots of jobs for someone of your caliber."

She gave me a long look while she chewed her underlip.

"They're all the same," she said. "You think any of them are any better? You know how long I'm working for your father? Since the day he went into business. I was only fourteen. I lied. The way I was built I could get away with it."

"I don't understand it," I said. "I *have* to put up with him. I *can't* quit. But you."

"Oh, he's all right, your father," she said. "That's just the way he is. But fair's fair, he's someone you can count on."

"What do you mean?"

"He's as good as his word: He's an honest, dependable man."

She really liked my father. It was beyond all understanding, though I strained.

"You know what he makes me feel?" she said. "Safe. My own old man was much worse. He used to chain me to the bed so I wouldn't go out and screw with boys. After him, your father's a saint."

My mother appeared then so I took my leave of Agnes and went back to the models' room where we got down to business. Forewarned, I was wearing a clean, practically new slip, but oh, how I hated to stand there in it between selections with all sorts of people, including Cohen and Feldman, walking through. No privacy and everyone a kibitzer.

"That looks very nice on you," my mother said. "Don't you think that looks nice, Allegra?" I glanced into the mirror and made a face. "Well, do you like it or don't you? You're the one who's going to have to wear it." What was there to like about a dress? Or to choose between one and another? Either it had buttons down the front or it didn't; it had a collar or it hadn't; the collar was pointed or round. No choice when it came to sleeves as all Gold-Mode frocks, except in summer, had bracelet-length sleeves, very flattering to skinny arms and bony wrists.

Sophie, who was kneeling on the floor at my hem, said through the pins in her mouth, "That's *her* color. Look how it makes those eyes look."

"It's a little too long in the front," my mother said.

"I'm fixing. Don't worry, it'll be perfect."

"Stand up straight," my mother said.

My father, passing through, glanced at me with genuine displeasure and, not pausing, said, "*Shlump.*"

"Shoulders back, stomach in. Like this," Marlene said, coming out of her coma and actually getting up off her chair to demonstrate standing.

"Gorgeous," Feldman said on his way to the toilet. "Next year she can come and model for us."

"It isn't right up here," my mother said to Sophie, pointing at my chest where the dress, as always, sagged dispiritedly.

"We'll put darts," Sophie said, sticking in pins. "I'll tell you what you should do, Allegra darling, just in the meantime till they grow in. Wear a brassiere and stuff it with socks."

"Glunk," I said.

"I mean it. You'd be surprised how many women do it."

"Fa chrissake," I said.

"How do you like this nice polka dot, Allegra? It has a nice little bolero jacket. It'll cover up your chest."

"How the hell many dresses are you getting her, fa chrissake?" my father said, passing through now in the opposite direction. "Where the hell is she going in all those dresses, on a cruise?"

"Yeah? Where the hell am I going?" I said.

"All what dresses?" my mother said. "Two, so far."

214

"You know what that number sells for?" my father said of the polka dot with the little bolero. "Forty-nine fifty wholesale. That's a hundred-dollar number in Bonwit's."

"I don't even want it," I said.

"Never mind," my mother said for my father's benefit. "Your cousin Sonia never walks out of here with less than eight dresses at a time. You're certainly entitled to two, the boss's daughter."

"I have a headache."

"You want some aspirin, darling?" Sophie said. "I have some aspirin right by my machine."

"Walk away, Allegra. Let me see how that looks walking."

I did my cripple's walk.

"Allegra! Walk properly."

I did my regular walk. My father, slashing through the room again in time to observe this, said, "Can't she learn to walk like a human being?" Once again Marlene tore her eyes from her reflection and rose to her feet, this time to give lessons in walking.

"Like this, dear heart. Make believe you've got a book on your head. Wait, I'll go find an actual book and you can try it," she said, vanishing gracefully.

"She's at the awkward age," my mother said to anyone present who happened to need that information.

"I've got a splitting headache," I whimpered. Socks on my chest, books on my head, what next?

"Little Cuban heels, that's the ticket," Feldman said on his way back from the toilet. "That number don't look so hot with saddle shoes."

"Where's Cohen?" I said. "We're waiting for his comments."

"Oh, look at this smart little spectator sport, Allegra," said my mother. "It's just the thing."

"Not one single goddamn book in this entire place," Marlene reappeared to say. "Nothing but phone books and ledgers and they're too heavy."

"Thanks anyway," I said, "but we're finished walking."

"Try this on, Allegra," my mother said. "It's adorable, even though it isn't your size."

"We'll put darts," Sophie said.

"I can't get out of this one," I said. "It's pinned to my slip. Maybe to my flesh. I think I have to throw up."

"Stop that nonsense, Allegra," my mother said while Sophie unpinned me from the little polka-dot number. "It's all in your head."

"It is?" I said, and a moment later it was out of my head and all over the cute little bolero.

PART 4

The Past as Present: The 1980s

The Shawl

Cynthia Ozick

S TELLA, COLD, COLD, the coldness of hell. How they walked on the roads together, Rosa with Magda curled up between sore breasts, Magda wound up in the shawl. Sometimes Stella carried Magda. But she was jealous of Magda. A thin girl of fourteen, too small, with thin breasts of her own, Stella wanted to be wrapped in a shawl, hidden away, asleep, rocked by the march, a baby, a round infant in arms. Magda took Rosa's nipple, and Rosa never stopped walking, a walking cradle. There was not enough milk; sometimes Magda sucked air; then she screamed. Stella was ravenous. Her knees were tumors on sticks, her elbows chicken bones.

Rosa did not feel hunger; she felt light, not like someone walking but like someone in a faint, in trance, arrested in a fit, someone who is already a floating angel, alert and seeing everything, but in the air, not there, not touching the road. As if teetering on the tips of her fingernails. She looked into Magda's face through a gap in the shawl: a squirrel in a nest, safe, no one could reach her inside the little house of the shawl's windings. The face, very round, a pocket mirror of a face: but it was not Rosa's bleak complexion, dark like cholera, it was another kind of face altogether, eyes blue as air, smooth feathers of hair nearly as yellow as the Star sewn into Rosa's coat. You could think she was one of *their* babies.

Rosa, floating, dreamed of giving Magda away in one of the villages. She could leave the line for a minute and push Magda into the hands of any woman on the side of the road. But if she moved out of line they might shoot. And even if she fled the line for half a second and pushed the shawl-bundle at a stranger, would the woman take it? She might be surprised, or afraid; she might drop the shawl, and Magda would fall out and strike her head and die. The little round head. Such a good child, she gave up screaming, and sucked now only for the taste of the drying nipple itself. The neat grip of the tiny gums. One mite of a tooth tip sticking up in the bottom gum, how shining, an elfin tombstone of white marble gleaming there. Without complaining, Magda relinquished Rosa's teats, first the left, then the right; both were cracked, not a sniff of milk. The duct-crevice extinct, a dead volcano, blind eye, chill hole, so Magda took the corner of the shawl and milked it instead. She sucked and sucked, flooding the threads with wetness. The shawl's good flavor, milk of linen.

It was a magic shawl, it could nourish an infant for three days and three nights. Magda did not die, she stayed alive, although very quiet. A peculiar smell, of cinnamon and almonds, lifted out of her mouth. She held her eyes open every moment, forgetting how to blink or nap, and Rosa and sometimes Stella studied their blueness. On the road they raised one burden of a leg after another and studied Magda's face. "Aryan," Stella said, in a voice grown as thin as a string; and Rosa thought how Stella gazed at Magda like a young cannibal. And the time that Stella said "Aryan," it sounded to Rosa as if Stella had really said "Let us devour her."

But Magda lived to walk. She lived that long, but she did not walk very well, partly because she was only fifteen months old, and partly because the spindles of her legs could not hold up her fat belly. It was fat with air, full and round. Rosa gave almost all her food to Magda, Stella gave nothing; Stella was ravenous, a growing child herself, but not growing much. Stella did not menstruate. Rosa did not menstruate. Rosa was ravenous, but also not; she learned from Magda how to drink the taste of a finger in one's mouth. They were in a place without pity, all pity was annihilated in Rosa, she looked at Stella's bones without pity. She was sure that Stella was waiting for Magda to die so she could put her teeth into the little thighs.

Rosa knew Magda was going to die very soon; she should have been dead already, but she had been buried away deep inside the magic shawl, mistaken there for the shivering mound of Rosa's breasts; Rosa clung to the shawl as if it covered only herself. No one took it away from her. Magda was mute. She never cried. Rosa hid her in the barracks, under the shawl, but she knew that one day someone would inform; or one day someone, not even Stella, would steal Magda to eat her. When Magda began to walk, Rosa knew that Magda was going to die very soon, something would happen. She was afraid to fall asleep; she slept with the weight of her thigh on Magda's body; she was afraid she would smother Magda under her thigh. The weight of Rosa was becoming less and less; Rosa and Stella were slowly turning into air.

Magda was quiet, but her eyes were horribly alive, like blue tigers. She watched. Sometimes she laughed—it seemed a laugh, but how could it be? Magda had never seen anyone laugh. Still, Magda laughed at her shawl when the wind blew its corners, the bad wind with pieces of black in it, that made Stella's and Rosa's eyes tear. Magda's eyes were always clear and tearless. She watched like a tiger. She guarded her shawl. No one could touch it; only Rosa could touch it. Stella was not allowed. The shawl was Magda's own baby, her pet, her little sister. She tangled herself up in it and sucked on one of the corners when she wanted to be very still.

Then Stella took the shawl away and made Magda die.

Afterward Stella said: "I was cold."

And afterward she was always cold, always. The cold went into her heart: Rosa saw that Stella's heart was cold. Magda flopped onward with her little pencil legs scribbling this way and that, in search of the shawl; the pencils faltered at the barracks opening, where the light began. Rosa saw and pursued. But already Magda was in the square outside the barracks, in the jolly light. It was the roll-call arena. Every morning Rosa had to conceal Magda under the shawl against a wall of the barracks and go out and stand in the arena with Stella and hundreds of others, sometimes for hours, and Magda, deserted, was quiet under the shawl, sucking on her corner. Every day Magda was silent, and so she did not die. Rosa saw that today Magda was going to die, and at the same time a fearful joy ran in Rosa's two palms, her fingers were on fire, she was astonished, febrile: Magda, in the sunlight, swaying on her pencil legs, was howling. Ever since the drying up of

Rosa's nipples, ever since Magda's last scream on the road, Magda had been devoid of any syllable; Magda was a mute. Rosa believed that something had gone wrong with her vocal cords, with her windpipe, with the cave of her larynx; Magda was defective, without a voice; perhaps she was deaf; there might be something amiss with her intelligence; Magda was dumb. Even the laugh that came when the ash-stippled wind made a clown out of Magda's shawl was only the air-blown showing of her teeth. Even when the lice, head lice and body lice, crazed her so that she became as wild as one of the big rats that plundered the barracks at daybreak looking for carrion, she rubbed and scratched and kicked and bit and rolled without a whimper. But now Magda's mouth was spilling a long viscous rope of clamor.

"Maaaa—"

It was the first noise Magda had ever sent out from her throat since the drying up of Rosa's nipples.

"Maaaa . . . aaa!"

Again! Magda was wavering in the perilous sunlight of the arena, scribbling on such pitiful little bent shins. Rosa saw. She saw that Magda was grieving for the loss of her shawl, she saw that Magda was going to die. A tide of commands hammered in Rosa's nipples: Fetch, get, bring! But she did not know which to go after first, Magda or the shawl. If she jumped out into the arena to snatch Magda up, the howling would not stop, because Magda would still not have the shawl; but if she ran back into the barracks to find the shawl, and if she found it, and if she came after Magda holding it and shaking it, then she would get Magda back, Magda would put the shawl in her mouth and turn dumb again.

Rosa entered the dark. It was easy to discover the shawl. Stella was heaped under it, asleep in her thin bones. Rosa tore the shawl free and flew—she could fly, she was only air—into the arena. The sunheat murmured of another life, of butterflies in summer. The light was placid, mellow. On the other side of the steel fence, far away, there were green meadows speckled with dandelions and deep-colored violets; beyond them, even farther, innocent tiger lilies, tall, lifting their orange bonnets. In the barracks they spoke of "flowers," of "rain": excrement, thick turd-braids, and the slow stinking maroon waterfall that slunk down from the upper bunks, the stink mixed with a bitter fatty floating smoke that greased Rosa's skin. She stood for an instant at the margin of the arena. Sometimes the electricity inside the fence would seem to hum; even Stella said it was only an imagining, but Rosa heard real sounds in the wire: grainy sad voices. The farther she was from the fence, the more clearly the voices crowded at her. The lamenting voices strummed so convincingly, so passionately, it was impossible to suspect them of being phantoms. The voices told her to hold up the shawl, high; the voices told her to shake it, to whip with it, to unfurl it like a flag. Rosa lifted, shook, whipped, unfurled. Far off, very far, Magda leaned across her air-fed belly, reaching out with the rods of her arms. She was high up, elevated, riding someone's shoulder. But the shoulder that carried Magda was not coming toward Rosa and the shawl, it was drifting away, the speck of Magda was moving more and more into the smoky distance. Above the shoulder a helmet glinted. The light tapped the helmet and sparkled it into a goblet. Below the helmet a black body like a domino and a pair of black boots hurled themselves in the direction of the electrified fence. The electric voices began to chatter wildly. "Maamaa, maaamaaa," they all hummed together. How far Magda was from Rosa now, across the whole square, past a dozen barracks, all the way on the other side! She was no bigger than a moth.

All at once Magda was swimming through the air. The whole of Magda traveled through loftiness. She looked like a butterfly touching a silver vine. And the moment Magda's feathered round head and her pencil legs and balloonish belly and zigzag arms splashed against the fence, the steel voices went mad in their growling, urging Rosa to run and run to the spot where Magda had fallen from her flight against the electrified fence; but of course Rosa did not obey them. She only stood, because if she ran they would shoot, and if she tried to pick up the sticks of Magda's body they would shoot, and if she let the wolf's screech ascending now through the ladder of her skeleton break out, they would shoot; so she took Magda's shawl and filled her own mouth with it, stuffed it in and stuffed it in, until she was swallowing up the wolf's screech and tasting the cinnamon and almond depth of Magda's saliva; and Rosa drank Magda's shawl until it dried.

Remnants: A Family Pattern

Ivy Goodman

B ASED ON THE DISORDERLY instructions of Lake Greenberg, named
after her grandmother, Laka Brint Shromm, who died the Friday
before the Monday Lake was born.

Front pockets: Cut two hand-sized squares and set aside.

The twins, Drancha and Deeta Shromm, were born to Yaakov
Harold and Laka Brint Shromm during the early winter of the couple's
third married year. Drancha, who decided which identical outfits the
two would wear each day for their first nineteen years; Drancha, who
became a nurse; Drancha, who missed second grade due to a severe
back problem which left her bedridden for seven months; Deeta, who
passed second grade alone but repeated it to keep Drancha company
when she returned to school; Deeta, who married a weak-hearted man;
Deeta, a sobbing arthritic who said she would just die without tele-
phones, who just died.

Legs: Double cloth and cut two. Stitch inner leg seams separately,
then baste at center front, crotch, and center back. Join permanently,
easing fullness and matching notches.

Laka Brint, born on the new continent and accustomed to jewelry
from her father's shop and black silk stockings embroidered with white
sheaves of wheat, shaved her head during the sweat of a scarlet fever.
The only hair that grew back was a very soft down.

With seven brothers, Yaakov Harold Sh_____, a journeyman
tailor, fled his homeland to escape conscription and marauding bands
of Cossacks. On the new continent officials certified some of the eight

224

youths Shromms, some Shramms, though they were all brothers from the same region, all sharing the same harsh name together. Yaakov was a Shromm and with his savings bought a fringed horse and matching fringed wagon and peddled housewares through the provinces. When he stopped at the town of P_____ and sold Mrs. Brint a metal colander and spools of gray and red thread at her open kitchen door, he met Laka, who was bald but beautiful. They were married that fall.

As a wedding present, Mr. Brint gave the couple a hillside men's clothing and tailoring shop with a two-story apartment above the store. Its kitchen led onto a dank yard and a cobblestone alleyway.

"Personally, I'm surprised that anyone married her," Brint said to his brother over poached fish at the luncheon after the ceremony.

"Don't complain," his brother said.

"Did I? Oh, no. I'm thankful."

After they returned from a weekend trip to a seashore resort, Laka cooked all morning, every morning, and at noontime set the table for a hot meal on Yaakov's treadle sewing machine. She crocheted seashells found on her honeymoon onto the borders of doilies and napkins. She organized flatware. She planted moss in iron pots around the yard walls. At night when she slid off Yaakov's thimbles, he whispered to her and stroked her tufts of hair.

Zigzag topstitching sprawling the entire finished garment: Zigzag, everywhere.

Laka conceived during the fourth month of her marriage, and from the tenth week of pregnancy on, was incapacitated. Her separating pelvic bones painfully pinched her sciatic nerve, her breasts tingled, she was constipated, and both ankles and seven toes swelled. She lay on the floral chaise lounge in the second parlor, silver needles, crochet hooks, skeins of pastel baby yarn, three yards of ribbon trim, and white linen infant smocks, merely basted together and waiting to be sewn, scattered around her. Her mother, upright on a straight-backed arm chair, started a new row of her knitting and said, "Be stern with yourself, Laka. Sit up. Start stitching."

Laka moaned and readjusted a towel over her head. "Oh, close the drapes, Mother. The light bothers me. What did you just say? I didn't hear you."

The baby kicked often and terrified Laka when she felt the shape

225

of its foot bulging out of her stomach. "Yaakov," she whispered in the middle of the night, catching her breath again, letting go of the brass rung of their headboard. "What is it growing inside me?"

The delivery was speedy but left the imprint of forceps on the baby's head. Named Dovid, he refused his mother's aching breasts and alone in his crib, trembled. He didn't sit until he was two, he didn't walk until he was three, and when he talked at four, his words vibrated with his shudders.

Detail, front pockets: Hem all edges. Add zigzags.

With Dovid creeping about between her legs, Laka swelled with two more babies. Four feet kicked at her, and she doubled over. She napped and dreamed her stomach was glass and saw an eight-limbed creature growing bristles and claws within her. "A monster," she told her mother. To Yaakov she said, "I hope for something better," and handed him Dovid.

"I blame the doctor," Yaakov said to everyone, to strangers whose clothes he tailored. While Laka rested, Dovid twitched in the store among pants legs and knocked over boxes.

"Twins?" Laka asked after laboring. A nurse handed her scowling Drancha and the tinier Deeta. "Twins?"

"It's compensation," Yaakov told her.

When the cranky twins learned to walk, Dovid learned with them. He stumbled through the house shaking dead fowls in his hands, trailing feathers, laughing while the twins ran to hide in their closet. They were frightened of trees; he waved branches in their faces and made them look up at elms. "Red birds," he would say, pointing skyward. They would glance up, expecting cardinals, and shriek when they saw only treetops.

His mother swatted him with brooms and said, "This hurts me more than you, Dovid," while in a garbled voice he shouted out, "Police! Help! She's beating a cripple."

Fob pocket: Cut a one-inch slit at rib level and bind with strips of folded cloth (see diagram). Then stitch shut because the watch is lost.

Ephraim was Laka's and Yaakov's fourth-born, a pale, bruise-kneed child who walked the town holding his left forefinger in his right hand. At three, he was the first in the family to wear eyeglasses. For close work, such as copying in his blue copybooks, he also peered through a small magnifying lens. While the twins uprooted moss in the yard and Dovid cursed them from the kitchen steps, Ephraim lay on his stomach in the alleyway behind them, reading newspapers and selected copybooks. He was run over and killed there by a man driving a convertible.

Back pocket: Cut crookedly then stitch on left rear without bobbin thread. When the pocket falls off, reattach quickly with a straight pin.

Marvya was the baby Shromm, the last-born, the reckless one who stuffed tailored trousers meant for delivery down sewer grates, tore her coat on fences, owned a bicycle, was a Yo-Yo champ until she died, and during high school, played basketball. She never married. "But I won't die a virgin," she told her mother on the morning of her nine-teenth birthday. For five years, until a friend explained it, she believed the stain of her menses was the blood of dying babies. "What luck, another miscarriage," she shouted monthly from her bedroom.

Over vest: Use a thick, opaque fabric, but to no avail because the back and fronts are too short, and there aren't any fasteners.

They were a wonderful family, standing arm in arm by the kitchen wall in their photographs. But one was killed, one went crazy, two were exactly alike, not much even when added together, and the last was defective to begin with. The wigged mother died a slow death of diabetes, the father a quick one, causes unknown, while he slept beneath a quilt made of trouser cuffs.

Body: Cut on the bias, across years. Stitch sides and shoulders, and let hang from a wire hook, diagonally.

Laka squared: her hips, her shoulders, her head, and the short straight banged wig she tugged over it. She rolled endless jelly rolls. "You look like sponge cake," Dovid said to her. "Everything you cook tastes bad." With sugar-gritty hands, she pulled his hair and shouted, "Go out to a restaurant." The twins set the table and argued over where the forks belonged. Hiding in the bathroom, Marvya made her Yo-Yo walk like a dog. Ephraim lay dead in the sitting room. The next day they would bury him.

Yaakov, the tailor-merchant, shortened trouser legs and counted silver dollars hoarded in a button chest. Customers stopped by, ordered suit coats, skimmed newspapers in the shoe department. "Ephraim used to read to me, but now he's gone," Yaakov complained. "So read

227

yourself," answered Dovid, powdered white with lime, jerking suddenly out of the basement doorway. "My Dovid," Yaakov announced. "He's grown." Then, remembering the daily folded in his hand, he traced a line of newsprint and said, "I still can't understand this language." But in piles of weekday papers he discovered articles (with photographs) and salvaged them: wearing skimmers and floral lounge pajamas, the twins at a Brownie garden party; the twins lost on their way home from a movie theater; Dovid in a car he tried stealing; Ephraim and the way he died; Marvya in the dark with three luminous Yo-Yos; an older Marvya with a basketball.

"You're a gentle man, Yaakov," Laka said to him. "But you gave me too many of the wrong children, and I make you suffer for it."

"But I help you," he said.

"Oh, yes. You cut their fingernails."

"I'll take care of the twins," he answered. "And find the men to marry them."

But they didn't want to marry. Drancha said, "I'm going to be a nurse," packed her suitcase, and left for a hospital. "No, I won't go with her," Deeta said after Dovid suggested it. "I hate blood and white, and the dead upset me." She entered a typing pool. "Look for a man," her mother warned. "If you want a life ahead of you."

She was scared of men. On a hay ride a boy who tried to kiss her had knocked her glasses off. "You'll break them," she said.

Then seven years later a fellow merchant telephoned Yaakov. "My nephew's here, suntanned from a stay at the beach. What are your daughters up to?"

Drancha was on ward duty, Marvya on a ball court, Deeta, a twenty-three-year-old, by herself in the sitting room. "You're going," Laka told her.

She stood in the corner of the kitchen near the wash tub. "Certainly, I'll always remember that tartan plaid dress, her prominent teeth, and those glasses. Gold-framed. What glasses," the nephew, Harmon Greenberg, later said.

"I hated him at first," Deeta said. "It was a danger signal, but despite it, we were married."

And on the wedding trip he went wild in a tunnel under the Hudson where his car stalled. When he kicked the wooden bumpers, wood chips blew in his eyes. He gritted his teeth loose. Through tears he

228

looked at his wife and said, "Why did I ask you? I don't know why I asked you."

She answered, "But it's done with. You asked me."

Drancha married an engineer, mechanical. His name was Silverstein.

And Marvya didn't marry. "As desirable as I am," Dovid said. "Who wants her?"

But men gave her flowers as big as onions and stood on their hands and knees in front of her in the parlor. She refused them. She spun out Yo-Yos, drew them back. She dribbled basketballs. "I'm talented," she said. "I want to tour. I'll demonstrate in the aisles of department stores." Then she took a job at the five-and-dime as a night clerk and alternate cashier.

"Oh, Marvya, why not marry someone?" Yaakov asked. "Have babies."

"Please, if only for my sake," Laka said. "I'm dying."

"You? You're as healthy as a horse," Dovid told her.

But her eyes blurred, her head throbbed, her ears itched. She cooked a boiled dinner. "It's constant pain," she said. Three days later she fell over in a diabetic coma.

Deeta rushed in and cried at Laka's bedside with her year-old baby, a daughter, Ellen. Drancha arrived with her husband Bert from another city. In a white-bibbed uniform and white-winged cap, she ordered everyone out of Laka's bedroom. "You'll pay me for private duty," she told Yaakov; then to the others she said, "What Mother needs most now is quiet."

When Deeta got home, she coaxed Harmon into bed and conceived another baby.

In the projection booth in the theater where he worked, Dovid howled then switched to the second reel of a grainy pornographic movie.

Yaakov, in the kitchen, said to Bert, "At least he has a trade now. Those projectionists even let him join their union."

Laka awoke, saw cobwebs in her eyes and a white-capped shape before her. "Who are you?" she asked.

Ignoring her, Drancha leaned into the hallway. "Everyone, listen. She's snapped out of that coma."

But for months she slid in and out of it, and with each emergence, the world looked dustier. "Deeta," she said one afternoon, "Yaakov just told me. You're in your twenty-ninth week, and I didn't even know you were pregnant."

"But it doesn't show on me." Deeta lighted another cigarette. "I'm so worried about you that I can't eat anything."

"But your baby," Laka said. "What will happen to it?"

It was tiny and furry, a girl, born three days after Laka's midsummer funeral. "Named Lake," Deeta said. "In Mother's memory."

"What good does that do?" Dovid asked. "She's a baby. Mother's dead. Who'll take care of us?"

"I look to Marvya," Yaakov said, blotting his forehead with the ribbons of mourning.

But Marvya wouldn't leave her room. She sat in the dark, in the heat, in a pile of Yo-Yos. "I don't understand," she said. "Where's Mother gone? I don't want to work in the five-and-dime. I don't want to live this way."

Yaakov covered her hands with his. "Time heals. And we have to help each other."

"Ha! No, never." Gasping, she laughed at him in horrible spasms. "No, I won't slave for you, the two of you. That's what you're asking. And I won't marry a man to avoid it. Shift for yourself. Everyone for himself, do you hear me?" She pounded her walls and hurled Yo-Yos. "I won't do it. I refuse to. Do you hear me?"

"Dovid, what to do with her?" Yaakov asked.

"Have the court commit her."

Deeta and Drancha came once, but no one else visited Marvya at the state institution. "Grow up," Drancha said. "Life is hard. Face reality."

Marvya said, "Please excuse me. I have to use the bathroom."

A year later they were notified when she hanged herself from the curtain rod in the women's shower stall.

"Sick," Yaakov said. "She put herself in and out of misery."

He and Dovid, two bachelors, lived alone, ate in restaurants, and teased their waitresses. While Yaakov slept late, Dovid unlocked the store and shaking, sweating, waited on morning customers. Every night he sat sprawled alone in the bright booth off the balcony of a narrow theater. "What I know about life and love," he said, "I know from these movies."

On alternate weekends, Deeta left her husband and in her car packed her children, chickens, and pots. Laka's old kitchen warmed with reheated soup while Yaakov sucked wings and Dovid complained, "It's even worse than Mother ever made." Deeta's two girls, Ellen and Lake, cracked wishbones then riffled through trouser racks and played in the storeroom. Yaakov pried open button tins, handed out quarters. When the girls were old enough, he made them guards, watching for shoplifters. "If you spot one, signal. Use these words." Then he spoke to them in his old language.

The morning after Yaakov died, Dovid found him, his tailor's hands crusted, clutching bedclothes hand-sewn from pants scraps.

"I can't believe it," Dovid sobbed in Deeta's living room. "My only friend is gone."

"Where can Dovid live?" Deeta asked after the funeral. "He can't stay alone. If he just tried to make coffee, he'd burn himself."

"Not with me. No thank you," Drancha said. She took a train back to her husband, their family.

Deeta said, "I don't want him to, but what choice is there? Can he live with us?"

Her husband Harmon fluttered in his bedroom. "Oh, all right," he finally said. "But he has to give us something. In repayment."
Sleeves: Cut two, stitch sides, ease caps into armholes. Turn cuffs. These are hands for the pockets.

Harmon Greenberg was a sickly man who lived a convalescent life in an attic above his family: a wife, two daughters, and later, his brother-in-law, Dovid. "Men make mistakes in life," he said. "Personally, I should never have married. Stomach problems, heart problems." He patted himself. "I don't like anyone. So why should I love them?"

Bert Silverstein, son of a milkman, sent himself to college, married, and had a son and a daughter. "At least we can choose our friends," he told Drancha, "if not your family." Often he demanded things: cake, ice cream, sex, sandwiches. But on generous days he dropped coins in a salt box, and Drancha spent them on fur coats and a beach house for the children, Carl and Candy.
Inside left front pocket: Add lining and buttons.

"I'm a widow with these girls to raise," Deeta said after Harmon died and left her. "I'm thankful for my brother, who provides us with money." Then Ellen went away to school, and Deeta telephoned very early every morning. "What are you up to? Who are your boyfriends? You're my life, you and Lake. Except for both of you, I would wish, like your father, that I hadn't married."

In the kitchen Dovid spilled his milk. "Good girl," he said when Lake brought him another. "Do as he says," Deeta told her. Each week she set up folding chairs then tore tickets at the back door for his Thursday stag movies. But she mapped her days to avoid him. She ran from floor to floor; she hid in closets and behind furniture. "She's a loon," Dovid laughed. "Like our Marvya." Nearby with a heavy-heeled shoe in her hand, Lake wanted to slay him. From a crack in a door, she watched him clean his toes with a knife while he cried over radio melodrama.

"What Dovid wants, I anticipate," Deeta said. She ran to him with hot dogs, comics, hash-browned potatoes. "I do it for money, for both of us, Lake." Then rubbing her hips, she complained of arthritis.

And Ellen never came home again. "I know better than that," she wrote Lake in a letter. They never learned what happened to her, though Deeta thought she married a lawyer.

Recommended fabric: Winter worsted, but in the left pocket, slip a scrap of tropical.

When arthritic Deeta fell from a ladder and died, only Dovid and Lake troubled to bury her. "Where are the others?" Dovid asked. His feet slid and kicked gravel down the path at the cemetery. "But Lake's here. My Lake. You'll take care of me?"

"No."

And she disappeared to a warmer part of what once was called the new continent.

Afterword of Dovid Shromm, survivor, a palsied man in worsted top-stitched sport clothes: pants, pocketed gown, and skimpy over vest. He lives in a black room, an album lined with photographs (see drawing and caption, back of pattern envelope): So this is what she makes of us. That crazy girl. Who knows what happened to her. But she asked for it, when she left us. We're her family.

Note from Lake, stapled to the flap of the pattern envelope: Though the fabric tears, unravels, you can't forget things. You can never run away. They're behind me; they are with me. I am wearing them. They're my family.

The Opiate of the People

Lynne Sharon Schwartz

DAVID, WHEN HE WAS FEELING HAPPY, used to dance for his children. The war was over, the Germans defeated. Once again he pranced across the living room raising his knees high in an absurd parody all his own, blending a horse's gallop and a Parisian cancan. Lucy, his youngest, would laugh in a high-pitched delighted giggle— David looked so funny dancing in his baggy gray trousers and long-sleeved white shirt with the loosened tie jerking from side to side. His business clothes. He wore them all the time, even at night after dinner. Sometimes at breakfast he wore his jacket too, as he stood tense near the kitchen sink, swallowing orange juice and toast and coffee, briefcase waiting erect at his feet.

When he stopped dancing he would smooth down his wavy dark hair modestly and catch his breath. "You like that, eh?"

Lucy was six. She wanted her father never out of her sight. She felt complete only when he was present.

"Yes. But why can't we have a Christmas tree?"

Lucy was eleven. They had a large family with many cousins, nearly all older than she was, and always getting married. At the big weddings the band music was loud and ceaseless. After the fruit cup and the first toast to the newlyweds, at some point during the soup, the popular dance tunes would give way to a rapping syncopated rhythm with the pungency of garlic and the ringing tone of a shout or a slap. The grownups leaped away from their bowls to form circle within circle,

233

holding hands. Anna, Lucy's mother, was a leader. She was heavy, but moved nimbly. Her head would bounce up and down to the music as she pulled a line of dancers under a bridge of arms.

"You can do it too, Lucy," she called out. "Come on."

And the circle opened, hands parted to let her in.

David did not dance these dances. She saw him at the edge of the circle, his tie neatly knotted, observing keenly, lighting an olive-colored cigar.

He waltzed. He waltzed with her mother, the two of them floating with stiff, poignant grace. His face, sharp-boned, alert, was tilted up proudly, his hand spread out flat against Anna's broad back.

"But why," Lucy asked, "can't we have a Christmas tree?"

"Don't you know yet?" He was annoyed with her. "It's not our holiday."

"I know, but it doesn't really mean anything," she protested, leaning forward against the front seat of the car, flushed with the champagne they had let her taste. "It's only a symbol."

She could see the edge of his smile and knew he was smiling because she had used the word "symbol." She felt clever to have charmed away his annoyance.

In the morning she accosted Anna.

"Why is he so against it?"

Anna did not turn to face her. She was putting on mascara in front of the mirror, and the tiny brush she held near her eyes looked like a flag. "Because they made him wear a yellow arm band when he went to school."

"But . . ." Lucy said. These bizarre facts tossed out at chance intervals made her feel another world, a shadow world, existed at the rim of their own. "But that was in another country."

"It makes no difference. The tree is the same."

She grasped that David was keeping something back from her, something that touched herself as well as him.

"What was it like when you were growing up?"

"We were poor," he said. "We worked, we studied. We lived where your grandmother used to live. It was very crowded."

"No, I mean before that. Before you came here." She whispered the last words shyly, for fear of somehow embarrassing him.

"I don't remember."

"You must remember something. You were the same age as I am now, and I'd remember this even if I moved away."

He tightened his lips and turned to the bridge game in his *New York Times,* sharpened pencil poised.

Saturdays, driving into the city to visit aunts and uncles, they sped through shabby neighborhoods with once-fine brownstones, down streets where men in long black coats and fur hats and unruly beards shambled in the path of oncoming cars. They had hanging curls in front of their ears, delicate straggly locks that gave Lucy a feeling of weak revulsion.

"It's Saturday," said David, "so they think they own the streets. No one should drive." He had to brake to avoid a group of teen-aged boys with unnaturally soft, waxy skin. Rolling down the window, he shouted, "Why don't you stay on the sidewalk where you belong?" Then, "Someone's got to teach them a little English," he muttered at the steering wheel.

"You sound like some ignorant peasant." Anna's eyes followed the group of boys sorrowfully. "Why can't you live and let live? And drive like a normal person?"

"Filthy refs," muttered David.

"What are refs?" asked Lucy from the back of the car.

"Refugees," said Anna.

With an inner leap of glee, she thought she spotted an inconsistency in David's thought, usually so logical. "Well, weren't you one too?"

"That's different."

"How?"

"They have no business looking like that. They give the rest of us a bad name. Lenin was right. Religion is the opiate of the people."

"Who was that again?" Lucy asked.

"Lenin. Vladimir Lenin."

"Oh, what kinds of things are you teaching her!" Anna exclaimed. "Leave her be."

He pronounced Vladimir with the accent on the second syllable. Lucy made a mental note of that.

"What was it really like back there?"

"I don't remember."

But she was fifteen now, strong with adolescence and nearly full

235

grown; she stood over him and waited while he turned the pages of his newspaper.

Finally he yanked off his glasses and looked up at her. "You really want to know? They came around at night and chased people out of their houses, then set them on fire. You were afraid to go to sleep. They sent you to the army for twenty years. They said we poisoned their wells and chopped up their babies. So everyone came here. One at a time. First Saul, he was grown up, then Peter, then Avi, then I came with my parents and the girls, because I was the baby. It stunk on the boat. People vomited all day long. All right?"

"All right, all right." She cringed and drew back from the brittle voice shouting at her. "All right, forget it."

Most of the time, if secretly, David was very proud of the way his life had turned out. Considering. He was proud of having married a good-looking American-born girl he fell in love with in high school. Anna kept a good home and took excellent care of the children, and when they went out to meet people she was just right, friendly and talkative, never flirtatious. He took pride in that wholesome, free tone of hers, so American. She was loving to him, though she might tease grudgingly if she thought he wanted her too often when the children were small and wore her out. Spirited, also: they disagreed often and loudly over petty things, but never over big things like right or wrong or decency or bringing up the family.

He was proud of their children, their house, and their car. He was proud most of all, though he would never have admitted this, of his perfect English, no trace of an accent. At school he had imitated the way the teachers spoke and stored their phrases in his keen ear. Walking there and home he moved his lips to practice, and when other boys ridiculed him he withdrew silently, watching with envy as they played in the schoolyard. He used to play too, back there, but now, after the trip and the ordeals of a new household in an incomprehensible land, he could not launch into games. His father never wearied of saying the four boys must work very hard to show they were as good as the others. They might not have much, but they had brains better than anyone else's. In this country lurked fortunes waiting to be snatched up by boys with heads on their shoulders. After two years of effort

David's speech was flawless, untainted, and he hoped that with the language embedded in his tongue he could do whatever he chose, that no one need ever know how foolish and awkward and alien he had once sounded.

His older brothers fared well too, and their English was fluent. More than fluent: they spoke with style and a feeling for diction and phrasing. Luckily, the family was gifted that way. But when he listened to them now, Avi and Peter and Saul, he detected a flavor of the foreign born. He couldn't place it—not any mispronunciation or inflection, but something. He wished them no ill, these nattily dressed brothers with flourishing businesses, but secretly he was glad to have been the youngest, best able to reshape the habits of his tongue. His sisters, already grown when they arrived, and pushed promptly into factories so that the boys might go to school, would always sound foreign. The oldest, Ruth, who had diligently mastered her English grammar, still kept an antique musical lilt, like a catch in the voice. It could take him unawares, even now, and bring unwanted, artesian tears to his eyes.

Their second night off the boat, an old uncle who had come two years earlier sat David's father down at his oilcloth-covered kitchen table. Along with countless bits of advice and lore, he instructed that the paper to read was the New York Times, and so David's father bought it daily, sending one of the boys out to the newsstand in the gray of morning with pennies in his pocket. The words "New York Times" were among the first in David's vocabulary.

Each night after ten hours bent over ledgers in the asphyxiating office of a Hebrew school, his father sat at the kitchen table learning English from the New York Times. No one was permitted to disturb him while he studied. Every two or three minutes he would look up a word in a black leather-bound dictionary, wetting the tip of his forefinger to turn its pages, which were thin and translucent like the wings of an insect. He was insect-like too, a small man with a small pointed graying beard, lined skin, and a black skullcap on his head. His shoulders were narrow and rounded. The sleeves of his white shirt were rolled up and his arms spread out over the open newspaper as in an embrace. When David recalled him now it was in that pose, hunched in the unshaded glare of the kitchen light, studying as he used to, except back there it was the Talmud and here the Times. He

237

remembered how, near midnight, finished at last, his father would gather the family together and summarize for them the contents of the major articles in the *New York Times*. Then they could go to bed. And remembering, David was assailed by an irritating mixture of pride and shame and nostalgia, which he tried to evict from his soul.

David went to law school. He was a dashing sort of young man, he liked to think, and he enjoyed reminiscing about his bravado in taking the bar exam. Hardly studying, for he was busy driving a cab in his spare moments, he passed the first time, usually a practice run. He hadn't even bothered checking the school bulletin board, but waited to find out the results from the list published in the paper. The achievement of passing the bar exam was rivaled only by the achievement of having his name printed in the *New York Times* for all the world to behold. It was while studying law that he came to appreciate and to love—though David was not a man who acknowledged love readily—the peculiar genius of his adopted country, and to feel deep affinities with it. He responded to the Constitution as an artist to an old master. A nonbeliever, in this he believed; he even admitted to feeling awe for the men who wrote it, though again, he felt awe for his fellow man rarely, all expectations and assessments of humanity having been incised on his spirit early on, in the years of the yellow arm band and the pogroms. He learned the Constitution by heart and remembered it—this was another of the achievements he took pride in. And on days when the Supreme Court (pinnacle of his favorite branch of government, for he was, by temperament and heritage, judgmental) struck down or upheld laws in accordance with David's interpretation of the Constitution, he was happy, and on those days he danced for his children.

He and Anna had two boys close together and then, ten years later, Lucy, who received the doting care spent usually on an only child. The boys turned out well, David thought, one a lawyer himself, the other an engineer; they married suitably nice girls, made money, and gave him and Anna grandchildren. And Lucy, he trusted, would be fine too. She had his head, quick and secret and sharp; though her temper flared up easily, like his, she didn't stay angry long. She could take care of herself and she was good-looking, which was important for a girl. All in all, a fine American girl.

Sometimes she made him worry, though. It was one thing to quote Marx and Lenin with righteous indignation—David did that himself— but another thing to take them seriously, especially here where matters were arranged otherwise, and it was just as well, too, for people like themselves. Lucy took it all far too seriously. She joined groups and recklessly signed her name to endless, dubious petitions. When David and Anna refused to sign or even to read those long sheets of paper she waved in their faces—for once you had signed your name who could tell where it would end up, no country is perfect, look at the business with McCarthy not so long ago—she got angry and made passionate speeches. And if David defended the way things were, she retorted that his narrow-minded and selfish mode of thinking was precisely the trouble with this country. Moreover, he and Anna were stodgy, unadventurous, needed broadening. "Why don't you travel? You have the money. Go to Europe. See another culture, how other people live, for a change."

"I've been to Europe," said David with a sneer and a tilt of the head. Then he saw her face turn hurt and ashamed, and he was sorry.

By middle age, when the boys were already young men, he had grown slightly pompous. He could hear it in his voice, but felt he was entitled to it, after all. He had made a certain amount of money, had a certain status, and spoke with an authoritative air, in well-sequenced paragraphs expounding his views to his thriving family on political, economic, and moral issues. Anna, who had heard it all before, put-tered in the kitchen; sometimes she would interrupt with a remark or anecdote that she mistakenly thought illustrated one of David's points. But the boys listened respectfully, and even Lucy looked raptly atten-tive. Now and then he might stop to paraphrase something for her in simple terms and she would nod gravely, but he was never sure how much she understood. His vocabulary was studded with multisyllabic little-used words he enjoyed hearing spoken in his own voice. Among his favorites were "belligerent," "manifest," "deteriorate," "pejorative," complex words he had deliberately mastered years ago, words difficult not only to say but to use accurately, and on occasion he adjusted his thoughts to create opportunities to utter these words, feeling pride at the casual, indigenous way they slid off his tongue.

Sometimes he wished he had made more money. He was never

239

quite sure he had made as much as his father had expected, when he told him, so many long years ago, to learn and show he was as good as the others. But since his father was dead now he would never know exactly how great those expectations had been. In any case, he had made enough. It was only when he thought of his brothers, and of childhood friends who had made more, that such doubts pricked him.

The first day of college, Lucy's roommate, a blond girl from Virginia whose father was in the foreign service, asked where she was from, and Lucy replied, "New York City."

"No, I know that, it was on the list. I mean *really* where you're from." As Lucy stared at her quizzically, she added, "Where you were born."

"New York. I told you." And then Lucy stared, with some unease, at the twin beds, twin dressers, twin desks, all squared off and bland. David had warned that at a school like this one, a "classy" school, as he called it, she would find bigotry, and she had brushed his warning off. For she had never, to her knowledge, experienced bigotry while growing up in New York City.

"I'm sorry," the girl, Patty, said with a harmless smile. "It's just that you have such a striking face, I was sure you were foreign. Middle East, Mediterranean, or something. I have a talent for placing faces— my parents dragged me all over the world, my whole life. Listen, all I mean is some people are lucky, that's all." Patty turned to the mirror in mock dismay, screwed up her ingenuous features, attempted a glamorous expression. "I mean, just look. No one would ever find *me* exotic." They both laughed, Lucy with relief. Patty was no bigot: *exotic*, she thought.

For months Lucy was exhilarated, as if she had discovered an intriguing new acquaintance; each evening she scrutinized her face, searching for what Patty had seen. It was true, a few of her aunts, with their olive skin, high cheekbones, and broad, almost Oriental faces, did look distinctly foreign, but she did not resemble them. Her jaws sloped down sharply to a strong chin. Her nose was straight and perfect, as her friends used to say enviously, her mouth small and finely curved. She had a high, smooth forehead with dark hair falling over it in calculated disarray, and dark, opaque eyes like David's. It was a good face—she was satisfied with it, but had never dreamed it might be *exotic*. She would not mention the incident to David, for she knew instinctively that he would not be pleased. David liked her to look like everyone else, and to wear whatever the girls were wearing that year. Often he asked her if she needed extra money for clothes, and when she came home for Christmas and Easter that first year he appraised her up and down and commented, in his understated way, "You look very nice. What do they call that kind of sweater?" Or coat. Or dress.

The following year she took an individual reading program in the nineteenth-century Russian novel. At the end there was an oral exam given by a panel of professors. She telephoned David long-distance the night before to find out the correct pronunciation of all the Russian names. Her ear was acute. If David said them over the phone a few times she could copy them. And then, in her fantasy, the professors would say, "Where did you get such a fine Russian accent?" and she would respond, with nonchalance, "Oh, my father is Russian."

Smerdyakov, Nozdraev, Sviazhsky, Kondratyevna . . . He resisted at first, but she coaxed until finally he said them for her, warmly, the heavy, earthy syllables rushing through miles of telephone wire into her ear. Saying them, he sounded like a stranger. She penciled accent marks in the proper places and repeated the names after him, but was shy about repeating them as well as she could have done. She sensed David might not like her assimilating the alien sounds too perfectly.

Except the next morning at the exam she found that several of them were wrong. At least the professors pronounced them differently. Lucy felt a shudder of fear, as if the room had suddenly gone cold. Who was David, really, and where was *he* from, if anywhere? And what did this make of her? The fantasy—"Where did you get such a fine Russian accent?"—never happened.

It could never have happened, she realized later. She had forgotten what Anna once told her privately, long ago. "Being Russian is one thing. Being Jewish, from Russia, is something else."

She learned also, in a history course, that it was Marx who first said, "Religion is the opium of the people," not Vladimir Lenin.

Months later, riding in David's car, Lucy said, "All those Russian characters in the books I studied for that course last year. They all had this great passion about life. Do you know what I mean?"

"Yes. Yes."

"Like your sisters. The women reminded me of them. And of me. They were all passionate about different things, but underneath it was the same."

"Yes."

"Do you feel that way sometimes?"

"What way?"

"Passionate. About life, I mean," she added when she saw him shift uncomfortably in his seat.

David moved into the left lane to pass a car. A truck appeared over the crest of the hill, approaching them. Speeding up, David swerved to the right, and in a reflex action, as he used to do when she was a child, shot his arm out in front of Lucy's chest to shield her. Safe again, he settled back and cleared his throat. "They always had much more respect for their great writers than we do here. You have to say that for them." It was understood that they never discussed his rash driving.

"Tell me, what was it like?"

"I don't remember."

"You must remember."

"It's so long ago, I can't."

"You left a brother over there, didn't you?"

"Yes, Mordecai."

"Well, what happened to him? Why didn't he come?"

"He was a grown man, established, with a wife and children and a job. It would have been hard for him to leave."

"Didn't you ever write to him?" She could almost touch it in the space between them, her own passionate urgency pressing him, and his resistance. "Didn't you ever want to know what happened to him?"

"He's probably dead now. Or else a very old man. Chances are he's dead."

"But why didn't you ever write? You could still try to . . ." She was warm and full of energy; like those women in the novels, she could set out on a sacrificial trek to trace this lost brother or his descendants, if David would only ask.

"How could we write? There were wars and pogroms. You think it

242

was as easy to correspond by airmail as it is now? . . . Well, we did write, at first, then we lost touch. There were . . . incidents. Killings. Didn't you learn any history? Didn't you learn about that famous ravine? That was our city." He pulled into the garage and leaned over to open the door for her. "You can afford to have passion." He smiled and patted her hand. "Come into the house."

Lucy was twenty-six. The last of her many cousins was getting married and she was taking Allan to the wedding. She had met him during a trip to Mexico, at an outdoor market in a dusty village. He was buying oranges. The way he stood at the fruit stand, tall and lanky, in faded blue jeans and work shirt, handling each orange thoughtfully, tenderly even, before dropping it into his net sack, appealed to her. She moved nearby, hoping he would notice her and start a conversation, which he did. But first he held out an orange. She always remembered that, how even before he spoke he offered her something.

No doubt some of the aunts and uncles would comment teasingly about Allan's beard. Men like David and his brothers shaved fastidiously, beards being part of the detritus they had left behind them. She had also prepared him for their sly remarks about marriage; he had a gentle face and they would take liberties: "So what are you kids waiting for? See, it's painless!"

For surely David or Anna would not have told anyone that they already shared an apartment. That fact was a thorn to David, and she was sorry to inflict it on him in his vulnerable years. Anna didn't seem to mind as much. She kept up with changing times, wore pants suits now, read articles in magazines about drugs and venereal disease, and even thought the ponytail on her oldest grandson was cute. But David's views were ancient and changeless.

"This must be the place," said Allan wryly. He found a space in the crowded parking lot. "Simplicity itself."

"I warned you, didn't I? We don't do things in a small way."

Inside, all plate glass and draperies and potted plants, they were ushered past a chapel, a ballroom for the dinner and dancing to follow, and onto a terrace overlooking a bright green lawn. A bar was set up at one end; at the other a band played a waltz. Men in dark suits and women in long gaily colored dresses flecked the grass in the sunlight

243

of the early June afternoon. A few couples danced on the terrace.

Lucy caught Allan's hand and pressed it. "It's beautiful, though, isn't it? A garden party."

"Very nice," he admitted. "All right, let's plunge in. Lead me to the slaughter."

"I'll start you on the young ones—they're easier. Then you can work your way up."

"Save me a dance."

"What kind of dance do you want?"

"Oh, any kind," said Allan. "I can do them all."

David rushed up to where they stood talking with a group of cousins. His walk had slowed lately, but just now he strode with the energy of his youth, reminding Lucy of the vigor of his absurd dances. He took her hand and held her away from him, appraising.

"You look lovely. What do they call that funny business up on top?"

"An Empire waist."

"Very nice." His eyes traveled the length of the dress, wine-colored, down to where it shimmered out in folds. "Come, I want you to meet some people. Excuse us, Allan, just for a few minutes. I'll send her right back." And he tugged her off by the hand excitedly, through the clusters of guests, the way she used to tug him in the zoo to show him some rare species she had found.

They stopped at a table where a few gray-haired people were gathered.

"This is my daughter, Lucy," said David, pushing her before him. "My scientist," he added, with his special blend of pride and mild mockery; she never could tell which was dominant.

There were a married couple, Victor and Edna Rickoff, with kind worn faces, and a tall man standing up, Sam Panofsky, broad and dapper, his thin white hair combed straight back from his forehead and stylishly long. Panofsky smiled all the time, leering beneath bushy white eyebrows. From the set of his jaw Lucy knew he thought well of himself and his appearance. In his navy-blue suit adorned with a wide orange tie, he moved rigidly, like a man much older than he looked. His body had a well-kept yet tenuous solidity, as though he stayed firm by artificial means, by laborious hours on machines in expensive health clubs. He watched Lucy; his lips closed, then opened, and he wet them with his tongue.

244

"A scientist?" he echoed.

"Damn right," replied David. Then, turning to Lucy, "We grew up together. Victor's house was right next door. We all went to school together."

"Sure," said Rickoff. "Did he ever tell you, Lucy, the crazy things we used to do?"

She shook her head.

"Oh, did we have times!" Rickoff's milky eyes lit up behind thick glasses. "Remember that back yard where we played bandits, how we dug in the dirt for bags of gold? And those poor chickens we chased?"

"You chased everything that moved." Mrs. Rickoff was fair and frail, and smoked with a long black cigarette holder. "Such wild boys. Like wild animals, bobcats."

Lucy sat down with them. "So you were childhood friends? This is amazing."

"Friends!" cried Rickoff. "More like family! At a wedding, like today, we used to sneak under the grownups' feet to get in the dance. You should have seen your father jump around. Some little dancer, that one, they used to say."

"And what else?" said Lucy.

"Your father was some smart-alecky kid. Remember, David, one morning you broke the ruler the teacher used to smack us with?" Rickoff tossed his benign and balding head. "So he smacked us with half! And sent us out to stand in the freezing cold for an hour!"

"Those winters were so bitter," said Mrs. Rickoff. "Snow up to your eyes. You had to melt ice to wash. But the summers." She leaned towards Lucy in a sudden surge, her voice deepening. "The summers were gorgeous. That sky, not like anything here. Very wide, with a funny yellow light on the trees. There was a certain time of day, four, five o'clock, when even those old houses had a golden look, from the light. We went around barefoot, jumping in puddles. The ground was hot under our feet."

Lucy was transported. It was just such privacies she had craved, like something out of a book, alien, exotic, transcendent. If only the Rickoffs had been her parents, she might have tasted that vanished spicy air. . . . Then turning to David, who was lighting up an olive cigar, his face bland and impenetrable, she felt a traitor.

"Barefoot, sure," Rickoff said to his wife. "Who had shoes?"

245

"Yes, you're leaving out the best parts," said Panofsky. "Sky, puddles! Why don't you tell her about the czars? Tell her what fun our boys had in the army." Panofsky moved stiffly towards Lucy and laid a hand on her shoulder. "But a pretty girl like you isn't interested in such things. Would you care to dance?"

She hesitated and looked at David again, foolishly, as though he could tell her what to say.

"Well, maybe a little later. I just got here." She gave a diffident laugh. "I want to hear some more." And then she felt embarrassed for wanting so obviously to possess it the easy way, the way she had taken possession of the old novels, reveling in the abrasive names that exercised her tongue, and in the improbable lusts and sufferings.

"You like this old stuff, eh? Sounds like a TV special, from this end. Right, David?" Panofsky snorted. "But she's lucky. Nice straight nose, good face. No one would ever take her for . . ."

"What do you mean? Take me for what?"

"You could be right off the *Mayflower*. . . . You know you have a few gray hairs already? Why don't you cover them up? A young woman like you with gray hair—no need, in this day and age. In this country, especially, you can change yourself into anything you want. Let me see, I bet you're not a day over . . . twenty-three?"

"Twenty-six."

"And not married yet? What's the matter?" He laughed and turned again to her father. "The young boys not good enough for her, David? You spoiled her?"

David stood up. "I'm going to go and see how your mother's doing." He paused a moment by her side.

"Go on. I'll be right over." She turned away from Panofsky and towards the others. "Is it so foolish to want to know something about your own history? I mean—" Then she stopped and thought once more how hopelessly naive she must sound. She saw her past as swaddled in secrecy, infused with a vast nostalgia for something she had never known, something which perhaps had never even existed, except as a mystery she herself had created and nourished. From the corner of her eye she noticed David walk briskly away; she felt both abandoned and yet finally free to unearth what she wanted. She gazed at the Rickoffs as though they were artifacts, archaeologists' finds, and

246

then dropped her eyes, reproaching herself: they were ordinary people, and she was tongue-tied.

Mrs. Rickoff must have sensed her discomfort. "Tell me something, Lucy. Did you ever see your father eat a banana?" she asked with a grin.

"A banana? I don't know. I don't remember."

"Fifty-five years in this country," she said nodding towards her husband, "and still he won't eat a banana. Because they didn't have bananas where we came from. He eats only what he ate as a child. That's how it sticks."

Everyone laughed, and Lucy relaxed. "Caviar," she said. "That's what my father passed on to me. Caviar every Sunday morning."

David went to sit with Anna, but over his shoulder he kept glancing at Lucy, still with the Rickoffs. A beautiful girl, it was undeniable, and the maroon dress suited her. She had turned out well. At school, first she had studied languages, then unexpectedly changed to bio-chemistry, more practical anyway, he decided. Now she had a job in a laboratory, working on an epilepsy research project and making good money, for a girl. Only the business with the boyfriend grated on his heart. Not Allan himself—he was a fine young man with a future, exactly the type he would have picked out for her himself. The beard was not worth making an issue of. When she had first brought him home to meet them David was pleased, and assumed it was only a matter of time.

"So," he teased the next day over the phone, "will we be seeing more of him?"

"I imagine so," she replied in the same tone.

"Good. I presume you see a lot of him?"

"Oh yes. As a matter of fact he's sharing the apartment. I was going to tell you, soon."

He hung up. In the kitchen he found Anna and shouted at her in a rage made worse because she went on quietly chopping onions while he flung his arms about and ranted.

At last she said, "What did you think she was doing with him? Times have changed. Maybe it's better."

He couldn't fathom Anna's attitude. It gnawed at his insides that

Lucy could turn against him so. In his mind he had to stop himself from calling her filthy names in a foreign tongue; alone, he would cover his ears and nod his gray head back and forth like an aged man grieving. Back there, women who did that were called those names, and when respectable women saw them they crossed to the other side of the street.

Anna advised him to say nothing about it to Lucy. His pain dulled, or he became accustomed to it. At least the boy was Jewish, he consoled himself wryly. The other he couldn't have been able to tolerate. She continued to visit with Allan, and David got through these visits by behaving as if they were married. They seemed so, in every way but the license. He would have liked to take her on his arm and walk down a flower-scented aisle, leaving her in the middle for Allan to fetch. And be host to all the relatives, showing what a fine wedding he could give. Surely he deserved it, after all his efforts? Yet this fantasy might never happen.

"But what will happen?" he would ask Anna petulantly.

"What will happen," said Anna calmly, "is that one fine day she will accidentally or on purpose get pregnant, and then they'll get married like everyone else, and you will have nothing to worry about."

He smoked and watched her at the table a few yards away. They were all talking and laughing loudly, except for Panofsky, who sat a bit apart, staring at Lucy as David himself was doing. Rickoff was telling some story, thrashing his arms about wildly, tossing in Yiddish and Russian phrases, and Lucy threw her head back and laughed. Then she leaned forward eagerly to ask him something. Rickoff sobered and gave her a long reply, his facial muscles moving in an old, foreign pattern, in a language counterpoint to his spoken English. Mrs. Rickoff joined in, also waving her hands, and as the three of them talked at once, it seemed to David that Lucy was taking on their old-fashioned expressions and gestures—extravagantly raised eyebrows, pursed lips, rhythmic shrugs and nods, lively winks and puckers and thrust-out chins and jaws. She said something with a swift dramatic flick of her hand that suddenly brought his mother back to life. David could not hear most of their words, but he imagined she was taking on their rough-edged foreign accents as well, her voice falling into a nasal, singsong intonation. He felt a chill: it was as if she were being transformed before his eyes, as if he had delivered her over to the very powers he had been shielding her from all these years, and she was all too willingly drawn in, drawn back. For a split second he glimpsed her not in her stylish silky dress but in heavy shapeless skirts and shawls, a dark scarf wrapped around her shaved head, her fine features coarsened by endless childrearing, scrubbing, cooking, and anxiety. When he blinked the image vanished.

He saw Panofsky lean forward to whisper in her ear. Lucy looked confused, then rose, reluctantly, it seemed, and let him lead her by the elbow to the middle of the terrace, where he swung his arm around to pull her close for the dance. His large hand pressed into the small of her back; her hand rested on his shoulder lightly, barely touching. Panofsky was more than a head taller than she, and he looked down at her, grinning. From David's distance Lucy seemed fragile and helpless in the flimsy dress with the bare back, though he knew she was neither. Still, Panofsky was holding her tightly, and she looked uncomfortable. Panofsky, that old lecher, burrowed his face against her hair for a moment, and David leaned forward as if ready to spring from his seat. Could Panofsky know, by any rumors, that she was living with a man, not married? He had made that nasty crack about her being too spoiled to marry. An old panicky tremor rose in David's stomach, a sickening tremor he knew from years ago on the boat, and later in school. Panofsky's face was red, his eyelids drooping, as he tightened his arm around Lucy's waist.

David was sick to his stomach and had to put out his cigar. The very air, dotted with the aging, familiar faces of transplanted people like Panofsky trying desperately, uselessly, to be carefree and self-assured, to be new and free and American, suddenly smelled fetid to him. And it seemed that in the idiotic, the nearly senile yet firm embrace of Panofsky was everything old and reeking of foreignness that he had labored so hard to protect her from. For himself he accepted it, it would cling to him no matter what fine words or clothes or houses masked it. But for his children, especially for her—ah, he had wanted them new, untainted, bred without that ancient history.

Panofsky gripped her hand and bent his cheek to her hair again. David saw Lucy draw back so that his head jerked awkwardly. Panofsky shifted and pulled her against him with the pressure of his thick wrist.

249

With relief, David watched her push at his shoulder and extricate herself from his hold, leaving him standing ridiculously, arms open in dance posture, in the middle of the sunny terrace. Would she come to them or go over to Allan, standing at the bar with the young people? He could not bear the thought of her shaming him in front of Allan, telling, in her voice which could be so harsh and mocking, about his crude, his unredeemable friends.

But she was coming towards him and Anna, sweeping over royally, head high, face flushed, holding up the bottom of her dress to walk faster. Before she said a word she whisked Anna's drink off the table and gulped it down.

"Christ, that one is the original dirty old man! Who let *him* in?"

"He's still a friend of your uncle Peter's," said David remorsefully. Unable to look his own daughter in the eye—was this what it had all come to?

"He was unbelievable! Blowing in my ear, practically. What a nerve! If he weren't an old friend of yours I would have told him exactly what I thought of him." She sat down and lit a cigarette.

Anna, the perenially serene, said, "Panofsky's always been like that, with anyone he can get his hands on. Once he got me out on the dance floor and I told him off good and proper. It's nothing to bother about."

David was relieved to see Lucy's frown beginning to turn slightly amused. Only an outburst of the moment, perhaps, a summer storm. She would forget it.

"Gray hair," and she laughed. She pulled a random hair from her head and studied it, then flicked it away. "Silly old fool. But seriously," and she put her hand on David's arm, "I liked your friends. The others." She paused and looked straight into his eyes, her anger spent. "It meant a lot, meeting your friends. They were wonderful. They told me your father was famous as a scholar. I never knew that. I never knew he managed an estate, either."

"For one of *them*," David sneered.

"That's not the point," she said.

"What is the point? You want to feel you came out of a book by Tolstoi? That's what you want? You didn't."

"Oh, Dad," she groaned. She turned in despair and looked at Anna, but Anna's face was closed and absent, as if she had witnessed this many times before and grown weary of it. Lucy sat silent for a few moments, then said, "They told me I looked like your mother. Is that so?"

"There's a resemblance." He shrugged. "For a few months in her life, maybe, she had a chance to look like you."

The band was playing a slow and stately waltz, the kind he used to dance with Anna. He could still do it well enough, he was quite sure. He edged forward in his chair, glancing first at Anna, then at Lucy, and hesitating. He saw her face brighten, but it was for Allan, who was approaching from across the terrace. Before he could reach them Lucy leaned up close; her hasty whisper was like a hiss. "Would it have cost you so much to tell me some of those things? Would it?"

David's face burned hot with shame, with an unspeakable confusion, just as Allan stepped up, smiling broadly, innocently, to take her hand. He wanted her to waltz.

A Good Deal

Rosellen Brown

M Y FATHER DOES NOT LIVE in what I would call a "home." We'd never have considered anything that even resembled the word, with its hypocrisy built right into its name (home cooking, comforts of home). I like to think he is in a sort of benign arm of the Catskills out on Long Island, a brightly decorated and well-kept hotel complete with live entertainment and a built-in synagogue a few blocks from the ocean. The air outside his hotel has that sharp salty extra dimension that makes you realize you are standing in something nourishing, almost tangible, not transparent, nonexistent, like most air. He won't go out in it because for him the extra dimension he anticipates (besides mugging or murder) is germs—a cold, bronchitis, pneumonia: who wants to smell *air?* Not at his age.

When we visit, we take him walking once around the building as if "outside" were a destination in itself. He's got his hat—a pale yellow golf hat for our summer visit, a formal fedora for the winter, the kind the FBI used to wear before they started passing as hippies and stoned collegians. "Come on, let's go for a walk," I suggest as soon as I see my wife and the kids sinking into torpor on his room-mate's bed in the room on the fourth floor.

This time we have brought him a little radio with earphones because the room-mate complains about noise, any and all, after 8:30 and the management will not "mix in," either out of scrupulous fairness or their (correct) suspicion that reason is destined for defeat here among the elderly with their habits that have turned to stone. Jane has correctly

252

predicted his reaction again—she maintains that my father is the only person she knows who has never said an unexpected thing. He is, for some reason I can't fathom, bewildered by the radio dials and I can see that it will go unused, he will leave it in its little blue box on his half of the closet shelf, another failed toy alongside the hearing aid and the electric razor. Inertia overpowers energy, impossible as it sounds. Entropy makes promises; someday I suppose I'll know what it is saying.

He has embraced his grandsons, offered them small dusty-looking cookies that he's saved from lunch in a napkin. They are touched, Timmy especially (he is the little one), at a sign of awareness that they were coming, that they might have needs or pleasures he could gratify. They don't ask or expect much—some rudimentary consciousness, a sign. They take one cookie apiece and chew it carefully, as if they are thinking hard. I ask more, although I don't get it. Well, I am his son, the remoteness of the third generation has not made me forgiving.

So we troop downstairs, Jane ahead of us, wearing her glorious red hair that made my father, when he first saw her, call her a Yankee; the two boys trying ceremoniously not to step on each other's heels, giving off, though, with every gesture the suppressed air of kittens in a sack, all frisky irresistible quenched movement. The elevator is one machine Pop seems to have mastered; not only does he hold the door, assured, while we file in, but he smiles and keeps his hand on the OPEN button for another tenant of his floor, a short, vividly-muumuued woman who hobbles on slowly inside a walker. As we move down the floors, sinking so hard our stomachs rise up into our chests and Josh says "Gulp" out loud, she looks at us, smiling, and then, apologetically at her aluminum contraption and shakes her head. "Don't get old, *kinder*, that's all I can say."

After she's gone—we politely wait for her to drag herself out and disappear around the elevators toward the gift shop—my father says "So who asked her? We need her opinion on anything, we'll remember to ask her."

Jane opens her mouth and closes it; so do I. We are going to berate him for his lack of generosity but instead we berate ourselves: the same impatience that bit her into speech bit him into anger. The hotel is fine, we assure ourselves, it is age that's depressing.

But no. I watch my father walk toward the door slowly but securely.

It is mostly women who are seated, watching, in the purple and yellow leather chairs on both sides of the aisle, because life seems for the most part to be a widowing. He has very few real complaints, considering what a man his age can expect—even the Bible would agree. It is all that has never changed that rankles: he is the same father I've always had, lacking a few appurtenances (teeth, hearing, hair, a wife) but otherwise stock still the same. "Kill me!" he pleaded after my mother died. "It's a mistake, how could such a mistake happen! I was always going to go first." I don't know how much losing her cost him. But he was terrified to face his life alone without a mother, that I know. He was bewildered, and he's still bewildered—how could it be that he has come through eighty-two years intact when strong men, men twice his size and a hundred times more vigorous and full of will, have died and left these women?

Timmy pushes on the hotel door with all his weight and the live air opens to us, edgy with salt, the sky bright blue as pure deep water. "Oy," my father says, turning his face back toward the building. "I'm climbing into my grave out here. What are you doing, Joey, punishing me with this cold?"

I wish I could find a sin in my father's past. I thought this once when I was embroiled in an episode of, what shall I call it, a brief unsanctioned lust—Janie never did find out, no harm was done—because I was caught in a paradox. My father didn't drink (a little schnapps on *shabbos*, gone in a blink) and neither did I; he was a dutiful bread-winner, earnest in his work, and so was I, give or take the moments of insolvency any writer is heir to. His shortcomings were all of omission, never of commission. He and my mother, however they had begun, had endured a marriage of convention and dependency. They mocked and quibbled, demanded and berated, my father thrust his neck out to be shamed and my mother enthusiastically did her best to shame him, and how they had me is hard to envision. As a teen-ager (like all teen-agers who have everyone experimentally in bed with everyone else, their teachers, their friends' mothers, the President!) I could never manage to imagine them so much as acknowledging each other in the Murphy bed they pulled down from the living room closet. (It was a tiny apartment; their son got the bedroom for his more hallowed activities.) But just as people unquestioningly needed marriages in those days, so did those marriages need children. I suppose I was a duty and they did me.

But then, as I said, the moment presented itself when I was less than dutiful and I found myself gathering up the odd ingredients for a great stew of justifications. I found myself thinking, I am not my father repeated once down the line. Even though you could confuse us in the dark by the shape of our bodies, the nap of our hair, he is a man in whom the blood beats weakly, whom the traces bind. Admirable and not admirable, those things. I didn't know just where I stood on virtue just then. It seemed to me, but only in flashes, as if there were a blinking sign at the corner of my vision, that virtue was only safety and safety was timidity. Cowering. Then that sign would blink again and I wasn't so sure. I saw Janie's face, innocent of worry (though I tried to see it anywhere but in the bedroom) and I saw the blond, thoroughly gentile, slim-hipped woman (a student of mine, not, to be honest, as innocent as my wife) who wanted me enough to put a lot of foregone conclusions in danger, hers and mine; and it was my father who seemed, or at least ought, I thought, to be begging me to *do* it, leave the strait and narrow, seize the hour and be bad.

I was bad; I could achieve badness with the best of them (only perhaps not as a recidivist). As it happened, I didn't enjoy it much, either in anticipation or in retrospect, only in the single blinding instant, gone as quickly as that ritual fire-in-the-throat whiskey after *kiddush*, that drives all of us every time, in the dark, on the sly, the animal instant that slaughters reason. And perhaps I enjoyed this colloquy too: Pop, I thought, a man has to dare to dare. Then I would ask myself why. To be able to say he dared? Say it to whom? I wasn't telling *him*. If my father, who was too simple and decent to lie or even give short-weight, wasn't good, only frightened, what was a good man? Sometimes he seemed to me, all of a sudden, not so naive as I had thought: telling me about a gangster neighbor, a philandering cousin, his aunt who took in boarders and then took off with one. He had noticed there was a world out there. But his own record, I thought, that was clean enough to be an incitement. In retrospect I see I was averaging my guilt over two generations. In my own way I was a coward too.

A few months ago, the night before we were to make our biennial trip to the city to see him, he called me. A call up here to Providence— "the country," he calls it—is a long-distance affair, very daunting. He hazards it rarely and only in emergencies. His voice had broken through distance to me, quavering, when he went into the hospital with pneumonia a few years ago, and once when his brother Abie died in Miami to weep for twenty minutes while he cursed himself for the bill he was running up. This time, hearing his voice saying "Joey?" as if he doubted it was really me, I was alarmed.

"What's the matter, Pop? Are you okay?" Our suitcases were already out on the bed waiting for our New York City clothes.

"I'm okay, a little cold, I cough, but I'm okay," he told me and his equivocal voice seemed to wait there for me to tell him why he had called.

"Listen, sonny," he said finally, "I got to ask you something."

"Couldn't it wait? We're—"

"I wouldn't bother you without a reason. I don't need a phone call on my bill, you know."

"Well—" I hadn't intended to be so uninviting. It was all to the good when he made himself push against the world; using the telephone was the challenge to him that climbing up a sheer rockface would be to me. I could see him pacing while he held the phone; I do that too.

"Listen. What do you think if—I want you should tell me if you think this is such a good idea."

"Right. Okay." I imagined he was going to ask to change rooms and be done with his room-mate's *mishugas* once and for all. Play the tv till midnight. Sing in the shower.

"What?" he asked.

"All right, go ahead."

"What head?"

"Nothing. Tell me what you want to tell me." Janie and the kids sometimes come running when they don't know I'm on the phone with him. "Who are you shouting at?" they ask. He must hear me as if we had one of those ancient undersea connections. "Pop. What idea?"

"I'm thinking I might get married, Joey. But I'm not so sure."

256

I bit my lips closed to keep from laughing. Then, guilty, I made my voice approximate simple interest and possibly even approval. "Married," I yelled. "Married?" The world was an astounding place; maybe if I leaped out the bedroom window I could fly.

"I don't want you should think this has to do with Mommy," he began, and I listened speechless while he explained. Then I went downstairs and told Jane he had finally said something surprising.

And so we were ready to meet Frieda the next day. "Is Frieda grandpa's fiancée?" Timmy asked, saying the words as if he were holding a fishbone by its repulsive tip. I said I didn't know. My father had asked my advice but I hadn't given any.

Usually he was seated just inside the front door of the hotel so that he could jump up anxiously at the sight of every clump of people who approached. This time, confirming my understanding that all his routines had changed, there was no one waiting for us.

The woman at the desk rang his room; no one answered. (His room-mate, he had told me incidentally, was in the hospital for tests—"He was falling down"—and, although such an intimation of mortality had always frightened and depressed him before, not for the room-mate's sake but for his own, this time he was too distracted by his own changing fortunes to take much notice.)

The receptionist suggested we try the card room where they were having their daily bingo. "He's in there a lot," she told us amiably. "And *she's* a hot one at games," she added indiscreetly. "Let me tell you, she wins real money!" We were dealing with common knowledge, then. The boys giggled and Jane looked grim.

We walked down the long hall that had the mildly antiseptic, beige, asensual ambience of a Holiday Inn. The door to the card room was open and I could see him from the hall, seated next to the cage in which the bingo pieces flopped and fluttered like lottery tickets, so that he could hear the caller with his better ear. Which one was Frieda, then?

On one side of him sat a dishevelled woman with hair twice as red as Jane's but slightly purple at the roots, as if it were emerging from a wound. She had the look of someone on loan from a back ward. On his other side sat a *kotselah*, a little cat, smaller, under what looked like a real lace shawl: my mother would have called her quality. She had a good hairdresser for her dry sherry curls (or was it a wig?) and a vaguely European tinge of irony, or tolerance, to her smile. Everyone here was European, of course, but I don't mean Poland, I don't mean Odessa, I mean, say, middle-class Prague or Vienna. *Café mit schlag.*

And she was raking in the chips. "Good Lord," Janie breathed at my side. She was thinking, I know it, of my mother's orthopedic shoes, the plastic flounce and flowers that spread like a rash to cover every undefended piece in the now-dispersed apartment, the Decline of Rome wall decorations, all pillars and crumbling temples, or Gainsborough ladies in gilt frames. She was thinking of the little piece of paper we had found in my mother's coat pocket when we were going through her "effects," the rain check from Waldbaum's for a 39¢ cauliflower. This Frieda, you could tell from a hundred yards, knew her antiques, her armoires, her netsukes; a hundred to one she kept sachet in her bureau drawers.

Pop introduced us but not until he had pulled everybody into the hall so that we wouldn't impede the next bingo round. "You look as if you've won enough for one day," I said to Frieda as pleasantly as I could. "You must have talent."

She laughed and shrugged self-deprecatingly. Even her teeth were a cut above the hotel average. Her winnings had gone into a delicate purse that closed with a businesslike snap of finality.

What had they agreed to? I couldn't tell—on the phone my father had simply said she had "asked him" and he was "thinking about it." She had been widowed fairly recently and was lonely living alone, and so she had (admirably? shamelessly?) come to see whom she could meet here. To make a deal. She had her own money and apartment and didn't need his, her own children and grandchildren ditto. On the phone that had made sense: a frightened little woman, permanent immigrant-class like Pop, toward whom, not on purpose, I had been— I and my generation, I mean—condescending since we were children.

But this Frieda was something else again. She entertained us. I had suggested we do something besides the usual tour around the shabby block and she suggested a nice little restaurant, "strictly Kosher"— with a calculating smile at Pop that would have passed, in his book, for "consideration." It was nearby, her daughter had found it and they'd gone there for brunch just last week. "It has privacy," she promised. "Booths. Nice. Upholstered."

The boys were ostentatiously enjoying all this. I could see they liked this new wrinkle in the dull fabric of their grandfather's life. She looked like the kind of grandmother who could reach into her purse or her pockets—not that she'd done so yet—and produce charming surprises, more interesting than plain butter cookies. At very least she was an impressive gambler. Or maybe it was relief at the chance to do something besides sit in the blank air of a dozen old people with their canes and cataracts and forced cheerful Happy-to-meet-yous and their self-absorption.

As I say, she knew she was charming and so she entertained us. She told stories, in a firm quiet voice, about her father who had been a scholar in Cracow (therefore a pauper here, untrained to do a dayswork). Her husband, continuing the tradition of useless luxury—a philistine she was, but honest—had been a violist. Whatever are you doing *here*, I wanted to ask her. What do you want of my poor father? He will make a woman like you more lonely still.

Well, the violist had dreamed of music, as it happened, but worked in "clucks"—that's cloaks and suits—like the rest of his *landsmen*. A cutter, then a presser at Waranow Togs on 35th Street. An unhappy man, unreconciled. For forty years, music on the side.

And that was how she had met my father, all those years ago. Some kind of garment workers' union picnic, wives invited. A rare Sunday in a park on Staten Island. An unforgettable day.

"How you met my father?" I echoed stupidly. Pop was eating a bagel, trying to negotiate it in spite of his insecure teeth. He looked at me shyly, blinking.

"He didn't tell you? Sam—" She lay one wrinkled but manicured hand on his bare arm. She was a woman who made disappointment into a charming pretext for flirtation. How my mother would have laughed. "Sam! A *tschotskele!*" she'd have said. A little trinket. But Frieda turned her widened eyes on all of us with innocent enthusiasm. "Yes—he didn't tell you we knew each other in the old old days? So when I met him here, what a surprise. A shock! Children—" and she fixed them, unfairly I thought, in her softening gaze and put one hand helpless on her chest as if to still her heart's persistent amazement.

259

"Can you imagine, this old tired lonely lady comes out here to a strange place, she doesn't know a single soul—but, you know, my daughter, my son thought it would be good for me to get out from my apartment, they said it wasn't healthy to be all the time alone. And they were right, now I can see that!" The boys were attentive to her gaiety even if it was the kind of love story that only brought forth from them retching noises when it concerned the young and the beautiful. "And who do I meet the very first day, I'm sitting next to him at supper, they put me there, you know, just like that, and they bring the soup and I look at him—"

My father is embarrassed. He struggles with the cream cheese, which will not spread evenly on his bagel. Timmy reaches across unsmiling and does it for him. "Thanks, sonny," Pop says, shamefaced. Do you know you will be a nursemaid? I want to ask this stranger. Do you know he gets lost on his way to the bathroom? He lived with us for a year after my mother died, and there wasn't a day I came home not expecting the house to have burned down because he'd left the gas on again, long after the kettle had gone dry.

I wasn't used to complex and contradictory feelings in my father's presence, I have to admit that—except for the contradiction of loving someone you don't respect. About myself and the way I live my life, he is impossibly ignorant, try as I might to enlighten him. Beginning back when I first refused to put on my galoshes for the rain, that old story, I have been a confusing rebellious undutiful son whom he has loved, as I love him, in spite of all. (Had I been lovable on his terms I'd have killed myself long ago.) That I should have become (happy or not) an impecunious writer instead of a doctor or, at worse, a businessman, has been an unforgiveable affront to his dreams for me. My working wife, the dishevelment of our house—no bedroom set, no wall-to-wall—have only been corroborations. He is a straightforward little man desperate for solvency, invisibility, silence. Tit for tat, I failed him, he failed me.

Now what am I to think?

Why does this woman want him? He is a live male, in better shape than most—two eyes, however cloudy; two ears, however shot; vestiges of a sense of humor, though that was better when he could hear. No stick to lean on, no apparent illnesses. Perhaps that makes him a prize.

Is he flattered? Does he want to get out of this hotel because, comfortable as it is, you live in public here? Does he see her as a woman? What would he *do* with a woman besides hand her his dirty socks, his underwear?

We do not talk marriage; or, that is, we talk around it by admiring her proferred proofs of ownership: pictures of her Sheryl, a teacher; her Arthur, a podiatrist with blow-dried hair and stunning practice; their children; a polaroid of her living room, which is not so different, actually, from my mother's: Italian Renaissance chairs, pseudo, only no plastic to protect them from the depredations of use. It is not so much her dowry as the bride-price, I am thinking, studying the stubborn hairs that sprout like weeds from my father's nearest ear.

Later, when we'd left her—awkwardly—in the lobby of the hotel where she claimed she had some business with a friend but hoped she'd see us again soon (were we off to Providence immediately or would we take advantage of the wonderful city, the shops, the shows?) I went up to my father's room alone with him. He looked deflated, though for a man who hasn't much wind in his small sails to begin with, that's a matter of conjecture. "You like her, Joe?" he asked me, afraid to meet my eyes.

"She's—fine, Pop. A lovely woman. Very well-preserved." I hated to say that, it always made me think of embalming, on the one hand, and a feat against great odds on the other. But I sometimes found myself purposely blunt with him, if not downright cruel. Partly it was to fulfill his disappointment in me, to rub his nose in it since he'd think it anyway. But also I think I did it out of disrespect, as if I knew his hide was so thick nothing I said could penetrate to sting him. How could I ask what she saw in him? I made it a question about calculation which he, ever the paranoid, could appreciate.

"What she wants? I don't know, Joey, but it's true. Living alone is no way. Especially a woman, all the way out there on Ocean Parkway by herself. . . ." He left the meaningful details to my imagination. "She's a good woman. Not selfish. Anyway, she's got her own."

"A little—fancy, maybe—in her habits? Do you think?"

He shrugged. "You know, I told her she wouldn't get much from me in the—you know—that department." He raised his eyebrows on "that," which made it sound like what my mother had darkly referred

261

to as "dorten"—"down *there*," that island that was to be isolated from thought, speech, and most important, touch. "Not like before."

I assumed the "before" was his marriage. "Well, there are lots of ways men and women can be friends," I said, and wondered if that sounded as pious as it felt. "She's probably not interested in—she just sounds lonely."

"Before she was always very—she's a modest woman, considering she's what you would call attractive."

The conversation was getting deeper than I tended to expect with my father. "Before she was modest? Pop, what do you mean, before?"

"Be*fore*."

"When you met her on that picnic, you mean?"

His eyes lit for just an instant with a warmth I had myself seen often before I was, say, twelve.

"You met her—more than at that picnic? You got to know her?"

He shrugged again, this time not for vagueness but for its opposite: detailed memory he did not care to discuss. I sat down gingerly on his room-mate's bright blue bedspread and clasped my hands between my knees. "A lot of things I wouldn't tell you, sonny. A father wouldn't tell his son certain things. You shouldn't be mad—"

"You knew her—well? For very long?"

He was looking out the window, though the blinds were three-quarters closed. "Oy, sonny," he said the way he did when something hurt him. "What can I say? Not long enough."

"Did—" I couldn't ask if my mother knew about it. "It" was not so very horrible, considering the facts of their marriage, or not even considering: my marriage is perfectly fine. But I had no memory in forty years of having addressed a single sentence to my father's back.

"Nobody knew it, Mommy never, you never. Not even Harry either."

"Harry."

"Her husband, Harry Abrahams. He was a nice man. He had some temper but when he wasn't mad. . . . Not what you call a hard worker but a nice man." He twirled the string of the blinds in his hand. "We only wanted nobody should get hurt." He looked at me briefly, to check my face. All I knew about my face was that it felt very red, hot, inflamed with confusion.

262

"What happened, then?" I managed to ask. I think I was stuck somewhere between laughter and a huge chest-clearing shout, a massive bleating beyond good or bad taste, beyond a son's discretion. "What?!" I wanted to yell. "What?!" like Archie's father in the comic strip.

"Once we almost—people were asking a lot of questions. So we couldn't take no more chances."

"Pop," I said from where I sat. I wanted to touch him, comfort both of us, but he was very calm, very distant from this tumult in my chest. "Were you glad? Did it—" I looked down, embarrassed. "Were you happy?"

"Happy? With her?" He hadn't mentioned her name once. He laughed. "I was all the time looking over my shoulder Mommy shouldn't find out. I don't know if that was so happy." He ran his hands hard along the sides of his head, where the remaining fringes of his grey stubble grew; it was not a gesture I recognized, probably something he did when he had a full head of hair. "So anyway, Joey, you children with your happy, all the time happy this and not-so-happy that—how do you know what this happy feels like?"

It was the thing that had separated us, really: my choice to be happy in my life, not simply "comfortable." "You'd have known," I said with a bitterness I thought nervy but couldn't take back. "Well, then, why did you do it? Why would you take such a chance?" If it wasn't for joy, I meant, if it wasn't for ecstasy. I saw him trudging up from the subway with the Journal-American under his arm, and sometimes the Daily News or the Post if he had found one abandoned on the train, summer, winter, all the time except the slack season when there was no work. I couldn't imagine the mechanics of an affair in the life of a man of such regular habits. Did he really go to union meetings when he said he did? Or to play pinochle?

"Why?" he echoed. He had sat down facing me, in his familiar defeated slouch. All his life my father has looked as if the chairs and mattresses he sat on were too soft. "Why?" He shook his head. "She was a nice woman, I told you. Very lively. A good talker. She dressed good, it was a pleasure to sit by her." He looked to see if I understood. "And miserable, all the time he made her sad. I don't know about his problem, what it was. Maybe the music. He thought he was a genius,

263

a Heifetz, the world should see it, so all the time he was taking it out on her. How she suffered by him! I don't know what it was."

No matter what kind of English a man spoke he could be an adulterer, I thought. The word seemed hollow, as if its meaning had spilled out of it, leaving a dry pod with no mischief in it. I still felt as if I'd fallen hard on my stomach, though, the way I used to when I was a kid. And he was not apologizing. I was impressed.

"So are you going to marry her? Have you been dreaming of this ever since you were—"

He shrugged and looked into his baggy lap. "I don't know, sonny, it's not the same thing now. After all. Then I was, you know. . . . A man. Now." My father pulling his clothes off in a frenzy, not taking the bills and coins out of his pockets, his glasses, his comb, not laying his slacks scrupulously over the back of the fat brown armchair with the clawfoot legs to keep the crease, not putting on the pajamas my mother had ironed, striped or figured with one of those aimless silly patterns, green or gray. I used to run the drawstring through with a pin when it came out in the wash. No, my father locking the door, approaching her, this Frieda, slowly, to draw out the pleasure a little longer. I knew the dream ritual too in which everything moves incredibly fast and incredibly slowly, both. It is forbidden pleasure that leaves a scar. Memory heals ragged when it isn't repeated a thousand times. He would know, if I said that, he would recognize the crater where the shame and jeopardy lay, and the sharp ridge of healing. Everything in me heaved once, the feeling in the elevator that had made my son say "Gulp" and press his palm to his stomach.

"Well, think about it, then. You don't have to decide right now." I stood up as if this had been a routine conversation. I was glad to find my knees steady. "See how it feels to think about it. Waking up with somebody there besides old Morris." I hit Morris's bedspread with my hand.

"I don't know, Joe. Ocean Parkway, what am I going to do all the way out there?" Being with Frieda didn't seem to loom large in this proposal.

"What do you do here?" You can sit in a chair anywhere, I thought. You can wrap your *tfillin*, eat your poached egg, huddle out of the wind.

264

"If she could drive a car. I got my doctors' appointments, and the *shul* maybe isn't so close. Here it's convenient under one roof." He was teetering. A shove either way could do it. I embraced him, showed him how to work the radio one more time, went down to the lobby by the stairs two at a time, agitated, while he stood bewildered beside the elevator whose button he had pushed for me hospitably, the way a host watches till the car departs, taking you with it.

We began the drive toward the city in silence. Jane asked me what was wrong and I snapped at her. "Why are you angry?" she said, though I swore I wasn't angry. My father rising from the warm rumpled bed and pulling on his rough layers of clothing, shrugging on his coat, his muffler, his gloves, and coming home to the Bronx, to me and to my mother standing over the endlessly steaming *tup* of soup. Steam coming out of his mouth as he turned the corner from the hilly avenue and headed toward me where I sat in front of the apartment house, on its two wide brick steps, in exactly the same place every day, even preposterously (and to my mother's irritation) in the dead heart of winter. It was my challenge to myself, my hardship, my fifty-pound weights, my four-minute mile, my swan dive, to sit with my corduroy knees drawn up in the three-quarter dark, tears of cold in my eyes, my gloveless hands jammed in my pockets, waiting for him, knowing it was only my secret endurance that made him come.

The Gittel

Marjorie Sandor

THERE IS A TRADITION in our family that once in a while a dreamer is born: an innocent whose confused imagination cannot keep up with the civilized world. This person walks around in a haze of dreams, walking eventually right into the arms of the current executioner, blind as Isaac going up the mountain with his father. Nobody knows who started this story—my mother used to say it was a second-rate scholar out to impress the neighbors—but apparently there are characteristics, traits peculiar to this person, and two hundred years ago people knew a catastrophe was on the way if such a person came into their midst. Once, when was a little girl, I asked Papa to name the traits. He said he couldn't; they'd been lost. All he knew was that this dreamer, before vanishing, always left behind a dreaming child, and that sometimes he thought he was such a child.

My father was a modest man; he came to Ellis Island with his eyebrows up, and they never came down. Furthermore he was the kind of storyteller who rarely got past the scenic details, since every time he let his imagination go his children had nightmares for a week. I remember: I was eight years old, sitting with him on the kitchen stairs, my bedtime cup of milk between us. My mother was scrubbing a pot with steel wool, making that sound that hurts the smallest bones in the body, and in the parlor the alabaster lamp had been lit for my grandmother Gittel's yahrzeit.

The lamp looked different than it does now. We hadn't converted

266

it yet to electric, and it glowed pale orange behind the alabaster. As a child I could look at it for hours, imagining miniature cities on fire, or ladies in a golden room. It didn't have the long crack you see running down the left side. My daughter Rachel did that when she was ten years old, running like a maniac through the room and tripping over the cord. She won't go near it now; at nineteen she thinks it's her destiny to break it. She's a little careless, it's true, but nothing some responsibility wouldn't cure. I'm waiting for her now—she said she was taking the 4:30 bus from the city. I've been thinking about things, and tonight, after we eat, I'm going to tell her she can have the lamp when she and Daniel move into the new apartment.

So, where was I? With Papa? Yes, he was looking away from me, at the lamp in the parlor.

"We don't really know when she died," he said. "Not the exact date. But sometimes I wonder—what if these dreamers are common, nothing extraordinary, people you have to fight to recognize as a sacrifice, a warning. . . ." He bent lower, opening his mouth to speak again. Something rough and wet scratched my wrist; it was the steel wool, all soapy, in my mother's hand.

"Don't romanticize, Bernard," she said. "It's common knowledge that Gittel was a selfish woman who should have had the good sense to stay single. Sacrifice, my foot."

Sometimes I wish I were more like her and less like my father. No matter how many questions a daughter had, she knew when to talk and when to keep quiet. Before my wedding, young as I was, she didn't tell me anything. "Why frighten a person unnecessarily?" she said later. Papa was different. He couldn't hide anything from me. It's from him we get the insomnia and the bad dreams—he always left his children to finish his stories in their sleep.

"The Gittel," he used to say, as if she were a natural phenomenon. A little beauty at sixteen, she had red-gold hair to her waist, fine features, and tiny feet. Thank God, Rachel inherited her feet and not mine. Lucky girl. Tiny feet, this Gittel, and a good dancer and musician. The red in her hair and the musical sense came from the Hungarian; the rest was German going all the way back to the seventeenth century, when the Shapiros settled illegally in Berlin. By 1920 the family was in a good position: respected by the new Berlin intellectuals. Of course it wasn't really the brains, but the red-gold hair and the fine noses that made them comfortable. You can bet if they'd looked more Semitic they'd have caught on sooner to the general news.

She was eighteen then. Her father, along with a handful of other Jewish scholars, had been granted a professorship in the University of Berlin, and the family was able to establish itself in a brick house on Grunewaldstrasse, with real lace curtains and a baby grand. Being her father's pet, Gittel took whatever she liked from his library shelves, and sometimes sat with him when a colleague came to visit. Soon after her eighteenth birthday, she came into his study to borrow a book—without knocking, just like my Rachel. She had just mastered the art of the entrance, and paused where the light from the alabaster lamp would shine best on her hair.

"Papa," she announced. "Where is the Hoffmann?"

Shapiro was deep in conversation with a slender, bearded visitor whose trousers, according to Gittel's standards, were a little short. "Read something else," said her father. "The Romantics are anti-Semitic."

"Not Hoffmann," cried Gittel.

The visitor turned. He cursed himself for having put on his reading glasses, since at that distance he could not see her face or her eyes. He saw hair lit to the color of his own carefully raised flame roses and a brown merino skirt, very trim at the waist. "You enjoy Hoffmann as well?" he asked, squinting.

His name was Yaakov Horwicz: thirty-five years old and a scholar from Riga, Latvia. Like Shapiro he was enjoying the new generosity of his government. For the first time in his professional life he had had enough money to take the train to Berlin for a lecture series: Shapiro's on Western Religions. After the lecture and a three-hour discussion in the Romanische Café, he had received an invitation to coffee in the professor's home.

He was delirious, first to stand in Shapiro's study, then to make the acquaintance of his household. And still wearing those ridiculous spectacles, the cheap frames warped from the weight of the lenses. He took off his glasses for the formal introduction. His eyes, which had seemed to Gittel to be unnaturally large behind the lenses, now had a fine, granular brilliance, like her mother's antique blue glass vase. It was his eyes that kept her standing there, and his eyes that made

Shapiro think to himself: he can't help but be honorable. It's not in his veins as a possibility, unfaithfulness. She's young, but better to send her with a scholar than watch her run off at twenty with a young gentile going through his mystical phase.

Professor Shapiro is not to be blamed. I can imagine his concern, for Gittel was famous for her lively behavior with students. A young man would come to the house on Grunewaldstrasse, stand in the front hall, and within minutes a figure in petticoats would appear running down the curved staircase, shouting "Mama, Mama, I can't get the buttons in back!" Mrs. Shapiro was no help either, in the long run. She wore her hair in a neat coil, fastened her own innumerable buttons without assistance, and on top of that made bread from scratch. Just like my mother, she wouldn't let her daughter into the kitchen until dinner was safe in the oven. "You're a little girl yet," she'd say. "There's plenty of time to learn." I vowed I'd be different with mine. She would make her bed the minute she started to talk back, and help me in the kitchen whenever it was convenient. I wasn't going to make the same mistake.

Mrs. Shapiro got the message from her husband and invited Horwicz to stay to supper that evening. That meal nearly cost them a suitor, for despite the intensity of his vision and the shortness of his trousers, Horwicz had a fondness for table manners, and Gittel's were wretched. She tapped her fingers on the white linen, rearranged her cutlery, and sometimes hummed a phrase of music, as if she were alone in her room. He blushed, torn between embarrassment and desire. She, on her side, glanced at him only long enough to compare his eyes to those of Anselmus, the student-hero of a Hoffmann tale, noting that each time she looked at him, a feverish color stained his cheeks. I know this kind of girl: not happy unless she's in the midst of charming someone into his downfall. Gittel hummed and smiled and asked Horwicz if, after supper, he would turn the piano music for her.

Horwicz raised his napkin awkwardly to his lips.

"Go ahead," said Shapiro. "We'll finish our discussion later."

Horwicz had never before turned pages of music for a lady, young or otherwise, and here Gittel sealed her fate. *Turn*, she said, trying out a low husky cabaret voice. *Turn*. It was easy to obey such a voice. Horwicz imagined going on and on, watching her narrow, lightly freckled hands touch the keys and lift under the lamplight. Her fingers trembled a little; his heart swelled under his ribs, wanting to protect. . . . When at last she released him into her father's study, he had forgotten Western Religions and inquired after Gittel's status. Shapiro was standing by his desk, a book in his hand.

"Tell me about Latvia," he said. "Things don't flare up there the way they do here, isn't that so?"

"That's true," said Horwicz. "The nationals have been very liberal."

Shapiro smiled a small, lopsided smile. "She will be a lovely wife, a delight," he said. "And Latvia is good."

Picture the night Gittel was told of her destiny. They stand in the front parlor, and she turns pale yellow, like a late leaf, and begins looking through her music for something she says she's been missing for a long time. Finally she stops looking and says to Horwicz: "We will live here, in town?" He takes her hands, surprised at the firmness of the thin fingers, the tautness of the palm. The hands don't tremble now.

"I have a house of my own, and a garden," he says. "In a suburb of Riga."

"Mother," cries Gittel. *"Riga?"*

Mrs. Shapiro ushers her daughter from the parlor. Imagine the sounds of their two skirts rustling, and how Horwicz felt watching them leave the room—the upright mother and the daughter, long fingers gripping her skirt. The two men wait in the parlor like displaced ghosts; Professor Shapiro trying over and over to light his pipe; Horwicz holding himself perfectly still, blinking and pale as if he'd just stepped out of his study into broad daylight.

When Gittel appeared in the doorway again her back was needle-straight. She stepped up to Horwicz and held out her hand. "Let me play you something," she said.

"Chopin," muttered her father. "Another anti-Semite."

Horwicz escorted her to the piano, where she played for him the Sixth Prelude, her favorite. It's a strange piece: half delight, half dirge. They say he wrote it during a night of terrible rains. A messenger came to his door: George Sand and her three children had been killed in a carriage accident. He kept composing, unable to leave the piano bench. He wrote the last notes in the morning, just as there was another knock on the door, and her voice . . .

Mrs. Shapiro did not come back into the parlor until Horwicz was ready to leave. She was as gracious as ever, a remarkable woman; I know how she felt. I can see her face, almost as fragile as her daughter's, the eyelids only a little pink, only a little. I admire that woman.

The wedding picture is right there—on the mantel. When my Rachel was small, she used to take it down and touch her tongue to the dusty glass.

"Don't do that," I'd say.

She'd look at me, already the archaeologist, and say, "I'm cleaning it off for you."

Somewhere in her teens she lost interest; she could walk by that picture without even a glance. I can't do that. I walk past and there's Gittel in the dress her mother made for her by hand: a creamy, flounced thing. Her waist is unbelievable. She's tiny, but then the bridegroom is no giant himself. Great mustaches hide his lips, and he's not wearing his glasses. Without them his eyes appear pale and wide awake, as if when the shutter came down he saw something astonishing. I don't know anything about his childhood or bachelor circumstances; why he should have such eyes on his wedding day I can only attribute to foresight. He was like Shapiro that way. So much foresight he couldn't enjoy the wedding cake.

Beside him the Gittel is serious too; only on her, seriousness doesn't look so sweet. Her lips are set tight together, and her pupils are so dilated that her green eyes look black as caves. Rachel used to look at those eyes.

"I don't like her," she'd say. Somehow even a child knows it's not the usual bridal worry that's in Gittel's eyes. Ten years old, holding that picture in her hand. "Mom," she says to me. "Do I have to leave home like her if I'm bad?"

She gave me a nice shock. When had I ever spoken of Gittel leaving home at eighteen? I played innocent. "Who told you that, Rachel?" I asked.

"You talk in your sleep," she said.

She made me nervous then, she makes me nervous now. At the time, I thought: what good will it do to tell a ten-year-old that when the time comes, she'll be good and ready to leave home?

"You're not a Gittel," I said. "Nobody is going to make you leave home. We just want you to be happy."

She bit her lower lip and big terrible tears dropped on her T-shirt.

"Rachel, you're breaking my heart," I said. "What's the matter?"

"It's okay," she said. "I'll go and pack."

Thank God that phase is over—although with Rachel it's hard to tell. Last month when we looked at that picture together she laughed.

"I used to have nightmares about her," she said.

I acted nonchalant. "Like what?"

"I don't remember. Big melodramas, everybody in the world disappearing—"

"Go on," I said.

Then she gave me such a look. "Mom," she said. "All kids have dreams like that."

"About the end of the world?" I asked.

"Yes."

Sometimes she hurts me with her quick answers. Every family has its stories, why should she deny hers? Besides, she traps me. She was all eagerness: "Mother, what finally happened to Gittel?"

What am I supposed to do? If I start to tell it, and she's in a modern mood, she cuts me off. If she's not, she gets all dreamy on me. Naturally I start thinking about her and Daniel and their archaeology studies, and so I say to her, "Rache, tell me honestly what you plan on doing with those old pots? Read the newspapers, look around you!" I raised her to read the newspapers so nothing should take her by surprise, and she winds up in the ancient ruins. Last week on the phone she said to me: "Mother, I read the newspapers and so does Daniel," and I knew she was biting her lip. It's a bad habit. "I'm coming this weekend," she said, "so you and I can have a talk." I made up my mind right then and there that I wouldn't mention Gittel unless she promises not to interrupt . . .

Gittel bore her husband seven sons in ten years. Papa was number four, Gittel's favorite because he had his father's eyes and could listen to her at the piano without speaking or tugging on her skirt every three minutes. Sometimes she would stop playing and say to him: "Shut your eyes, Bernard, and imagine that this is a baby grand instead of an upright, and that across from us is a maroon divan, where grandpapa sits reading, his glasses slipping down his nose." Other times she took him into the courtyard and lifted her fine nose into the air. "Smell," she said. "Today it smells exactly like April at home." He listened to

272

her describe where the alabaster lamp had stood in the other house (she had it next to the piano in Riga) and how her mother had given it to her, along with the brass candlesticks, the five handmade lace doilies, and her own key ring to wear at her waist. "A good housekeeper is never without her keys," her mother had said, knowing everything in advance.

Once a week a letter arrived from Grunewaldstrasse, and the family gathered in the parlor to hear Gittel read it. Papa remembered later how his father leaned against the mantel listening carefully to letters that seemed to be about nothing but the weather and fifteenth-century religion. His mother's hands trembled as she read—her voice, too—and sometimes afterward he heard them talking in their bedroom, their voices soft to begin with, then rising, rising.

Gittel captured the little suburb. For months after her departure people talked of how the young mother would be stirring soup in the kitchen and suddenly remember a dream she'd had the night before. Off she'd run to the neighbor's house, bursting in: "Marta, I forgot to tell you what I dreamed about your boy!" Her friends seemed to love this, especially the burning of the soup that went hand in hand with the piece of news, the almost forgotten dream, the stories about Grune-waldstrasse. It was rare in that time and place to find a woman for whom dreams and stories came before soup, and a miracle that, given her dizzy mind and her husband's library heart, any of the seven boys grew up. "Luck," Papa would say to me if Mother was in the room. "Destiny," he'd say if she wasn't.

He was five years old when his father died. Diabetes: that's where Papa got it, and now I have to be careful too. Gittel was twenty-eight, and after the seven boys she still had her figure and her lovely hair. Papa's memory of her is of a woman in a new black silk dress and fine shoes, hushing a baby. It was at his father's funeral that he began to be afraid of her.

The service was held on a little rise in the Jewish cemetery outside Riga. It was a fine March day, the kind of day when the tips of the grass look caught on fire, and gulls go slanting across the sky as if they can't get their balance. The kind of day where you want to run in one direction and then turn and see the figures of people you've left behind, tiny and unreal as paper dolls. Papa wanted to break out of the circle

273

of mourners and run across the knolls and valleys of the cemetery, all the way down to the shore, where the Gulf of Riga stretched endlessly away.

"Come here, Bernard," said Gittel. "Stand in front of me."

She placed one hand lightly on his shoulder, but every time he shifted his weight, her fingers tightened. His brothers stood all around him: Johan, the eldest, almost ten and already a tall boy; Aaron and Yaakov beside him. Pressed tight to their mother's skirt were the two young ones, whose names Papa later forgot, and on her hip, the baby. She stood absolutely still, while around her Horwicz' friends and relatives rocked back and forth. Papa turned once and looked up at her face. Her narrow jaw was marble white, and her eyes, clear and unreddened, were trained on a tuft of grass blowing beside the open pit. People whispered: "Poor thing, she's in shock. He was everything to her." Only Papa, watching the dark pupils, knew that she was not thinking about her husband. When the rabbi closed his book, Gittel sighed and bent down to Bernard.

"Very soon," she said, "we can go back."

"Back to the house?" said Bernard.

"No," she replied. "Grunewaldstrasse."

For five years no one but Papa knew Gittel's mind. They thought she would pull herself together and become a good manager with all the help she was offered by her women friends. Everybody should be so fortunate; Horwicz' cousins in the city came by often to take the boys out for a drive, and ladies were always bringing hot dishes by. "With seven boys she must be desperate," they said. The neighbors began to wonder, though, how with seven wild boys they would be hearing Chopin and Mozart four hours together in the morning. Certain shopkeepers began to talk. The dishes stopped coming, and the cousins, after a lecture or two, stopped coming to get the boys. "Let her suffer like other human beings," they said. "A lesson is what she needs."

Maybe by that time it was too late for lessons. I suppose she tried. She worked in her husband's garden, coming up with small, deformed carrots and the smallest heads of cabbage imaginable. She sent the three eldest boys to serve one-year apprenticeships in town, and when they came home for the Sabbath they brought her things from the city, and part of their wages. Bernard she sent to school: Bernard, who wanted nothing more than to be a carpenter like his big brother Johan, whom he worshiped for his muscles and his talk of America. Every day after school Bernard went to the carpenter's house to drink tea with Johan, and every day Johan showed him the tin with the money in it. "They say you can't keep kosher there," he'd say. "But otherwise it's paradise."

Home in the evenings, Bernard let his mother caress his face. "You have the eyes of your father, and the brains of mine," she'd say. "He is a great teacher in Berlin, and so will you be, when we go home."

"We are home," he'd say, looking at his feet.

"No," she said. "You wait and see."

Gittel's looks were beginning to go. Her hair was no longer that burnished gold color, although the ladies told her she could fix it easily with a little lemon juice and a walk in the sunlight. But Gittel wasn't listening. She played loud, crashing pieces by Chopin and Liszt, and sent Bernard to do all her errands in town so she wouldn't have to face the helpful remarks of the shopkeepers. When he left for school she sent him with letters to mail to Grunewaldstrasse, which came back marked *wrong address*.

One day a letter came from the Shapiros—with another address, in a district of Berlin Bernard had never heard his mother mention. In the morning, he waited beside her writing table while she finished a letter. Over her shoulder he read: *I don't care if it's smaller, we're coming. People stare at me in the street.*

"I'll be back in a minute, Mama," he said. Upstairs in his room he packed a school satchel and hid it in his closet. He would know when she began to pack up her lamp and her candlesticks.

That night Gittel went to the carpenter's house and wept at his table. "We're running out of money," she said. "Can you keep Johan for another year?" The carpenter was surprised; he knew Gittel's people in Germany were well off, that she could get money any time she wanted. He told people later that his first reaction was to refuse: "Lie in your own bed," he wanted to say, but she looked almost ill. Her lovely skin seemed blue, as if she were turning to ice inside. "All right," he said.

Two days later the shoemaker received a visit, and under the pressure of her tears, offered to keep Aaron for a second year. "He works like the devil," he said later, "better than my own sons, and doesn't waste his money." But telling the story, he shook his head: "It's a terrible thing to see a woman trying to give away her children."

The third boy, Jacob, was finally taken by the Horwicz cousins, though not until they had given Gittel a piece of their minds. Now that Horwicz had passed on, they revered him like a saint. "If our Yaakov were alive, what would he say to all this?" "If your Yaakov were alive," she answered, "would any of this be happening?" She was gaunt and smoky-eyed as a gypsy, and sometimes, in the two weeks that followed, she looked at Bernard with such passion that he ran out of the house and took a streetcar to Johan's, where he stayed till suppertime. Late one night, as he was working in his copybook for school, she knelt beside him.

"Bernard," she said. "Are you still having your special dreams?"

He hadn't been able to remember his dreams for weeks. Instead he heard voices all talking at once: the voices his father had called "demons" because they distorted every word that came into the mind. "No," he said.

"I have," she said, touching his arm. "You are now my eldest son, and we are taking our family home."

"We are home," he said.

"Home," she repeated. "My mother's—"

Something was kicking inside his ribs. Where his heart should be was a small, clawed animal coming loose. He scrambled up onto his chair and stood towering over his mother. "You can't make me," he shouted. "Because I am going to America with Johan and Yaakov and Aaron."

She stayed on her knees a moment, then tried to get up—too suddenly—and swayed forward as she did. Bernard flushed with shame; she looked like a drunk girl clutching the table edge.

"You are my son, and you will do as I say," she said.

The pressure in his chest built higher. He looked at the woman before him, and for an instant, the curve of her nose, the tiny velvet mole beside her mouth, were as alien to him as the landscapes of Asia in his schoolbook. "I don't know you," he cried, closing his eyes against the sight of her hand rushing toward his face.

276

"Go to bed," said Gittel. "In the morning we will talk."

At dawn Bernard crept out with his satchel and took the first streetcar to the carpenter's house. Every day he waited for the knock on the door, for the sight of his mother and the three children standing on the step, a cart piled high with belongings. The world seemed to him to have closed its mouth; the gulls, the bright grass, the wide and silent gulf—all seemed to have grown bolder in their colors to judge him. A week passed.

One evening Johan came home from work and took his hand. "Come," he said. "I want to show you something." They took a streetcar out of the city and walked down the street to their own house. It was unlocked. Inside the furniture gleamed, the rug lay bright and soft on the floor, and the pots and pans—always before in the sink—hung clean and polished on the kitchen wall. Under the alabaster lamp was a sheet of paper. *To my beloved Bernard I leave my mother's alabaster lamp, her brass Shabbas candlesticks, and the key ring, so that in America he will remember his mother.* The rest of the letter divided up the household items among the other boys. In an envelope they found the deed to the house.

It was the station porter who had told Johan; he was the last person in the suburb to see Gittel and the three children. He said her fingers quivered when she tried to hand him the four tickets to Berlin. He had never seen her up close before, and told people later that she was a little girl. "Magnificent hands, though," he said. "Like a slender man's, strong and nicely shaped. The kind of hands you don't expect to tremble, and she didn't expect them to either. I could see she was embarrassed, so I said, 'Going for long?' 'Oh no,' she said. 'Just to visit my parents and take the children to a magic show.' She put her hands in her coat pockets. 'I'm terrible about traveling,' she said, smiling."

The silence of the world then was different; it wasn't the silence of waiting, but the kind that comes after a mistake, with disbelief caught in it like a maimed bird. The three oldest brothers swore never to allow their mother's name to cross their lips as long as they lived—not even if she wrote and begged their forgiveness, or became ill. They worked hard, and Johan spoke continually of passage costs and departure dates. And Bernard began to dream. He dreamed he was sitting beside his mother on the piano bench, both of them dressed for his father's funeral service. Suddenly she rose from the bench and gripped his arm. "Come with me," she cried, "into the piano where it's safe." Bernard looked out the window. At the door and all the windows of the house stood a hundred men in fine suits, knocking politely. He bit his mother's hand, but she kept her grip, drawing him to her and into the open piano. The lid came down, suffocating . . .

After school Bernard sometimes went to the station to listen to the porter, who was still elaborating on Gittel's departure: how she looked, how the three little boys clung about her asking, "Will there be an acrobat there? Will there be a fat lady and a thin man? Will they cut somebody in half and make him come out whole?" Every day the story got longer. The porter got better tips, and his tongue lightened as if it were a balance scale tipping in one direction. "Terrible circles under her eyes," he said. "And the children: I swear the youngest knew it was for more than three days—"

Such stories the Gittel could tell you—about strangers in town, or what happened to the neighbors yesterday, or a terrifying dream that would haunt you for weeks, as if you yourself had dreamed it. But when it came to newspapers, she was a fool. Thank God that's not the case with Rachel, although from the look on her face sometimes, and the news of the world, I think: "What's the difference?" She will argue with me about Gittel, too, but newspapers or not, Gittel wasn't thinking about current events. She was sleepwalking, imagining the lovely carpets, the curved staircase, her mother coming down the hall to greet her, her father sitting down to chat with a student.

I should stop the story here. For one thing, Rachel's bus gets in any minute, and the way she walks, she'll be here before I can clear the table of these papers. . . . But I remember how it used to drive me crazy when Papa began to describe the tiniest details of Gittel's traveling dress and people and things he had never seen. He could never get to the end of the story. *Next time*, he'd say, and next time he'd start all over at the beginning, lingering until Mother called us in to supper. Some habits are hard to break, he used to say.

On the train Gittel took her children into an empty compartment, but you know how it is; someone always comes to interrupt your dreams. This time it is an elderly gentleman, the first German she's seen since she got on in Riga. During the first hour of the ride nobody speaks. The children keep their heads lowered, once in a while glancing up at the stranger, who is smart and alternates his gaze between the countryside and his own shoes. You know how the eye roams when you're traveling. Maybe at this moment my own daughter is sitting in the window seat of a bus, a stranger beside her. Any minute he could turn and look at her face and say, "Going home?" The stranger in Gittel's compartment is polite, and Gittel is busy telling her children about magic shows and lace curtains and hot potato kugel. "Grandpa and Grandma have moved," she says, "but I'll take you to look at the old house. She'll have a lunch for us, too. A hot lunch."

She has a nice voice, thinks the stranger. He lets his eye rest on a piece of hand luggage at her feet, and suddenly, coming awake, he sees the name *Shapiro*. He turns pale and leans forward.

"Frau Shapiro?"

She looks at him, startled, and the children hide their faces in her coat.

So much goes through the stranger's mind when he sees the face of the Gittel: a face that cannot shed its innocence, even when the eyes in it look out the compartment window at the new red and black flags in the station windows—seen quickly, because the train goes so fast. The stranger holds out his hand.

"I knew a Shapiro at university," he says. "I am proud to say. I am proud."

He holds her hand too long; he won't let it go even when the conductor comes into the compartment and says: "Passports, please." Her eyes grow dark with surprise.

"Excuse me, please," she says, pulling her hand away, reaching into her bag for her passport.

"Wait," he says.

But Gittel, with a nervous laugh, had handed hers over. She doesn't change expression when the conductor takes a long look at it and says: "You will report to the Bureau of Immigration as soon as you arrive. Your passport needs changes."

The conductor is gone. The stranger wants to tell her something, but her face speaks to him like marble, like a desert statue that knows either everything or nothing.

What can he do but ask her where she is going, keep her in conversation until the train comes into the station? So he asks, and she begins a story. A story about a lovely house, a mahogany mantel, a fireplace, a smoking chimney, a girl who is coming at this moment through the front door, having for once remembered her key; a girl capable, after all, of surprising her mother.

The Legacy of Raizel Kaidish: A Story

Rebecca Goldstein

IN 1945 THE FOLLOWING INCIDENT took place in the death camp of Buchenwald. There were two young Jewish girls who had become very devoted to one another during the few months of their imprisonment. Each was the last survivor of her family. One morning one of them awoke too weak to work. Her name was put on the death list. The other, Raizel Kaidish, argued with her friend that she, Raizel, should go instead. She would tell the Germans there had been a mistake, and when they saw how strong and fit for work she was, it would be all right. Someone informed on the girls and they were both gassed. The informer was rewarded with Raizel's kitchen job.

I am named after Raizel Kaidish. My mother knew her from the camp. It is noteworthy that although the war took all her relatives from her, my mother chose to name her first child, her only child, after someone outside the family, after the heroine of block eight, Buchenwald.

My mother's moral framework was formed in the camp. Forged in the fires, it was strong and inflexible. One of her central concerns was that I, without myself suffering, would come to know all that she had learned there.

My moral education began at an early age. It consisted at first of tales from the camp. People in my real life were nice or mean, usually a little of both. But in the tales there were only saints and sinners, heroes and villains. I remember questioning my mother about this, and her answer to me: "When times are normal, Rose, then normal people are a little nice and a little mean together. But when there are

281

hard times, when there is not enough to eat or drink, when there is war, then you don't find a little nice and a little mean mixed together. You find only greatness. Very great badness and very great goodness."

The people in my life did not seem so real to me as the people in the tales. When I closed my eyes I couldn't picture the faces of my friends or family. All that I could make out of my father was a vaguely sad face around the glinting rimless glasses. (It seemed, in my child's mind, that the light bouncing off from those polished lenses gave the wrong impression, suggesting something hard and resistant, whereas I knew that everything in my father yielded to the touch.) Even my mother's features wouldn't come into focus, only her outline: tall and always erect, in the grey or dark blue suit and the white blouse, her light brown hair in a low bun at the nape of her neck.

But my images of the camp were vivid and detailed. The pink rosebuds on my wallpaper were not as real to me as the grey and drab green of the barracks, the brown of the mud. It seemed to me that I knew the feel through decaying shoes of the sharp stones in the main square, the sight, twice daily, of the terrifying roll-call. It seemed I too had quickly glanced up at the open sky and wondered that others outside saw the same sky.

My father, a doctor like my mother, did not approve of the tales:

"She's too young. You'll give her nightmares, traumas. A child this age shouldn't know."

"A child this age. Don't be a hypocrite, Saul. You know you would never consider her old enough to know."

"And why should she know? Can't we forget already? Can't we live like others?"

"No. We can't. I wouldn't even want to. Would you really want it, Saul, to think and live like the others? To join the sleepwalkers, with the glazed eyes and the smug smiles? Is that why we lived when the others didn't? Is that what we want for our daughter?"

And at this point I can hear my father's sigh, the deep drawn-out sigh so characteristic of him, which had always seemed to me, when I was young, to have the slight tremor of a sob. My father's sadness was something I felt I could almost reach out and touch, like my mother's goodness.

The arguments between my parents continued throughout my childhood. And my father, so gentle, was a man who hated to fight. In the quiet of the night, awake in my bed, I would catch the cadences of their voices, my father's sad and low, so that I missed much of what he said, my mother's burning with her quiet blue fury.

But the lessons continued, the simple stark tales of cruelty and sacrifice, cowardice and courage. And always she came back to the story of my namesake. She would tell me that she had honored both Raizel and me in choosing my name. (She called me Raizel or even Raizele sometimes, in rare moments of tenderness, stroking back my hair.) She hoped that I too would be capable of real courage, of giving another's life just as much importance as my own.

When I reached fourteen, my mother, deeming me to have arrived at least at the age of reason (and also the age at which Raizel had sacrificed herself), began to instruct me in the moral theory she had worked out in Buchenwald. The theory is elaborate and detailed, reminiscent of the German my parents spoke to one another: complications nesting within complications. The brief account I give here is necessarily inadequate, and perhaps not intrinsically interesting. But the picture of my mother is incomplete without a description of her moral viewpoint.

My mother believed that the ethical outlook is the impersonal outlook. One is morally obliged to look at a situation without regard for one's own identity in it and to act in the way which is dictated by this impersonal view; to act in the way one believes will minimize the sum of suffering. My mother's emphasis was always on minimizing pain and suffering, never maximizing happiness or well-being. She explained this to me once when, much older, I questioned her: "I know what is evil. To know suffering is to know evil. None of the attempts to identify the good have this same certainty."

So far there is nothing, except for its pessimistic cast, to distinguish my mother's view from the great bulk of utilitarian theories. The special twist comes in the foundations she claimed, and it is a twist that mirrors her personality: her uncompromising rationality. The expression of this came in her denial of the "separateness" of the ethical realm. Ethics for her was nothing but a species of logic. The moral obligation is nothing over and above the obligation to be logically consistent, and virtue reduces to rationality.

Why is this so? Because to deny the obligation of acting on the impersonal viewpoint, one would have to maintain that one's self has some special metaphysical significance, that it makes a difference that one is who one is. And how can this consistency be maintained once one has recognized the existence of other selves, each of whom is who he is? (Only the solipsist can consistently be unethical.) To use one of her favorite analogies: the person who acts only in his own interest is like a person who says there is always something special about his location, because he can always say "I am here," whereas everyone else is merely there. Once one has granted that there are other subjects of experience, other selves which suffer, then one can maintain that one's own pain matters (and who would deny this?) only if one grants that the pain of everyone else matters in exactly the same way.

Raizel Kaidish's behavior was paradigmatically ethical. Viewing the situation impersonally, this fourteen-year-old saw that the stronger child would have a better, though slim, chance to survive. She acted on this view, undeterred by the fact that it was she who was the stronger, she who was unnecessarily risking her life.

After the liberation my mother returned to Berlin to continue her formal training in medicine. She also began her lifelong study of philosophy. She was curious to see who among the philosophically great had shared her discovery. Kant she considered to be the most worthwhile ethicist. Socrates she loved for his devotion to the ethical questions, for his conviction that nothing ought to concern us more than the questions of how to live our lives. (Hanging over my bed, the only piece of embroidery I've ever known her to do, was the Socratic quotation: "The unexamined life is not worth living.") But for the most part my mother found the great philosophers of the past a disappointment. The truth, so simple, had eluded them, because they had assumed the separateness of the ethical realm. Some had grasped pieces of it, but few had seen the unseamed whole.

It was contemporary philosophers, however, particularly the positivists and their "fellow travelers," who aroused her wrath. For here were philosophers who dismissed the possibility of all ethical reason, who denied the very subject matter of the field. Instead of conducting inquiries into the nature of our moral obligations, they have offered analyses of the grammar of ethical propositions. She would look up from some contemporary philosophical book or journal, her eyes blazing their blue fury:

"Positivists." The intonation she gave the word was similar to that she gave "Nazi." "They don't see because their eyes aren't turned outward but inward, into the blackness of their own minds. To forsake the important questions for this dribble! To spend your life examining quibbles!"

And I? How did I feel about my extensive moral training? The object of so much attention, of all the pedagogical theorizing, the fights in the night, I felt ignored, unloved, of no significance. And, especially as I grew older, I felt angry—a dumb, unacknowledged outrage. It was not just a matter of the rigidity of my upbringing, the lack of laughter in a home where one could reach out and touch one's father's sadness and mother's goodness. It was not just the fact that I was always made to feel so different from my friends, so that I often, though always with a great sense of guilt, fantasized myself in another family with parents who were frivolous and happy and had no numbers burned into their arms. But it was something else that infuriated me. There is, of course, nothing unusual in a child's resentment of a mother. My friends, from early adolescence onward, were always annoyed with one or another of their parents. But theirs was the pure clean indignation which is unashamed of itself. Mine was an anger also angry at itself. Hadn't she suffered enough? Shouldn't I try to do everything to make it up to her? By hating her I joined the ranks of her enemies. I allied myself with the murderers.

And so the resentment, folded back on itself again and again, thickened and darkened. Never once did I ever say, not even to myself, "I am angry at this woman." This acknowledgement came years later, after she was dead, during the time in which I deliberated over having a child of my own. (The mental delivery of this decision was so much more painful than the actual physical delivery.) In debating the reasons for having a child, I asked myself whether any reasons could be right, whether one was ever justified in bringing a person into being for some reason of one's own? But if not for one's own reason, then whose?

It seemed a moral inconsistency woven into the very fabric of human existence. And then I realized that the *act* of parenting need not bear any of this moral compromise: it is possible for the reason one had for

285

creating a child to recede into significance in the face of the fact of that child's existence. The ends for which one bore the child lose themselves in the knowledge of the child itself. This is the essence of good parenting, and it was exactly what I felt to be missing from the relationship between my mother and me. I knew what no child should ever know: that my mother had had me for some definite reason and that she would always see me in terms of this reason. I sensed this in my mother, and I hated her for it.

I said that my anger never showed itself. Actually there was a brief rebellion whose form was so typical of the oddity of my family that now, years later, even I can see its comic aspects and smile. My first semester of college, while my friends developed their own conventional modes of rebellion, I worked out mine. I became a positivist. I took Introduction to Philosophy with a self-intoxicated young professor, a new Ph.D. from Harvard, and, although this would not be his own description, a neo-positivist. He told us during the first lecture that he was going to show us, over the course of the semester, why we were lucky, insofar as we were philosophy students, to have been born now; that it was now possible to see that previous generations had devoted themselves to pseudo-questions concerning the nature of Reality, Truth, and The Good; and that such questions were expressions of logical confusion. These fine big words don't name anything, and thus there is nothing there whose nature is to be explored.

I sat there drinking in his words, thinking, "This is it. This is why I came to college." All through that term, Monday, Wednesday, and Friday, from ten to eleven, while others dozed and doodled, I listened in a state of delirium, following the arguments with a concentration I have never attained since. My mind bubbled over with the excitement of this illicit doctrine, this forbidden philosophy. And the most forbidden, and therefore delicious, view offered in the course was that devoted to ethics, or rather the dismissal of ethics.

I memorized whole passages out of my favorite book, A. J. Ayer's *Language, Truth and Logic:* "We can now see why it is impossible to find a criterion for determining the validity of ethical judgements. It is not because they have an 'absolute' validity which is mysteriously independent of ordinary sense-experience, but because they have no objective validity whatsoever. If a sentence makes no statement at all, there is obviously no sense in asking whether what it says is true or false. And we have seen that sentences which simply express moral judgments do not say anything. They are pure expressions of feeling and as such do not come under the category of truth and falsehood." I was moved by the sparse beauty and elegance of the arguments. How had I never seen if before, never seen that my mother's unshakable theory was nothing but a floating airy fabrication of pseudo-statements?

My preparations for final exams were trivial compared to my cramming for the visit home during intercession. I arrived back about eleven at night, too late for philosophical debate. But my mind was so teeming with positivist arguments that when my mother wished me "good night" I almost challenged her: "What do you mean by that? What do you mean by 'good'?"

The next evening, after my mother and father arrived home from the hospital, we all sat in the living room while Bertha, our house-keeper, finished dinner. I was waiting for the right moment for launching my attack, any comment which was mildly speculative. But my perverse mother was all practicality that night. She asked me about the food at school, about my roommate, even told a funny story about her own roommate, in Berlin before the war. Then finally:

"You were always so brief on the phone when I asked you about your classes. Tell me more about them. You seemed to have enjoyed them very much."

"Yes, they were wonderful. Especially philosophy. I'm going to major in it."

"Really? I've always thought it a rather funny kind of profession. Every person should of course think about philosophy, but it seems an odd way to earn one's living."

"But what about teaching, Marta?" my father, the eternal peace-maker, asked. "Don't you think it's important to have people teaching philosophy?"

"Well yes, that's true. But I suspect that most of them don't think of themselves primarily as teachers, but as thinkers, professional thinkers, however strange that sounds. Well, we can ask Rose here. What do you fancy yourself, a teacher or a philosopher?"

"A philosopher of course. The need for professional training in philosophy is no different than anywhere else, no different than in medicine. People think they can just jump in and start philosophizing and that they'll make sense. They rarely do. It takes technical training."

"Oh? I disagree very much, as you know, with this emphasis on technical training. Instead of humanizing the mathematical sciences they try to mathematize the humanities. Translating into a lot of complicated symbols doesn't show the truth of what you're saying."

"But it does often show its meaninglessness."

"Oh really? Yes, I can see how that might often be true."

Impossible woman! What was wrong with her? Her kindling point was usually so frighteningly low, but tonight she would not burn. She wouldn't even flicker. (The explanation would have been obvious to anyone not occupying my vantage point. She was, quite simply, very happy to see me.)

I had no more patience. I abandoned my hopes for a smooth transition.

"Mother, there's a question about ethics that has been bothering me."

There. I had opened the door. Now I had to walk through.

"Yes? Tell me about it. Perhaps I can help."

"You've always said that the moral obligation is nothing but the obligation to be logically consistent. But why do we have to be logically consistent?"

"I must say you surprise me. Such an anti-rationalist question. And after a semester of college. The answer is, of course, that the truth is important. And logical inconsistencies can't be true. If you ask me why the truth is important I can't give you a non-circular answer. Anything I say is going to presuppose the importance of truth, as all rational discourse presupposed it. And this impossibility of a non-circular answer is itself the answer."

"I don't understand a word you're saying!" I exploded. "The Truth! The sacred lofty Truth! What's the Truth? Where's the Truth? Let me see you point to it. What does it mean to say 'The Truth is important'? What cognitive content can it possibly have? It's nonsense. And the same with all the other so-called truths of your so-called theory. You claim to be so rational, but you're only emoting. Eternally emoting. And I'm sick to death of it!"

My speech was not delivered in that cool voice of detached reason

I had so diligently rehearsed. Instead it tore out of me with a force that amazed me, sweeping me along.

The effect was immediate. My mother's face had the same capacity for instantaneous transformation I have observed in my infant daughter. (I often find myself wondering whether this is a trait characteristic of infancy, or whether it is something my Marta has inherited from her grandmother, along with her name.) My mother had never raised her voice to me, and she did not do so now. As always her eyes did all the screaming.

"Positivist." Her introduction was not the usual one. There was outrage and contempt, but it was muffled by sadness.

"After all that I have taught you, you speak that way? You lose everything in one semester of college? Have you so little substance that at your first exposure to the jargon of these anti-thinkers you disintegrate?"

I had no answer. The brilliant arguments cramming my head only the night before were all gone. My head was so hollow it felt like it was floating away from the rest of me. The numbing fog of shame and guilt was settling back over everything. I dimly saw my father sitting there, staring out at us over the wall of his sadness. My mother's voice burned through the haze.

"You disappoint me. You disappoint us all. You are not worthy to be named after Raizel Kaidish."

Soon after my wedding, when my mother was fifty-six, she learned that she had cancer of the uterus and had no more than six months to live. She reacted to her impending death as if she had been preparing for it her whole life, as indeed she had been. She looked at it with her customary objectivity: Yes, she was relatively young, and there were still many things that she would have liked to experience, particularly grandparenthood. But that she, a Jew from Berlin, had been given these past thirty years was a fact whose response was gratitude, not the greedy demand for yet more years.

She never complained. Her greatest worry was the mental pain her illness was causing my father and me. She died as I had always known her to live: with superhuman discipline and courage.

A week before she died she told me that it had been she who had informed on Raizel Kaidish. She asked my forgiveness.

Midrash on Happiness

Grace Paley

WHAT SHE MEANT by happiness, she said, was the following: she meant having (or having had) (or continuing to have) everything. By everything, she meant, first, the children, then a dear person to live with, preferably a man (by *live with*, she meant for a long time but not necessarily). Along with and not in preferential order, she required three or four best women friends to whom she could tell every personal fact and then discuss on the widest deepest and most hopeless level, the economy, the constant, unbeatable, cruel war economy, the slavery of the American worker to the idea of that economy, the complicity of male people in the whole structure, the dumbness of men (including her preferred man) on this subject. By dumbness, she meant everything dumbness has always meant: silence and stupidity. By silence she meant refusal to speak; by stupidity she meant refusal to hear. For happiness she required women to walk with. To walk in the city arm in arm with a woman friend (as her mother had with aunts and cousins so many years ago) was just plain essential. Oh! those long walks and intimate talks, better than standing alone on the most admirable mountain or in the handsomest forest or hay-blown field (all of which were certainly splendid occupations for the wind-starved soul). More important even (though maybe less sweet because of age) than the old walks with boys she'd walked with as a girl, that nice bunch of worried left-wing boys who flew (always slightly hand-icapped by that idealistic wing) into a dream of paid-up mortgages with a small room for opinion and solitude in the corner of home. Oh do you remember those fellows, Ruthy?

Remember? Well, I'm married to one.

Not exactly.

O.K. So it's a union co-op.

But she had, Faith continued, democratically *tried* walking in the beloved city with a man, but the effort had failed since from about that age—twenty seven or eight—he had felt an obligation, if a young woman passed, to turn abstractedly away, in the middle of the most personal conversation or even to say confidentially, wasn't she something?—or clasping his plaid shirt, at the heart's level, oh my god! The purpose of this: perhaps to work a nice quiet appreciation into thunderous heartbeat as he had been taught on pain of sexual death. For happiness, she also required work to do in this world and bread on the table. By work to do she included the important work of raising children righteously up. By righteously she meant that along with being useful and speaking truth to the community, they must do no harm. By harm she meant not only personal injury to the friend the lover the coworker the parent (the city the nation) but also the stranger; she meant particularly the stranger in all her or his difference, who, because we were strangers in Egypt, deserves special goodness for life or at least until the end of strangeness. By bread on the table, she meant no metaphor but truly bread as her father had ended every single meal with a hunk of bread. By hunk, she was describing one of the attributes of good bread.

Suddenly she felt she had left out a couple of things: Love. Oh yes, she said, for she was talking, talking all this time, to patient Ruth and they were walking for some reason in a neighborhood where she didn't know the children, the pizza places or the vegetable markets. It was early evening and she could see lovers walking along Riverside Park with their arms around one another, turning away from the sun which now sets among the new apartment houses of New Jersey, to kiss. Oh

I forgot, she said, now that I notice, Ruthy I think I would die without love. By love she probably meant she would die without being *in* love. By *in* love she meant the acuteness of the heart at the sudden sight of a particular person or the way over a couple of years of interested friendship one is suddenly stunned by the lungs' longing for more and more breath in the presence of that friend, or nearly drowned to the knees by the salty spring that seems to beat for years on our vaginal shores. Not to omit all sorts of imaginings which assure great spiritual energy for months and when luck follows truth, years.

Oh sure, love. I think so too, sometimes, said Ruth, willing to hear Faith out since she had been watching the kissers too, but I'm really not so sure. Nowadays it seems like pride, I mean overweening pride, when you look at the children and think we don't have time to do much (by time Ruth meant both her personal time and the planet's time). When I read the papers and hear all this boom boom bellicosity, the guys outdaring each other, I see we have to change it all—the world—without killing it absolutely—without killing it, that'll be the trick the kids'll have to figure out. Until that begins, I don't understand happiness—what you mean by it.

Then Faith was ashamed to have wanted so much and so little all at the same time—to be so easily and personally satisfied in this terrible place, when everywhere vast public suffering rose in reeling waves from the round earth's nation-states—hung in the satellite-watched air and settled in no time at all into TV sets and newsrooms. It was all there. Look up and the news of halfway round the planet is falling on us all. So for all these conscientious and technical reasons, Faith was ashamed. It was clear that happiness could not be worthwhile, with so much conversation and so little revolutionary change. Of course, Faith said, I know all that. I do, but sometimes walking with a friend I forget the world.

Homage to Isaac Bashevis Singer:
A Story

Susan Fromberg Schaeffer

I T SO happened that she began to worship Isaac Bashevis Singer.

She was afflicted with a high fever that would not go down. It rose to 103 degrees in the mornings and evenings and then dropped to normal. When her fever was high, she shook all over; when it dropped, she felt healthy as a horse, but tired. The doctor said she had to go to the hospital. She said she was sure she could shake it off at home. She could take her aspirins herself. She would set her alarm to ring every four hours. Besides, one of her neighbors sat in her living room all day long, so she was not alone. She had a television and her neighbor did not and the woman was addicted to many programs. Probably, if the truth were known, Mrs. Klopstock venerated the television, which she regarded—without awareness—as the custodian of her safety.

The doctor said she could not live forever with a fever of 103 and admitted her to the hospital. That same night, her doctor came to see her. "I want to go home," she said. "Everyone's dying here." She was on a bad floor. Virtually everyone was dying. The doctor said she could go home as soon as she was finished with her tests. He told her to forget about the other patients. *She* was not dying. Mrs. Klopstock said she would be glad to forget about the other patients, especially since there was nothing wrong with her. She had a fever, she told the doctor, because she was upset. "You've been upset before," he said. "Being upset could cause a fever," she said. "Please," said the doctor.

293

"No one could be that upset." "They could," she said, "if they had my daughter." "One daughter," he said, "to cause all this trouble?" "I have troubles even I don't know about," said Mrs. Klopstock. He didn't say anything.

Mrs. Klopstock remained in the hospital. In spite of herself, she grew fond of her roommate, Mrs. Smith, who was dying of brain cancer. One night, Mrs. Smith soiled herself and cried for an hour because she was afraid to call the nurse. Mrs. Klopstock called the nurse. The nurse shouted at Mrs. Smith. She said she was worse than a baby. She said she had a 90-year-old patient who could do more for herself than Mrs. Smith could. Mrs. Smith cried for hours. She would not eat her snack; she was afraid of soiling herself again. "The patients are all dying," said Mrs. Klopstock to her doctor, "and the nurses are killing them." "Don't exaggerate," he said. She demanded to know why they were holding her there. The doctor said she was in a hospital, not a prison, and she had a fever of unknown origin. Mrs. Klopstock was worried about her health insurance; she asked if that was a disease. "Of course it's a disease," he said. She raised her eyebrows; she was not so sure.

She persuaded Mrs. Smith that she wanted to get out of bed and sit up on a chair. The nurses were always after her because she lay quietly in bed in the hospital position, curled up like a shrimp, her back to the door. Mrs. Klopstock noticed that she, too, had taken to looking out the window curled on her side, back to the door. Mrs. Smith agreed that she would like to sit up and surprise her daughter by greeting her from the chair instead of the bed. Mrs. Klopstock rang for a nurse. The nurse said she didn't have time to sit anyone up now. Mrs. Klopstock asked the nurse her name and began to write on a pad she kept near her pillow. The nurse wanted to know what she was doing. Mrs. Klopstock said she was writing to the hospital administrator. The nurse dragged Mrs. Smith from her bed and pushed her down on a chair. It was an empty victory. Mrs. Smith's daughter did not come that night and the nurse found no time in which to help Mrs. Smith back to bed. At 10 o'clock, Mrs. Klopstock buttonholed a doctor, dragged him after her and brought him over to Mrs. Smith, who was crying from exhaustion. He put her back to bed. The next day, Mrs. Smith refused to stir. Two days later, she was taken to the hospital nursing home.

Mrs. Klopstock's next roommate was a Chinese woman who made her, at 60, feel young. She did not speak a word of English and once a month came into the hospital for chemotherapy. She was a very quiet, very clean woman and Mrs. Klopstock felt she knew her. She might have been Jewish had she not been Chinese. With the help of Mrs. Wu's family, she and Mrs. Wu established a kind of sign language. When that failed, Mrs. Wu called her daughter at her place of business and told her what she wanted. Then she handed the phone to Mrs. Klopstock and her daughter translated what her mother had said. Taking care of Mrs. Wu distracted Mrs. Klopstock, who nevertheless was uncomfortably and furiously aware that the doctors did not yet know what was wrong with her. Once night, Mrs. Wu, who had been attached to an intravenous, began to flail about in her bed. Mrs. Klopstock got up and went to see what the trouble was. Mrs. Wu called her daughter, spoke to her, and then gave Mrs. Klopstock the phone. "Her arm is bleeding," said the daughter, "and the needle hurts her." Mrs. Klopstock went off to get a nurse. "Her arm is not bleeding and it does not hurt," said the nurse. "There is blood on the floor," said Mrs. Klopstock. "It's old blood," said the nurse.

"I see," said Mrs. Klopstock, "the angel of death in long white robes and he's hovering over your head." She watched in fascination as the angel floated above the nurse's head and paused at the entrance to the room just before hers. "Besides," said the nurse, who didn't seem to have heard her, "you don't speak Chinese, do you?" Mrs. Klopstock did not answer. The vision did not cheer her. On this floor, the angel of death did not come for nurses.

She was not surprised when she heard the Code Nine alert; the noise on the other side of the wall was no surprise to her. It took longer than she thought. "Where is Mr. Stein?" she asked the next morning. "In Intensive Care," said the first nurse. "Gone home," said the second. So she knew. Later, she heard two young doctors talking. "I didn't think he'd go down the tubes so fast," one of them said. Mrs. Klopstock planted herself in front of them. "They told him," she said, "there was nothing wrong with him and that he was just a crybaby and that he had to stop asking them for ice all the time." The doctors looked at her, appalled. They thought she was crazy. She went back to her room and curled up, back to the door. "Your programs are coming on," said a nurse. Mrs. Klopstock ignored her. They only tolerated her because she could walk. She pretended to be asleep.

At last, her doctor said, they knew what was wrong with her. Mrs. Klopstock sat up. "You have an infection of the heart valves," he said. Mrs. Klopstock clutched her chest. "You're in no danger," he said. Mrs. Klopstock looked up. Nothing was hovering in the air above them. "I want to go to another hospital," she said. "They kill people here." "You have to trust your doctor," he said. "The angel of death lives here," she said. "I hate to start in with psychiatrists," said the doctor. "Wait," she said. "Someday you'll be sick and they'll put you in here and you'll see for yourself." He looked at her oddly. Silence unrolled itself between them like the map of an unknown country. "At least," he said, "we think you have an infection of the valves of the heart. We can't find any other cause of the fever. You have a murmur. People with murmurs are particularly susceptible to these infections. Sometimes the bacteria don't show up on our tests." "Then you're not sure I have it," she said. "No," said the doctor, "but we have to treat it. It's the only way to rule it out. If you have it and we don't treat it, you'll die." "I don't have it," said Mrs. Klopstock. "It's in my head." "The only thing in your head is that silly idea," he said. "Stop telling the nurses it's all in your head. They won't come when you call them." "And if you treat me and I don't have it?" she asked. "You'll have germ-free blood," he said.

"How do they treat it," she asked, "an infection of the heart?" "Oh," he said, as if waking up, "six weeks of antibiotic therapy." "I'll go home in the morning," Mrs. Klopstock said with relief. "Oh no," he said, "you have to stay here. The medication is given intravenously." Mrs. Klopstock began to protest—it would never work, the doctors were irresponsible, the nurses were worse, they never changed an I.V. bottle until the tubes from them were filled with blood. The doctor was not listening to her. He was staring into the hall. "Well?" she demanded. "I thought I saw someone in a hospital gown," he said, "on a ladder." "That was no patient," she said. He avoided her eyes.

They had her at last. She was plugged into the I.V. She was too nauseated to walk. The doctor gave her something for the nausea and she slept for three days. Her neighbor came and brought her the alarm watch she had left behind on her dresser so that she could wake herself up every three hours and remind the nurses to replace the empty I.V. bottles with full ones. Mrs. Wu was sent home. The nurse told her she would be happy to hear that her next roommate was "only" diabetic. Then why, wondered Mrs. Klopstock, when they laid the new woman on the bed next to hers, was a white figure hovering over her? Mrs. White was losing her toes and her sight. She prayed constantly, both alone and in company. Mrs. Klopstock was disgusted by the smell of her decaying feet which seemed, in some dreadful way, to incorporate the odor of prayer. She was terrified by the way Mrs. White, who was long and thin and flat, rocked and swayed in the air like a snake. Mrs. Klopstock watched her, horrified. Finally, she realized that Mrs. White swayed in the hope of seeing something more clearly.

One day, then another, passed. Mrs. Klopstock's dread of her roommate grew. Her small head at the top of the long, thin column of her body was wrapped in a turban. Mrs. White seemed about to change into something else, something not human. Mrs. Klopstock lay on her side and stared out the window. From her bed, she could see only a square of grey sky and an occasional sea gull. She lay there, hour after hour, waiting for her doctor. "You've got to get me out of here," she said. "Or get her out. I was here first." "What's wrong with her?" asked the doctor, who had inspected Mrs. White many times already. Mrs. Klopstock said that she didn't know why, but the woman gave her the creeps. "The creeps?" the doctor echoed. "Where did you get an expression like that? The creeps?" "She does, she gives me the creeps," Mrs. Klopstock insisted, starting to cry. "I'll see what I can do," he said. Mrs. Klopstock knew he wouldn't be able to do anything. She cried harder. Later, she got up and drew the curtains around her bed. She turned on the t.v. and adjusted the curtain so that all she could see from her bed was the screen. She felt as if she had been sent into the desert.

The nurses tried to get her to draw the curtains, but she was ferocious. If no one would remove the terrifying Mrs. White, she would remove herself into her little room of striped cloth walls. Day after day went by. She heard Mrs. White pray with her minister, a faith healer and many friends. She had always hated religion. Sealed in her tent, she bit her tongue to keep from jeering at them. They loved *The*

Book of Job. She could not avoid listening to them. They were the most unfortunate people she had ever heard of or known: their lives were plagued with calamities she never knew existed, and yet they were continually praising God. Mrs. Klopstock decided that they were either stupid or deranged. Still, something about Mrs. White awed her. Mrs. White spent half her life in hospitals. She was in the hospital or she was home. She was equally happy in either place. She *was* happy. Mrs. Klopstock was outraged. How could she not know what life was doing to her? Was she too stupid to be crushed? "It's quiet in here," she heard Mrs. White's current visitor say. "*Too* quiet," Mrs. White said pointedly. Mrs. Klopstock sighed in her tent and wrapped herself around her pillow. She looked up at her I.V. bottle. In 15 minutes, she would have to make her way through the newest group of psalm singers, into the hall, after the nurse. It was too much for her. She fell asleep.

When she awoke, the room was dark. She looked up at her I.V. bottles. Miraculously, they had been replaced. It was quiet. Outside, it was foggy and the traffic lights turned the mist red. She turned from the window toward the door. Something, she could see it clearly, was floating over the curtain which separated her bed from Mrs. White's. It seemed to be looking at her. She got up, and, pulling her I.V. after her, went over to inspect Mrs. White's bed. She called to her, but Mrs. White neither answered nor moved. She pushed the button and the nurse's intercom came on. "I think Mrs. White is in a coma," she said. She heard the nurses running down the hall. "Is she in a coma?" she asked. "Sure is," said the nurse. She called the office and the office paged the doctor. Mrs. Klopstock watched in fascination while the team assembled and treated Mrs. White. A white spirit rose from Mrs. White's body, floated up toward the ceiling, then sank until it touched her lips. It was as if her breath had become visible. But the thing was creature-like, human sized. She heard Mrs. White gasp and the white, vaporous being seemed to disappear into her lungs. "She'll be all right now," said the doctor. "I am completely crazy," thought Mrs. Klopstock, "or I will be if I don't get out of here." But no one seemed able to move her from Mrs. White or Mrs. White from her.

Another week went by, then another. Three weeks had passed and then a fourth, and still Mrs. Klopstock insisted on living inside her own tent. Meanwhile, she caught a cold which settled in her ears. People came into the tent and she thought they were teasing her by moving their lips without speaking. She realized that she could not always hear, but she never knew when she was going to be deprived of her hearing. Her vision, too, was becoming blurry. The eye doctor who came to examine her said the fever had irritated the membranes and nerves of her eyes. She knew she was losing interest in life. She no longer answered the phone. There was no one to whom she could talk. More and more, she left the phone off the hook altogether. What could she tell them? That she was dying? Not of the fever, which was in her mind, but of something else, something worse.

The doctors insisted that there was nothing wrong with her. They pointed at the I.V. bottles and insisted that she was getting stronger every day. Sounds reached her from far away, as if she were underwater. She stopped watching television. She lay on her bed and thought. For the first time, she thought of herself as a collection of sensors bound together by a personality. She knew, when she closed her eyes, just where her mind was attached to her body. She could put her finger on the place. The two were joined loosely, as by a large, clumsy knot. Any fingers—fingers clumsy and sticky with youth—could undo it. She could feel the threads loosening. The sensors were malfunctioning. In dreams, she was a bird whose instincts had failed. She was flying over a dark sea and no longer knew which way to fly or how to stay in the air. She was dying. It was only a matter of time. She looked up and was not surprised to see a white shape floating above her. She had no desire to breathe it back in. She woke up in Intensive Care. "Potassium shock," said the nurse. She fell asleep.

Her doctor was standing over her. "We're sending you home next week," he said, "before something really happens to you." "Do you still think I have an infection of the heart?" she asked. "No," he said. "Why?" she asked. "Your fever didn't drop the way it should have; if you'd had that kind of infection, it would have dropped down within one or two days. Once we started, we had to finish." "See?" she said. "It's all in my head! I told you! I told you from the start!" "Let's not start on that again," he said.

The next day, Mrs. Klopstock, who had been returned to her room, came out of her tent. "You're looking white," said Mrs. White. "Pretty

299

pale and awful." Mrs. Klopstock said she wasn't surprised. Mrs. White said that while Mrs. Klopstock had been away in Intensive Care, she had almost signed herself out because her husband had been taken to Kings County with a seizure. Mrs. Klopstock drew the curtains back and sat on the edge of her bed. Now that she was going home, she did not fear Mrs. White. She began to like her. Mrs. White exhorted her to get up. "The bed," she said, "takes all your strength." Mrs. Klopstock suggested that it was the fever, not the bed, which had worn her down. "It's the bed," said Mrs. White. "It sucks out all your strength. You don't start in walking now, you'll be an invalid when you get home. Go get us some ice." Mrs. Klopstock, filled with foreboding, set off for ice. "I made it back!" she said, dumping some ice into Mrs. White's water pitcher. "I told you," said Mrs. White. "A few more trips and you won't even be panting like an old hound out in the swamp."

As the day of her release approached, Mrs. Klopstock grew sicker and sicker. Her hearing flickered on and off as if she were a radio with many bad tubes. She was cold, then hot. Her eyes focused unexpectedly and equally unexpectedly blurred. One morning, sitting on a chair while the nurse made her bed, she thought she would shake herself from her seat onto the floor, she was so nervous. "I've never been so jumpy," she said to Mrs. White. "You're not used to it, that's all," said Mrs. White. "I'm ready to get in that bed with you," said Mrs. Klopstock. "Come on in," said Mrs. White, "I'm waiting for you." When Mrs. Klopstock was released, she kissed Mrs. White goodbye and promised to call her. But she knew, in leaving, she was escaping. She had begun adjusting to Mrs. White, who was losing herself, piece by piece, and when she did so, she had turned her face from the land of the living toward the land of the dead.

When she got home, she was more dead than alive. She still had a fever, although now it was considered low-grade. She was convinced that she was going to die. Nothing anyone said changed her mind. She knew how she felt.

And so it happened that she came to worship Isaac Bashevis Singer. Her daughter had left three paperback volumes of his stories in the apartment. Her eyes had improved enough so that she could now read. She had not read a word during the eight weeks she spent in the hospital, but now she read the stories one after another. They were just the right length. She read one each time she took her temperature. Gradually, she came to believe that reading the stories lowered her temperature. At first, she was annoyed by Singer's characters. So many of them seemed crazy. But then she remembered the angels she had seen floating through the air in the hospital. His characters were no crazier than she was. Gradually, she began to think of Singer as the actual creator of actual creatures who were so much like her. He was like a God. He understood his creatures; he rarely judged them. He knew more than an ordinary human. She grew to believe that God had chosen Singer as his representative on earth. He had suffered so that he could testify. He had been rewarded for fulfilling his mission by great powers. So she began to pray to Isaac Bashevis Singer.

Now Mrs. Klopstock knew that it was forbidden to pray to a living person, but she remembered her mother appealing to the spirits of dead ancestors in times of trouble. She told herself she was doing nothing her mother had not done. She was only hurrying things up. Singer was not dead yet, but someday he would be. Why wait to pray to him? So she fell into the habit of calling upon Isaac Bashevis Singer when she felt as if it were a great effort merely to breathe in and out. "Isaac Bashevis Singer, save me!" she would cry to herself. And she began to feel better. Soon, she was better. Her daughter called to say she would be coming to see her and asked how she was. "Better," said Mrs. Klopstock. "First, I could do nothing. Now I can do next to nothing." "That's progress," said her daughter in a bored voice. "When are you coming?" she asked her daughter. Her daughter was vague. Mrs. Klopstock decided to try writing stories herself. There was no point in sitting around waiting for her daughter. She would, of course, dedicate the stories to the master. She prayed to him continually, out of habit, out of devout belief.

Mrs. Klopstock and her daughter were sitting in the kitchen. The walls were egg-yolk yellow. Her daughter insisted that she had not visited her mother in the hospital because hospitals frightened her. Her mother knew that, she said. With a fingertip, she traced figure eights on the table. What, Mrs. Klopstock asked herself, was she doing with this large, middle-aged, alien child? She would die without ever having tried to talk to her. "You know, Elsa," she said, "those books you left here? By Singer? I read them." "That's good," said her daughter. "And now I pray to him," said Mrs. Klopstock. "He healed me." "You're not serious, of course," said her daughter. "Oh yes I am," she said. Her daughter would not look at her. "Don't worry, I'm not crazy," said Mrs. Klopstock. "You sound," said her daughter, "crazy as a bedbug." "He has the power to answer prayers because he writes," Mrs. Klopstock said. Her daughter stared at her. "You," she began, "you haven't started writing?" "Oh yes I have!" Mrs. Klopstock said triumphantly. "Writing gives me strength." "But you can't do that!" her daughter sputtered. "You can't give away family secrets! You can't do things like that!" "What makes you think I'm writing about the family?" her mother asked. (In fact, she was.) She watched her daughter; she could hear her thinking. "Are you going to show him the stories?" her daughter asked at last. "Who?" asked Mrs. Klopstock.

"Singer!"

"Oh, Singer. God forbid. I don't want anyone, especially him, to know what they're about." Her daughter looked at her as if to say that she shouldn't worry; the stories probably weren't about anything anyway. "They are about something all right," said her mother. Her daughter looked at her with something like fear. "Ma," she said, "don't tell anyone about this business. This worshipping Singer stuff." "Whose business is it?" Mrs. Klopstock asked rhetorically. "You know," she said, "last night I had the most curious dream. I dreamed I found a beautiful doll's head right on the kitchen table and the doll had the most beautiful brown hair you ever saw. So I showed it to my parents, and to grandma, she was there too, and they all said, but the doll doesn't have a body. And that confused me because I hadn't noticed. So I put the doll's head back down on the table and I saw there were crumbs there and they would get in the doll's hair and I was afraid rats would come and chew on her hair, and I couldn't figure out how to get the crumbs out of her hair. And they kept saying that she didn't have a body, but when I looked at the doll, I could see it even if they couldn't. What do you think it means?" "God knows," said her daughter, shuddering. "I used to make dolls," said her mother. "Not the heads but the bodies. That's how you made them in those days. You bought the heads and hands and feet and made the bodies yourself." "Let's change the subject," said her daughter. "I used to keep extra heads. In case one broke," said Mrs. Klopstock. "Mother!" exclaimed Elsa.

"I know what it means," said Mrs. Klopstock. "What does it mean?" asked Elsa. "You wouldn't understand," said her mother. "Who would," asked her daughter, "Singer?" Her daughter was upset, sarcastic. This was not the mother she knew. "It's a dream about the mind and the body," said her daughter smugly. "What about them, Miss Smartypants?" asked her mother. Elsa didn't answer. "You don't know," said her mother. "Who does?" asked her daughter. "Singer knows," said Mrs. Klopstock.

She got up and brushed some imaginary crumbs from her skirt and went to the stove to look after their tea. "Do you dream a lot?" her daughter asked wistfully, but Mrs. Klopstock was running water in the sink and did not hear her. Her daughter pressed both her hot palms to the cool enamel table. She knew she would be afraid to reread the Singer stories now. Her mother was smiling to herself and humming. A white cloud of steam rose in the air and hovered there. For a moment, the room tilted and then it seemed to right itself.

Electricity

Francine Prose

A NITA SAILS THE BABY over her head. "Earth to Spaceship Bertie," she says. "Earth to Spaceship Bertie. Can you read me?"

The baby's laugh sounds forced, like Johnny Carson's when he's blown a joke. Last week she caught Bertie practicing smiles in the mirror over his crib, phony social smiles for the old ladies who goo-goo him in the street, noticeably different from his real smile. It occurs to her that the baby is embarrassed for her. Lately she's often embarrassed for herself. This feeling takes her back fifteen years to her early teens, when she and her parents and her younger sister Lynne used to go places—Jones Beach, Prospect Park—and she'd see groups of kids her own age. At the time she had felt that being with her family made her horribly conspicuous; now she realizes that it probably made her invisible.

The house is quiet. Now since she's back is the first time Anita can remember being in her parents' home without the television going. She thinks of the years her father spent trailing her and Lynne from room to room, switching lights off behind them, asking who they thought was paying the electric bills. Yet he never turned the TV off; he'd fall asleep to the *Late Show*. Now the TV is dark, the house is lit up like a birthday cake, and her father is down in the finished basement, silenced by the acoustical ceiling as he claps his hands, leaps into the air, and sings hymns in praise of God and the Baal Shem Tov.

304

In the morning, when Anita's father goes off to the *bet hamidrash*, the house of study, Anita and her mother and the baby watch *Donahue*. Today the panel is made up of parents whose children have run away and joined cults. The week Anita came home, there was a show about grown children moving back in with their parents. It reminds Anita of how in high school, and later when she used to take acid, the radio always seemed to play oddly appropriate songs. Hearing the Miracles sing "What's So Good about Goodbye?" when she was breaking up with a boyfriend had made her feel connected with lovers breaking up everywhere. But now she hates to think that her life is one of those stories that make Donahue go all dewy-eyed with concern.

The twice-divorced mother of a Moonie is blaming everything on broken homes. "Don't you *ever* become a Moonie," Anita whispers, pressing her lips against the back of the baby's neck. Another mother is describing how her daughter calls herself Prem Ananda, wears only orange clothes, has married a boy the guru's chosen for her, and, with her doctorate in philosophy, works decorating cakes in the ashram bakery.

"Cakes?" says Anita's mother. "That's nothing. Only my Sam waits till he's fifty-seven to join a cult. After thirty-three years of marriage, he'll only make love through a hole in the sheet."

"A hole in the sheet?" Repeating this, Anita imagines Donahue repeating it, then realizes: incredibly, she and her mother have never talked about sex. Not ever. Imagining her mother on Donahue, Anita sees only close-ups, because if the camera pulled back, it would see up her mother's housedress to where the pale veined thighs dimple over the tops of her support hose.

Anita goes over and hugs her mother so hard that Bertie, squeezed between them, squawks like one of his bath toys. The baby starts to cry, her mother starts to cry, and Anita, not knowing what else to do, presses Bertie against her mother and pats and rubs them as if trying to burp both of them at once.

Anita takes nothing for granted. When she lifts her foot to take a step, she no longer trusts the ground to be there when she puts it down. She used to say that you could never really tell about people; now she knows it's true. She never once doubted that Jamie loved her, that he

305

wanted the baby. When he came to visit her and Bertie in the hospital and began crying, she was so sure it was from happiness that she literally did not hear him say he'd fallen in love with somebody else.

She'd made him repeat it till he was almost shouting and she remembered who this Lizzie was: another lawyer in his office. At a garden party that summer Lizzie had asked to touch Anita's belly.

Just as Jamie was offering to move out of the house they had rented for its view, for their vision of children standing at the Victorian Bay window watching boats slip up the Hudson, a nurse wheeled the baby in, in a futuristic clear plastic cart.

"Spaceship Bertie," said Jamie.

Anita's sister Lynne says that men do this all the time: Jamie's acting out his ambivalence about fatherhood, his jealousy of the mother-infant bond. This sounds to Anita like something from *Family Circle* or *Ladies' Home Journal*. Lynne has read those magazines all her life, but now that she's going for her master's in women's studies, she refers to it as "keeping up." Lynne can't believe that Anita never had the tiniest suspicion. A year ago, Anita would have said the same thing, but now she knows it's possible. Whenever she thinks about last summer, she feels like a Kennedy-assassination buff examining the Zapruder film. But no matter how many times she rewinds it, frame by frame, she can't see the smoking gun, the face at the warehouse window. All she sees is that suddenly, everyone in the car starts moving very strangely.

Anita's mother believes her. Overnight, *her* husband turned into a born-again Hasid. Perhaps that's why she hardly sounded surprised when on the day she and Anita's father were supposed to drive up to Nyack to see the baby, Anita called to say that she and Bertie were coming to Brooklyn. Over the phone, her mother had warned her to expect changes. Daddy wasn't himself. No, he wasn't sick. Working too hard as usual, but otherwise fine. Her tone had suggested something shameful. Had he, too, fallen in love with somebody else?

Pulling into her parents' driveway, Anita thought: He looks the same. He opened the door for her and waited while she unstrapped Bertie from his car seat, then sidestepped her embrace. He'd never been a comfortable hugger, but now she missed his pat-pat-pat. She held Bertie out to him; he shook his head.

"Bertie, this is your grandpa," she said. "Grandpa, this is Bertie."

"Has he been circumcised?" asked her father.

"Of course," said Anita. "Are you kidding? My doctor did it in the hospital."

"Then we'll have to have it done again," said her father. "By a *mohel*."

"Again!" yelled Anita. "Are you out of your mind?"

Attracted by the noise, her mother came flying out of the house. "Sam!" She grabbed the baby from Anita. "Can't you see she's upset?"

The commotion had comforted Anita. Everything was familiar— their voices, the pressure of her mother's plump shoulder pushing her into the house, the way she said, "Coffee?" before they'd even sat down.

"I'll get it," said Anita. "You hold the baby." But her mother headed her off at the kitchen door.

"It's arranged a little different now," she explained. "Those dishes over there by the fridge are for meat. These here by the stove are for milk."

That night they couldn't eat till her father had blessed the half grapefruits, the maraschino cherries, the boiled flank steak, the potatoes and carrots, the horseradish, the unopened jar of applesauce, the kosher orange gelatin with sliced bananas. During the meal, Bertie began to fuss, and Anita guided his head up under her shirt.

"Is it all right if the baby drinks milk while I eat meat?" she asked. Her mother laughed.

"Edna," said her father, "don't encourage her."

Bertie cried when Anita tried to set him down, so she was left alone with her father while her mother did the dishes.

"What *is* this?" she asked him. "You never went to *shul* in your life. Aunt Phyllis and Uncle Ron didn't speak to us for a year because on the Saturday of Cousin Simon's bar mitzvah, you *forgot*—you said—and took us all to Rip Van Winkle's Storybook Village."

"I did forget." Her father laughed. "Anyhow, we didn't miss any-thing. Simon was bar-mitzvahed in the Reform temple. The church."

"The church!" repeated Anita. "Dad, what's the story?"

"The story, Anita?" Her father took a deep breath. Then he said:

"Once upon a time, a jeweler was taking the subway home to East Flatbush from his shop on Forty-sixth Street. At Nostrand, he finally got a seat and opened his *Post* when he heard loud voices at the far

307

end of the car. Looking up, he saw three Puerto Rican kids in sneakers, jeans, and hot pink silk jackets which said 'Men Working' on the fronts, backs, and sleeves. When he realized that the jackets had been stitched together from the flags Con Ed put up near excavations, he found this so interesting that it took him a while to notice that the kids had knives and were working their way through the car, taking money and jewelry from the passengers and dropping them into a bowling bag. Then he thought: Only in New York do thieves wear clothes which glow in the dark. The boys didn't seem to be hurting anyone, but it still didn't make the jeweler comfortable. He thought: Is this how it happens? One night you pick the wrong subway car, and bingo! you're an item in the morning paper.

"Halfway down the car, they reached an old lady who started to scream. Then suddenly, the lights began to flash on and off in a definite pattern: three long blinks, three short blinks, three long blinks. By the fourth SOS the muggers had their noses pressed against the door, and when it opened at the station, they ran. 'Thank God, it's a miracle!' cried the old lady.

"Meanwhile the jeweler had his head between his knees. He was trying to breathe, thinking he must have been more scared than he'd known. Then he looked up and saw a young Hasidic man watching him from across the aisle.

" 'It wasn't a miracle,' said the Hasid. 'I did it. Follow me out at the next stop.'

"Normally, this jeweler wasn't the type to follow a Hasid out onto the Eastern Parkway station. But all he could think of was, had his wallet been stolen, he'd have had to spend all the next day at the Motor Vehicles Bureau replacing his license and registration. He felt that he owed somebody something, and if this Hasid was taking credit, keeping him company was the least he could do.

"On the platform, the Hasid pointed to a bare light bulb and said, 'Look,' The light blinked on and off. Then he waved at a buzzing fluorescent light. It blinked too. 'I lied before,' said the Hasid. 'It wasn't my doing. Everything is the rebbe's. . . .' "

Anita's father stopped when her mother came in, drying her hands. "Bertie!" Anita's mother cried, picking the baby up and waltzing him into the kitchen. "Don't listen to this nonsense! A whole life ruined for one blinky light bulb!"

308

"It wasn't the light," said Anita's father.

Anita wanted to ask if his story really happened or if he'd made it up as a metaphor for what happened. She thought: *Something* must have happened. In the old days, her father didn't make up stories. But she forgot her questions when she heard her mother in the kitchen singing "Music, Music, Music" to Bertie, singing "Put another nickel in, in the nickelodeon," sounding just like Teresa Brewer.

Now, five months later, watching the parents of cult members on Donahue, Anita decides that her father's story left out all the important parts. Such as: why he really joined. There's no overlooking the obvious reasons: old age, sickness, death. If they'd been Protestant and he'd converted to Catholicism, no one would have wondered why.

She remembers a weekend this past summer when Jamie was away on business—with Lizzie, she thinks now—and her parents came up to see her. Her father drove her to the supermarket to shop for their visit and for Jamie's return. At the checkout stand, the kid who packed their order insisted, over her father's protests, on wheeling the cart out and loading the bags into their—the old man's, the pregnant woman's—car. Like her father, Anita was angry at the kid. Couldn't he see that her father could have done it? Not for nothing did he swim fifteen laps at the JCC pool every Sunday morning. But the crazy thing was, for the whole way home, Anita was mad at her father.

Her father is still in shape. And despite all the rushing to *shul* every morning and from there to work, he seems pretty relaxed. What's hurting her family, Anita decides, is the unpredictability, the shaky sense that everyone is finally unreliable. What's bothering her mother is that the man she's shared her bed with for thirty-three years has suddenly and without warning rolled to the opposite side. She must wonder if the sheet with the hole in it has been there all along.

Anita wants to tell her mother that there's no guarantee; you can't know anything about anyone. She wants to ask: What's so strange about a man wanting to sing and dance his way into heaven? But if they've never even talked about sex, how can they talk about this?

Anita bundles Bertie up in so many layers that he does look like a spaceman, and takes him to the library. On the subway, she notices that the lights flash on and off. The train is almost empty and she thinks about muggers in hot pink Con Ed jackets, but feels that Bertie is a kind of protection. Babies are unpredictable, like crazy people; she's heard you can sometimes scare muggers away by pretending to be crazy.

The librarians in the Judaica section eye Bertie so suspiciously that he exhausts himself trying to charm them and falls asleep in Anita's arms. Juggling baby and purse, she pulls out some reference books on Hasidism and sits down.

She's surprised at how much she already knows, what she has picked up from growing up in New York, from college, reading, and sheer osmosis. She starts Martin Buber's *Tales of the Hasidim*, then decides she must have read it or else heard the stories somewhere. She thinks of Jamie's friend Ira who'd visited once a year from his Orthodox commune in Cambridge, bringing his own food in an Empire Kosher Poultry shopping bag. She can't remember him telling stories.

For information about her father's sect, she's directed to the microfilm section. The librarian hands her a flat box, then seeing that it's impossible for her to thread the machine while holding Bertie, gives her a sour smile and does it for her.

For some reason, they've microfilmed whole editions of the city papers. Anita likes flipping back through the pages; it's like reading a story when you already know the end, only eerier. Meanwhile she learns that fifteen years ago, her father's group came from Hungary via Israel to their present home in Brooklyn. In the centerfold of the *Daily News*, there's a photo of the rebbe walking from Kennedy airport to Brooklyn because his plane from Jerusalem had landed on the Sabbath, when he wasn't allowed to ride. Taken at night, the picture is blurred, hard to read. The rebbe is all white hair and white beard, Mr. Natural in a beaver hat. On the next page is an ad for leather boots from Best and Co.—thirty dollars, fifteen years ago, an outrageously low price.

Ironically, the reason Anita can't concentrate is that she's being distracted by the noise from the Mitzvahmobile parked on Forty-second Street, blaring military-sounding music from its loudspeakers. She pictures the Hasidim darting from one pedestrian to another, asking, "Excuse me, are you Jewish?"

One afternoon, not long after she and Jamie first fell in love, they were approached by the Mitzvahmobilers, and Jamie said yes, he was Jewish. They dragged him—literally dragged him—into the trailer. The weather was nice, and nothing in those days seemed like an imposition, so Anita had waited on the library steps till Jamie emerged, looking pale.

Apparently, the Hasidim had tried to teach him how to lay *tefillin*, but he just couldn't get the hang of it. He froze, his hands wouldn't work. Finally they gave up. They put the phylacteries in his hands, then covered his hands with theirs and just held them, one on his forehead, and one on his arm near his heart.

On Friday nights, Anita's father sleeps at the *bet hamidrash* so he won't have to travel on the Sabbath, and her sister Lynne comes for dinner.

As children, Anita and Lynne fought, as their mother says, tooth and nail. Now it's simpler: they love one another—so Anita feels disloyal for thinking that Lynne is just like Valerie Harper playing Rhoda. But it's true, and it's not just the curly hair, the tinted glasses, the running shoes, and the tight designer jeans. It's Lynne's master's thesis, "The Changing Role of Women as Reflected in Women's Magazines, 1930–1960." It's her job as a social worker in a family-planning clinic and her boyfriend Arnie, who's almost got his degree as a therapist and is already practicing on the Upper West Side.

Lynne and Anita kiss hello. Then Lynne puts her arms around their mother, who's stirring something at the stove, and hugs her for so long that Anita starts feeling uncomfortable. Finally she zeroes in on Bertie, ensconced in his yellow plastic recliner chair on the kitchen table.

"Look how he holds his head up!" says Lynne.

Bertie's been holding his head up since he was two weeks old, and Lynne's seen it, but Anita refrains from pointing this out. Together they set the table, then Lynne pulls her into a corner and asks what she hears from Jamie.

"Oh, he's coming to see Bertie tomorrow."

Lynne stares at Anita, trying to ascertain if this "means" anything. Then she gets her purse and starts rummaging around. She takes out a tortoiseshell case, brushes tobacco dust off it, and gives it to Anita, who knows what it is before she opens it: eye shadow, a palette of different colors.

"Thanks," says Anita. The gift moves her and reminds her of what she's always known: her sister is less of a feminist or a Rhoda than a real magazine reader, a girl who believes in her heart that eye shadow can change your luck.

For Lynne, their mother has cooked the same company dinner she made when Anita first came home. But without their father's blessing, the meat tastes greasy, the potatoes lukewarm; the gelatin has a rubbery skin. His absence should free them, thinks Anita, but he's all they talk about, in voices so low he might as well be downstairs.

With Lynne's coaching, their mother talks, and Anita sees she's been wrong: her mother's unhappiness isn't philosophical, it's practical. Imagine being forced to start keeping a kosher home at the age of fifty-three! Two sets of dishes! The doctor says salting the meat is bad for her heart. The smallest details of life now have rules which Sam won't let her break; she has to take the train to Essex Street to buy special soap for him.

If it gets much worse, Lynne suggests, she might consider a trial separation.

"Who would it help?" their mother asks. "Would it make me happier? Would it make Daddy happier?"

"I doubt it," says Anita.

"What would make me happy," their mother says, "is for Daddy to turn back into his normal self."

Anita wonders what would make *her* happy. Lately she's not sure. Bertie makes her happy, but it seems important to remember: he'll grow up and leave her. If you can count on anything, she thinks, it's that.

She senses that Lynne is talking less about happiness than about punishment. Lynne feels that their father is responsible for their mother's troubles, just as Jamie is for hers. Anita thinks that no one's to blame for her parents' situation; and in her own case, she's partly at fault.

Her first mistake was to gain so much weight when she was pregnant. Why should Jamie have faith she'd lose it when her own doctor didn't? Now she has, but, clearly, it's too late.

Her second mistake was to quit her job, even if it was the lowest editorial job in the world, the slush pile at *Reader's Digest*. Most of the submissions were for "The Most Unforgettable Character I've Ever

Met," and most of these had never done one unforgettable thing except die slowly of some horrible cancer. Jamie liked hearing about them; he said they made him feel better about *his* day. And after she quit and took to reading long novels—anything, so long as it went on for more than four hundred pages—it wasn't the same. She'd try to tell Jamie about the Baron Charlus or Garp's mother, and he'd be staring past her. Once, to test him, she said, "My doctor said it's going to be triplets," and he just kept gazing beyond her out the dark kitchen window at the lights moving slowly up the Hudson.

Which reminds her of her third mistake: they never argued. Lynne, who fights with Arnie over every little thing, has told her that she and Jamie were afraid of their anger. Maybe so. Even when Jamie told her he was leaving, Bertie was there, listening to what for him was their first conversation. How could they have fought?

Anita wonders what happened to that part of her that used to fight tooth and nail with Lynne. She imagines Jamie and Lizzie litigating over every avocado in the supermarket. It's the only way she can stand thinking of him in the supermarket with somebody else.

Once, visiting friends in Berkeley, Anita and Jamie went to an all-night supermarket for orange juice. They took a joint for the ride and got so stoned that, when they got there, they couldn't move. They just stood near the vegetable bins, talking, laughing, marveling over the vegetables, those California vegetables!

Once more, Anita feels like she's watching the Zapruder film. She's the only assassination buff who can't even handle a magnifying glass, who wouldn't know a smoking gun if she saw one.

Anita's wasted the morning trying to imagine her conversation with Jamie. She's afraid she'll have nothing interesting to say. She blames this on living in her parents' house, where nothing interesting ever happens. She feels that living there marks her as a boring person with no interesting friends she could have stayed with. But that's not true. She and Bertie would have been welcome in the editing room of Irene's SoHo loft, on the couch in Jeanie's Park Slope floor-through. But being home is easier, she doesn't have to be a good guest. If Bertie cries at night, her mother comes in and offers to sing him Teresa Brewer.

One thing she could tell Jamie is what she's noticed at the Pathmark:

more and more people seem to be buying huge quantities of specialty items, whole shopping carts full of apricot yogurt, frozen tacos, Sprite in liter plastic jugs. She's heard that American families hardly ever sit down to dinner together. So who knows, maybe there are millions of people out there, each eating only one thing. She could tell him how she took Bertie to the park to see some other babies. He slept the whole time, leaving her with the other mothers, none of whom even smiled at her. At one point, a little boy threw sand at a little girl. The girl's mother ran over, grabbed the boy's ankles, and turned him upside down. Anita expected coins to rain out of his pockets like in the movies, but none did. After a while, the boy's mother came over, and, instead of yelling at the woman who was shaking her upside-down son, said, "I'm glad it's you and not me." Anita felt as if she'd stumbled in on a game already in progress, like polo or a new kind of poker with complicated rules which no one would stop to explain.

But the last thing she wants is to sound like some pitiful housewife drifting back and forth between the supermarket and the playground. She wonders what sort of lawyer Lizzie is. Corporate taxes, she hopes, but fears it's probably the most interesting cases: mad bombings, ax murders, billion-dollar swindles.

She's tempted to tell Jamie about her father, how for a week or so last month he'd been instructed by his rebbe: instead of saying grace, he should clap his hands whenever the spirit of thanksgiving moved him. In the hour and a half it took to eat—with her father dropping his silverware, clapping, shutting his eyes as if smelling something sweet—Anita tried to predict these outbursts, but couldn't; she thought of the retarded people one heard sometimes in movie theaters, shouting out randomly, for no reason. She could tell Jamie how her father came home in a green velvet Tyrolean hat with a feather; apparently, the rebbe had given out dozens of hats to illustrate his sermon: the righteous man must climb this world like a mountain.

But she knows that telling Jamie would only make her angry at him for not being around tomorrow when she'll need to tell him the next installment. Nor does it make her happy right now to think that Jamie knows her father well enough to know that in the old days, he wouldn't have been caught dead in a Tyrolean hat.

The obvious subject is Bertie. Everything he does interests her; she thinks he's a genius. Why can't she tell Jamie about his practiced smiles, about his picking up his own Cheerios? Why? Because what could be more pitiful than thinking that anyone cares if your five-month-old can pick up his own Cheerios?

Bertie's victory over Cheerios should be their victory. Instead, she can hardly talk about Bertie; it's as if she's accusing Jamie. Bertie should be the mortar cementing them; as it is, he's part of the wall.

When Jamie rings the doorbell, Anita half hopes that Bertie, who hasn't seen his father for two weeks, will not recognize him and scream. Bertie looks at Jamie, then at Anita, then at Jamie, then smiles a smile which anyone could tell is his real one.

Anita's mother says, "Jamie! There's apple cake in the fridge if you kids get hungry." Then she backs out of the room. It's so uncomfortable they could be high-schoolers dating—except for the presence of Bertie and the fact that Anita and Jamie didn't know each other in high school.

"Can we go for a walk somewhere?" Jamie is staring to the side of Anita's head, at Bertie. Anita feels as if he's asking Bertie out and is one of those guys who's scared to be alone with his date. She's the friend he drags along, the chaperone.

"Sure," says Anita. Bertie's wriggling so hard his feet jam halfway down the legs of his snowsuit and Anita has to thread them through. She knows she's making herself look incompetent, making the process of dressing Bertie look harder than it is.

On the way to the park she can't think of anything to say. She doesn't want to discuss specialty items at the Pathmark or the upside-down boy. Of course she's done this before, rehearsed whole conversations that turned out to be inappropriate. But never with Jamie.

The playground is chilly, almost deserted. In one corner, two five-year-old boys are playing soccer while their parents—all four of them in ponytails—hunker on the ground, passing a joint. There's a dressed-up Orthodox family sitting in a row on a bench. By the swings, a young mother says to her daughter, "Okay, ten more pushes and we're going home." And finally there are some boys—ten, eleven, twelve—playing very hard and punishingly on the jungle gym and slide, as if it's the playground equipment's fault that they've grown too big for it.

"When is Bertie going to be old enough for the slide?" asks Jamie.

"Tomorrow," says Anita.

The mother by the swings counts to ten, and when the little girl says "Ten more!" grabs her daughter's hand and pulls her out of the park. Jamie sits down on one of the swings and stretches his arms out for Bertie. Holding the baby on his lap, Jamie pushes off. Anita can't look till she reassures herself: she trusts Jamie that much—not to drop Bertie. She sits on the other swing and watches Bertie, who is leaning forward to see where they're going before they get there.

"Look how he holds his head up," says Jamie. "That's my boy."

"He's been doing that for four months," says Anita.

Jamie trails his long legs in the sand and stops with a bump. "Anita," he says, "just what am I supposed to do? What do you want?"

Anita wonders what she does want. She's not sure she wants to be back with Jamie. Bertie or no Bertie, it's too late. Something's happened that can't be fixed. Basically, she wants what her mother wants: for everything to be the way it was before everything changed.

"I want to know one thing," she says. "Remember that garden party at Mel's?"

"What about it?" says Jamie.

Anita remembers a buffet of elegant, salty things—sun-dried tomatoes, smoked salmon—which by then she wasn't allowed to eat. "I want to know if you and Lizzie were already . . ." She thinks: If a woman could walk clear across a party to feel her lover's wife's belly, her lover's unborn child inside it, well then, you really can't know anything about people.

Jamie says, "Of course not," but in a tone that makes Anita suspect it began at that party, or thereabouts. She wonders: Did their fingers brush accidentally over a Lebanese olive? A long look near the pesto and sour-cream dip?

"It wasn't Lizzie." Jamie's swinging again, distractedly. "It wasn't you."

"Who was it?" she says. "Don't blame Bertie, he wasn't born yet."

"It wasn't the baby. It was me. Listen—" Jamie stops himself by grabbing the chain on her swing together with his. The seats tilt together crazily. "When I was in the seventh grade, there was a kid in my class named Mitchell Pearlman. One day we got to talking about our dads, and Mitchell said that his was a photographer. He'd been everywhere, done everything. Had he fought with the Mau Maus? Sure. Sipped tea with Queen Elizabeth? Of course. Lived with the Eskimos, crossed the Sahara on a camel? You bet.

"Naturally we thought he was lying till we went to his house for his birthday. The minute we met Mitchell Pearlman's father—mustache, jeans, big silver belt buckle—we began to think Mitchell was telling the truth. After the cake and ice cream, his father brought out the pictures of himself in front of the igloo, the camel, arm in arm with Jomo Kenyatta, dandling the baby Prince Charles on his knee. And for months after that, for years, I hated my own father. I wouldn't speak to him."

"So?" says Anita. "I don't get it."

"So, when Bertie was born, I suddenly thought: In a couple of years, he'll be me in the seventh grade. And I'll be my father. And he'll go out and find his own Mitchell Pearlman's father. And he'll hate me. I thought: We've made a terrible mistake! We should have waited to have Bertie till I was Mitchell Pearlman's father! Does this make any sense?" There are tears in Jamie's eyes.

Anita thinks: Not much. For one thing, the chronology's wrong. Jamie fell in love *before* Bertie was born. For another, Bertie isn't Jamie and Jamie isn't his father. Jamie's father owns a dry cleaners, while Jamie is a labor lawyer with interesting cases. She wants to shout at him that exchanging long looks with a lady lawyer over the pesto is nothing—nothing at all—like fighting with the Mau Maus. But she doesn't. She's beginning to see that her sister's right: this *is* something some men do. Jamie himself doesn't understand, any more than Mitchell Pearlman's father understood why he found it so easy to leave the wife and kids and take off across the Sahara.

She imagines Jamie ten years hence, taking Bertie out for the afternoon. He's one of those weekend fathers she never really noticed till she was pregnant, and then she saw them everywhere. She could always tell how uneasy it made them to take their kids places whole families went. Recently she read in the *Times:* there's a health club in Manhattan which, on Saturdays and Sundays, caters exclusively to single fathers and their children. Ten years from now, there will be hundreds of these places.

She imagines men and children lolling in a steamy pool, pumping

317

exercycles, straining on Nautilus machines. There are no women in her vision, it's as if all the mothers have died of some plague. She hears the cries of the children, sees the shoulders of the fathers rounded as if from the weight of the children tugging their arms.

The only thing she can't picture is how Bertie will look in ten years' time.

For weeks, her father has been asking her to come to a service in his *shul.* "The worst that'll happen is that you'll have fun," he says. It's made Anita a little nervous, like having a Moonie ask her to go away for the weekend. But the day after Jamie's visit, she agrees. There's nothing but football on TV.

"Can me and Bertie sit in the same section?" she asks.

"Don't be smart," says her father.

When she comes downstairs in a turtleneck and good brown corduroy jeans, she sees him really suffering with embarrassment. She goes and changes into a long skirt from the back of her closet, Indian print from the sixties.

On the drive down Eastern Parkway, Anita and her father don't talk. Again she has the peculiar feeling of being on a date. There's not much traffic on this Sunday, and everything seems so slowed down that she's slow to notice: her father's whole driving style has changed. He used to zip around like a cabbie, teeth grinding, swerving, cursing. Now he keeps to this lane, he's got all the time in the world. His elbow is out the side window, and cold air is rushing into the car.

"Can you shut that?" says Anita. "The baby."

"Sure," says her father. "Sorry."

"What kind of service are we going to?"

"A wedding."

"Turn the car around," says Anita.

"Don't be stupid," says her father. "Would you have preferred a funeral? All right—next time, a funeral."

"What next time?" says Anita.

"You'll be interested," says her father. "The ceremony is outside, under the stars."

"Stars you can see from Crown Heights?" says Anita. "I'll be interested."

In the old days, her father used to start looking for parking places miles in advance. She remembers hours of accelerating, then falling forward as the brakes squealed in the search for a spot in Chinatown. Now as they pull up to the block in which hundreds of Hasidim are milling around, her father cruises smoothly into an empty space.

The short winter afternoon is darkening. The street lights come on. The air is crisp and clear. The men wear nearly identical black coats, the women's are of various subdued hues. Most of the women are in high, good leather boots which remind Anita of the ad on the microfilm. It's easy to spot the converts like her father in his fur-collared car coat, the young men in denim and down; it annoys her that several young women wear paisley skirts much like hers.

The crowd spills off the sidewalk, blocking the northbound lane, but the two cops parked in their squad car ignore it. Leaning on other cars, Puerto Rican kids in sweatshirts and down vests idly hump their girlfriends as they watch the Hasidim assemble. The wedding canopy is already up, held by four men who keep switching the pole from hand to hand so they can warm the free hand in their pockets.

Suddenly everyone's buzzing like bees. Anita's father leans forward and says, "The rebbe."

Anita stands on tiptoe. But from a quarter block away, the rebbe looks pretty much like the photo: Mr. Natural. That's another reason she could never join this sect: being female, she'd never get closer to the rebbe than this. She turns to say this to her father, but he's gone—drawn, she imagines, toward his rebbe.

The crowd buzzes again when the bride and groom appear. The bride's leaning on some women, the groom on some men. They both look ready to drop. When Anita gets a good look at the groom—gangly, skin the color of skim milk—she understands why the bride can hardly walk. How could anyone marry *that?*

Nearly rigid in his quilted snowsuit, Bertie's getting heavy. Anita holds him up though she knows he's too young to focus on the center of attention, too young to know there is a center. To Bertie, everything's the center: the scarf of the woman in front of him, his own inaccessible fist.

Anita thinks: the bride must be freezing. Maybe that's why she's so hunched over as the women lead her in circles around the groom. Under the veil, she could be anything—old, ugly, sick, some covered-up temple idol. No wonder the groom is so panicky!

Even with all the Hebrew prayers, the ceremony is over in no time. They always are, thinks Anita, except when people write their own. Real religions and even the state seem to know: if it drags on too long, somebody *will* faint. Anita and Jamie got married impulsively in a small town on the California-Nevada border. What she mostly remembers is sitting in a diner in Truckee, writing postcards to all their friends saying that she'd just been married in the Donner Pass by a one-armed justice of the peace.

Her thoughts are interrupted by cheers; the groom has broken the glass. Then bride and groom and wedding canopy disappear in the crowd bearing them—and Anita and Bertie—into the hall.

Just inside the door, the men and women peel off in opposite directions. Anita follows the women into a large room with a wooden dance floor surrounded by round tables, set with centerpieces of pink carnations in squat crystal vases and groupings of ginger ale and seltzer bottles.

No one's saving places or jockeying to be near friends. The ladies just sit. Anita stands for a minute or so, then sees two women beckoning and patting the chair between them, so she goes and sits down. She soon understands why the women have found places so quickly: it doesn't matter where they sit, no one stays put for more than two seconds. They kiss and gab, then get up, sit next to a friend at another table, kiss and gab some more. Meanwhile the waiters are weaving through with bowls of hot soup, shouting to the women to get out of their way. But no one's paying attention.

The woman to Anita's right is middle-aged and kind of pretty. She's Mrs. Lesser. When the waiter brings Anita's soup, Mrs. Lesser pushes it away so Anita won't spill it in her struggle with Bertie's zipper.

"Your first baby?" asks Mrs. Lesser.

"Yes," says Anita.

"I had my first when I was sixteen. Can you believe I'm a grandmother?"

Anita might not have thought it, but she can believe it; she doesn't know quite what to say.

320

"Can you believe it?" Mrs. Lesser puts her big face near Bertie's little one, and Bertie rewards her with his most radiant, sweetest, and most inauthentic social smile.

"Look at this baby smile!" Mrs. Lesser says to the whole table. "Look at this sweetheart!" It's Anita's introduction to the room at large, and all at once it's open season on Bertie. Mrs. Lesser gets up and someone else sits down and starts stroking Bertie's cheek.

These women have children and grandchildren of their own, thinks Anita. Why are they so interested? But they are, they're full of questions. How old is he? What's his name? Does he sleep through the night? Is he always so good?

Anita feels like Bertie's ventriloquist. She has to make an effort to speak in her normal voice as she says, "His name's Bertie. He's five months old. He can pick up his own Cheerios."

"Cheerios?" cry the women. "At five months? He's a genius!"

The partition separating the men's and women's sections stops a few feet from the ceiling. Anita's facing it when suddenly she sees three furry brown things fly up, then plummet, then fly again. Just as she figures out someone's juggling hats, she hears applause from the other side of the plywood.

With each course, a different woman is making Bertie smile and nibbling from whatever plate the waiter has put down. First comes stuffed derma, then a platter of thick roast beef, little round potatoes, canned peas. Anita picks up a forkful of peas. She isn't very hungry, it isn't very good. No one's eating much; even the fleshiest ladies are just tasting. But every woman who sits down offers to hold Bertie for Anita, or to cut her roast beef. They say to Bertie, "Too bad you can't eat roast beef, pussycat," and "Next year at this time you'll be munching little brown potatoes."

*   *   *

Slowly at first, the men begin dancing. Anita feels it through the floor before she hears it. Stamp, stamp. Soon the silverware is rattling, the peas are jumping on her plate. The stamping gets faster, there are shouts. Anita wonders if her father is dancing. Probably he is. The door between the two sections is open, children are running back and forth. No one would stop her from looking. But she doesn't, she just doesn't.

Singing, clapping, the men make their own music. The women have help. Two men come in with an accordion and a mandolin. The women dance sweetly in couples, a dance that seems part waltz, part foxtrot, part polka. Mrs. Lesser reappears, and when a sprightly gray-haired lady to the far side of her makes swaying motions with her arms, Mrs. Lesser says, "If you're asking, I'm dancing," and away they go. A tiny old woman approaches Anita and says, "Would the baby care to dance?"

All the women want to dance with Bertie. Young and old, they keep cutting in, passing him around. Anita catches glimpses of him, first with this one, then with that, sailing, swaying to the music, resting his cheek on their pillowy breasts. When Mrs. Lesser sits back down, she asks where the baby is.

"Dancing," says Anita.

Mrs. Lesser cranes her neck. "He's smiling," she says. "He's the belle of the ball!"

Suddenly there's a whoop from the other room, and Anita sees the groom's head and shoulders over the partition. From the angle of his head, the stricken expression, she knows that this is the part where the men hoist the groom up in a chair and dance. Then the women gather and raise the bride's chair. The music gets louder, and the women begin circling the bride, dancing with such intensity that Anita goes and finds Bertie and takes him back.

At last the bride's head is nearly touching the ceiling. Above the partition, she and the groom look at each other. Anita wants to study this look. She thinks it's something she should pay close attention to. But she's only half-watching. Mostly she's concentrating on not dropping Bertie, whom she's holding up above her head.

"Look, sweetheart," she's saying. "Look at the lady in the chair!"

Bertie sings when he nurses, a sweet satisfied gulping and humming high in his nose. That night, after the wedding, Anita falls asleep while he's nursing, and his song turns into the song in her dream.

In her dream, Bertie's singing "Music, Music, Music" just like Teresa Brewer. He's still baby Bertie, but he's up on stage, smiling one of his phony smiles, making big stagey gestures like Shirley Temple or those awful children in *Annie*. One of these gestures is the "okay" sign, thumb and forefinger joined. The circle his fingers make reminds her of the Buddha. It reminds her of a Cheerio.

Anita wakes up laughing, wondering how a little baby could know words like "nickelodeon." She gets up, and without detaching Bertie from her breast, slips a bathrobe over both of them and goes downstairs. Except for her parents' bedroom, where earlier she heard her mother preparing for sleep, every room is lit up. In the kitchen, light is shining from around the edges of the cellar door. Anita and Bertie go down.

Opening the door to the family room, she sees her father sitting cross-legged on the cork-tiled floor. His eyes are shut and tears are shining on his cheeks. But he's not so out of it that he doesn't hear her come in. Looking up, he seems frail and embarrassed, an old man caught doing something he's not supposed to do.

Anita wants to apologize and leave. Then it dawns on her that she's not down there to bother him. There's something she wants to ask, but she's not sure what it is. She wants to ask why all the lights in the house are always on. She wants to ask who he thinks is paying the electric bills.

Anita's father stands up and dries his eyes with his palm. Then he says, "Hold up your hand."

Anita holds up her hand and he lifts his, palm facing hers, a few inches away. He asks if she feels anything.

She feels something. A pressure.

She remembers how when she was in labor with Bertie, she held Jamie's hand. Just before the nurses let her start pushing, she turned to Jamie and said, "I don't think I can do this." "Sure you can," he said, and squeezed her hand so hard she'd thought it was broken. By the time it stopped hurting, the contraction was over and she knew she could go on. Now she sees that Jamie didn't mean to hurt her. He was scared too.

Her father's hand is still a few inches away, but its grip feels as tight as Jamie's. She can almost feel electrons jumping over the space between them, electricity drawing them as close as she is to Bertie, who just at that moment lets go of her breast and sits up, watching them.

323

A Letter to Harvey Milk

Lesléa Newman

for Harvey Milk, 1930–1978

I

THE TEACHER SAYS we should write about our life, everything that happened today. So *nu*, what's there to tell? Why should today be different than any other day? May 5, 1986. I get up, I have myself a coffee, a little cottage cheese, half an English muffin. I get dressed. I straighten up the house a little, nobody should drop by and see I'm such a slob. I go down to the Senior Center and see what's doing. I play a little cards, I have some lunch, a bagel with cheese. I read a sign in the cafeteria, Writing Class 2:00. I think to myself, why not, something to pass the time. So at two o'clock I go in. The teacher says we should write about our life.

Listen, I want to say to this teacher, I.B. Singer I'm not. You think anybody cares what I did all day? Even my own children, may they live and be well, don't call. You think the whole world is waiting to see what Harry Weinberg had for breakfast?

The teacher is young and nice. She says everybody has something important to say. Yeah, sure, when you're young you believe things like that. She has short brown hair and big eyes, a nice figure, *zaftig* like my poor Fannie, may she rest in peace. She's wearing a Star of David around her neck, hanging from a purple string, that's nice. She gave us all notebooks and told us we're gonna write something every day, and if we want we can even write at home. Who'd a thunk it, me—Harry Weinberg, seventy-seven-years old—scribbling in a notebook like a schoolgirl. Why not, it passes the time.

So after the class I go to the store, I pick myself up a little orange juice, a few bagels, a nice piece of chicken, I shouldn't starve to death. I go up, I put on my slippers, I eat the chicken, I watch a little TV, I write in this notebook, I get ready for bed. *Nu*, for this somebody should give me a Pulitzer Prize?

II

Today the teacher tells us something about herself. She's a Jew, this we know from the *Mogen David* she wears around her neck. She tells us she wants to collect stories from old Jewish people, to preserve our history. *Oy*, such stories that I could tell her, shouldn't be preserved by nobody. She tells us she's learning Yiddish. For what, I wonder. I can't figure this teacher out. She's young, she's pretty, she shouldn't be with the old people so much. I wonder is she married. She doesn't wear a ring. Her grandparents won't tell her stories, she says, and she's worried that the Jews her age won't know nothing about the culture, about life in the *shtetls*. Believe me, life in the *shtetl* is nothing worth knowing about. Hunger and more hunger. Better off we're here in America, the past is past.

Then she gives us our homework, the homework we write in the class, it's a little *meshugeh*, but alright. She wants us to write a letter to somebody from our past, somebody who's no longer with us. She reads us a letter a child wrote to Abraham Lincoln, like an example. Right away I see everybody's getting nervous. So I raise my hand. "Teacher," I say, "you can tell me maybe how to address such a letter? There's a few things I've wanted to ask my wife for a long time." Everybody laughs. Then they start to write.

I sit for a few minutes, thinking about Fannie, thinking about my sister Frieda, my mother, my father, may they all rest in peace. But it's the strangest thing, the one I really want to write to is Harvey.

Dear Harvey:

You had to go get yourself killed for being a faygeleh? *You couldn't let somebody else have such a great honor? Alright, alright, so you liked the boys, I wasn't wild about the idea. But I got used to it. I never said you wasn't welcome in my house, did I?*

325

Nu, *Harvey, you couldn't leave well enough alone? You had your own camera store, your own business, what's bad? You couldn't keep still about the boys, you weren't satisfied until the whole world knew? Harvey Milk, with the big ears and the big ideas, had to go make himself something, a big politician. I know, I know, I said, "Harvey, make something of yourself, don't be an old* shmegeggie *like me, Harry the butcher." So now I'm eating my words, and they stick like a chicken bone in my old throat.*

It's a rotten world, Harvey, and rottener still without you in it. You know what happened to that momzer, *Dan White? They let him out of jail, and he goes and kills himself so nobody else should have the pleasure. Now you know me, Harvey, I'm not a violent man. But this was too much, even for me. In the old country, I saw things you shouldn't know from, things you couldn't imagine one person could do to another. But here in America, a man climbs through the window, kills the Mayor of San Francisco, kills Harvey Milk, and a couple years later he's walking around on the street? This I never thought I'd see in my whole life. But from a country that kills the Rosenbergs, I should expect something different?*

Harvey, you should be glad you weren't around for the trial. I read about it in the papers. The lawyer, that son of a bitch, said Dan White ate too many Twinkies the night before he killed you, so his brain wasn't working right. Twinkies, nu, I ask you. My kids ate Twinkies when they were little, did they grow up to be murderers, God forbid? And now, do they take the Twinkies down from the shelf, somebody else shouldn't go a little crazy, climb through a window, and shoot somebody? No, they leave them right there next to the cupcakes and the donuts, to torture me every time I go to the store to pick up a few things, I shouldn't starve to death.

Harvey, I think I'm losing my mind. You know what I do every week? Every week I go to the store, I buy a bag of jellybeans for you, you should have something to nosh on, I remember what a sweet tooth you have. I put them in a jar on the table, in case you should come in with another crazy petition for me to sign. Sometimes I think you're gonna just walk through my door and tell me it was another meshugeh *publicity stunt.*

Harvey, now I'm gonna tell you something. The night you died the

*whole city of San Francisco cried for you. Thirty thousand people
marched in the street, I saw it on TV. Me, I didn't go down. I'm an
old man, I don't walk so good, they said there might be riots. But no,
there were no riots. Just people walking in the street, quiet, each one
with a candle, until the street looked like the sky all lit up with a
million stars. Old people, young people, Black people, white people,
Chinese people. You name it, they were there. I remember thinking,
Harvey must be so proud, and then I remembered you were dead and
such a lump rose in my throat, like a grapefruit it was, and then the
tears ran down my face like rain. Can you imagine, Harvey, an old
man like me, sitting alone in his apartment, crying and carrying on
like a baby? But it's the God's truth. Never did I carry on so in all my
life.*

*And then all of a sudden I got mad. I yelled at the people on TV:
for getting shot you made him into such a hero? You couldn't march
for him when he was alive, he couldn't shep a little naches?*

*But nu, what good does getting mad do, it only makes my pressure
go up. So I took myself a pill, calmed myself down.*

*Then they made speeches for you, Harvey. The same people who
called you a shmuck when you were alive, now you were dead, they
were calling you a mensh. You were a mensh, Harvey, a mensh with
a heart of gold. You were too good for this rotten world. They just
weren't ready for you.*

Oy Harveleh, alav ha-sholom,
Harry

III

Today the teacher asks me to stay for a minute after class. *Oy*, what
did I do wrong now, I wonder. Maybe she didn't like my letter to
Harvey? Who knows?

After the class she comes and sits down next to me. She's wearing
purple pants and a white T-shirt. *"Feh,"* I can just hear Fannie say.
"God forbid she should wear a skirt? Show off her figure a little? The
girls today dressing like boys and the boys dressing like girls—this I
don't understand."

"Mr. Weinberg," the teacher says.

"Call me Harry," I says.

"O.K., Harry," she says. "I really liked the letter you wrote to Harvey Milk. It was terrific, really. It meant a lot to me. It even made me cry."

I can't even believe my own ears. My letter to Harvey Milk made the teacher cry?

"You see, Harry," she says, "I'm gay, too. And there aren't many Jewish people your age that are so open-minded. At least that I know. So your letter gave me lots of hope. In fact, I was wondering if you'd consider publishing it."

Publishing my letter? Again I couldn't believe my own ears. Who would want to read a letter from Harry Weinberg to Harvey Milk? No, I tell her. I'm too old for fame and glory. I like the writing class, it passes the time. But what I write is my own business. The teacher looks sad for a moment, like a cloud passes over her eyes. Then she said, "Tell me about Harvey Milk. How did you meet him? What was he like?" *Nu*, Harvey, you were a pain in the ass when you were alive, you're still a pain in the ass now that you're dead. Everybody wants to hear about Harvey.

So I tell her. I tell her how I came into the camera shop one day with a roll of film from when I went to visit the grandchildren. How we started talking, and I said, "Milk, that's not such a common name. Are you related to the Milks in Woodmere?" And so we found out we were practically neighbors forty years ago, when the children were young, before we moved out here. Gracie was almost the same age as Harvey, a couple years older, maybe, but they went to different schools. Still, Harvey leans across the counter and gives me such a hug, like I'm his own father.

I tell her more about Harvey, how he didn't believe there was a good *kosher* butcher in San Francisco, how he came to my store just to see. But all the time I'm talking I'm thinking to myself, no, it can't be true. Such a gorgeous girl like this goes with the girls, not with the boys? Such a *shanda*. Didn't God in His wisdom make a girl a girl and a boy a boy—boom they should meet, boom they should get married, boom they should have babies, and that's the way it is? Harvey I loved like my own son, but this I never could understand. And *nu*,

328

why was the teacher telling me this, it's my business who she sleeps with? She has some sadness in her eyes, this teacher. Believe me I've known such sadness in my life, I can recognize it a hundred miles away. Maybe she's lonely. Maybe after class one day I'll take her out for a coffee, we'll talk a little bit, I'll find out.

IV

It's 3:00 in the morning, I can't sleep. So *nu*, here I am with this crazy notebook. Who am I kidding, maybe I think I'm Yitzhak Peretz? What would the children think, to see their old father sitting up in his bathrobe with a cup of tea, scribbling in his notebook? *Oy, meyn kinder*, they should only live and be well and call their old father once in a while.

Fannie used to keep up with them. She could be such a *nudge*, my Fannie. "What's the matter, you're too good to call your old mother once in a while?" she'd yell into the phone. Then there'd be a pause. "Busy-shmusy," she'd yell even louder. "Was I too busy to change your diapers? Was I too busy to put food into your mouth?" *Oy*, I haven't got the strength, but Fannie could she yell and carry on.

You know sometimes, in the middle of the night, I'll reach across the bed for Fannie's hand. Without even thinking, like my hand got a mind of its own, it creeps across the bed, looking for Fannie's hand. After all this time, fourteen years she's been dead, but still, a man gets used to a few things. Forty-two years, the body doesn't forget. And my little *Faigl* had such hands, little *hentelehs*, tiny like a child's. But strong. Strong from kneading *challah*, from scrubbing clothes, from rubbing the children's backs to put them to sleep. My Fannie, she was so ashamed from those hands. After thirty-five years of marriage when finally, I could afford to buy her a diamond ring, she said no. She said it was too late already, she'd be ashamed. A girl needs nice hands to show off a diamond, her hands were already ruined, better yet buy a new stove.

Ruined? *Feh*. To me her hands were beautiful. Small, with veins running through them like rivers, and cracks in the skin like the desert. A hundred times I've kicked myself for not buying Fannie that ring.

V

Today in the writing class the teacher read my notebook. Then she says I should make a poem about Fannie. "A poem," I says to her, "now Shakespeare you want I should be?" She says I have a good eye for detail. I says to her, "Excuse me Teacher, you live with a woman for forty-two years, you start to notice a few things."

She helps me. We do it together, we write a poem called "Fannie's Hands":

> *Fannie's hands are two little birds*
> *that fly into her lap.*
> *Her veins are like rivers.*
> *Her skin is cracked like the desert.*
> *Her strong little hands*
> *baked challah, scrubbed clothes,*
> *rubbed the children's backs.*
> *Her strong little hands*
> *and my big clumsy hands*
> *fit together in the night*
> *like pieces of a jigsaw puzzle*
> *made in Heaven, by God.*

So *nu*, who says you can't teach an old dog new tricks? I read it to the class and such a fuss they made. "A regular Romeo," one of them says. "If only my husband, may he live and be well, would write such a poem for me," says another. I wish Fannie was still alive, I could read it to her. Even the teacher was happy, I could tell, but still, there was a ring of sadness around her eyes.

After the class I waited till everybody left, they shouldn't get the wrong idea, and I asked the teacher would she like to go get a coffee. "Nu, it's enough writing already," I said. "Come, let's have a little treat."

So we take a walk, it's a nice day. We find a diner, nothing fancy, but clean and quiet. I try to buy her a piece of cake, a sandwich maybe, but no, all she wants is coffee.

So we sit and talk a little. She wants to know about my childhood in the old country, she wants to know about the boat ride to America, she wants to know did my parents speak Yiddish to me when I was growing up. "Harry," she said to me, "when I hear old people talking Yiddish, it's like a love letter blowing in the wind. I try to run after them, and sometimes I catch a phrase that makes me cry or a word that makes me laugh. Even if I don't understand, it always touches my heart."

Oy, this teacher has some strange ideas. "Why do you want to speak Jewish?" I ask her. "Here in America, everybody speaks English. You don't need it. What's done is done, what's past is past. You shouldn't go with the old people so much. You should go out, make friends, have a good time. You got some troubles you want to talk about? Maybe I shouldn't pry," I say, "but you shouldn't look so sad, a young girl like you. When you're old you got plenty to be sad. You shouldn't think about the old days so much, let the dead rest in peace. What's done is done."

I took a swallow of my coffee, to calm down my nerves. I was getting a little too excited.

"Harry, listen to me," the teacher says. "I'm thirty years old and no one in my family will talk to me because I'm gay. It's all Harvey Milk's fault. He made such an impression on me. You know, when he died, what he said, 'If a bullet enters my brain, let that bullet destroy every closet door.' So when he died, I came out to everyone—the people at work, my parents. I felt it was my duty, so the Dan Whites of the world wouldn't be able to get away with it. I mean, if every single gay person came out—just think of it!—everyone would see they had a gay friend or a gay brother or a gay cousin or a gay teacher. Then they couldn't say things like 'Those gays should be shot.' Because they'd be saying you should shoot my neighbor or my sister or my daughter's best friend."

I never saw the teacher get so excited before. Maybe a politician she should be. She reminded me a little bit of Harvey.

"So nu, what's the problem?" I ask.

"The problem is my parents," she says with a sigh, and such a sigh I never heard from a young person before. "My parents haven't spoken to me since I told them I was gay. 'How could you do this to us?' they said. I wasn't doing anything to them. I tried to explain I couldn't help being gay, like I couldn't help being a Jew, but that they didn't want to hear. So I haven't spoken to them in eight years."

331

"Eight years, *Gottenyu*," I say to her. This I never heard in my whole life. A father and a mother cut off their own daughter like that. Better they should cut off their own hand. I thought about Gracie, a perfect daughter she's not, but your child is your child. When she married the *Goy*, Fannie threatened to put her head in the oven, but she got over it. Not to see your own daughter for eight years, and such a smart, gorgeous girl, such a good teacher, what a *shanda*.

So what can I do, I ask. Does she want me to talk to them, a letter maybe I could write. Does she want I should adopt her, the hell with them, I make a little joke. She smiles. "Just talking to you makes me feel better," she says. So *nu*, now I'm Harry the social worker. She says that's why she wants the old people's stories so much, she doesn't know nothing from her own family history. She wants to know about her own people, maybe write a book. But it's hard to get the people to talk to her, she says, she doesn't understand.

"Listen, Teacher," I tell her. "These old people have stories you shouldn't know from. What's there to tell? Hunger and more hunger. Suffering and more suffering. I buried my sister over twenty years ago, my mother, my father—all dead. You think I could just start talking about them like I just saw them yesterday? You think I don't think about them every day? Right here I keep them," I say, pointing to my heart. "I try to forget them, I should live in peace, the dead are gone. Talking about them won't bring them back. You want stories, go talk to somebody else. I ain't got no stories."

I sat down then. I didn't even know I was standing up, I got so excited. Everybody in the diner was looking at me, a crazy man shouting at a young girl.

Oy, and now the teacher was crying. "I'm sorry," I says to her. "You want another coffee?"

"No thanks, Harry," she says. "I'm sorry, too."

"Forget it. We can just pretend it never happened," I say, and then we go.

VI

All this crazy writing has shaken me up inside a little bit. Yesterday I was walking home from the diner, I thought I saw Harvey walking in front of me. No, it can't be, I says to myself, and my heart started to pound so, I got afraid I shouldn't drop dead in the street from a heart attack. But then the man turned around and it wasn't Harvey. It didn't even look like him at all.

I got myself upstairs and took myself a pill, I could feel my pressure was going up. All this talk about the past—Fannie, Harvey, Frieda, my mother, my father—what good does it do? This teacher and her crazy ideas. Did I ever ask my mother, my father, what their childhood was like? What nonsense. Better I shouldn't know.

So today is Saturday, no writing class, but still I'm writing in this crazy notebook. I ask myself, Harry, what can I do to make you feel a little better? And I answer myself, make me a nice chicken soup.

You think an old man like me can't make chicken soup? Let me tell you, on all the holidays it was Harry that made the soup. Every *Pesach* it was Harry skimming the *shmaltz* from the top of the pot, it was Harry making the *kreplach*. I ask you, where is it written that a man shouldn't know from chicken soup?

So I take myself down to the store, I buy myself a nice chicken, some carrots, some celery, some parsley—onions I already got, parsnips I can do without. I'm afraid I shouldn't have a heart attack *shlepping* all that food up the steps, but thank God, I make it alright.

I put up the pot with water, throw everything in one-two-three, and soon the whole house smells from chicken soup.

I remember the time Harvey came to visit and there I was with my apron on, skimming the *shmaltz* from the soup. Did he kid me about that! The only way I could get him to keep still was to invite him to dinner. "Listen, Harvey," I says to him. "Whether you're a man or a woman, it doesn't matter. You gotta learn to cook. When you're old, nobody cares. Nobody will do for you. You gotta learn to do for yourself."

"I won't live past fifty, Har," he says, smearing a piece of rye bread with *shmaltz*.

"Nobody wants to grow old, believe me, I know," I says to him. "But listen, it's not so terrible. What's the alternative? Nobody wants to die young, either." I take off my apron and sit down with him.

"No, I mean it Harry," he says to me with his mouth full. "I won't make it to fifty. I've always known it. I'm a politician. A gay politician. Someone's gonna take a pot shot at me. It's a risk you gotta take."

The way he said it, I tell you, a chill ran down my back like I never felt before. He was forty-seven at the time, just a year before he died.

VII

Today after the writing class, the teacher tells us she's going away for two days. Everyone makes a big fuss, the class they like so much already. She tells us she's sorry, something came up she has to do. She says we can come have class without her, the room will be open, we can read to each other what we write in our notebooks. Someone asks her what we should write about.

"Write me a letter," she says. "Write a story called 'What I Never Told Anyone.' "

So, after everyone leaves, I ask her does she want to go out, have a coffee, but she says no, she has to go home and pack.

I tell her wherever she's going she should have a good time.

"Thanks, Harry," she says. "You'll be here when I get back?"

"Sure," I tell her. "I like this crazy writing. It passes the time."

She swings a big black bookbag onto her shoulder, a regular Hercules this teacher is, and she smiles at me. "I gotta run, Harry. Have a good week." She turns and walks away and something on her bookbag catches my eye. A big shiny pin that spells out her name all fancy-shmancy in rhinestones: Barbara. And under that, right away I see sewn onto her bookbag an upside-down pink triangle.

I stop in my tracks, stunned. No, it can't be, I says to myself. Maybe it's just a design? Maybe she doesn't know from this? My heart is beating fast now, I know I should go home, take myself a pill, my pressure, I can feel it going up.

But I just stand there. And then I get mad. What, she thinks maybe I'm blind as well as old, I can't see what's right in front of my nose? Or maybe we don't remember such things? What right does she have to walk in here with that, that thing on her bag, to remind us of what we been through? Haven't we seen enough?

Stories she wants. She wants we should cut our hearts open and give her stories so she could write a book. Well, alright, now I'll tell her a story.

This is what I never told anyone. One day, maybe seven, eight years ago—no, maybe longer, I think Harvey was still alive—one day Izzie comes knocking on my door. I open the door and there's Izzie, standing there, his face white as a sheet. I bring him inside, I make him a coffee. "Izzie, what is it," I says to him. "Something happened to the children, to the grandchildren, God forbid?"

He sits down, he doesn't drink his coffee. He looks through me like I'm not even there. Then he says, "Harry, I'm walking down the street, you know I had a little lunch at the Center, and then I come outside, I see a young man, maybe twenty-five, a good-looking guy, walking toward me. He's wearing black pants, a white shirt, and on his shirt he's got a pink triangle."

"So," I says. "A pink triangle, a purple triangle, they wear all kinds of crazy things these days."

"*Heshel*," he tells me, "don't you understand? The gays are wearing pink triangles just like the war, just like in the camps."

No, this I can't believe. Why would they do a thing like that? But if Izzie says it, it must be true. Who would make up such a thing?

"He looked a little bit like *Yussl*," Izzie says, and then he begins to cry, and such a cry like I never heard. Like a baby he was, with the tears streaming down his cheeks and his shoulders shaking with great big sobs. Such moans and groans I never heard from a grown man in all my life. I thought maybe he was gonna have a heart attack the way he was carrying on. I didn't know what to do. I was afraid the neighbors would hear, they shouldn't call the police, such sounds he was making. Fifty-eight years old he was, but he looked like a little boy sitting there, sniffling. And who was *Yussl*? Thirty years we'd been friends, and I never heard from *Yussl*.

So finally, I put my arms around him, and I held him, I didn't know what else to do. His body was shaking so, I thought his bones would crack from knocking against each other. Soon his body got quiet, but then all of a sudden his mouth got noisy.

"Listen, *Heshel*, I got to tell you something, something I never told nobody in my whole life. I was young in the camps, nineteen, maybe twenty when they took us away." The words poured from his mouth like a flood. "*Yussl* was my best friend in the camps. Already I saw my mother, my father, my Hannah marched off to the ovens. *Yussl* was the only one I had to hold on to.

"One morning, during the selection, they pointed me to the right,

335

Yussl to the left. I went a little crazy, I ran after him. 'No, he stays with me, they made a mistake,' I said, and I grabbed him by the hand and dragged him back in line. Why the guard didn't kill us right then, I couldn't tell you. Nothing made sense in that place.

"*Yussl* and I slept together on a wooden bench. That night I couldn't sleep. It happened pretty often in that place. I would close my eyes and see such things that would make me scream in the night, and for that I could get shot. I don't know what was worse, asleep or awake. All I saw was suffering.

"On this night, *Yussl* was awake, too. He didn't move a muscle, but I could tell. Finally he said my name, just a whisper, but something broke in me and I began to cry. He put his arms around me and we cried together, such a close call we'd had.

"And then he began to kiss me. 'You saved my life,' he whispered, and he kissed my eyes, my cheeks, my lips. And Harry, I kissed him back. Harry, I never told nobody this before. I, we . . . we, you know, that was such a place that hell, I couldn't help it. The warmth of his body was just too much for me and Hannah was dead already and we would soon be dead too, probably, so what did it matter?"

He looked up at me then, the tears streaming from his eyes. "It's O.K., Izzie," I said. "Maybe I would have done the same."

"There's more, Harry," he says, and I got him a tissue, he should blow his nose. What more could there be?

"This went on for a couple of months maybe, just every once in a while when we couldn't sleep. He'd whisper my name and I'd answer with his, and then we'd, you know, we'd touch each other. We were very, very quiet, but who knows, maybe some other boys in the barracks were doing the same.

"To this day I don't know how it happened, but somehow someone found out. One day *Yussl* didn't come back to the barracks at night. I went almost crazy, you can imagine, all the things that went through my mind, the things they might have done to him, those lousy Nazis. I looked everywhere, I asked everyone, three days he was gone. And then on the third day, they lined us up after supper and there they had *Yussl*. I almost collapsed on the ground when I saw him. They had him on his knees with his hands tied behind his back. His face was swollen so, you couldn't even see his eyes. His clothes were stained with blood. And on his uniform they had sewn a pink triangle, big, twice the size of our yellow stars.

"*Oy*, did they beat him but good. 'Who's your friend?' they yelled at him. 'Tell us and we'll let you live.' But no, he wouldn't tell. He knew they were lying, he knew they'd kill us both. They asked him again and again, 'Who's your friend? Tell us which one he is.' And every time he said no, they'd crack him with a whip until the blood ran from him like a river. Such a sight he was, like I've never seen. How he remained conscious I'll never know.

"Everything inside me was broken after that. I wanted to run to his side, but I didn't dare, so afraid I was. At one point he looked at me, right in the eye, as though he was saying, *Izzie, save yourself. Me, I'm finished, but you, you got a chance to live through this and tell the world our story.*

"Right after he looked at me, he collapsed, and they shot him, Harry, right there in front of us. Even after he was dead they kicked him in the head a little bit. They left his body out there for two days, as a warning to us. They whipped us all that night, and from then on we had to sleep with all the lights on and with our hands on top of the blankets. Anyone caught with their hands under the blankets would be shot.

"He died for me, Harry, they killed him for that, was it such a terrible thing? *Oy*, I haven't thought about *Yussl* for twenty-five years maybe, but when I saw that kid on the street today, it was too much." And then he started crying again, and he clung to me like a child.

So what could I do? I was afraid he shouldn't have a heart attack, maybe he was having a nervous breakdown, maybe I should get the doctor. *Vay iss mir*, I never saw anybody so upset in my whole life. And such a story, *Gottenyu*.

"Izzie, come lie down," I says, and I took him by the hand to the bed. I laid him down, I took off his shoes, and still he was crying. So what could I do? I lay down with him, I held him tight. I told him he was safe, he was in America. I don't know what else I said, I don't think he heard me, still he kept crying.

I stroked his head, I held him tight. "Izzie, it's alright," I said. "Izzie, Izzie, *Izzaleh*." I said his name over and over, like a lullaby, until his crying got quiet. He said my name once softly, *Heshel*, or

337

maybe he said *Yussl*, I don't remember, but thank God he finally fell asleep. I tried to get up from the bed, but Izzie held onto me tight. So what could I do? Izzie was my friend for thirty years, for him I would do anything. So I held him all night long, and he slept like a baby.

And this is what I never told nobody, not even Harvey. That there in that bed, where Fannie and I slept together for forty-two years, me and Izzie spent the night. Me, I didn't sleep a wink, such a lump in my throat I had, like the night Harvey died.

Izzie passed on a couple months after that. I saw him a few more times, and he seemed different somehow. How, I couldn't say. We never talked about that night. But now that he had told someone his deepest secret, he was ready to go, he could die in peace. Maybe now that I told, I can die in peace, too?

VIII

Dear Teacher:

You said write what you never told nobody, and write you a letter. I always did all my homework, such a student I was. So nu, I got to tell you something. I can't write in this notebook no more, I can't come no more to the class. I don't want you should take offense, you're a good teacher and a nice girl. But me, I'm an old man, I don't sleep so good at night, these stories are like a knife in my heart. Harvey, Fannie, Izzie, Yussl, my father, my mother, let them all rest in peace. The dead are gone. Better to live for today. What good does remembering do, it doesn't bring back the dead. Let them rest in peace.

But Teacher, I want you should have my notebook. It doesn't have nice stories in it, no love letters, no happy endings for a nice girl like you. A bestseller it ain't, I guarantee. Maybe you'll put it in a book someday, the world shouldn't forget.

Meanwhile, good luck to you, Teacher. May you live and be well and not get shot in the head like poor Harvey, may he rest in peace. Maybe someday we'll go out, have a coffee again, who knows? But me, I'm too old for this crazy writing. I remember too much, the pen is like a knife twisting in my heart.

One more thing, Teacher. Between parents and children, it's not so easy. Believe me, I know. Don't give up on them. One father, one mother, it's all you got. If you were my tochter, I'd be proud of you.

Harry

Glossary

Spellings are those which appeared in the stories as originally printed.

alav ha-shalom May his soul rest in peace.

Baal Shem Tov Eighteenth-century mystic who founded Hasidism.

bet hamidrash House of study or prayer; synagogue.

bar mizvah; bar mitzvah Ceremony in which a thirteen-year-old boy is initiated into the religious community and performs his first act as an adult, the reading in the synagogue of a weekly portion of the Torah (equivalent for girl is *bat* mitzvah).

chaver Boyfriend.

Chad Gadyo Song about a little goat, symbolizing the Jewish people, sung at the end of the Passover seder.

challah Braided egg bread baked for the Sabbath and festive occasions.

dorten There.

El Yivneh Hagalil Folk song of Zionist movement.

faygeleh Homosexual (literally, "little bird").

fresser Eater.

gefullte (fish) Fish cakes or loaf, made of chopped fish.

Gemara Second part of the Talmud, consisting of commentaries on the Mishnah, its first part.

gemutlich   Comfortable, cozy.

golem   A creature without a soul, created by magical means.

Gottuniu, Gottenyu   Dear God.

goy   A Gentile.

Hasidism   Populist religious movement among Eastern European Jews in the eighteenth and nineteenth centuries; current forms flourish in many parts of the world.

heder   Hebrew school.

hentelehs   Little hands.

hora   Jewish folk dance.

Humesh   The Pentateuch, the five books of the Torah.

hutz la'aretz   Abroad.

kibitzer   Someone who jokes or teases.

kiddush   Ritual that sanctifies the Sabbath and Jewish holy days.

kinder   Children.

Kol Nidre   Introductory prayer of Yom Kippur (Day of Atonement) service.

kosher   Ritual dietary laws.

kosher yid   Observant Jew.

kotselah   Little cat.

kreplach   Dumplings.

landsmen   People from the same hometown in the old country.

maabara   Temporary immigrant camp life.

matzoth   Unleavened bread.

mensh   An upstanding human being.

midrash   Commentaries on the Bible.

mikweh   Ritual bath.

meshugeh   Crazy or mad.

Mogen david   Star of David.

mohel Man who circumcises male baby in Brith Milah.

momzer Bastard.

mezuzzah Small wall plaque containing verses from Deuteronomy, fixed to doorpost.

nosh Snack.

nudge Pest.

ozeret Maid.

Pesach Passover.

rav Spiritual authority.

rebbe Hebrew schoolteacher; rabbi.

rebbetzin Female schoolteacher; rabbi's wife.

Rosh Hashonoh High Holy Day that celebrates the Jewish New Year.

schmegeggie Jerk.

shabbas, shabbos Sabbath.

shalom Hello; good-bye; peace.

shanda Shame.

shala Question.

Shema (Yisroel) Jewish credo, "Hear O Israel," asserting the unity of God.

shep naches Receive pleasure.

shickser Gentile woman.

shtetl Small Jewish town.

shlepping Dragging or pulling.

shmaltz Rendered chicken fat.

shule Synagogue.

Talmud Comprehensive, multivolume compilation of Jewish law, consisting of the Mishnah and the Gemara.

tfillin, tefillin Phylacteries.

tochter Daughter.

Torah The five books of Moses, broadly construed as the teachings of Judaism.

tref Unkosher, defiled.

tsotskele Plaything; toy; doll-like woman.

tup Pot.

vay iss mir Woe is me.

yahrzeit Observance of the anniversary of a death.

Yiddishkeit Jewishness.

zaftig Juicy; plump.

Biographical Notes

Mary Antin (1881–1949)

Mary Antin emigrated to the United States with her Russian-born parents at the age of ten and was educated at Girls' Latin School in Boston; Teachers College, Columbia; and Barnard College. Her first book, *From Polotzk to Boston*, was published in 1899. Her most celebrated work, *The Promised Land*, appeared in 1912, after serialization in the *Atlantic Monthly. They Who Knock At Our Gates: A Complete Gospel of Immigration* (1914), which protested against restrictive immigration laws, was her last book.

Rosellen Brown (b. 1939)

Rosellen Brown is the author of three novels, *The Autobiography of My Mother* (1976), *Tender Mercies* (1978), and *Civil Wars* (1984), two books of poetry, *Some Deaths in the Delta* (1970) and *Cora Fry* (1977), a book of short stories, *Street Games* (1974), and, with her husband, Marvin Hoffman, a documentary play about Russian Jewry, *Dear Irina*, produced in Houston in 1988. Brown, who lives in Texas, received an award from the American Academy and Institute of Arts and Letters in 1988.

Hortense Calisher (b. 1911)

Born in New York City, Hortense Calisher graduated from Barnard College, married shortly after, and was a full-time wife and mother for thirteen years. Her first short stories were published in 1948. Calisher's works comprise volumes of short fiction—*In the Absence of Angels* (1951), *Tale for the Mirror* (1962), *Extreme Magic* (1964), *The Collected Stories of Hortense Calisher* (1975), and *Saratoga, Hot* (1985); eleven novels and several novellas, including *Textures of Life* (1963), *The New Yorkers* (1969), *On Keeping Women*

345

(1977), *Mysteries of Motion* (1983); and *Herself: An Autobiographical Work* (1972). She has served as president of PEN, and is currently president of the American Academy and Institute of Arts and Letters.

Edna Ferber (1885–1968)
Edna Ferber wrote many short stories, collected in such volumes as *Buttered Side Down* (1912) and *Cheerful By Request* (1918). Her first best-seller, *So Big*, won the Pulitzer Prize in 1924. Her novel, *Show Boat*, published in 1926, was adapted for the stage the following year and has since been in constant production. Ferber's career included two volumes of autobiography, theatrical collaborations with George Kaufman—*Minick* (1924), *The Royal Family* (1927), *Dinner at Eight* (1932), and *Stage Door* (1936)—and eleven additional novels, among them *Saratoga Trunk* (1941) and *Giant* (1952), both made into highly successful movies.

Gloria Goldreich (b. 1934)
Gloria Goldreich studied at Brandeis University and at the Hebrew University of Jerusalem. Her novel, *Leah's Journal*, received the National Jewish Book Award for fiction in 1979; another novel, *Four Days*, won the Federation of Jewish Philanthropies Arts and Letters Award for 1981. Her short stories and essays have appeared in such magazines as *Midstream, Commentary, Moment, Haddassah Magazine, Ms., Ladies Home Journal, McCall's*, and *Redbook*. She has written children's books and novels for young adults, and is the editor of *A Treasury of Jewish Literature From Biblical Times to Today* (1982). She lives in Westchester, New York.

Rebecca Goldstein (b. 1950)
Rebecca Goldstein received a B.A. from Barnard College, a Ph.D. in philosophy from Princeton University, and has taught philosophy at Barnard and at Rutgers University. The author of two novels, *The Mind-Body Problem* (1983) and *The Late-Summer Passion of a Woman of Mind* (1989), she currently writes in New Jersey.

Ivy Goodman (b. 1953)
Ivy Goodman received a B.A. from the University of Pennsylvania and an M.A. from Stanford University. She has held fellowships from the National Endowment for the Arts and the Fine Arts Work Center in Provincetown. Her book of short stories, *Heart Failures*, was published in 1983; stories from this volume have been anthologized in *Prize Stories: The O. Henry Awards, The Ploughshares Reader*, and *The Signet Classic Book of Contemporary Short Stories*. She lives in Maryland with her husband and infant son, and is at work on a novel.

346

Joanne Greenberg (b. 1932)

Born in Brooklyn, New York, Joanne Greenberg graduated from American University. She is the author of the autobiographical novel, *I Never Promised You a Rose Garden* (1964), published under the pseudonym Hannah Green. Other fiction (published under her own name) includes the historical novel, *The King's Persons* (1963), *The Monday Voices* (1965), *In This Sign* (1968), *Founder's Praise* (1976), *A Season of Delight* (1981), *The Far Side of Victory* (1983), *Simple Gifts* (1986), *Age of Consent* (1987), and *Of Such Small Differences* (1988). She is also the author of three collections of stories, *Summering: A Book Of Short Stories* (1966), *Rites of Passage* (1972), and *High Crimes and Misdemeanors* (1979). She received the Fromm-Reichmann Award of the American Academy of Psychoanalysis in 1967 for *I Never Promised You A Rose Garden* and the Daroff Memorial Award for *The King's Persons*. She lives with her husband in Colorado.

Fannie Hurst (1889–1968)

Fannie Hurst wrote seventeen novels, including such best-sellers as *Back Street* (1931) and *Imitation of Life* (1933), more than two hundred short stories, and scores of film and radio scripts, articles, and pamphlets. Mostly published in women's magazines, many of her stories also appeared in the annual Best American Short Story prize volumes. Sixty-three of them were reprinted in nine books published between 1914 and 1937.

Johanna Kaplan (b. 1942)

Johanna Kaplan grew up in the Bronx and attended Music and Art High School in Manhattan. She received a B.A. from New York University and a master's degree in special education from Teachers College, Columbia. Her collection of short stories, *Other People's Lives* (1975), and her novel, *O My America!* (1980), each received the Jewish Book Award for Fiction. Kaplan has taught writing at the Bread Loaf Writers' Conference in Middlebury, Vermont and reviews contemporary fiction for the *New York Times Book Review* and other journals.

Edith Konecky (b. 1922)

Edith Konecky was born in Brooklyn and currently resides in Manhattan. She is the author of two novels, *Allegra Maud Goldman* (1976), and *A Place at the Table* (1989). Her short stories and poetry have appeared in *Saturday Evening Post*, *Esquire*, *Open Places*, *Mademoiselle*, *Kenyon Review*, *Cosmopolitan*, *Virginia Quarterly*, and *Aphra*.

Lesléa Newman (b. 1955)

Lesléa Newman was born in Brooklyn, New York, and currently resides in Western Massachusetts, where she teaches women's writing workshops. She is the author of the novel *Good Enough to Eat* (1986), a book of poetry, *Love Me Like You Mean It* (1987), a collection of short stories, *A Letter to Harvey Milk* (1988), and the children's book *Heather Has Two Mommies* (1989). She is also the editor of *Bubbie Meisehs by Shayneh Maidelehs*, a collection of poetry by Jewish women about their grandmothers (1989).

Tillie Olsen (b. 1913)

Born in Omaha, Nebraska, Tillie Lerner Olsen worked as a union organizer during the Depression, when she began to write. Interrupted by marriage and four daughters, Olsen published her first work, *Tell Me A Riddle*, in 1961; the title story, originally published separately, won the O. Henry Award. In 1974, Olsen published *Yonnondio: From the Thirties*, the first chapter of which had appeared in *Partisan Review* in 1934. Her collection of essays on women's writing, *Silences*, appeared in 1978. At her suggestion, the Feminist Press reprinted Rebecca Harding Davis' *Life in the Iron Mills* (1972), for which Olsen wrote an introduction. She has received several fellowships and an Award for Distinguished Contribution to American Literature from the American Academy and the National Institute of Arts and Letters. She is currently writing fiction in San Francisco.

Cynthia Ozick (b. 1928)

Cynthia Ozick was born in New York City. She earned a B.A. from New York University and a master's degree in literature from Ohio State University. She is the author of the novels *Trust* (1966), *The Cannibal Galaxy* (1983), and *The Messiah of Stockholm* (1987), three collections of short fiction, *The Pagan Rabbi and Other Stories* (1971), *Bloodshed and Three Novellas* (1976), and *Levitation, Five Fictions* (1982), and dozens of critical essays, many of them collected in *Art & Ardor* (1983) and *Metaphor and Memory* (1989). Among the awards she has received are the National Book Award, the American Academy of the Arts Award for literature, the Edgar Lewis Wallant Award for fiction, the Jewish Heritage Award, the Distinguished Service in Jewish Letters Award from the Jewish Theological Seminary, and the American Academy of Arts and Letters Strauss Living Award. She is a three-time first-prize winner of the O. Henry Prize Stories Award (for "The Shawl," its sequel, "Rosa," and "Usurpation").

Grace Paley (b. 1922)

Born in the Bronx, Grace Paley attended Hunter College. Her short stories have appeared in *The New Yorker*, *New American Review*, *Esquire*, *Atlantic Monthly*, and other journals, and have been collected in *The Little Disturbances of Man* (1959), *Enormous Changes at the Last Minute* (1974), and *Later the Same Day* (1985). She received the literary award for short-story writing from the National Institute of Arts and Letters in 1970, the Brandeis

University Creative Award Citation in Fiction in 1978, and was elected to the American Academy and Institute of Arts and Letters in 1980. Active in the peace movement for many years, she has taught at Columbia University, Sarah Lawrence College, and Syracuse University.

Francine Prose (b. 1947)
Born in Brooklyn, New York, Francine Prose received a B.A. and an M.A. from Harvard University. Her novels include *Judah the Pious* (1973, winner of the Jewish Book Council Award), *The Glorious Ones* (1974), *Marie Laveau* (1977), *Animal Magnetism* (1978), *Household Saints* (1981), *Hungry Hearts* (1983), and *Bigfoot Dreams* (1986). She is also the author of *Stories from Our Living Past* (1974), a collection of Jewish folktales, and of short stories and articles published in the *Atlantic*, the *Village Voice*, *Commentary*, *The New Yorker*, the *New York Times*, *Tikkun*, and *Mademoiselle*. She has taught at Harvard, Sarah Lawrence, the University of Utah, the Bread Loaf Writers' Conference, and the Iowa Writers' Workshop, and currently lives in upstate New York with her husband and two sons.

Marjorie Sandor (b. 1957)
Marjorie Sandor grew up in Southern California and was educated at the University of California, Davis, and the University of Iowa Writers' Workshop. Her stories have appeared in *The Best American Short Stories* (1985 and 1988), *The Pushcart Prize XIII*, and *Twenty Under Thirty*, as well as in literary magazines. Her first collection, *A Night of Music*, was published by The Ecco Press in 1989. She is currently on the faculty of the Creative Writing Program at the University of Florida, and lives with her husband in Gainesville, Florida.

Susan Fromberg Schaeffer (b. 1941)
Susan Fromberg Schaeffer was born in Brooklyn, New York, where she still resides. She received her B.A., M.A., and Ph.D. from the University of Chicago. She is the author of six novels, *Falling* (1973), *Anya* (1974), *Time in Its Flight* (1978), *Love* (1980), *The Madness of A Seduced Woman* (1983), and *Buffalo Afternoon* (1989), a collection of short stories, *The Queen of Egypt* (1980), and five books of poetry, including *Granite Lady* (1974), nominated for a National Book Award. *Anya*, a novel about the Holocaust, won the Friends of Literature Award and the Edward Lewis Wallant Award.

Lynne Sharon Schwartz (b. 1939)
Lynne Sharon Schwartz grew up in Brooklyn, New York, attended Barnard College, and did graduate work at Bryn Mawr College and New York University. Her novels include *Rough Strife* (1980), nominated for the American Book Award and the PEN/Hemingway First Novel Award; *Balancing Acts*

(1981), *Disturbances in the Field* (1983), and *Leaving Brooklyn* (1989). Her stories are collected in *Acquainted with the Night And Other Stories* (1984) and *The Melting Pot and Other Subversive Stories* (1987), and have appeared in *Best American Short Stories* and *O. Henry Prize Stories*. She is also the author of *We Are Talking About Homes: A Great University Against Its Neighbor*. She lives in New York City with her husband and two children.

Jo Sinclair (b. 1913)

Jo Sinclair (the pen name of Ruth Seid), was born in Brooklyn, New York, but spent most of her life in Cleveland. She is the author of many short stories, which have appeared in *Harper's, Esquire, Saturday Evening Post, Collier's, Reader's Digest,* and the *New Masses,* among other journals, and of essays, poetry, and plays. Her four published novels include *The Wasteland* (1946), *Sing At My Wake* (1951), *The Changelings* (1955), and *Anna Teller* (1960). She is currently at work on a new novel at her home in Pennsylvania.

Tess Slesinger (1905–45)

Tess Slesinger wrote one novel, *The Unpossessed* (1934), and many short stories, some of them collected in *Time: The Present* (1935), before moving to Hollywood where she became a screenwriter and an activist for the Screen Writer's Guild and Anti-Nazi League. She died of cancer at the age of thirty-nine, shortly after completing the screenplay for *A Tree Grows in Brooklyn* in collaboration with her second husband, Frank Davis; her other major scripts include *The Good Earth, The Bride Wore Red,* and (with Davis) *Dance, Girl, Dance, Remember the Day,* and *Are Husbands Necessary?* An enlarged edition of *Time: The Present,* entitled *On Being Told That Her Second Husband Has Taken His First Lover,* was published in 1971.

Anzia Yezierska (ca. 1885–1970)

Anzia Yezierska emigrated to New York's Lower East Side from Plinsk, Russia in her early teens. She taught domestic science (which she had studied at Teachers College, Columbia) before beginning her writing career. Yezierska's first two books were sold to the movies and led to a screenwriting contract, but she was unhappy in Hollywood and soon returned to New York. In addition to her autobiographical novels, *The Bread Givers* (1925; revised edition 1975, edited by Alice Kessler Harris), and *Red Ribbon on A White Horse* (1950), she wrote *Salome of the Tenements* (1923), *Arrogant Beggar* (1927), and *All I Could Never Be* (1932) (which fictionalizes her unconsummated relationship with John Dewey). Her short stories are collected in *Hungry Hearts* (1922), *Children of Loneliness* (1923), and in *The Open Cage* (1979, edited by Alice Kessler-Harris).

Leane Zugsmith (1903–69)

Born in Louisville, Kentucky, Zugsmith studied at Goucher College, the University of Pennsylvania, and Columbia University. She worked as a copy editor, journalist, and screenwriter. She is the author of the novels, *All Victories Are Like* (1929), *Goodbye and Tomorrow* (1931), *Never Enough* (1932), *The Reckoning* (1934), *A Time to Remember* (1936), and *The Summer Soldier* (1938). With her husband Carl Randau, she collaborated on *The Visitor*, a mystery story adapted as a Broadway play in 1944, and *The Setting Sun of Japan* (1942), an account of their trip through the Far East. An anthology of her short stories, *Home is Where You Hang Your Childhood*, was published in 1937, and another, *Hard Times with Easy Payments*, from the New York newspaper *P.M.*, in 1941.

Credits